OUR OWN WAY 2
by Misty Vixen

D1527931

CHAPTER ONE

"We should probably discuss what organizing our new life together actually looks like," Ellen said as she slipped her robe on.

It was one of the few things she'd salvaged from her previous life.

"Yeah," Gabe agreed, belting his jeans and then grabbing his t-shirt.

Their excitement had naturally led to a different kind of excitement and they had just finished showering from that.

He pulled his shirt into place. "What does it look like to you?"

Ellen laughed and then sighed, tying her robe belt just above her broad hips. "Of course you ask me first. I don't know. And the problem is that I'm still too...I don't know, I'm still recovering and mired in my job. I feel like I'll have a better capacity to really dig into it when I finally get fired. I know it has something to do with visual design. I like art."

"Is there a reason you don't want to quit?" he asked.

"Yes. Absolutely. When you get higher up into salaried positions with a bit more security, traditionally, if a company has to let you go or fire you, they typically like to protect themselves from any sort of repercussions. And in my experience, the chances of that happening go up if they treated you like shit. Which they have."

"So...what, they'll bribe you not to start shit?" he asked.

"Essentially, yes. Typically in comes in the form of a 'severance package' that you must sign a legally binding agreement to get. And that agreement says: I won't sue you."

"*Could* you sue them?"

She pursed her lips. "Possibly. There's definitely some shit they've pulled. But in truth, I don't want to deal with a drawn out lawsuit and lawyers and all the fucking hassle that the American 'justice system' entails. It's a gamble anyway. They have very good lawyers, and they can afford to wait me out."

"Huh. Interesting. And depressing. But all right, that makes sense. So, you want to get fired, take a vacation, and then, once the mental and emotional dust finally settles, you want to reexamine yourself and your life to determine a path forward."

"Yes. Exactly."

"Okay."

He was still formulating his own response, because there was a lot to consider, or at least it felt that way, when she frowned and sat down at the foot of the bed.

"You all right?" he asked.

"Mostly, just...are you really okay with this? I mean, are you *truly* okay with having an out-of-work girlfriend?"

Gabe resisted his instinct to immediately say yes and really thought about it for a moment. Was he? He sure felt like that. They had money, in that Ellen had a fair amount of money, and they were in a living situation that they could sustain theoretically for years.

Half a decade even. That was a really long time.

"Unless I'm missing something really obvious: yes, I am okay with that. I'm happy with it," he replied. "Are *you* comfortable with it?"

"I...mostly am? The problem is the fear. I know

that some of this is me just being terrified of the idea of going against what is essentially my core ideology. I feel like I'm trying to leave a cult. Which I guess I kind of am? We basically worship jobs and work and careers and overachieving and working yourself to fucking death."

"That's true," he muttered.

"And I've been doing it since I was in high school. You'd think it'd be easy to just stop, but I'm afraid. I'm not even sure *why* I'm afraid."

"I think you're worried that you aren't sure how much of you will be left after you remove this massive part of yourself you've been building for two decades."

She looked up finally, staring at him, almost startled. "I...yes. That actually makes a lot of sense. Which sounds horrifying and stupid. Why is so much of my identity wrapped up in my goddamned job?"

"Because you, like most of the rest of us, were forced into it. People roll their eyes at phrases like 'capitalist propaganda' but we are *literally* indoctrinated with actual, real propaganda designed by real people and blasted twenty four seven at us since birth. We are indoctrinated into worshiping hard work and money and status. They're capitalizing on a biological impulse, several of them, and twisting them into something seriously fucked up."

"Is it that bad?" she murmured.

"Yes! When the average job is treated as: 'you should be *thanking* me for the opportunity to be abused and exploited as you work yourself to death while surviving on the most minimum possible resources', yes, that is absolutely screwed beyond belief."

"...yeah. That makes sense. And the fact that

people actually defend that...yeah." She shifted uncomfortably. "I just don't want you to think I'm a lazy bitch who's only with you for money."

"How could I *possibly* think that?! I mean, first of all, you have all the money."

"Yeah, right *now*. But that will change naturally as time goes on. If I'm not bringing any in, and you are, then you'd end up being the one making financial decisions because you're the one with the money. And I don't know the statistics of how likely you are to succeed at writing, but I think the odds are in your favor."

"Maybe. We'll see about that. But I don't think that, and I won't. Even if we end up in a situation where I'm bringing in loads of cash and you're bringing in nothing, it's not like I'd make all the financial decisions with an iron fist."

"Why?" she asked. "You'd have absolute power in that situation."

"I wouldn't because this is a *relationship,* as in a *partnership.* I mean, even practically speaking I know that you are smarter than me. In general, but very specifically with relation to finances. Why wouldn't I get your advice? But more significantly, I don't want to just make unilateral decisions in the relationship.

"Not unless it falls under something you just don't want any input on. We're still separate people and, to a certain degree, we still have our own lives, but we are now making the decision to entwine our lives together. What I do affects you and vice versa. Trying to make huge decisions, let alone huge financial ones, without your input, would be not just stupid, but cruel."

Ellen stared at him for a long time, not saying anything. He waited, wondering if he'd hit some nerve or crossed some line without realizing it.

Finally, she blinked a few times and gave her head a little shake. "Wow."

"What?" he asked.

"I'm just...it's actually coming to me just how different you are from everyone else I've dated or really known. I don't think any man I've ever dated before would even be able to successfully articulate that, let alone actually *tell* it to me. The best I've ever gotten is: let's keep our finances separate. You do you and I'll do me," she replied.

"That's not a *terrible* idea."

"No, but it's *safe*. In a very individualistic way. It's safe *from the other person*. I don't want to be safe *from* you, Gabe. I want to be safe *with* you. And I want you to feel safe with me."

"I do."

"I know...and I feel the same way. But it's just-this keeps happening. I keep realizing that you're not just a great boyfriend but an *amazing* one. And I keep looking back and wondering how the hell I ended up in such awful relationships..." She sighed heavily and pinched the bridge of her nose for a moment, closing her eyes, then dropped her hand and took a deep breath.

Letting it out it, she opened her eyes back. "But we need to focus. What I was saying is that I'm frightened of the future. If I get fired from my job and I don't go seeking another one pretty quickly, I could be destroying a career that I've been building for over a decade now. Because let's say I stop working and everything goes well for a decade, but then we get screwed over and I need to find a job again. I can't just go back to the level I'm at now, almost certainly. A ten year gap in employment? I'd be virtually *unemployable.*"

"And that's terrifying," he murmured, sitting beside her now.

"Yes. It is. What if I'm throwing away everything on a whim? I could theoretically fuck myself over for the rest of my life."

"I think..." He hesitated, looking down at the floor between his feet.

"What? You might as well just be real with me."

"All right. I think this is coming from a place of fear. Which you've admitted, but I think this is coming from a place of irrational fear. Or...more to the point: not-quite-rational fear. I think you aren't necessarily wrong about this stuff, but I do think you're making it out as worse to be than it really will be. I think you're smart enough and motivated enough that if it came down to it, you could and would find some way to make it work."

She chuckled a little grimly. "You sure that's not just coming from a place of worship? You called me an apex predator of a girlfriend and a goddess more than once. Clearly you're biased."

He laughed, rubbing the back of his neck. "Yeah...I am. But I say that with as much lack of bias as I can. Maybe this will help, though: whatever happens, I think *we* can make it work. Five years from now, ten, twenty, fifty, we can figure it out."

"Man, fifty? Sounds like you're proposing to me," she murmured, putting her hand over the back of his.

"I, uh..."

Ellen laughed. "Wow that really threw you just right off your game, huh?"

"Yeah."

"I'm sorry, I didn't mean to, I was just teasing.

But you're right. I've said it before, I'll say it again: I believe in us. And I need to remember that, especially in the face of terror." She was silent for a moment, contemplating. "You're right. I should trust myself, and I should trust you, and us. It's a leap of faith, but I'm willing to take it. And I shouldn't not take it just because I'm familiar with a certain level of misery. Now, you go. We've established I'm a mess and I will be until I get fired. Your turn," she said, turning to face him more.

"All right. Obviously, I want to tackle my job harder and take it more seriously. Produce more, faster. And you have offered to help, and I want to take it. You offered to give everything a more serious edit and also to help me with the cover art. Are we still on for that?" he asked.

"Very much so, yes. What I've done so far has been fun. So, give me all the most recent versions of all your work that is finished and I will give it a serious, more thorough edit and send it back. I will also start putting together cover art for you. I have ideas and we can work together on that."

"Perfect. Thank you. It is deeply appreciated." He paused, then grinned. "I never really thought I'd have a girlfriend who would actively participate in my writing."

"I am very happy to."

"So am I. Okay, next thing. I need to sit down and actually make more of a plan for the future. Figure out what I want to do. But basically, I know I want to keep doing this. I want to keep writing erotica and romantic stuff and publishing it myself. I want to set up more of my own little corner of the internet, but that's what I want to do," he said.

"Perfect," she replied.

"You don't think I should be more ambitious? Have backups?"

"I think those things would be smart but...I also think you should live your life how you want and within your means. And right now, our means are very forgiving. Three hundred bucks a month plus gas and groceries and internet? We can survive on probably five hundred a month if we really have to. That's amazing. I think we should work on whittling down our debt as fast as we can, but that can wait for now. And I think we've pretty much nailed down the pertinent facts. And..." She smiled suddenly. "I think I want to go on a date with you today. We haven't really done that. Unless there's something else you want to do."

"We haven't really done a traditional date," he replied. Gabe smirked suddenly and slipped a hand along her thigh, beneath the robe. "There *is* something else I'd like to do..."

"*Gabe!*" she cried, laughing and grabbing his hand. "Oh my God-how are you *this* horny? We *just* did it!"

"I'm dating *you*," he replied, opening up her robe a bit, "I mean just *look* at you."

She sighed heavily and blushed, pulling her robe closed. "I appreciate it but-seriously! How are you *this* horny? After what we did, and everything you did with Holly!?"

"I have a lot of catching up to do," he replied with a shrug.

"Fine. Fair enough. But I'm serious, let's have a date. And we can end it with some more personal fun in this bed. Not before, though. I need...a little break."

He kissed her forehead. "All right. What do you want to do?"

She pursed her lips in consideration for a moment, then her eyes lit up abruptly. "You know what? You decide. That's what I want. I want you to make this date happen."

Gabe thought about it for a moment, wondering briefly, almost instinctively, if this was a 'you'd better guess what I want' situation, but he passed that out of hand.

Ellen was not that kind of woman.

"I'll make it happen."

CHAPTER TWO

Ellen giggled. "Gabe...I don't think I've ever seen you like this before."

"Like what?" he replied, rolling to a stop as the light up ahead turned red.

"You look like you're swinging between extremely confident and deeply worried."

"Uh...yeah, that's a fair assessment."

She laughed again. "Gabe, come on, you know you've got my pussy on lockdown, right? You'd have to *try* to fuck up bad enough that I won't be in the mood when we get back."

"I, uh, well that's good to know," he replied, "but it's more than that."

"What's got you so worried?"

"This is our first real date. You've put it completely in my hands–which, to be clear, is fine– and I'm scared of...not even screwing it up. But not doing a good enough job for you. I'm-I guess, my point is, I'm after more than just hoping you'll get naked for me at the end of it. I really want you to have a good time," he explained.

She was silent for a moment. "Gabe. I appreciate that. A lot. Honestly, hearing you say that by itself just makes the night. It's extremely romantic, largely because I know you really mean it. But I have something to put you at ease. I'm very confident that I'm going to have a good time, whatever it is that we do, because I'm going to be with you. And that's a good time."

"You're sure?" he asked.

"Gabe! Yes, I'm sure. I feel like if I was having a bad time, like I just wasn't enjoying whatever it was we were doing, you'd be able to pick up on that, and you'd react accordingly instead of just ignoring me or trying to talk me into not bringing the mood down. And, to be clear, I'm okay with putting up with something that's annoying for you, if you're *really* into it and I'm just not, but that's not the same thing.

"My point is, you have enough caring and emotional intelligence to notice. Honestly, you have more emotional intelligence than most of the people I've met in my life. And self-awareness."

"Really?" The light turned green and he began driving again, making his way towards their first destination for the night.

"Yes. Good lord *yes*. You've taught me a lot about myself and given me ways to articulate things I never really thought that much about before. Just...identifying emotions and responses and habits. Emotional intelligence, I am realizing, is something that has been severely lacking in my life. From both myself and the people around me."

"Good to know, then. I just hope it isn't too miserable," he murmured.

"What isn't?"

"Self reflection...uh, not that you should feel miserable reflecting on yourself. It's just, the frequent reaction to being alone with one's self seems to be one of misery. It can be for me, definitely."

"Oh. Yeah, that tracks, actually. We're all imperfect and we all make mistakes, and it's got to hurt, realizing something you did was actually really shitty, or realizing you keep doing stupid things. And then trying to actually make up for it or correct it. Ugh, that's another concern. What if I'm a workaholic? What if I *can't* stop?" she asked.

"Well, in that case, first we'd have to find you

something that you can put that energy towards, something that will make you feel happy and fulfilled, or at least one of those things, and secondly, we'd have to figure out a work-life balance for you," he replied.

"You know, I know that I'm intelligent, but there are times where I wonder if you're wrong, and you are the smarter one."

"I think the reality of the situation is that there are so many different kinds of intelligences, and so many different things to be good at, that we're never going to get a meaningful comparison."

She laughed. "See, that's something a really smart person would say."

"Maybe. I don't know. I've never felt particularly intelligent."

"Gabe, trust me, you're smart. Did you do well in school?"

"No."

"Then you aren't academically inclined. There are lots of people who did bad in school who are very intelligent."

"I'm guessing you did well."

"...mostly. In the beginning it was all As all the time. After my work began, my grades started suffering. I missing more days and my parents felt that the work was more important than the school. Still managed mostly As and Bs though. I would've been valedictorian if it weren't for them," she muttered.

"Sorry. That's still so insane to me," he replied.

"Me too, actually. I keep looking back and realizing how crazy that was. There's so many things that I didn't realize were abuse. I feel like too many people have this terrible idea about abuse, that if you aren't punched in the face it doesn't count. I mean, God, what Holly said, about how he wasn't hitting her so basically none of it was a big deal...ugh. Anyway. Where are we going?"

"It's a surprise, but not a huge one. We've been there before," he replied.

"It's all right, Gabe, you don't have to temper expectations. Oh. Also, I really should've said this before, but I'm going to pay this, whatever it is we do," she said.

"Are you sure?"

"Yes. I'm positive. I'm the one that asked for the date, but I'm also the one with money right now."

"All right."

A few moments later, they pulled into a familiar parking lot and he found a space in the lot beside the park that they'd gone walking in not all that long ago. It was somewhere in the high fifties today and the clouds in the sky were few in number.

"This is where it starts," Gabe said, killing the engine.

"This is a good start," Ellen replied.

They got out and began walking along the path between the dead trees.

"I'd intended to find a bigger, better park, but then got kind of impatient to get the date started. I know there's a few other parks in the city and I think one has a lake in it. Or pond? I don't know, somewhere between a lake and a pond. It's big enough that it takes a bit to walk around. I've been to it once before," he said.

"I'd love to see it, and this one is still fine to walk around in," Ellen replied.

He took her hand and she laced their fingers together.

"I was thinking..." Ellen said after a bit longer.

"Yeah?"

"Holly."

"What about her?"

"I want to invite her back again soon. Honestly I wish she didn't have to leave today. But I think we should take her on a date. Like a real date, like this."

Gabe nodded. "Yeah, I'd be very down for that. She could use it. She seems so stressed out. And lonely. There are so many times when having something like that would've been amazing and would've gone a long way towards making me feel better...although is it weird? I'm not that well-versed in *typical* dating, let alone dating another person while already in a relationship. Like, should just one of us take her?"

"I don't think so. I think she's already very cozied up to the idea that she's with *both* of us."

"Is she? I mean *with* us, not with both of us," he replied.

"Well, that's not exactly what I meant. It's still early. But we're headed that way. We should both go with her, she'd liked that." Ellen paused for a long moment. "So, I want to be completely clear on something, I'm not steamrolling you on this, right? I know I'm kind of aggressively pursuing her but I *want* that girl for both us. And to help her. But if you don't want to bring someone else into the household, you can tell me. You *should* tell me."

"So we're really talking about her moving in?" he asked.

"I mean *eventually*. Like I said, it'll still be a while."

"You aren't steamrolling me. I think we're pretty well aligned on the situation. I guess I'm more trying to caution you, or maybe soften your expectations, in case she sees this as a passing fancy?" he replied.

She snorted. "*Passing fancy?*"

"You know what I mean."

"Yes, I do. And you're wrong."

"In what?"

"She does *not* view this as a passing fancy." She giggled. "You have the weirdest phrases. Or I guess oldest? It sounds like something a nineteenth century poet would say. Anyway. Gabe, that girl is well on her way to being in love with us. You should *see* the way she looks at you. I mean, you saw it in the video."

"Yeah but we were fucking."

"Gabe." She stopped, looked around, then walked them over to a bench and took a seat. He sat beside her, still attached to her at the hand. "Fucking or not, Holly is *very* into you. She's into me, too, but I think she's still scared of me. You are her...I don't know, hero? Maybe that's too much, but you get what I'm trying to say."

"Seriously?" he asked.

"Yes! You really don't see it?!"

"I don't, but I guess I'm not sure what it would look like for me to be able to recognize it. I'm still coming to terms with the fact that you think I'm amazing and you love me. But Holly, too? *Two* women who are kind and fun and *perfect tens?* Are you kidding me? That's like a double lottery. It seems impossible."

"Gabe, I am *not* a perfect ten."

"You so are."

"Oh shut up," she muttered, blushing and pursing her lips. He chuckled. "I said shut up! My point stands: she is falling for us, especially you. So I think you should seriously be considering the reality of moving another girl into your house and your bed. She wants you very badly."

"I think you're projecting a little, and we also have to be careful not to steamroll *her*."

"That's a good point. Holly's obviously very submissive and I...am intimidating. And so are you, in your own way. But I don't think I'm projecting. *Perhaps* I'm jumping the gun a little bit. Perhaps. But trust me, she wants us." Ellen paused, leaned back against the bench for a moment, a thoughtful look coming onto her face.

"What?" he asked.

"I was just thinking...I understand what you're saying, that I want the situation to be a certain way, so I need to be careful not to just assume it is or read what I want into it. But you're doing the same thing, just from the other direction, I think," she replied.

"How?"

"I want, but you worry. You're worried she isn't into us, and you might be reading too much in that direction."

He considered that for a moment, then slowly nodded. "Okay, yes. You have a point. But I think that's safer. Not just for me, but for other people. How many people pressure others into doing something because they're wanting instead of worrying? When you worry, you aren't pressuring another person, you're just pressuring...yourself, I guess?"

"I get that, and up to a certain point you are correct, but I think you also need to realize that damaging yourself is not always the best thing to do. Because you start thinking that it's the only real option available. All of your choices are not: hurt someone else or hurt myself. It's okay to be reserved, but you really need to keep an eye on it because if you let it go on for too long eventually you'll find yourself assuming everything you want is out of your reach so why bother?"

Gabe was silent for a long time as he considered that, staring into the forest beyond the park. The trees were mostly dead now, like skeletal hands reaching up against a pale gray sky.

"I'm sorry, that got pretty serious," Ellen murmured.

"I'm not upset," he replied. "I was just thinking. You have a point. A good one. Managing expectations is a good thing, but you have to keep an eye on it, keep your hand on the wheel...now *I'm* sorry, because it got so serious. This is a date that you wanted, it's supposed to be more lighthearted."

"Gabe...it's not *supposed* to be anything other than a meaningful experience. And that covers a really broad range of emotions. It's not like I expect or even want the date to be all fluff all the time," she replied. "I'm not—"

"What?" he asked when she didn't continue.

"I was just about to say I'm not scared of intense or unhappy or serious conversations, and that's true, but I realized all at once that I used to be. All the time. I was...maybe scared isn't quite the right word, but I always wanted to avoid more serious conversations with anyone close to me. Because it always, *always* ended up being used against me somehow. But it isn't that way with you. At all. Just being able to talk about being insecure about my height or my weight with you has been such an unburdening relief, not just because I know you *like* those two things about me, but because I honestly believe you would never use them against me to hurt me."

He slipped his arm around her waist and scooted closer to her. "I'm glad you trust that. I want to say I'll never hurt you, but I can't promise that. No one can. Because at some point, I'm going to piss you off, and you're going to piss me off, and we'll have a fight. And that will suck. But...I think we're going to be okay when it comes to fighting."

"I hope so," Ellen whispered. "I have turned into an absolute savage bitch because I've had to fight for *so* much, and I hate that. And I'm only just recently truly beginning to realize just how savage I've had to be before, and I'm terrified it's going to come out one day in a fit of rage, and I'm going to say something unforgivable, and lose you."

"Whatever happens, I feel like I'd give us a fair chance to work it out," he replied.

"That's the reason," she paused, "*one* of the reasons I'm in love with you."

He chuckled, then shivered slightly as a hard gust of cold wind blew across them. "Come on," he said, getting up, "let's move onto the next part of the date."

"Lead on," she replied as she got up.

They shared a kiss and began walking back to the car.

CHAPTER THREE

Ellen was amused, and Gabe was happy to see that, but he was also a little confused.

He certainly wanted her to be happy, and she was, but now she seemed just amused by something and he wasn't sure what it was.

After the park, he had taken her to a little burger place that he knew she'd been eyeing for a bit and discovered it was really good. Now, with the sun heading for a horizon that was promising rain, they were pulling into a huge, half-empty parking lot in front of a movie theater.

Gabe often felt bad that he enjoyed the fact that the pandemic seemed to bring down the general amount of people at a given location, because a lot of people discovered that they'd just rather stay home and that was easier than ever to do now that everything could be delivered or somehow provided to a given household.

He really loved being in a place that was undercrowded as opposed to overcrowded. Maybe that was anxiety talking, or just general introversion, but it was almost soothing.

"All right, I'll bite," he said, finally breaking his silence as he parked and killed the engine. "What's got you so amused?"

"Whatever do you mean?" she replied.

"Oh do *not* give me that," he said, turning and staring at her more deliberately. "Something has you incredibly amused."

"Maybe I'm just happy."

"You are happy, but this is more than that. Something happened around the burger place that changed your smile to a smirk."

"Hmm...okay, I'll level with you: I'm afraid if I tell you it will stop, and I kind of don't want it to stop."

He considered that response for a moment. "Now you have me *very* curious."

"It's something you're doing and I think you're doing it mostly without realizing it, and I like it, but also find it a little funny."

"You can't say all that and then not tell me. Come on."

"All right, fine. I can't keep anything from you, not when you ask directly, at least. You...are strutting."

"*What?*" Whatever he'd been expecting to hear, it was absolutely not that.

"You are showing me off."

"...I am?"

"Yes."

"You're sure?"

"I am."

He was silent for a few moments, trying to think about the restaurant. Going into and out of it. Was he...strutting? Had he ever done that before? It didn't really seem like a thing he did, or would do, given his personality.

"I'm not mad," she said.

"You sure? I remember that was a problem you had with your last boyfriend," he replied.

"It's...a little more complicated than that, I'm learning. There was some stuff that I thought I hated, or just put up with, but I am learning that it was the person doing it, not the action itself. And while a lot of guys were threatened by my height, some leaned into the...I guess you could call it the 'wow factor'?

"I know that I really stand out. I don't look like most other people. Sometimes it makes me want to run and hide, sometimes I enjoy and lean into it. With you, I'm leaning into it. Even if you don't realize it, you're walking around in public with me and your body language is one hundred percent 'look at this chick who is with me' and 'that's right, she's with me', and there is absolutely a certain part of me that really likes that."

"So should I lean into it?" he asked.

She laughed. "I think...you shouldn't necessarily lean into it, but you also shouldn't lean away from it. See, this is exactly why I didn't want to tell you. Because now you're thinking about it. It was a subconscious thing."

"Well...not entirely," he admitted after thinking about it. "I *do* feel that way. Having a six foot five goddess with me in public? Yes, I am proud of that, even if that might not be the healthiest mindset."

She sighed and shook her head, and when he looked at her again he saw she was blushing. "Be careful with that goddess shit," she murmured, "it's going to go to my head."

"There are worse things."

"...fair enough. But yeah, I agree with you. It *is* nice to show off...a little bit. Not too much."

"So basically, keep it confident but don't get cocky?" he asked.

"Well...I like a *little* cockiness."

"Noted. Now come on, we've still got some time to spare and I want to hit that arcade they've got in there."

"Hmm," she said as they got out.

"Hmm what?"

"I used to hit up this arcade when I was in high

school all the time. I fucking loved the first person shooters with the actual guns, and the racing games. But then I fell out of it. People kept giving me shit because 'girls don't play video games'."

"That's such fucking bullshit," he said. "Trust me, I am *extremely* happy to play video games with you, or to help facilitate the playing of them if you want to do it alone."

"I have to admit, it's an appealing idea. I've liked what I've seen so far watching you. And I am actually very excited to hit this arcade with you."

"Good."

They started walking across the chilled parking lot towards the entrance of the huge theater, holding hands again. He tried to get a sense for whether or not he was walking differently than he normally did, but how did he normally walk?

After a moment, he decided she was right and he just shouldn't think about it.

They went into the theater and paid for their tickets. Ellen became even happier when she discovered they were going to see a new fantasy movie that had dropped last week. He'd heard her mention it a few times and he was pretty curious to see it as well. Once they had the tickets, they headed for the arcade.

It was only about a third full, though he noticed that most people glanced over when they walked in and heard Ellen talking, and their glances lingered for at least a few seconds when they saw her. Gabe felt continually reminded that Ellen was right: she was something of a spectacle or a marvel. Being taller than most women was one thing, but being taller than most men was another. And being that much taller, and attractive, made her stand out a lot.

As they turned bills into tokens and began making their way around the arcade, looking for a good two-player game, he considered that.

It was a basic rule of human psychology that people liked to be seen attached to attractive people, and having an overtly attractive significant other was sort of the apex of the pyramid in that case. His first girlfriends had been beautiful, in their own ways, but not in ways that were recognized by the general public when they were out and about.

Gabe hadn't cared. He thought they were pretty and he let them know that often enough. In truth, with every girlfriend he'd ever had, he'd thought he was dating out of his class to varying degrees. His final girlfriend before Ellen, though, had been hot.

Hot in a way that everyone knew.

He'd felt good about it at first, but as the relationship began to deteriorate, it just came to feel like a liability more than anything else. Increasingly he found himself coming to the conclusion that she was going to leave, because she could do so much better than him.

It didn't help that she sometimes hinted at that when they were fighting.

But it was different with Ellen.

He knew what it was because, as she had said, he was emotionally intelligent and self-aware. Though he would personally have described it as being burdened with self awareness. He knew that a lot of guys wanted the woman he was with, but with Ellen, he knew they were bulletproof. There was nothing anyone could do to convince her to leave him.

Probably.

He mentally checked himself as he thought that. No. Not probably. Life was uncertain, the universe was inherently unstable and chaotic, but he wanted, or maybe even needed, to have more conviction and certainty in his life.

More faith in his relationship with Ellen.

She was also right that he was setting himself up to be betrayed by life, because that's what had happened so many times.

But he trusted her, and he believed in her, and what they had together.

And to complicate things more, he knew it was immature. Wanting to show off how hot his girlfriend was in public, but some part of him flashed with anger at that thought. So fucking what? After all the absolute horseshit he'd endured his entire life, being on the other end of that particular dynamic was something he fucking deserved.

Maybe more than that, something he'd felt that he'd earned.

He'd paid his goddamned dues in misery and suffering for decades now and he was going to be happy and enjoy this, even if it meant indulging in a bit of strutting.

"This one," Ellen said, stopping suddenly.

Gabe looked at the arcade cabinet and grinned. It was one of the big ones, it could accommodate four players and had incredibly detailed sci-fi looking rifles and pistols. It was about an alien invasion.

"Let's do it," he replied.

They stepped up, fed the tokens to the machine, and started playing.

They kept going until they were almost late to the movie.

. . .

"Are you still awake?" Ellen asked softly.

"Yeah," Gabe replied.

"What are you thinking about?"

"...it's kinda dumb."

She laughed and rolled over, the bed shifting beneath her, and he felt the strangest little burst of lust run through him. For a moment, he couldn't even figure out why her rolling over had turned him on, even just for a few seconds, but as he looked at her, he realized it was because feeling the bed shifting beneath him as much as he had reminded him of how tall and thick she was.

Sometimes it still surprised him just how into her, and certain aspect of her, he was.

"Tell me anyway, I don't care if it's dumb," she replied.

"You want to hear everything I'm thinking?" he asked.

She reached out and dragged her fingertips slowly down one arm. "Maybe I do."

He laughed. "All right, fine. That game we played tonight...it got me thinking really, really strongly about writing an erotica."

"Seriously?"

"Yeah. I don't know what it is...I think my brain is already being rewired to think about 'how would people hook up in this scenario?', you know? I just feel really compelled to write about survivors or maybe resistance soldiers hooking up during an alien invasion. But that's stupid."

"I mean...is it? Why?"

"It just feels like...like when they try to theme a porn, you know? I mean that whole 'lonely MILF does the pizza guy' thing is kind of ridiculous enough, but the stuff that's like 'it's the apocalypse and we should fuck to keep the human race going' is usually beyond cringe."

Ellen laughed and took his hand suddenly. "Gabe, those things are ridiculous and embarrassing because that's what most porn comes off as, because most porn is acted out by people who look good fucking, not who are good at acting. Or written by people who are not good at writing. Everything is presentation and execution, Gabe. And you are *good* at those two things."

"You think so?"

"I *know* so. And I'm not just blowing smoke up your ass, I mean it. You are a good writer. I really want to read your stone age porn. I'm super interested in reading this alien invasion hookup idea. I mean if you think about it, people fuck in basically every situation if they can. Yeah no one shows the actual sex scene in the alien invasion movie, but it totally happens. They don't focus on that because that isn't the point of the media in that case, but in this case it *is* the point. I'm sure there are *lots* of people out there who would be into the idea."

He was silent for a long moment. "You have a point," he murmured finally. "I don't know why it's so hard to get out of this mindset. I sort of feel like...I'm afraid to take this seriously."

"That makes sense. A lot of sense," Ellen replied.

"You think so?"

"Yes. You are creating something, first of all, and secondly, you are creating something in a field society has traditionally shunned and mocked. I think a lot of people have an instinct to not take things too seriously. It's sort of like that 'I was just kidding' fallback. If someone mocks what you create, you can say 'well I wasn't trying very hard', like an escape hatch. But...you know what's a much better stance to have that has a benefit of being really hot?"

"What?"

"Make something, and then stand by it, and say, 'I made this'. Take it seriously. It's a lot harder to do, and sometimes you'll be embarrassed or even humiliated, but you'll learn to take this in stride. And the people trying to humiliate you don't deserve the time of day from you. You'll learn to ignore them."

He found himself nodding. "That's a really good point. And you're right...fuck this. I'm going to take this more seriously, and stop questioning everything, and just do what makes sense."

"Good. You've been doing that more and more since we've gotten together, and I am really proud of you for that." She kissed him and he slipped a hand over the back of her neck and deepened the kiss. He felt her tongue come into his mouth.

When she broke the kiss, they were both breathing heavily.

They looked into each other's eyes in the dim moonlight filtering in through the window, listening to the sound of the soft rainfall tapping the roof.

They didn't even need to ask.

"Can you be on top again?" he asked.

She let out a breathy laugh as she threw back the blanket. "Of course."

CHAPTER FOUR

Gabe glanced over as his phone buzzed.

He quickly picked it up and activated it, then grinned as he saw it was a text from Holly. Opening it up, he found himself looking a picture of her shaved pussy.

It came with a message: *Is this too slutty?*

He chuckled and immediately began responding: *It's very acceptably slutty and you have such a hot pussy.*

"What are you laughing about in here?" Ellen asked as she came into his office.

"Check it," he replied, passing her the phone.

"Oh wow. So nice," she murmured, looking at the phone.

While she did that, Gabe turned back to his laptop and wrapped up what he was doing.

The last nearly four days had been very busy. Ellen had been burning through his work, rereading and editing everything with a much more intense eye. She had also been working on putting together some cover art. Based on what he'd seen so far, it became immediately obvious that she had a very sharp eye for art and aesthetic.

Gabe had been working furiously.

In between re-reading and applying Ellen's edits whenever she got him one, he was working on the final story in Tall, Blonde, and Beautiful. At twenty five thousand words, it was already the longest thing he'd ever written.

Well, for himself anyway.

And in between both of these things, he was throwing together a plan for not just his stone age erotica idea, but a sequel series to Tall, Blonde, and Beautiful. It had been bugging him for some time now and he was still figuring it out.

Gabe finished typing up the part that he was working on, then saved the document, closed out, and turned back around to face Ellen.

She was smirking into the phone, her face lit up with lusty delight.

"What's she saying?" he asked.

"She sent me a pic of her tits. We are *corrupting* that girl, Gabe, and I am so fucking happy to be doing this with you," she replied.

"Same," he agreed.

As she passed his phone back, she lost her smile, her expression instead becoming a little concerned.

"What?" he asked.

"I was just thinking...it feels kind of weird. I can't escape the fact that this thing I have going with Holly just feels a little weird."

"Why?"

"I'm not sure. Some of it has to do with the fact that she's over a decade younger than me. In some ways, she's really mature for her age. In other ways...I don't know, it shows. I'm twelve years older than her. It feels weird sometimes. But that's not it, not really. I think...there's a bit of conflict coming from the fact that I absolutely want to corrupt her sexually and fuck her like crazy and use her like a sex toy, but at the same time I also want to take care of her and make sure she's safe and happy? Those are two different instincts. Very different."

"Okay," he replied after thinking about it, "I can see where you're coming from. But isn't that how you feel about me?"

Her frown deepened. "Yes...but it's not the same.

And I'm not sure why. Maybe because it's more 'normal'? Expected? Traditional? You're my boyfriend, of course I want to have sex with you and also take care of you and do fun, domestic, cozy things with you. But with Holly...ugh, I'm not sure. It's not her fault, whatever it is, it's something about me."

"So do you still want to fuck her?" he asked.

"Oh yes. So very much. That isn't going away. I know that much. What do you think I should do?"

"Embrace it," he replied.

"It's that easy?"

"I didn't say it was *easy,* but it's simple. Yeah, embrace it. Fuck her and then make sure she's getting enough sleep and food and listen to her when she wants to talk. Treat her like...your girlfriend. Our girlfriend," he replied.

"Hmm."

He waited. While Ellen chewed over that, his phone buzzed. He checked it. Holly again.

So are we still cool for me to come over and spend the night and...everything else?

He grinned and responded: *Emphatically yes.*

She sent a response almost immediately: *Awesome! I am coming now!*

"She's coming," he said, shutting down his laptop and getting up.

"Good, I'm fucking horny. And you need a goddamned break."

"I don't need one that bad," he murmured.

"Gabe! You've been working like ten or twelve hour days, back to back!"

He paused as they reached the living room. "...have I?"

"Yes! I didn't want to say anything because I've

been working hard, too, but you've been in your office so much. Also, to be clear, this is not me feeling neglected. You've been good about coming out and spending time with me. This is me worrying about *you*. You need a break, Gabe, or you're going to break. I've seen it before."

He thought back over the past few days and then realized, suddenly, how mentally exhausted he was. "You might have a point."

"Damn right I do," Ellen replied. They both sat down on the couch. "Now, love of my life, you are going to take the night off and enjoy your little fucktoy."

"First of all..." he paused, "am I really the love of your *life?*"

"Yes. Have I not made that abundantly clear?" she replied with a small but growing smile.

"You have," he said, "I just...nevermind. I was going to say, isn't she more of *our* fucktoy?"

"Yes, and if she's down with it, I want to have a full-on threesome tonight. I'm thirty four and I've never actually had one," she replied.

"Really? Wait, did last time not count?"

"Yes, really. And last time...was very fun. But I want a more full contact threesome, where all three of us are actively participating at once," she replied.

"So do I."

Ellen pursed her lips and studied him more closely. "What?" she asked finally.

"What what?" he replied.

She laughed and rolled her eyes. "Don't give me that, something's bugging you. What is it?"

"It just...feels a little weird, referring to Holly as our fucktoy."

"Ah. Don't worry about that...well, okay, that's

not entirely accurate. Keep aware of it. It would be different if we were trying to impose that role and name on her, and she only reluctantly went along with it because she didn't want to rock the boat. But we're both very aware people, and you can trust that Holly is throwing herself happily into that role. It's a good instinct, though…"

"You think so?" he replied. "It's not too anxious?"

"No. Our relationship with Holly is two things, for the moment. First, it's still young. We've had one date. Second, she is the submissive to our, primarily *your,* dom."

"I think that's more you than me," he said.

Ellen shook her head. "No, love. She's intimidated by me. That isn't the same thing. We'll have that sub-dom dynamic to be sure, but it's going to even out. You are the one she subs to."

"You seem to know a lot about this," he replied.

She laughed. "I had a *lot* of free time at certain points in my life and I've read a *lot* of erotica and romance novels, and gone delving into a lot of BDSM spaces online. I'm no expert, but I know the basics, and I can read people well. But my point is this: we are committing to the dominant role in the relationship, and she, both because of her submissive role *and* because of who she is as a person, is relying on us for a lot of things."

"Like?"

"Mainly: not to mistreat her. I mean, you heard her: she stayed with that loser for like a *year* after his anger issues became serious. She ultimately got out of her own will but Holly is definitely a 'I don't want to make waves and I hate confrontation' type of girl. I think we'll eventually get around to her feeling more comfortable with her telling us if something is bothering her, but for now, we are going to have to watch her and make sure she's having a good time."

Gabe thought about it. Everything Ellen was saying made sense, but he was quickly coming to realize this was a blind a spot.

He was still coming to terms with the idea that not one, but two amazing women were interested in him, one of them being the woman of his dreams, who was actually in love with him. But if that was something he was grappling with, then the notion that someone as attractive as Holly could and even would connect with him enough that he could hurt her inadvertently felt even farther beyond his reach.

It was a problem he'd dealt with before. He'd hurt people's feelings without realizing it primarily because he didn't even think they gave enough of a shit about him to allow themselves to be hurt. He'd rarely felt like he mattered enough to even register to most other people.

Holly seemed to have so much more power than him, and Ellen more than that.

The idea that she was coming to him and would willingly submit to him still felt just south of impossible.

Gabe came out of himself and his thoughts as he realized that Holly had to be close. He looked around as a thought occurred to him and then looked back to Ellen.

"Thank you for straightening up," he said, "I was going to do it but I got wrapped up in my work."

The smile that Ellen gave him felt a lot deeper and more intense than her usual smiles, and he could tell he'd touched on something. "Thank you for noticing," she replied.

They both straightened up as they heard a car engine passing by, getting closer, and then suddenly dying. Gabe got up but paused when he didn't hear a door open and close. He waited, they both did, listening still.

After a moment, he wondered if it was someone else who'd parked in a nearby driveway, though it sounded close enough. He walked over to the door and peered out the peephole, then frowned.

"Is it her?" Ellen asked.

"Yeah, but she's just...sitting in her car," he murmured.

"Is she crying? I...have definitely just sat in my car and cried more times than I care to admit," she asked.

"I can't tell. Doesn't look like it. Also, I'm sorry, that sounds miserable."

"It is, but also...it wasn't all bad." He looked at her. She gave a rueful little smile. "I know it sounds weird, but crying is definitely a release, and at some point I learned that I can dump a lot of tension and anger and misery by having a good cry by myself. Sometimes in the bathroom, or in my bed, or in the car. Nothing intense, just...is that really weird?"

"It makes sense," he replied, then looked back as he heard the car door open. She got out. She looked happy now as she closed the door and approached the house.

He pulled open the door before she could knock and she let out a startled sound.

"Oh! You scared me," she murmured.

"We've been waiting for you," he replied.

"That's...good to know," she said, grinning.

As she stepped into the house and began getting out of her hoodie and shoes, he closed the door and studied her.

She looked fantastic, though run down. She was wearing a buttoned t-shirt and a pair of bluejeans that looked amazing on her.

Right way, though, he could tell something was off.

Most of it was in her expression, like she was holding something back, but some of it was in her movements. She was stiff and at the same time a little clumsy. If it hadn't been for her expression, he would have written it off as exhaustion. Based on her texts, she was getting off after a nearly ten hour shift, and, young and fit or not, that was often exhausting work for a waitress.

She had on makeup but he could still see dark shadows beneath each eye, both of which were a little bloodshot.

Gabe glanced at Ellen. He could tell she was picking up on it, too.

"So...how was your day?" he asked, taking her hand when she finished with her shoes and leading her over to the couch.

"Ugh, fucking exhausting," she replied.

He sat down and gave her a gentle tug. She smiled more genuinely and sat down on his lap, then kissed him on the mouth suddenly.

It was a long, pleasant kiss.

When she pulled back, she suddenly lost some of her smile and shot a furtive glance towards Ellen.

"This is still...weird," she murmured. "I'm so scared I'm going to piss you off."

"It's all right, Holly, you aren't going to piss me off," Ellen replied, reaching over and taking one of her hands. She flipped it over and then began pressing her thumbs into her palm.

"Oh. *Oh.* Oh my God," Holly whispered, closing her eyes. "How are-oh wow, Ellen, that feels amazing."

"You like it? I was looking up how to help writers unwind and...besides the obvious way a girlfriend can help her sexy writer boyfriend relax, this came up. Palm massage."

"She has the thumbs for it," Gabe said.

"I fucking love it. That feels-ah!" she cried as something popped in her palm. "Holy shit! I didn't even know my hand could pop!"

"Gabe said almost the exact same thing," Ellen said, looking pleased with herself. "Here, give me your other one."

"Gladly."

She kept working it and they glanced at each other as Holly closed her eyes again, her mouth slowly opening in pleasure as Ellen's thumbs worked her other palm.

"You're really tense today," Ellen murmured.

"Am I?" she replied.

"Yeah. Are you doing all right?"

There was a pause that lasted just a little too long and an expression that wavered across her face very quickly before she said, "I'm all right."

"You can tell us if you aren't," Gabe said, running his hand slowly up and down her thigh.

Holly shifted a little uncomfortably. "Oh, you know, I don't want to bring down the mood."

"Holly," Ellen said, then popped her other palm, making her gasp and then moan, "you don't have to talk about it if you don't want to, full stop. But, coming from a woman in her mid-thirties who kept a *lot* in to 'keep the peace' and 'not bring down the mood'? I can assure you that you'll typically feel a lot better if you talk about what's bugging you with people you can trust."

She remained silent for a moment, not meeting either of their eyes, and then finally she opened her mouth. "I just—"

She started crying.

CHAPTER FIVE

"I'm sorry," she managed, and seemed to struggle.

Holly looked like she wanted to get up, her face red.

"It's okay, Holly," Gabe replied.

She began to say something else, but another sob hit her, and then she leaned against him and wrapped her arms around him and buried her face in his chest. She began to cry harder. He suddenly felt transported back to the first night Ellen had reappeared in his life, the way she'd done just about the exact same thing.

He hugged her, one arm around going around her back, his other hand settling gently against the back of her head, her soft red hair.

"It's okay," he murmured.

Ellen reached over and placed her hand on Holly's back as well, below his arm, gently rubbing it through her shirt.

Holly tried to say a few things, muffled half-words coming out, none articulate, and then she gave up and just cried into his chest.

Even though he had experience with this already, he still felt uncertain and just a little frightened that he was going to say the wrong thing or make it worse. Whatever it was. That was another thing he was scared of.

What if something horrific had happened to her?

Gabe had come across a fairly recurring problem online from people who had more serious mental health issues hating how, whenever they opened up to someone, more often than not that person tended to pull away, either all at once or slowly. That was a really bad feeling, an awful reaction to get, and he'd even faced it himself before.

But he also had sympathy for the people who pulled back because, even if it was a selfish thought...it was a *lot* to just dump 'I'm suicidal' on someone. What if you said the wrong thing? In a way, even if it wasn't true, it felt like someone was abruptly shoving their life into your hands, and that was a horrifying, titanic responsibility.

It wasn't quite the same as what was happening right now, but it all fell under the umbrella of uncomfortably vulnerability.

Mostly, he was just afraid he was going to fuck up when Holly needed him, because she obviously needed him right now.

This was a really 'do or die' kind of moment, emotionally speaking.

But Ellen was right about the fact that he wanted a relationship with her, and pursuing a relationship meant accepting certain responsibilities. Like taking care of someone when they were having a crisis or even just a really shitty day.

Whatever it was, whatever Holly was dealing with, he knew he needed to step up and at least try to help her. He couldn't give up just because he was afraid. More than that, he very much wanted to help her, to comfort her, to try and help her feel better.

She stopped crying after a few minutes, but remained laying against him for a bit longer.

"I'm sorry," she said finally. "I'm so embarrassed." She sounded tired.

"Don't be embarrassed," Ellen said. "I did the same thing to him the first time I came to his place."

Holly shifted, sniffed, then sat up. "Really?"

Ellen laughed softly. "Yeah. Like the exact same

thing. I'd just been cheated on and everything was falling apart and...it's okay."

"I..." She hesitated, then sighed and sniffed again. "Shit. I'm sorry. I'll be right back."

"Take your time," Gabe replied.

She just nodded silently and got up, then walked out of the living room. The bathroom door closed. They heard her blowing her nose.

"I wonder what happened," he murmured.

"She's probably really stressed," Ellen replied. "You should take it as a compliment."

He looked over at her. "*What?*"

"That she cried on you, like I did. You think either of us would have done that if we didn't trust you? Feel safe around you?"

He thought about. "...yeah, all right. That makes sense." Gabe looked down at his shirt. "I need to change now."

"Just take it off," she replied.

"You sure? You don't think me being suddenly shirtless won't send mixed messages?" he asked.

"I think Holly is going to need some sex after that. Not immediately, but soon, tonight. And she also probably is worried that she just majorly turned us off. And I think it might help reassure her that she hasn't," Ellen explained.

He shrugged and took off his shirt as they heard the bathroom door open. Holly reemerged into the living room, paused as she looked at the two of them, then walked over and sat back down slowly on his lap.

"I guess I got snot and tears all over your shirt," she murmured.

"A little," he replied. "But it's all right."

"You got his shirt off at least," Ellen said.

Holly laughed, smiling for a moment. It was like sunshine breaking through clouds. Then she lost it, looking away. "I'm sorry."

"You don't have to be sorry," Gabe replied.

"I am. I came over here to have fun and you both are so nice to me and I reward that by walking in and crying. And over what? Nothing even happened to me! I'm just so fucking stressed...goddamnit," she muttered.

"Holly," Ellen said, firmly enough that she looked at her, "it's okay. We aren't mad, or annoyed."

"Are you sure?" she murmured, looking from Ellen to Gabe.

"We're sure," he replied. "Just because we seduced you and invited you over to our house to fuck doesn't mean we can't also do other things, or that we can't get serious if that's what you need. You're stressed, and that doesn't just go away because you want it to. And we don't just look at you as a hookup, Holly. You're our friend and we care about you. If you want to talk about it, we should talk about it."

"I...so you really just want to hear me bitch about nothing?" she asked.

"Holly," Ellen said, "it's not nothing. It's bothering you. We'll understand if you don't want to talk about it, but it's like I told you: I am the marathon runner of 'not talking about it'. I don't necessarily regret keeping a lot of stuff in, because I'm looking back and realizing that I was right to do it, but I *do* regret that I never really found anyone I could lean on, emotionally, and just spill to. Someone I could trust. I trust Gabe, and you can, too. You can trust both of us."

She seemed to chew over that for a moment.

Finally, she asked, "Can we still have sex later?"

They both laughed loudly and Gabe kissed her cheek. "Yes, Holly, we can absolutely have sex later. It doesn't have to be either or."

"Okay. I'll just...talk about it." She heaved a long, weary sigh. "It's dumb, though. I don't even know why I'm so stressed out. I just am. It's the same stupid bull as usual at my job. Rude customers, a jerk boss, long hours of running around, working my ass off. Everyone thinks being a waitress is a nothing job and just *so* easy and like, yeah, there's *way* harder jobs out there, but it isn't fucking easy and I'm so fucking sick of hearing that.

"Ugh, and then my friends. I *am* annoyed about that. They didn't fucking believe me! I showed them the pictures after telling them about my time with you two and they said I was lying! I was just making it up!"

"Wait, so what do they think the pictures are then? Because they're obviously real," Ellen replied.

"They think it's fucking AI generated! I guess you can do that now? I didn't even know that was a thing but yeah, that's what they said. I didn't feel like arguing, although I almost called you to help back me up," she said.

"We so would have," Gabe replied, "and yeah, I've seen some of that stuff. I guess there was some sort of breakthrough this year and it's terrifying what they can generate now. Like photo-realistic pictures and masterpiece paintings and stuff like that."

"Holy shit, seriously?"

"Yeah. It's fucking up a lot of industries. It's...terrifying, honestly. But why are they so hellbent on disbelieving you? They don't really sound like friends," he said.

"They're jealous," Ellen said.

"Do you think so?" Holly replied.

"Yeah, definitely. It sounds like jealousy. Which I know is what everyone says when someone's being shitty, 'you're just jealous', but I'm pretty sure in this case it's true."

"...I don't know," she murmured. "They're *really* pretty, and they don't have problems getting dates."

"You got a picture of them?" Ellen asked.

"Yeah, I do. Hold on..."

She got up and moved over to her purse, then crouched down and began digging through it. Gabe found both he and Ellen looking at her ass. It was so fantastically showcased by the jeans she was wearing, pulled tight across it.

"Here," she said, straightening back up and turning around. She paused. "You two look...funny."

"It's your ass," Ellen replied.

"What?"

"You have the hottest fucking ass," Gabe said.

"I...um...oh," she murmured, blushing now. She laughed awkwardly. "Well. Thank you." She came over and sat back down in his lap, then began navigating her phone. "Here they are."

Gabe took a quick look at the picture. He saw two women posing in a parking lot. They were both pretty attractive. One was about as pale as Holly, with blonde hair and a trim figure. She looked pretty fit. The other was taller, her skin a lot more tan, her hair black. He passed Ellen the phone.

"Oh yeah," she said after a few seconds. "Jealous."

"How can you tell?" Holly asked.

Ellen studied the phone a moment longer, then passed it back to her, looking vaguely uncomfortable.

"So...I'm not trying to throw shade, because girls tearing down girls is a terrible and all-too-easy mindset to get into, but...you're hotter than they are. By a lot. Don't get me wrong, they're very pretty, though less so now based on what I've heard about them, but while they are sevens or eights, you are a straight ten."

"Ah, come on with that...I-you know, you don't have to flatter me," she murmured.

"I'm not," Ellen replied flatly. "Holly, *I* am jealous of you."

"What!?" she asked, straightening up, seemingly startled by the admission. "That's-how? You're, like, a fucking model, Ellen. You're *so* beautiful. I was reading a romance novel recently and there was this phrase in it used to describe the female main character: staggeringly beautiful. That's what I think of when I think of you. You are staggeringly beautiful."

Ellen laughed. "I appreciate it, and I'm glad you think so. But you're easier on the eyes than I am, Holly. Just trust me. This isn't me putting myself down, or even me lifting you up, it's just me telling it like it is. I'm very happy to be with a pair of people who are enamored of my physical appearance, but if we entered into beauty contests, you'd win almost every time, Holly. You are *ridiculously* hot."

"You really are," Gabe said.

"I...okay. I guess I'll have to take your word for it. So they're telling me I'm lying because they're jealous?" she asked.

"Yes," Ellen replied. "I'm not proud to admit it, but that would've been me not too many years ago. Maybe not so aggressively, it sounds like they have very little subtlety, but I would be jealous...hmm."

"What?" Holly asked.

"Maybe we can help you. We can *prove* it."

"How?"

"Well they can't call you a liar if we're right there, backing you up, right?"

"No, I guess they couldn't," she murmured.

"I'll think of something," Ellen said, smirking. "Fuck those bitches...sorry, I know they're friends. Although I'm wondering if maybe they might be toxic 'friends'."

"I am...beginning to wonder that myself," Holly admitted uncomfortably.

She looked down at her phone again, frowning at the photo, then shook her head and turned the screen off.

"I'm probably too caught up in it, I should just let it go," she muttered, setting the phone aside.

"I don't know, it'd bug me if I hooked up with someone I thought was mega hot and I had photographic evidence and my friends were just like 'you're lying'," Gabe said.

"Yeah, it's so fucking annoying. Everything is annoying recently. Just bugging the shit out of me, even stuff that normally doesn't. It kinda makes me wish I could drink. It seems like being drunk chills you out," Holly replied.

"You can't drink?" Ellen asked.

"I'm not supposed to. I've got some kind of genetic defect or something that makes me not metabolize alcohol correctly? I'm not completely sure, but I know it fucks with my heart, I guess. Like, I won't die if I have a shot, but I really shouldn't, and I hate the taste anyway."

"That sucks really hard," Gabe muttered.

Ellen's face lit up. "Oh! What about weed? We

have some edibles and you could totally try some!"

"I…" Holly seemed to consider it for a moment. "You know what? Yeah. Give me some."

CHAPTER SIX

"Huh, that's not what I expected it to look like," Holly murmured as Ellen held the gummy in her palm.

"What'd you think it would look like?" she replied.

"Whenever I'd hear someone talking about gummies, I guess I'd always picture, like, a bear? Like those vitamin gummies? Or like a giraffe maybe?"

Ellen made an unhappy noise and Gabe felt himself tense up. Holly picked up on it almost immediately.

"What? What's wrong?" she asked.

"I-it's nothing," Ellen replied.

"No wait, it's something. Something upset you guys. What? Did I say something?" she asked, increasingly worried.

Ellen sighed. "It's just...the word. Giraffe. It's what people used to call me in high school and it's the *one* thing that really got to me. And it still does."

"Oh God, I'm sorry. Ellen, I would *never*–"

"I know, Holly. You had no idea, it's fine. It's just a reaction...it's fine. It's just that my ex-fiance screamed it at me when we were fighting and-you know, I don't want to talk about it." She regained her smile. "I'm not mad, I promise. I just want to have a good time. So, the gummy. Do you have any experience with weed or edibles before?"

"Only a little, none with gummies, though. I smoked a little like two years ago, but...mmm. Let's just say I don't have a very happy history with weed, but I want to try it again."

"So you want to get stoned with us?" she asked. "Yes."

"Okay. I want you to only eat half of this, all right? It can be powerful and we have to sort of test how much it affects you. Everyone's different."

"That makes sense." She took it out of Ellen's hand and studied it, then sniffed it. "Are you sure it's not laced with something?" she asked, then paused, a look of horror coming over her face. "Not that I think you guys are trying to dose me with something! I mean, I just want to be sure, where it's from, you know?"

"It's fine, Holly," Ellen replied. "It's a very reasonable concern, and yes, we're sure. We've had some and we got it from a legal distributor."

"Like...a store?"

"Yeah," Gabe replied.

"Holy shit, that's so weird. I can't believe we can just walk into a store now and buy actual weed." She began to put it in her mouth, then hesitated again. "Can I spend the night here? I worry about driving..."

"Yes you can and that's a very smart worry. Never drive while stoned," Ellen said.

"It would be great if you spent the night," Gabe agreed.

"Awesome!" She bit half the gummy off and then passed the rest back to Ellen as she began chewing on it. "Oh...man, I don't have to work tomorrow, but I should've brought clothes...ew, God, it tastes bad."

"Yeah, sorry, should've mentioned that," Ellen replied.

"It's like...a skunk? I don't know. Gross." She swallowed.

"Let me get you something to drink," Ellen said,

standing up. She paused, looking at the half gummy in her hand. "You want to split it, babe?"

"Sure," he replied.

They hadn't indulged since the last time. Ellen bit the remaining half in half, then passed it to Gabe, who ate what was left. She disappeared into the kitchen and then returned a moment later a pair of sodas.

"Thank you," Holly said, accepting it, popping it open, and quickly taking a deep drink.

"Where's mine?" Gabe asked with mock irritation.

Ellen laughed. "I thought we'd share one, lover boy. Just like we're gonna share Holly later on."

She snorted into her drink and started coughing. "Oh shit, I'm sorry!" she cried. "I spilled on you."

"It's fine," Gabe replied.

"You could lick it off," Ellen said.

"I...yeah, I could," Holly murmured.

She set the soda aside, got down on her knees and leaned in. The soda had ended up getting on his chest. She stuck her tongue out and dragged it slowly across his skin. He shuddered a little at the warm, wet contact and she grinned as she straightened back up.

"I feel like that was hot," she said.

"It was so hot," Ellen said.

Holly's smile slowly broadened. "So, uh...since I'm already down here on my knees..." She reached out and placed a hand over his crotch. "Oh wow, you're already hard."

"I think that's answer enough," Ellen said.

"Well, if you're offering I certainly won't say no," Gabe replied.

"I'm offering," Holly said.

"May I join you?" Ellen asked. "Gabe took me

on the nicest date recently and I have been meaning to do something really nice for him in return, and *I* think that joining our super sexy fuck friend in blowing him would be nice."

"Yeah, you can join me. I've never done something like that before," Holly said.

"That would be extremely nice," Gabe replied, feeling lust not just pulse through him but roar wildly as Ellen stood up and began taking her shirt off.

"Oh yeah, I should do that, too," Holly murmured, taking off her own shirt.

"Good fucking lord, you two have amazing tits," Gabe said as their shirts and bras came off. Well, Holly's bra, Ellen wasn't wearing one. "You both are going to be hot forever."

Holly laughed as she began undoing his belt. "I appreciate it, though I imagine my looks will start running out in twenty years or so, maybe twenty five."

"What?! No way! Holly, you and Ellen are going to be absolutely banging well into your fifties, sixties too, probably," Gabe replied.

"What? Come on, don't be ridiculous."

"He's right," Ellen said. "Although Gabe clearly has a taste for older women."

"He does? Oh, right. But...wait, you aren't *that* much older than him?"

"Oh no," Ellen murmured, unzipping his pants, "not me, honey."

"...who then?"

Ellen chuckled. "Let's just say that Gabe has the eye of a certified cougar. A fifty year old cougar. And he would *so* happily fuck her brains out. She *is* very hot."

"Are you fucking with me right now?" Holly

asked.

"No! I'm being serious. I can't really get into details, because it's private at the moment, but yeah, I'm telling the truth."

"Gabe," Holly said, looking at him now, "you'd fuck a fifty year old woman?"

"In a heartbeat," he replied. "Shit, I've seen women over the age of sixty who I would be absolutely down to fuck if they were."

"That's crazy," she murmured. "And cool. I just...hear a lot about how women should just stop trying to look sexy after they hit forty."

"Fuck that bullshit," Ellen replied, "hot for life. Now..." she murmured, freeing his erection from his boxers, "let us tend to this man that we both like so very much."

Holly giggled. "I *do* like him very much."

The entirety of the world seemed to drop away as both of them, topless and gorgeous and perfect, stuck their tongues out and leaned in. He could feel their hot breaths as they drew closer. Ellen looked happy and horny, Holly looked nervous, though that seemed to already be fading. Gabe groaned as both of their tongues made contact at the same time.

"I think he likes it," Ellen murmured, and Holly laughed.

Then Ellen gripped his shaft and both of them were licking his head, dragging their tongues across it and causing a symphony of hot, wet ecstasy to begin cascading through him. He found himself breathing heavily, flushing with heat as the pleasure came roaring into existence.

The sheer eroticism of seeing these two licking his dick was almost overwhelming.

They kept licking, dragging their tongues over

his most sensitive area, lighting him up with rapture. Ellen and Holly both stared at him. Ellen looked seductive and Holly looked horny and excited.

"Here, give me a little room, I'll show you something," Ellen murmured.

"Ooh, okay," she replied. "I've never done anything sexual at all with another woman."

"I am selfishly glad that I get to be your first girl. And, in many ways, you are mine," Ellen said. She raised up his erection. "See that part right there, just below the head? Suck on it. Gently. And use your tongue, too. It's crazy sensitive."

"All right."

Holly leaned in and tilted her head, then pressed her lips to the base of his head. Gabe groaned as she began sucking on it and flicking her tongue against it.

"See? Told you," Ellen said, grinning fiercely.

Holly looked pleased with herself and kept going. Gabe groaned louder as she continued pleasuring him and then, a few seconds later, he felt soft warmth against his balls. Ellen was cradling them, he realized. She began to massage them gently.

Holly continued with her pleasure until she pulled back suddenly. "Sorry," she murmured, "it's kind of hurting my neck."

"That's fine. That was fucking great," Gabe replied.

"My turn," Ellen said.

She leaned in and slipped his head between her lips, then continuing sliding them down his shaft until his entire erection was buried in her wonderful mouth. He kept staring, enraptured, as she held his eyes with her own, her head bobbing smoothly.

Ellen could really suck dick, he had been very happy to learn.

His tall, pale blonde goddess continued for another half minute, then took it out of her mouth and passed it to Holly, who took up the task eagerly.

"How do you want to come?" Ellen murmured, her voice a demure purr.

"Holly's mouth," he replied.

She laughed. "I figured. You look pretty close. Holly, give me a thumbs up and keep going if you're okay with that."

Holly raised her thumb.

"You okay to swallow?" he asked.

She raised her thumb again and Ellen laughed. "Well, take it away, red."

Holly kept going, increasing her speed, her lips slipping up and down his cock faster, blasting him with pleasure. Everything about her looked wonderfully sexual. Her hair was already getting messy, her eyes alight with lust, her big, pale, bare breasts swaying back and forth with the motion of her oral sex. All it took was her going at it like that for a few seconds more and staring into her eyes, feeling that intense sexual connection, to set him off.

Gabe groaned loudly, slipping a hand over the back of her head and pushing forward almost without realizing it. She didn't try to stop him, instead taking his head to the back of her throat as he started coming.

He let out another loud sound of pleasure as she swallowed, an eruption of ecstasy and sexual gratification exploding out from his core as she did it, all those tight, wet muscles contracting slickly around his orgasming dick.

Gabe came hard, his seed leaving him in intense, furious spurts, and it kept going until there was nothing left. Each time Holly swallowed it was another burst of pure bliss.

When it was over, he let go of her and fell back against the couch, panting.

She took his dick out of her mouth and coughed a few times.

"Sorry," he managed, "I should've warned you."

"It's fine," Holly replied, grinning as she accept her soda from Ellen, who had been holding it for her. "I've never had a cock jammed into my throat before." She took another drink, then laughed awkwardly. "I actually mean that in a good way. I liked it."

"I think we're all learning that you enjoy being...handled," Ellen said, getting up.

"Does that mean something specific? There was something about the way you said it," Holly asked, standing as well.

"What I mean is, I think you might be into rough play."

"I have more of an idea of what that means but..."

"Wow, you *are* innocent. Which is not a bad thing," Ellen said. "It means...well, typically speaking, people either enjoy holding others down and fucking them, or they enjoy being held down and fucked. I believe you enjoy being held down and fucked like a cheap whore."

"I, uh..." She laughed awkwardly, blushing hard now, "...yeah. That sounds, um...nice."

"Have you ever been tied up? Or handcuffed? While being fucked?" Ellen asked.

"No."

"But the idea turns you on?"

"Uh...I think so? I'm not sure, it's hard to know because I'm kinda horny right now in general," Holly murmured. She took another drink, then inhaled sharply. "Ow, fuck."

"You okay?" Gabe asked.

"Yeah, just...my back. It hurts."

"Sounds like an absolutely perfect excuse to get you naked and for Gabe to massage you," Ellen said.

"I'd really like that, actually," Holly replied.

"Let's do it," Gabe said.

CHAPTER SEVEN

"Oh my God that's amazing," Holly groaned.

Gabe laughed softly, running his hands slowly down her bare back. She was completely naked now. Actually, at this point, they all were.

Ellen sat down on the bed, watching them with that sultry smile of hers.

"Holly, what did you mean earlier, about weed?" he replied, working his way down to her lower back.

Ellen had told him that women with big breasts tended to have lower back problems, and Holly definitely had some big tits.

"Oh, that. It's nothing fucked up…" She paused. "Well, maybe it is. I don't know. I have to admit, meeting you two has me questioning a lot of things. In a good way. But, okay, yeah. So, it really has to do with my ex-boyfriend–" She paused, began to try and twist back to look at Gabe, but quickly gave up and settled for laying her head on its side, "is it weird to talk about my ex while I'm over here hooking up with you?"

"No. It's not like I'm jealous," Gabe replied.

She laughed. "You have nothing to be jealous of. You're better than him in every way. But okay then. So he was into smoking weed. Obviously, I wasn't, because of how I was raised. I used to be scared of it, but at some point I realized it was bullshit, everything my parents tried to scare me with. I wanted to try it. He seemed cool with it at first.

"So I tried it. And it was nice. I got high a few times, it was fun. But then he tried to stop me from smoking it. At first I didn't even notice. I'd do it maybe once a month when I was really stressed and it was a weekend. At some point I realized that he was still smoking, but whenever I wanted some, there was some excuse why I couldn't."

"That's weird," Gabe said. He popped something in her back and she let out a loud, long moan.

"Oh *fuuuuuck,* Gabe. That's...that one has been bothering me all week."

Ellen laughed. "I know exactly how you feel."

"I'll bet. I'm really jealous you get this every night...anyway, so, yeah, weird. After a while, I finally put two and two together, realizing he was still smoking pretty regular, but he never had any for me. I thought it was because he just wanted it all to himself, but I confronted him about it. He first told me he didn't want me to hurt my brain, because I was so smart."

"Which turned out to be a lie, I'm guessing," Ellen said.

"Yeah. I mean, I bought it. It actually made a lot of sense to me. But then later, like during the last few months of the relationship, we were having a fight, and it somehow came out that he made me stop smoking weed because he was afraid that if I turned into a stoner, I'd be more likely to cheat on him," she replied.

"How...does that make sense?" Gabe asked, pausing in his massage as he tried to piece that one together.

"So I basically asked the same thing. I guess it's a thing for guys to invite girls over and get them stoned, which gets them horny and more likely to just fuck, even if they're already dating someone? I don't know, but so yeah, that's my story with it. I didn't ever do it again after that because, I don't know, it just felt weird."

"I hope this will help overwrite that bullshit," Ellen said. "You feeling anything yet?"

"No, not yet...maybe a little? I don't know."

"It can take a while to kick in and it's kind of varied. You might also have a really high tolerance for it. I know some people who can eat five times what you just ate and feel basically nothing," Gabe replied.

"I don't think I have a high tolerance for it. It usually just took a few tokes for me to get stoned."

"Well, there's more if you want more, but I want to give it a good hour before that," Ellen said. She smiled and reached over, running one hand slowly down Holly's back. "I'm so glad you felt safe enough with us to try this."

"I trust you more than I've ever trusted anyone, I think," Holly murmured. "Is that insane? We've barely known each other a week."

"Sometimes, it's just...when you know, you know," Gabe replied.

"It feels so good to trust people and do stuff like this. Not even just the sex stuff, although that is fucking *awesome*. But just...being here together, telling each other stuff. I feel like...mmm, how do I put it? I feel like, when I'm here, I don't have to pretend to be anything. I don't have to pretend to be happy or cool or smart. I can just...be."

"Gabe has that effect," Ellen said. "Because I felt the *exact* same goddamned thing when we first started hooking up. I mean, when we were just talking to each other a few years ago, too, but it kicked in hard when we started being together. It's like a superpower or something. He pulls vulnerability out of us."

"Is that so bad?" Gabe asked.

"No, it just means we're way more likely to

spread our legs," Ellen replied.

Holly laughed. "How many other girlfriends you have around here?"

"Just you."

"And a cougar, apparently."

"I haven't slept with her. I haven't done anything with her," he said.

"Yet," Ellen murmured.

"Shut it," he said, looking at her.

"Mmm...maybe you should *make* me," she replied.

"It's extremely tempting," he said.

"Don't forget about Em," Ellen replied, smirking more broadly.

"Who's Em?" Holly asked.

Ellen laughed and Gabe sighed. "Right," he said. "So...wait, didn't we talk about this last time? Whatever. I swapped oral with Ellen's friend."

"My *married* friend. Me and her wife watched while they did it. In the back of a car. At a party," Ellen replied. "We have video of it, actually."

"Oh yeah! Okay I remember now. Sorry, it's just-a *lot* has been happening just recently thanks to you two," Holly said. "That still seems so wild."

"I watched you have sex with my boyfriend four days ago," Ellen said.

"Yeah, just...I don't know. I guess it just seems a little crazy to me...do you have any other pics or vids I could see?"

"Emily said she's cool with that," Ellen replied, getting up. "There's some pics she's been sending."

"Okay, here, lemme up," Holly said. Gabe got off of her and she began getting up, then she stopped, on her hands and knees now. "Oh. Ohhhh wow."

Gabe laughed. "You're feeling it?"

OUR OWN WAY 2

"Uh, yeah. Whoa. This is...whoooooa. My head is all...swimmy. Uh." She giggled. "This feels amazing. Like...this is definitely different from what I remember last time. This is a lot more intense. I guess that makes sense cuz it took longer to kick in."

"You feeling good about it?" Ellen asked as she kept hunting around for her phone.

"Oh *yes,*" Holly murmured, falling onto her side and giggling some more. "It's so good. *Wow* is it good. I love it and...oh my, I'm *horny*. Like *really* horny."

"Same," Gabe agreed.

"Yep," Ellen said, giving up her search for her phone.

"What should we do?" Holly murmured.

"I was hoping for a more full-on threesome this time," Ellen replied. "Are you comfortable with that?"

"Yes," Holly said immediately. "I want you two to make good use of me."

"Oh, you like the idea of being used like a piece of fuckmeat?" Gabe asked, running a hand down her thigh.

"*Yes,*" she groaned, shuddering under his touch. "I do. If it's you two. So much."

"Yeah? You want to be destroyed by Gabe here?" Ellen murmured.

"Yes. Very badly."

"I know this desire," Ellen said, grinning broadly.

Gabe pushed Holly over onto her back and then held himself up over her, staring down at her flawless, pale body, her flushed face, full of lust and the kind of shy, anxious energy someone who was exploring their sexuality in true depth for the first time had.

He leaned in and kissed her. She moaned and kissed him back. After a bit, he pulled back and slipped lower.

"She's never had two people suck her on tits at the same time," he said.

"That's right," Ellen murmured, "we should fix that."

"Oh, I...mmm, okay," Holly whispered, starting to pant as Gabe licked across one of her vividly pink nipples.

She let out a moan as Ellen did the same with her other breast, and then she started panting as they each began sucking on her big, firm tits.

"Oh wow," she gasped, "that's-oh my. Holy-oh that's good. *OH!*" she cried as Gabe started rubbing her clit.

Ellen laughed softly and joined him, slipping a hand down between her thick, smooth thighs and pushing a finger inside of her.

"Oh my God!" she yelled.

"Too much?" Gabe murmured, licking across her breast.

"Ye-no-I don't know just don't stop!"

He and Ellen both laughed and kept pleasuring her. He felt like they were playing her body like an instrument, she was so reactive and everything seemed to be going so perfectly. Holly was moaning and twisting and occasionally thrashing as they hit a sensitive spot. Sucking on her breast was a true pleasure, and seeing Ellen doing it at the same time just heightened the effect.

When Holly orgasmed, Ellen had to put a hand over her mouth because she was screaming so loud. She thrashed and twisted and spasmed as the climax ran wild through her body. Her pleasure continued for a good, long time and when it had passed, she was left gasping for breath, flushed badly, her hair a wild mess.

"You okay there, Holly?" Gabe asked.

"...yes," she whispered. "Oh wow. I...have never felt something like that before. Is it the weed?"

"I think it's the weed and also the fact that you're with two skilled, experiences fuckers," Ellen said.

"Yes," she murmured. "That tracks."

Gabe had to sit on an impulse to point out he didn't necessarily feel skilled or experienced. Holly seemed to have a pretty clear view of him and his abilities, and he had to wonder how much of that was psychological. And if it was, why should he do anything to erode that notion? They were all enjoying it. Why not lean into it, at least a little?

"We haven't even fucked yet," he said, running his fingertips down one sweat-slicked arm.

She made a weird sound and shuddered hard. "...that's also true."

"I think we broke her," Ellen said, laughing.

"I think so, too. I feel, um, just...amazing. I think that was the best orgasm I've ever had...I really want to be fucked right now."

"What a coincidence," Gabe replied, pushing her legs open wider and getting between them, "I really want to fuck you right now."

She laughed loudly, her breasts jiggling wonderfully, then she gasped as he made contact with her, rubbing his head between the wet, warm lips of her pussy. He was already rock hard and ready to go again.

Getting back inside of Holly was like a hard hit of harder drugs.

She let out a loud, long moan of pleasure as he penetrated her. He worked his way quickly inside of her, finding her wonderfully wet and inviting and oh so hot within, and then he laid down against her pale nude body, kissing her deeply. Holly immediately kissed him back, wrapping her arms and legs around him and screaming into the kiss as he began driving into her.

They continued like that for what felt like a while, both of them lost in the absolute bliss of sex. At some point he felt Ellen's hand on his back and he remembered that she wanted in on this, too. He pulled back, and had to spend a moment untangling himself from Holly's grabbing limbs. As soon as he was up, resting on his knees and still fucking her smoothly, Ellen leaned down and began making out with her and groping her big breasts.

They both moaned as they made out, tongues twisting together passionately. Gabe grabbed her ankles and held her legs up, spread wide, as he continued driving into her. Holly seemed to be having trouble keeping up with it all, breaking the kiss several times as he screwed her.

"Gabe," she murmured, "you should grab Holly's wrists and pin them to the bed."

"You want that, Holly?" he asked as Ellen moved out of the way again.

"Yeah, that sounds hot," she replied.

He grinned and grabbed her wrists, leaning forward and pinning them to the pillow over her head. He kept driving into her, staring down at her, and she let out a surprised moan.

"Holly fuck-why is this so hot!?" she cried.

"Knew it," Ellen said.

"You like, you little whore?" he asked, tightening

his grasp a little.

"I-uhn-*yes!*" she screamed and then she was orgasming again.

Gabe groaned loudly, feeling her pussy contracting and fluttering wildly around his erection as he kept thrusting into her. Each time he did she let out a new cry of bliss, a hot gush of sex juices escaping her as he fucked her brains out.

It was a monumental struggle not to come inside of her.

But somehow he managed, and when she had finished with her orgasm, he pulled out of her. He could sense Ellen's need to be fucked.

"Your turn, babe," he said, panting, sweaty now.

"On your back," she replied.

Gabe laid down as she made room and Holly watched them as Ellen mounted him, took him inside of her wet opening, and then began riding him, putting her immense hips to excellent use.

"Good fucking lord that is hot," Holly whispered.

"Gabe is the only guy I've ever met who is happy to let me ride him," Ellen said.

"What?! How!? Being ridden by you seems like it would be the best thing ever," Holly cried.

Ellen laughed. "You'd think so."

"Gabe looks, just, deliriously happy right now."

"That's a good way to describe it," Gabe replied distractedly, groping Ellen's enormous breasts as she kept fucking him, bouncing on his cock and banging him down into the mattress.

She kept riding him until she orgasmed, and somehow he managed to hold onto his own climax a second time, though he wasn't sure how.

"Okay, now you can do what you want," Ellen said, getting off of him.

"I know exactly what I want," he replied, sitting up. "Ellen, on your back. Holly, lay on her on your back as well."

"Ooh, I've seen this in porn," Holly murmured as they got into position.

He got them where he wanted them, then, once they were where he needed them, Gabe paused.

"What?" Ellen asked.

"I need a picture of this," he replied.

"Get it," she said.

"Yeah, I wanna see," Holly agreed.

For a moment he completely blanked on where he'd put his phone, then remembered it was in the living room, jogged out to grab it and hurried back. He was so desperate to continue fucking them that he almost dropped his phone as he tried to get the camera on.

"There," he said, snapping the picture of the two naked women.

"Film it!" Ellen said.

"Yeah!" Holly agreed immediately.

"All right," he said, getting his video camera function going and then climbing onto the bed again. Once he had it on, he rested on his knees between their spread open legs and penetrated Holly again. "You're both getting creampies."

"You already came once!" Holly moaned.

"Don't care, I'm fucking horny as hell right now," he replied.

There was an absolute surreality to fucking Holly as she laid atop Ellen, then pulling out, shifting down, and fucking Ellen, listening to both of them moan and cry out. It was even more surreal to be seeing it through a phone.

The pleasure was beginning to overwhelm him.

He kept going, driving furiously into them and listening to them moan and shout, switching back and forth between them, until he couldn't hold out any longer. He made sure he was in Ellen when he came first, given she was the one on the bottom.

"Oh shit, he's about to come," Ellen said, then moaned.

"How can you tell?" Holly murmured.

"Hard to say, I just...oh fuck!"

She moaned as he drove more furiously into her and then it happened, and he was unleashing his seed deep within her. He groaned loudly, almost dropping the phone, as he came inside of her. The ecstasy and gratification blasted through him as he filled her up.

When he was finished, he pulled out and put himself right back into Holly.

CHAPTER EIGHT

"So," Gabe said, feeling more than a little dazed after everything that had happened, and the hot shower that had followed, "how was everyone's first threesome?"

"Mind-blowing," Holly murmured sleepily.

They were all under the blankets, naked, Holly between the two of them.

"That pretty much sums it up for me," Ellen said. "It was beyond hot. I'm impressed. I honestly wasn't sure if you could come three times in under an hour."

"I wasn't either," he said, then groaned a little. "My dick kind of hurts."

"You have got to give yourself more of a break," Ellen replied.

"Oh don't *even* with that shit. I have the two of you, horny as fuck and naked and gagging for my dick, and you expect me to, what, say 'hold on, give me an hour'?"

They both giggled.

"He has a point," Holly murmured, then yawned.

"Okay, that's fair. We should probably sleep. Holly's fading fast."

"I'm here," she said, then yawned again. "I'm pretty beat, though. That fucking took it out of me."

"More like put it in you," Ellen said, and Holly giggled again.

"Sleep, cutie," Gabe said, and kissed her on the forehead.

"Yeah," Ellen agreed, kissing the back of her head.

"You guys are too nice," she said softly. "Why are you so nice? You coulda just fucked me and booted me, or even just ignored me."

"We *like* you, Holly," Ellen said.

"Yeah." Gabe took her hand and she smiled tiredly and gave it a gentle squeeze. "I know we haven't known each other for long, and I know we're more or less hooking up but...we care about you, Holly. And I know it seems like we're experienced but you have to remember, this is new for us, too. Even if it wasn't, though, we want to make sure you're taken care of and happy."

"You're doing a really, really, *really* good job then. Thank you. A lot."

"You're welcome. Goodnight, Holly," Gabe replied.

"Yeah, goodnight, pretty girl," Ellen said.

She laughed softly, her eyes already closed. "Night," she murmured.

"We should get to sleep, too," Gabe said.

"Very true," Ellen agreed. "I love you."

"I love you too, babe."

They shared a kiss over Holly, who had already slipped into sleep, and then settled in.

. . .

Gabe opened his eyes to a redheaded model staring at him.

"Shit," he muttered, jerking back a little.

"Oh! Sorry!" Holly said, then giggled. "I didn't mean to scare you."

"Were you watching me sleep?" he asked, rubbing one eye.

"Yeah."

"Why?...not that I'm complaining."

"Ellen told me you are insanely cute when you're

sleeping and that I should watch you. So I did. And I'm still a little buzzed from last night, so I guess I got a little distracted."

"Wait, so how long have you been watching?"

She laughed. "Not like *hours,* maybe like ten minutes?"

"Huh. Was she right?"

"Oh yeah. Big time. You're adorable when you're asleep."

He chuckled and pushed the blankets away. "Not sure how to take that."

"It's a compliment," she replied. "Can we shower together?"

"Yeah."

Gabe checked his phone, finding it to be just past ten in the morning. Ellen wasn't in the bedroom, though he could hear faint typing coming from, he assumed, the living room. He got up with Holly and then poked his head into the living room. Ellen was indeed stretched out in the couch, wearing her robe, frowning at her laptop.

"Morning, lovely."

She smiled and looked up. "Morning, handsome."

"Gonna take a shower and then...I was thinking. We should do something today, all three of us, out of the house," he replied.

"I was thinking the exact same thing. I can have this wrapped up in ten minutes, and I haven't had breakfast yet."

"Perfect."

He headed into the bathroom, where he found Holly standing before the mirror, brushing her teeth. She said something garbled and barely coherent to him as he started up the shower.

"Yeah, I don't mind," he replied.

She glanced at him, toothbrush still in mouth, then quickly finished up, rinsed and spat.

"How the fuck did you understand that?" she asked.

"Context, I guess," he replied.

"It's really not weird that I'm using your toothbrush?"

"Considering all the things we've done, no," he replied.

She laughed. "I guess that's a good point."

They switched places and he smacked her bare ass in passing. She gave a little sound of surprise, then giggled and got in the shower. Gabe washed off his toothbrush and then brushed his own teeth, then took a long leak and joined Holly in the shower.

"I have a question," she said.

"Shoot."

"You obviously think I'm really hot. What's it like for you, fucking me?" she asked.

"It's kinda like…" Gabe paused and considered it. "Well, to be honest, it's like how I imagined fucking a porn star would be like. Only better."

"How is it better?!"

"I'm a realist at heart, and so it kind of fucks with even my fantasies. It's harder to imagine a porn star being nice to me while we have sex, given I don't have a big dick, I'm not very attractive, and I'm not great at sex, at least compared to what they're used to," he replied. "You seem pretty obviously into the sex when we have it."

"I am. I so am," she replied. "And I don't know if it helps but…I made online friends with a porn star. Not, like, a *huge* one, but like that was her job. And she was always complaining."

"About what?"

"Everything. Porn isn't fun, apparently. Or, it's less fun for the girls. A lot of the positions are super uncomfortable, and it smells awful, and it's really annoying, having a camera on you all the time, everyone constantly trying to fuck you. But she said she hated dealing with giant dicks. She said there's size queens who are into that, which is cool, but past a certain point, and I mean not much beyond the average, it just hurt. That's why I was so relieved when I saw your dick."

He laughed. "It's kinda weird hearing that you're relieved I have a small dick."

"I didn't say small! I said it *wasn't* huge...are you mad at me?" she asked. "I didn't mean to insult you, I just–"

"I'm not mad, Holly. I was joking, mostly...why were so sure it was huge?"

"Ellen? She's, like, *so* fucking tall. And thick. It's just where my brain went. Happy I'm wrong. You are the *perfect* size. It feels amazing in me." She paused, then frowned. "Sorry, I feel like I'm making too big a deal out of this. I'm not and I know it's this whole thing...I just, I'm happy with your size, end of statement."

"Works for me," he replied. "How about you?"

"How about me what?"

"What's it like having sex with me?"

"Oh, man, just...hot. And fun. I didn't know it could be like this. We've only done it twice but...it's like you can read my mind. I barely have to think about something, like wanting to adjust, or wanting you to do it a little different, or faster, or slower, and you react immediately. You can read me *way* too good. Ellen's good too, but...you're something else."

She smiled suddenly. "Like fucking a porn star...but better. I really like that."

"So do I."

They switched after she finished washing up and she simply looked at him. "So...what are we doing today? Or am I assuming too much? Should I go?"

"We'd like to enjoy your company some more," he replied.

"Okay good. I've got today off and I was really hoping to spend it with you both."

"Excellent. I thought, because you're so stressed, Ellen and I could take you on a date day."

Her eyes lit up. "Really?! That would be amazing! I'd love it so much! What would we do?!"

He laughed. "Well, is there anything in particular you'd like to do?"

"Anything?" she asked.

"Anything within reason. Like...within the city and not insanely expensive," he said.

"Okay...oh! I know exactly what I would like to do. Across town there's this place, it's a combination bowling alley, mini-golf course, and arcade. I used to go all the time in high school. For some reason it was the only place my parents were cool with me going. I think they knew the owner and he pretended to be religious."

"You think he wasn't?"

"I know he wasn't. I know for a fact he did meth in the bathroom with his employees, and he was always hitting on high school girls who came around. I think maybe it got sold at some point, but I would *love* to go back there. I've been meaning to and I know it's still there and operating. It would mean so much if we could go!"

"Then we'll go," Gabe replied.

"For real? I could pay if you wanted me to."

"Holly, when you date Ellen and I, you don't pay," he said.

"Oh." She smiled. "I...like that." Then she slowly lost it. "Unless that's shitty to like?"

"How would it be shitty? I'm literally offering," he asked as he finished washing up and killed the shower.

They both grabbed towels and started drying.

"I know there's this whole thing about who should pay on a date. Guy or girl, or both? I feel like it's totally cool to split the bill, I mean, you're both going on a date together, but it's become like a battlefield or something. Some guys get offended if a girl tries to pay, some women not only expect a man to pay, but will go out of their way to try and order the most expensive shit. And then, like, politics gets dragged into it, like...somehow I'm letting down women everywhere by just rolling over and being like 'yes please pay for me man taking me on a date', you know?"

"I think...things have gotten really complicated over the past decade and a half, and it's only going to get worse, and what really matters the most is what the people actually involved in the situation think," Gabe said. "And I think if you and me and Ellen are all okay with us paying, then that's the end of it."

"...yeah," she murmured as she finished drying off and hung the towel back up, "I like that." She stepped over to the mirror, then wiped at it and frowned as she studied herself.

"Something wrong?" he asked.

"My hair...would you guys lose, like, a lot of attraction for me if I cut my hair kinda short? I want it short, but I keep hearing about how guys don't like girls with shorter hair."

"You should do what you want with your hair and fuck what anyone else thinks. It's *your* hair," Gabe replied.

"Yeah, but you've got a vested interest in me looking attractive, right?" she asked.

He laughed. "I mean, I do? But that doesn't matter. You should do what you want. Also, you're making the assumption that getting a shorter hairstyle would make you less attractive, and that is an incorrect assumption."

She laughed. "Is that so?"

"Oh yeah. I fucking *love* women with short hair. In fact, if you want, we could do that, too."

"You'd take me to get a haircut?"

"If that's what you wanted, yes."

"You're really sweet."

"I try to be," he said. "Now, come on, let's get dressed. I'm starving."

...

They had breakfast at a diner that was more upscale than the place where Holly worked.

She seemed practically bubbly in how happy she was. She kept smiling, talking eagerly about pretty much whatever caught her attention. She had a lot of questions for them, and they were only to happy to answer.

In a way, it made Gabe a little sad.

He knew he was seeing a person who had been miserable for a very long time suddenly being thrust into a state of happiness, and the little he knew about Holly so far seemed to paint a picture of a smart, kind, earnest young woman who had been mistreated by life in a rather harsh way. As they ate, he suddenly gained a stronger and deeper understanding of what Ellen had been talking about: that protective instinct.

He just wanted to take care of her and make sure she was okay.

He wanted to protect her, but there was an extra layer of complication wrapping that up because he was a guy and she was a girl. There were all sorts of bizarre societal twists as to why that complicated things, and he wanted to adhere to the standard he'd *just* set with her, about them making their own decisions within their own little group.

But he couldn't deny that even when it was just the three of them, alone together, they'd been warped by the society that had raised them.

All that being said though, Gabe was beginning to think that Holly really did just want someone to take care of her, and she did actually seem very enamored of him. So why not? As long as he wasn't taking advantage of her or hurting her, then why would it be a problem for him to be protective of her?

He kept all this inside his head and apparently did a good job, because neither Ellen nor Holly asked him if something was wrong.

Once the food was gone, they took her to a haircut place and, after some consideration, all three of them ended up getting a trim.

When it was over, they all stood together in front of the shop, looking at each other. Holly looked particularly anxious.

"Well? Come on, is it dumb?" she asked.

"No, not at all. It's hot," Ellen replied.

"You aren't just telling me what I want to hear, right?"

"It's really hot," Gabe agreed.

"Okay...I'm sorry. I just-I got my hair cut once when I was seventeen, shorter than this, and my parents just absolutely flipped out. They started screaming at me, they thought I was a lesbian all of a sudden? It was so awful."

"Your parents are the fucking worst," Ellen muttered. "You look fantastic, Holly. Beautiful. Now, how about we go to that bowling alley and just fuck off like teenagers again all day?"

"That sounds like an amazing plan," Holly replied eagerly.

Gabe led them back towards the car. "Let's go."

CHAPTER NINE

"Just so you two know, I'm going to dominate," Ellen said as they switched out their shoes.

"What makes you so confident?" Gabe asked.

Ellen smirked. "I know you dominate in bed, sweetheart, but not only do I have the massive height advantage, I also actually did bowl somewhat seriously for two years about a decade ago. I intend to sweep the floor with you two."

"Makes sense to me," Holly replied with a shrug. "I just like throwing the ball."

"I guess we'll see, won't we," Gabe said, tying his shoes.

"Is that a *challenge* I hear in your voice?" Ellen asked, her tone turning far more interested.

"Could be," he replied with a shrug.

"You're fucking on, babe."

"Why don't we make it interesting?" he asked, smirking at her.

Ellen glared at him.

"...man, she's staring daggers at you," Holly murmured. "I'd be wetting myself."

"What did you have in mind?" she asked, her voice low, somewhere between amused and irritated.

"First game, whoever has a higher score by the end...gets to receive oral sex from the loser. In the bathroom. Here," he replied quietly.

Her expression changed, but not by much.

"You are fucking on," she growled.

"I think you might've opened Pandora's Box or something," Holly murmured.

"I guess we'll see, won't we," he replied.

"Oh we'll *see* all right," Ellen growled. "I'm

gonna *see* you on your knees between my thighs in about twenty minutes."

"If you say so," he replied with a shrug.

"When did you get so fucking cocky?" she asked.

"Since meeting you," he replied.

"Why is this so hot?" Holly whispered.

"Roll, motherfucker," Ellen snapped.

As cocky as he was acting, Gabe did wonder.

He had admittedly started poking her for fun and he hadn't expected her to react so strongly. Then again, was it any wonder that a woman who had built her life on fighting for everything would have a *very* strong competitive streak? He wondered, suddenly, if he'd just discovered an interesting new aspect of their relationship.

Gabe stretched for a bit, loosening up, and then took his time selecting his ball. He was still testing them out when he heard Ellen go. He glanced over and saw she'd knocked down eight of the pins. The second her ball came back she hurled it again and knocked the rest down.

"Come on, Gabe. It's your turn," she taunted.

"Have a little patience, dear," he replied. "You can't be *that* eager to blow me."

"You're walking on thin ice, mister."

He glanced at her again. She was staring intently at him, a small, almost dangerous smile on her face. "You're *really* into this competition, aren't you?"

"Gabe, let's just say that...I don't lose."

For a moment he wondered if maybe he'd wandered into actually dangerous territory. He didn't want to piss her off. But he couldn't shake something his gut was telling him. That as much as she did want to answer his cocky call and trounce his ass, she wanted him to win more. She wanted him to dominate her.

Well, here was hoping he could. And that he was right.

Gabe found the ball that seemed best and moved over to the lane. Holly was watching raptly. He lined himself up and took a few practice swings. Then, focusing, he hurled the ball down the lane, releasing it and sending it rolling fast and hard right down the center.

It slammed into the pins and knocked over every last one.

"I seem to have gotten a strike," he said, turning to face Ellen.

She was staring at the pins but quickly turned her attention to him.

"I'd better not find out you're secretly a fucking expert at this," she muttered.

"I may have had some practice," he replied with an easy shrug, going and sitting down beside Holly. "Your turn, cutie."

"You two are getting scary," she murmured as she got up.

"Don't worry, it's all in good, if intense, fun," Gabe replied.

"Uh-huh," Ellen agreed, and seemed to make an effort to contain herself a little more.

Gabe couldn't keep the smile off his face, though.

This was going to be interesting.

...

Gabe stepped up to the line for the last time.

It had been a surprisingly tense game. It was obvious that Ellen was no slouch, not that he'd ever doubted her skill. But she was definitely good, and her great height definitely gave her more command of the bowling ball.

But he had somehow managed to luck into getting the gym teacher in high school who allowed his students to walk to the nearby bowling alley and practice bowling twice a week three years in a row, and he'd also played at least every once in a while, when he could afford it, to blow off some steam. Ellen had the power, to be sure, but he definitely had better aim.

And, apparently, that's what counted here.

The only way he was going to lose this was if he missed both throws here.

And, to be honest, he was feeling lucky.

He wound up and threw the ball.

It was a strike.

He heard Ellen groan loudly as he waited for his ball to come back. When it did, he wound up and did the exact same thing.

And got another strike.

"Oh come on!" she groaned.

As he wound up for his third and final throw for the last frame of the game, he briefly considered trying to gutter it, but quickly surmised that she would be insulted. So he aimed true and threw hard. And managed to get a third strike.

"Are you kidding me?!"

"Holy shit, that's amazing," Holly murmured.

"Well, well, well," Gabe said, turning around and smirking at Ellen, "looks like I won."

"Get in the fucking bathroom," she growled.

He said nothing, just walked towards her and then off towards the empty side of the bowling alley. At this point, he wasn't completely sure if he'd actually pissed her off or not.

"I'll just be here," Holly murmured.

Apparently neither could she.

Ellen marched silently after him.

"You don't have to do this if you don't want to," he said, growing serious as they approached the bathroom.

"I want to. Now get in there," she replied, giving him that sort of dangerous smile she had adopted.

He'd never quite seen her like this before.

Gabe looked around, making sure no one was watching, then scoped out the bathroom. He was relieved to find it small and empty, just a pair of stalls and a pair of urinals. He motioned for her to come in and she did, then locked the door behind them.

"Get over there," she said.

"Are you mad?" he asked, unable to keep from smirking a little.

"No," she said simply.

Gabe decided to take her at her word.

They moved over to the far stall, got in and closed the door. Ellen got down onto her knees. She sighed as she started unzipping his pants.

"This is going to be hell on my knees," she muttered.

"I guess you'll have make me come fast then," he replied.

She pursed her lips and glared up at him, and couldn't keep the smile off her face. He had to admit, this sort of playful antagonism was both interesting and arousing.

Without a word, she got his cock out and got to work.

She got him off in ninety seconds flat.

He'd never had such an aggressive blowjob

before, nor such an effective one. She was going for the kill immediately, and she got it.

He put both hands over the back of her head and jammed his cock as far down her throat as he could manage as he started coming, encouraged by her intensity. The pleasure was beyond intense, a hot surge of deeply gratifying ecstasy and release.

Ellen swallowed everything.

When she was finished and he released her, she stood up and then moved to the mirror, where she studied herself and fixed her hair, then washed her face.

"You...are not like anyone else I have ever dated before," he murmured as he put himself away.

"Nope," she agreed.

Then she finished up and walked out of the bathroom. Gabe lingered for a moment, contemplating the interaction. Something had definitely passed between them, something that hadn't before, and he knew he was seeing this side of her that he hadn't really before. What was making him a bit nervous though was the question of: was that interaction good or bad?

Or, maybe more specifically, healthy or unhealthy?

It was *fun*, that much was clear at least, and not just because he'd gotten blown.

The problem was that he couldn't really parse it. In some way, he thought that Ellen might have been...surrendering to him?

It made a certain kind of sense, he decided as he took a piss and then washed up.

A lot of people in positions of authority or with great skills tended to try and lord it over everyone else, and they loved to be challenged...but only if they were sure they could win. They weren't looking for a real test of skill, they were looking for a chance to look good.

Truly confident or skilled people, on the other hand, sought to either win or lose, and would accept both equally. In fact, he imagined that beyond a certain threshold, you got to the point where you wanted to lose.

Is that where Ellen was?

As he made his way back to the table, something occurred to him in a more obvious way.

Ellen had a dominant personality, but not completely. There was a part of her that was submissive, strongly so, but it was something she had to bury, because she couldn't trust anyone with that knowledge.

Too many people confused sexual submission with weakness.

And Ellen already had enough morons challenging her at every turn for the simple fact that she had a vagina, not because she showed some deficit in understanding or skill.

It felt somewhat dangerous to think this, but Gabe was almost positive that Ellen wanted to be put in her place by him. It was a dynamic that he never thought he'd genuinely encounter, but it was a massive sign of true trust.

She trusted him to be able to dominate her, sexually if not socially, but still respect her.

This was her fetish.

"You look happy," Holly said between blowing on a slice of pizza.

"I am very happy," he replied. "So it finally got here?"

"It's worth the wait," Ellen said after swallowing

her bite. "This pizza is amazing, just like you said."

"Yeah! It's crazy, I used to get this pepperoni pizza *every* time I came here. I'd come here *to* get it sometimes. And it's just like it was," Holly exclaimed merrily.

Gabe took a piece and bit into it.

They were right, it was unreasonably good.

"Shit," he muttered, and kept eating.

They both laughed.

"So, another game them?" Ellen asked after a few moments.

"Yeah," Gabe replied.

"Ellen, you seem a lot...calmer. Did you, uh...do more? In there?" Holly murmured.

She laughed. "No, just what I said I was going to do."

"And that calmed you down?"

"Yes."

"Why?"

"It's..." She considered it for a moment. "I'll try to explain later. Let's just say that I had a need and Gabe fulfilled it. Even if he doesn't fully realize it..." She looked at him closely. "Although I'm wondering if perhaps he does realize it."

"Perhaps he does," Gabe agreed.

"You two are so wild," Holly said. "And kind of scary intense sometimes. Not that it's a bad thing. It's weirdly exciting in a really, um, specific way."

"Good," Ellen murmured. "Now, let's continue this date of ours."

Holly grinned broadly and took another bite.

...

"How are you feeling, Holly?" Ellen asked as the

three of them headed back to the car.

"So good! That was so fun," she replied. "I haven't had a day like this in...fuck, years? Way too long. It's been grind, grind, grind." She lost her good cheer as they came to Ellen's car. "And I have to go back to work tomorrow. Goddamnit. I don't want to leave."

"You know, you *could* spend the night again," Gabe said. "Unless you live really close, you'd actually be closer to your job from our place."

"That's true, but...are you sure I wouldn't be imposing?"

"I'm sure. Ellen?" he asked.

"I'm happy with it. You might want to grab some clothes, though. And here, you sit in the front seat."

"Are you sure?"

"Yes, it's your date, cutie."

Holly let out that awkward shy laugh of hers and ducked her head a little. "Okay," she murmured. They got into the car and she sat beside Gabe as he got behind the wheel. "It wouldn't be weird if I brought some clothes over? I feel like that's one of those things that people see as, like...a line to be crossed? Like it means we're more serious if you bring clothes over, you know? And I don't want to impose that on you..."

"We're offering, Holly," Gabe replied. "We can swing by your place and grab a few days' worth of clothes and put it in the dresser. It'll be fine."

"Okay," she said, but she still seemed kind of worried now. "Uh...I guess get back onto Holland Street, going right, and follow it for a while. I'll guide you there."

"On it," Gabe replied, starting up the car.

As she guided them through the city to her

apartment, he noticed she seemed increasingly anxious. Was she really this worked up over the clothes thing? That didn't quite feel right. Maybe it was something about where she lived. Maybe she was embarrassed. He had sure felt embarrassed of the places he'd lived before now.

Before long, they pulled into the parking lot of what might be called an upper lower class apartment complex. It was a step up from where he'd been living not all that long ago, but it would never be mistaken for high living. Not that he was throwing shade. And, he had to keep reminding himself, the economy was in the toilet.

Landlords wanted not just fucking proof of income, but that income had to be *triple* the rent.

And, of course, rent was now insanely expensive.

Fucking fifteen hundred bucks a month for a one bedroom apartment, and this state was supposed to be low cost of living.

Who the fuck was making forty five hundred bucks a month nowadays?

"Okay, let me just run up and grab it, and I'll be right back," Holly said quickly as soon as they'd parked.

Then she was out and gone.

"She really doesn't want us seeing her apartment," Ellen murmured.

"I can understand the feeling," he replied. A moment of silence went by. "So...we're all good, right?"

Ellen laughed softly. "Yes, Gabe. What happened back there was...you tapped into my competitive side. Extremely effectively. And I'm quite happy with how it played out."

"Even though you lost?" he asked, smirking at

her in the rearview.

She stared back at him with a smile that conveyed both guile and love, and maybe perhaps just a single drop of danger.

"Yes," she said, "just...be careful. I'm mostly very chill nowadays about things, but once you push the go button on my internal competition machine, it can get intense."

"That sounds like a challenge to me," he replied.

"See, this is how I know this is it. This is the one relationship that's going to work. You're fucking with me, I *know* you're fucking with me, and it isn't pissing me off in the slightest. If anything, it's making me horny." She paused, seemed to consider something. "Although I am being serious: be careful. I have anger problems, and I see too many things as a fight, so...we have to be cautious with this. Plus, don't forget that while I *am* submissive, and I like being made to submit...I also am dominant, too."

"How can I tell when your pushback is legitimate and not an invitation to...put you in your place?" he asked.

"Hmm. I'd say that you've got good enough instincts to figure that out on your own, but I also like hedging my bets. So how about this: a safeword?"

"A...social safeword?"

"Yes, exactly. If you're beginning to legitimately piss me off, I will say...nascent."

"That is...quite the choice. But okay. Nascent."

"I've always liked the word but I never really seem to say it. I don't know why, it just conjures images of...cool outer space sci-fi? I don't even understand why that is. Probably it's similar to some sci-fi word I heard two decades ago and connected. How about you?"

"I don't think I'll need one," he replied. "It's hard to imagine you pissing me off."

Ellen frowned, then grew serious and leaned forward. "Gabe...it's important to me that you choose one. I honestly know how you feel, but that kind of thinking leads to resentment. Because eventually I *will* piss you off, but you won't want to say anything, and that will keep happening, and you'll get more pissed each time, because you aren't healthily releasing that frustration...do you see what I mean?"

"I do. And that's fair. All right...periwinkle."

She snorted. "What!? What even is that!?"

"Some blue flower," he replied.

"How do you even know that?"

"I have no idea. I think I read it in a book once. So, nascent and periwinkle. Our 'you're actually starting to piss me off' safewords...for the record, you *are* very good at bowling."

"Oh I know," she replied, regaining her smile as she leaned back.

He continued staring at her in the rearview. "You know, I'm glad I put you in your place. I think you need it, at least a little."

"Oh *do* I?"

"Yep."

"Maybe I'll put *you* in your place tonight."

"You could try," he replied.

"Motherfucker you are *on.*"

Holly reappeared at that moment, carrying a backpack. She hurried over and got back into the front passenger's seat. "Okay, I'm ready."

"Perfect. Let's go have a relaxing night together," Gabe replied, backing out of the parking space.

CHAPTER TEN

"Hey love, will you come in here?" Ellen called.

"Yeah, one minute!" he called back.

Gabe was focusing intensely on reading over her final edits on Tall, Blonde, and Beautiful Five. He was close to being finished. He tried not to hurry as he read over the last few paragraphs, not wanting to keep Ellen waiting but also not wanting to leave this undone, not now that he was so close to the end.

Finally, he read the last sentence and then sighed in relief.

Done, finally.

Gabe stood up and then grabbed his phone from off his desk, vaguely aware that he'd received a text message at some point. Unlocking it as he headed out of his office, he paused as he walked into the living room and found it empty.

Turning around, he headed for the bedroom and found her in bed with her laptop, scrutinizing it intensely.

"What's up?" he asked.

"Did you finish the edits?" she asked without looking up, clearly focused on her own thing.

"Yes. Just now. Tall, Blonde, and Beautiful is now completely edited. Including the bonus shit."

"Good. Excellent."

"...you okay there?" he asked.

"Hold on...sorry," she muttered, adjusting something on her screen. Finally, she exhaled sharply and sat back, then favored him with a smile. "When I called you in I thought I was done, but then I realized I wasn't quite, so I was fixing something. Anyway...here."

She picked up the laptop and turned it around.

Gabe took it from her, staring at the image on the screen intently.

"Whoa."

"You like, I take it?"

"Fuck yes, I like. This is amazing," he muttered. "How the fuck...this seems like a bit much."

"How's that?" she asked.

Gabe couldn't quite articulate it at first. He kept staring at the image. It was of a woman in a simple black dress, her face obscured by the title of the story, against a simple outdoors background that was very softly blurred. In some way that he couldn't put his finger on, he could tell that this was an older, mature woman, even without seeing her face.

This was to be the cover for the second short story that he'd written for Sadie. She'd actually texted him a request the second night that Holly was over, and given he'd been feeling particularly inspired, he'd managed to bang it out pretty fast. She had told him she was very happy with it and was fine with him publishing it.

This one had been...a bit more obvious.

It was about a mature woman who had just gone through an unhappy divorce getting an apartment and learning she had moved in next door to a cute guy less than half her age, and hitting on him, and then fucking him.

"I guess, this seems like the cover of an upscale, whole romance novel, or at least full erotica novel. This thing is barely ten thousand words long. This is really fucking good, though."

"I told you, I have an eye for aesthetic," Ellen replied, accepting the laptop back. "As for wasting a quality cover on a short story, I don't think that's the case. Let me tell you a lesson I learned the hard way, Gabe: presentation is *everything*. Okay? A quick story. The place where I work now, there was a guy working there in the next office over. He was...kind of a fucking dunce. However, he was absolutely sure that this plan he had of going off on his own and making a lot of money from launching an independent consulting site was going to take off.

"I managed not to laugh, because he was...to be blunt, he had his job because he was the CEO's daughter's fiance. He wasn't good at his job. Just good enough to get by. He launched a website, and a little 'how to' book, and got cards made. I looked over the website once, and...holy shit, it looked *slick*. And sharp. It looked legit and professional. And he was charging a *lot*. Like his highest package was two grand for 'professional accounting help'. He quit his job about two months after I came in."

"And?" Gabe asked.

"It worked. I overheard one of the upper managers talking about how the guy had launched a successful career as an independent financial advisor despite operating under the handicap of being an idiot. And he *was* an idiot, don't get me wrong. I'm not ragging on him for the hell of it, he had all these little short videos giving basic and more specific advice and yeah, they looked professionally produced and he was a pretty decent actor, but the advice was either 'a fucking moron could figure that out' or 'that's really stupid advice', but he was making it. Because of presentation."

"And that...doesn't seem fucked up to you?" he asked.

"Oh yeah, big time. Tons of people do it, though. How many 'influencers' or 'social media experts' or 'self help geniuses' are there out there who are saying some dumb shit that sounds profound if you're desperate or a little dumb and they're raking in money? I mean, they're evil grifters and they know it, but it clearly *works*. As for this?

"Here's the thing, Gabe: we aren't lying to anyone. It's not like we're promising a five hundred page prize-winning bestseller with this cover art. Presentation is fucking everything, Gabe, because people see that cover, and they are going subconsciously assume that they're looking at a great story, before they've even read a single word, which means they're going to go into it assuming it's great, again, without realizing it, and the thing about humans is that we tend to fill in the blanks. If we think something's gonna be great, our subconscious minds look for excuses for that to be true."

"...hmm." He thought about it for a bit. She had a point, and he knew it. "All right. I mean, bottom line: I'm not complaining. It's great. They've all been great so far. It just feels weird. But I'm grateful."

"Good," she said, smiling. "I know this feels slimy, but we aren't doing anything slimy. It's just that...people have expectations, even if they don't know it. Do you know how many shit novels get to be bestsellers just because they have slick cover art and good marketing?"

He sighed heavily and rolled his eyes. "Yes. I do. Don't even get me started on that."

She laughed. "Yeah, I figured. Okay, sit down, babe. I need to go over this list with you, double-check that everything's solid and we're both completely on the same page."

"All right, what list?" he asked.

"This list of your bibliography. There's a lot to

go over and we've been pushing hard for the past week and I want to make sure everything goes well for the relaunch. So...first thing on the list: your five original shorts."

"That's solid," he replied. "All the covers look great and the idea we came up with to bundle them and add a bonus short story is...I mean it sounds good, I'm just wondering if it'll even work. That also feels a little scummy? Like I'm trying to rip people off?"

"You aren't," she said, "it's not like you're forcing them to buy it. And bundles are reaching a different market. But on top of that, it gives people who like you a chance to support you more. They don't *have* to buy it, and they're missing out on a short story, not some crucial plot detail."

"Yeah...sorry. Part of me hates to keep being like this but another part of me doesn't? I hate...the idea of selling out? Although I guess I'm not sure if that's what this is?"

Ellen looked at him for a long moment, lips twisted in concentration. "You have to learn when to give and when to stand," she said finally. "You can't die on every hill, Gabe. To be clear: I respect you a lot for this. Being true to yourself and wanting nice things for your fans are both very good things. But at a certain point, you have to face the fact that this is your job. It isn't a passion project and it isn't a hobby, it's a job.

"And we have bills to pay, groceries to buy, and a capitalist hellscape to survive. I'm fine with not ripping people off, if anything, I encourage you to give people a fair deal and to always be honest and up front about things, but you have a kindness streak in you, and you have...temper it. You have to recognize that charging a reasonable price for a thing that you made is not bad."

"You're right," he said. "So, yes, that one is done. Covers are set, bonus short has been written, all the editing passes have been done, and all the formatting has been done."

"Excellent," she murmured, looking over her list. "Next, the trilogy about the one night stand turned romance."

"Same story, bonus short written, packaged and ready for relaunch," he replied.

"Second trilogy about the vacation sex?"

"Finished."

"Perfect. Tall, Blonde, and Beautiful? You said all editing is done?" He nodded. "Perfect." She frowned. "I'm having some trouble piecing together covers for it, and that's going to be one of the more important ones, because it's your highest seller."

"I imagine it's because it's so hard to find such a gorgeous woman as yourself?" he asked.

Ellen sighed and flushed. "Shut up," she muttered. "And yes, it's hard to find a six and a half foot model that is also...curvy. I'm still looking and thinking for those covers. How about Sadie's two stories?"

"First one is ready, second one I still gotta do the edits on."

"Okay. That covers everything that's already done. Where are we at with the stone age fucking?" she asked.

He laughed and shook his head. "I'm about halfway done with the first one."

"And you're still comfortable making three longer ones instead of five or six shorter ones?"

"Yes. I'm getting more confident about writing longer works. I'm aiming for them to be about thirty or thirty five thousand words apiece."

"Mmm...you're bumping up against the bare minimum of what could be considered a novel," she said.

"Really?"

"Yeah. Technically speaking, forty thousand words is recognized as a novel. How do you not know this?" she asked, then paused, closed her eyes for a second. "I'm sorry, that was rude."

"No, I mean, it's a fair question. I think I might've known it once but I forgot, but...I am not what you would call traditionally educated or trained. I just...write stuff, and read stuff, and cobble stuff together."

"Which makes your talent even more obvious," she said. "So, this is basically where I'm at. You know those crazy videos of someone lining up all the balls on the pool table and then hitting one and then they *all* go in?"

"Yeah?"

"That's what we're doing. I want to line everything up for maximum impact for this relaunch. We need to finish getting all the new covers made, all the editing done, and all the formatting prep work done. We will prep the packages for the shorts and the two trilogies and have them ready to go. We will then launch the three compilations, Tall, Blonde, and Beautiful Five, Sadie's second commission, and the first stone age erotica novella within the same day. Meaning we will have six things to launch simultaneously. We also need to make sure your website is up, functional, and linked to in your books, and get your social media updated before then."

"That's...a lot. How long do you think all this will take?"

"We're probably still at least a week or two out. It depends mostly on how long it takes you to get the stone age story written and how long it takes me to figure out what to do about the Tall Blonde cover art," she said.

"Man. Two weeks," he muttered.

"Or longer...also, do you need to respond to a text or something? You've been holding your phone since you walked in here."

"Oh, right, shit," Gabe muttered, unlocking it again. "I got a text."

"So did I. Are you cool with Abby coming here for lunch?" she asked as he opened up the text.

"Yeah, that's fine...just Abby? Or Abby and Em?"

Ellen smirked. "Hoping for another blowie?"

"Uh..." he chuckled awkwardly, "I mean I wouldn't say no..."

She laughed. "Just Abby. She wants to talk with us about something. Not sure what. But she's offering to buy lunch for us and bring it here, so what are you in the mood for?"

"Uh...tacos sound good. Could we do that one place, what was it...fuck. Um. Javier's? Javier's something," he asked.

"Yes. Just tacos?" she asked, grabbing her own phone and beginning to text.

"Yeah, like four tacos, and their super hot sauce," he replied. "Oh shit, it's from Sadie."

"Ooh, what's she say?"

"She says...'thank you for the story, it was very effective'."

"You should hit on her," Ellen said.

"What?! That doesn't seem kind of risky to you? What if I piss her off and we lose this insanely good deal we have living here?" he replied.

"Just...trust me. Come on, live a little. Flirt with the hot cougar you so desperately want to bang," she said, going back to texting with that fiery smirk of hers.

He sighed, staring at his phone for a long moment. He pictured Sadie. She'd given him a look during their first, and only, meeting, that he thought had been rooted in lust, but he'd never been able to convince himself of that entirely.

He imagined what she might look like naked.

Or on her knees, blowing him.

Naked, on her back, legs spread...

"Fuck it," he muttered.

"That's my man," Ellen said with a devious laugh.

He began typing a response: *Effective in what way exactly?*

It seemed like an innocent enough question but the content was erotic in nature. If it was effective that had to mean it made her horny, and getting her admit that outright felt like a step in the right direction.

He thought she might not respond right away, but then the little ... appeared.

Well, if you want the honest truth, it made me rather amorous.

A pause, then the ... appeared again.

Then: *I hope I'm not stepping over the bounds by saying this, but I masturbated to it. Twice. And it gave me very intense orgasms.*

"Whoa!" he said.

"What?!" Ellen cried, her head snapping up. "What'd she say?!"

"She just admitted that she masturbated really

effectively to the story."

"Ha! Knew it! Keep going!"

Gabe stared at the screen for a long moment, unsure of how to proceed, but then it came to him quickly.

That's really hot.

He didn't want her thinking she'd freaked or grossed him out. If anything, he really wanted to encourage this kind of talk because, well...he wanted to fuck her.

Really bad.

She responded: *That's good to hear.*

He waited to see if there was more, but there wasn't. He sighed softly after deciding not to respond.

"So?" Ellen asked, finishing her own texting.

"I said it was hot and she said that's good to hear. That's where it ended. I think it's best to let it stay there for now," he replied.

"That is a *great* instinct. Whenever you penetrate new ground, you want to give yourself and the other person time to get used to it. Push and then pull back." She smirked. "Like when you're pushing that dick into me or Holly."

He chuckled awkwardly. "I seriously didn't think you'd be this sexual."

"You bring it out in me," she replied. "So, Abby's gonna be here in about half an hour. Let's get ready."

CHAPTER ELEVEN

Abby looked around as she walked into their place, carrying two bags of food.

"I have to say, this is a nice place," she said. "A little stark, but nice...some old woman gave it to you?"

"A mature woman cut us a very sweet deal," Gabe replied.

"Why?"

"Because she is a cougar on the prowl for hot young dick. Specifically Gabe's," Ellen replied.

Abby's eyes bulged a little as she set the food down on the coffee table. "*Really?*"

"Ellen is...imaginative. She wants to be a patron of the arts. I'm a starving artist, she's well off enough to offer a sweet deal," Gabe replied.

"Huh...Ellen looks pretty confident," Abby said.

"Ellen's confident in everything, and she has an overactive imagination," Gabe replied.

"Yeah, *I* am the one with the overactive imagination in the relationship. Not the actual writer," Ellen said, rolling her eyes. They began digging into the bags, opening them up and pulling out the containers of food. "Trust me, she's playing the long game, she wants to take a ride on that dick."

"You seem really invested in this," Abby murmured.

"I think it'd be hot. She's hot. And...well, you know, as a woman who is getting older, let's just say that I like the idea of older women being able to pull cute young guys like Gabe."

"How old is she?"

"Fifty."

"Oh, wow. Nice."

"*Any*way," Gabe said firmly, "thank you for lunch."

Ellen laughed. "Yeah, thanks for lunch, Abby. How are you and Em lately?"

"Good," Abby replied.

"That felt a little...loaded," Ellen murmured.

Abby laughed softly and shook her head, then bit into a taco, chewed and swallowed. "It wasn't. It's more just...things are stable. And that's good. For the most part."

"For the most part, huh?" Ellen replied.

"Don't you fucking sass me, Ellen Campbell," Abby said firmly.

Ellen straightened up at that, her eyes flashing with...something.

"Oh my, what was *that* look?" she murmured.

"I don't like being challenged," Ellen replied.

"You sure about that?" Gabe asked.

She snapped her head towards him. "Don't *you* sass me," she growled.

"I don't know, I kinda want to see what that looks like," Abby said with a small smile.

"You–"

"Okay," Gabe said quickly, "this is really fun but I think we should probably derail this."

"Probably," Ellen agreed after a moment.

"Yeah," Abby said, looking a little disappointed. "This isn't really what I came over here for...fun as it is. You're smart, Gabe. I can see why you're doing so well with Ellen, and how you managed to land that amazingly hot redhead."

"Thanks," he replied.

"You're welcome. So. Em and I are good. Happy. Living a pleasantly domestic life now, largely free of the godforsaken misery that is 'work'."

"Fuck work," Ellen said, raising her cup.

"Fuck work," Abby agreed. "But I want to know how *you* two are doing."

"Very, very well," Ellen replied. "Gabe and I working on revitalizing his backlist. We're having a lot of fun together, and a lot of fun with Holly."

"What's she like? She looks so...innocent in those pics you sent," Abby asked.

"She is, but there's an absolute fucking freak inside, just gagging to get let out," Gabe replied.

Abby and Ellen both laughed. "That's exactly what I figured."

"Gabe was fucking the shit out of her a few nights ago and all he did was grab her wrists and hold them down and she came, like, immediately. Her body wants domination and restraint, and it has for a long time, she just hasn't been able to hear it properly. She grew up with extremely conservative parents."

"Oh. Ew."

"Yeah. The kind who hate sex ed and shove abstinence down everyone's throat...while at the same time cheating on each other, no doubt. But she's been very happy to open up."

"That's good," Abby said. A moment of silence went by as they ate, then she cleared her throat. "So there is a rather specific reason I came over today."

"I figured," Ellen replied.

"We've all talked about it before, and I've watched you put your dick in my wife's mouth and come down her throat," Abby said, looking at Gabe, "so I don't really want to dance around the issue: Em and I have been discussing the possibility of you and her going all the way. Before we dig any deeper into that, I'd like to know if this is a thing we are all comfortable with."

"Well...uh...yeah," Gabe replied after a brief hesitation when he realized Ellen wasn't going to say anything first. "I'm okay with that."

Ellen laughed. "Figured you would be. Yeah, I'm okay with it. I was kinda nervous about going all the way because I thought I might get jealous and I do *not* want to go down that road, but now that I've watched him fuck the shit out of Holly...I'm confident."

Abby smiled. "Good. I'm glad we're all on the same page. Emily wants to have sex with you, and I am okay with this happening. I basically want to iron out the details. Namely: I want to make sure everyone involved is safe. I can say for sure from our end that Emily and I have not been with anyone, in any capacity, since we got married. We also both had tests done six months ago for peace of mind, because there *are* ways to catch things that don't involve sex, and we're good. Emily got her tubes tied so she can't get pregnant. You two?"

"Gabe and I have only been with Holly. Besides Emily, obviously," Ellen replied. "We're good and we're confident that Holly is, too. There have been tests."

"Excellent. We don't know each other too well at this point, but Emily trusts you, and I trust Emily. And so far, I trust everything my instincts are telling me about the two of you...Gabe, you look uncomfortable," Abby said, and both she and Ellen looked at him again.

"Uh...I'm not," he replied. "I'm sorry. This is just-it's a little weird for me. We're talking about...me having sex with your wife like we're in a boardroom.

And I'm not complaining, I'm just having a hard time adjusting."

"I understand," Abby said, her tone softening just a little. "Sorry if I seem a little cold. I spent a decade preparing to be and being a lawyer. When I'm negotiating something, I slip right back into it. But I also personally prefer this. I hate dancing around things. Far too easy to misinterpret or read what you'd like to into a situation. Far, far better to simply flat out state it."

"Yeah, I agree," he replied. "In truth, I've wished for conversations to go like this my whole life. Flirting is fun but it's so...I don't know, dangerous? Too easy to misunderstand or even outright lie...should we run this by Holly? I feel like she has a right to know."

"I agree," Abby said. "Em and I have already discussed that. She should know, and get a say in this whole thing. If possible, we'd like to meet her."

"I'm sure she'd be happy to meet you," Ellen replied.

"How old is she, exactly?"

"Twenty two," Gabe said.

"Phew. Young. I'm jealous. I wish I could shed twelve years," Abby murmured.

"Really? Is it that much of a difference?" Gabe asked.

"Yes," both Ellen and Abby said at the same time. He looked at them more closely. Abby frowned, then twisted her lips in consideration.

"I think it's more...for both Ellen and I, our twenties were rough. And, honestly, our early thirties. Really, it's all been rough for Ellen. I got lucky with Em. I think it'd be different if it wasn't so rough. I've known women my age who still look and seem to be twenty two. It's...a complicated subject. But from where I sit, twenty two seems like a fucking lifetime ago. Hell, so does twenty six to be honest. But...it's nights like the two we had, when you came to the house and when we went to the party, that help wash away the years."

"Yep," Ellen agreed immediately. "And I feel a lot younger recently. Knowing that I'm going to be free of my job soon? Dating you, love? Actually being able to fucking *relax* in my own goddamned home? I feel like a teenager on summer vacation again. Like...a real one, not the ones I had to endure." She sighed. "Sorry, getting too heavy. So we're all down to fuck then?"

"Yes," Abby said.

"Yeah, I'm okay with this. We'll run it by Holly. Although I have a question."

"Shoot," Abby replied.

"Why isn't Emily here talking about this with us?"

"Yeah I was wondering that, too," Ellen said.

Abby chuckled. "Well, Emily is...surprisingly shy about this."

"*What?*" Ellen replied, immediately breaking into a broad grin. "Em? Shy?! *What!?* I have seen her get topless and dance on a table after losing a poker game at a party. How in the name of God can she be shy about this?!"

"I'm not completely sure myself, but I think...Gabe intimidates her. I also know for a fact you intimidate her still," Abby replied.

"Wait, why do *I* intimidate her?" Gabe asked.

"I know part of it is because she hasn't been intimate with a guy–besides what you two did in the back of that car–for years now. Like, a very long time. And this is going to be...different than the party. More intimate. And that's what she wants, but she's also worried about rejection, I think. But...to be honest, I'm not even sure if she knows why she's so shy about it."

"How in fuck's name could I reject her?" Gabe replied. "Like, 'oh, actually, I don't think I'll sleep with the insanely hot tattooed model'. There's no way she can think that's a possibility."

"Well, you have Ellen, dear," Abby replied. "And their relationship is...complicated."

Gabe thought of what Emily had told them when they'd first met, how scared she was of Ellen. He supposed it made sense from Em's perspective, though it still struck him as impossible. How could she not know how insanely hot she was? How could she not know that *of course* he was going to sleep with her if he had the chance?

"Ellen is my own personal goddess," Gabe said, "but Emily is clearly *ridiculously* hot."

"Oh my God, shut the fuck up, Gabe," Ellen whispered, blushing.

Abby laughed. "You two are really great together. And I know that, Gabe. Emily...well, we can discuss this more later. Are we all comfortable with unprotected sex?" she asked. "I am, given I have heard how much more...pleasing it can be. And Emily very specifically requested it."

"Damn, really?" Gabe replied.

"Yes. She wants you to fill her up. I'm going to do you a favor and just tell you now, Em has a big impregnation fetish. She just hates the idea of *actually* being pregnant," Abby said.

"Oh. Um. Interesting," Gabe murmured.

Ellen broke into a broad grin. "Do *you* have an

impregnation fetish, dearest boyfriend of mine?"

"I...might," he replied awkwardly, then cleared his throat.

"Oh my God he *so* does," Abby said. "You'll make her happy if you're the one to bring it up. And *don't* tell her I told you. She's...I don't know, it's a thing with her. She never told me I couldn't tell you, and I think she wanted to me to tell you without her knowing it. Emily can get so weird over some things."

"Noted," Gabe replied.

"I wonder if Holly wants to get knocked up," Ellen murmured. "I bet she would so get off her birth control for you and let you just-*wow*, babe, I can *see* your hard-on. This really does it for you, huh? Why have we never talked about this?"

"I...don't know," he replied, shifting awkwardly. "Just...I don't know."

"You're so cute when you're embarrassed," Ellen said.

"Gee, thanks."

"She's right, you are," Abby said.

"*Gee, thanks,*" he repeated more forcefully.

"It's a good thing!...sorry, I'm done teasing. It's in good fun, but I have to remind myself that it's only good fun if *everyone* is having fun," Abby replied.

"Are you not having fun, dear?" Ellen asked, then hesitated. "I meant that authentically but it came out so teasing. Fucking hell, I really can't turn it off sometimes."

"I'm fine," Gabe said, "just...having trouble adjusting to all this. And I'm okay with the teasing, just sort of riding the line between that and 'Jesus fucking Christ these women are so attractive I hope I don't say something stupid'."

"Am I really that attractive to you?" Abby asked.

"Yeah," he replied.

"I'll admit that I feel like I've never had a great grasp of my own attractiveness to men. Well, I did in high school, but that was...a different time. And a confusing one. Guys hit on me a lot, but I always turn them down because, well, lesbian. And I found increasingly that they would immediately come back with some variation of 'yeah well you're actually pretty ugly, I was trying to do you a favor'. So I...don't really know anymore? I've stopped caring, but it is something I'm curious about."

"Wow that's shitty," Ellen muttered.

"There's a lot of assholes out there," Gabe said, "but I think that's a thing that guys say. A lot of us don't tend to handle rejection well."

"Why is that? I mean I've seen women handle rejection *so* poorly but the ratio seems off. Way more guys blow the fuck up over being told no than women...or maybe that's just my perception? I will admit to the possibility of reading into it what I want to," Abby asked.

"I think it's really complicated but it mostly boils down to: we as a species are biologically hardwired to value reproduction above all else, and so everything gets put through that filter, and so your attractiveness and ability to attract are valued above all else, and this is understood across all societies, even if it's incredibly problematic, and women tend not to get rejected because men are so desperately lonely and also are often after something simpler than what women are after?" he replied.

"Huh," Abby murmured. "Are guys really that lonely?"

"Yes," Gabe replied, "we are. Go on one of the

big social media sites and ask: Men, what problem do you have that women just do not get? And I promise over half the answers will be isolation and crippling loneliness. I know some women have the same problem but...there's a good reason that the average suicide rate is three or four times higher in men, universally across nations."

He paused. "Sorry, that got dark. To answer your original question: Yes, you are pretty attractive and probably the vast majority of the men who asked you out agree with that sentiment, they just felt really shitty because you told them they were too unattractive to date."

"That isn't what I told them!" Abby replied. "Jesus, it was rarely fucking personal. I'm a *lesbian*."

"I know, sorry," Gabe said quickly. He sighed. "I should've led with: that's what they heard, not what you said...I should probably stop talking about this. We were having a good talk."

"Now *I'm* sorry," Abby muttered, "I didn't mean to get defensive. But...I don't mind talking about this stuff. I've only had a few male friends who I felt were okay with the fact that I wasn't going to fuck them. And it's been a long time, years, since I talked with any of them. It's nice to be able to talk about the real inner workings openly. Should probably dial it back right now, though. I get...intense. Side effect of working in law."

"I'm all right with blunt conversation," Gabe replied. "If anything, I'm coming to encourage it. Ellen has definitely been helping with that."

Abby chuckled. "Yeah, I can imagine that."

Ellen sighed. "I'm...learning. Or rather unlearning. Avoiding blunt honesty became a survival tactic for me. In my experience, almost no one wants to hear what you *really* think. Thankfully, though, Gabe is all about that brutal honesty."

"After my last relationship, I decided that I don't ever want to be with someone that I have to keep secrets from," Gabe said.

"Hell fucking yes to that," Ellen muttered, raising her cup before taking a drink from it.

"Yep," Abby agreed. She finished off the last of her meal, took a long drink, then brushed her hands off and returned her attention to the two of them. "So, it's a busy day for me today, and I have to get back to my life. To be clear: you two are one hundred percent onboard for Gabe having unprotected sex with Emily at our place soon?"

"Yes," Ellen said.

"Very much emphatically yes," Gabe replied, making them both laugh.

"Good. It'll probably be a few days. I need to talk with Em some more and we've got stuff going on, but it'll be soon. I really want to see this."

"Me too," Ellen murmured.

"Thanks for lunch, and the, uh, opportunity to rail your wife," Gabe said.

Abby laughed loudly. "You're welcome, Gabe...I can definitely see why Emily is into you. And Ellen. All right, farewell for now."

They wished her farewell and shut the door behind her after she'd gathered her things and left.

"So..." Ellen said, looking at Gabe.

"So?" he replied, gathering up the remains of the meal to throw away.

"I know you were telling her the truth, but...any further thoughts on this? I know this has to be a little weird."

"It is, but I'm pretty much good to go," he

replied, tossing the containers away and brushing away the remains of the meal from the tabletop. "It might be a different story when I'm actually in bed with Emily, but...well, this *does* feel pretty weird, to be honest. It feels weird that everyone is as cool with it as they are, and it feels weird because I can't help but be paranoid about the other shoe."

"Too good to be true?" Ellen asked.

He nodded. "Yeah, exactly. How about *you?* Are you feeling as good as you seem to be?"

"Yeah. I am. I feel..." She paused, then chuckled awkwardly. "It sounds weird, but how I feel about you having sex with other women is...you're *really* amazing. As in, you are a great fuck, but also you're really genuinely kind and considerate. Which helps massively with the sex. But how I feel is, I don't want to keep you entirely to myself. I look at it as helping other women get to experience fun, safe, and *good* sex. And, yeah, apparently I *really* like watching my boyfriend fuck other women, so I'm getting something out of it, too."

"You're an amazing girlfriend."

She smirked. "I know."

Gabe sighed. "You are so fucking cocky sometimes."

Her smirk broadened a bit. "I guess I am...you gonna do something about that?"

He grabbed her wrist and began guiding her to the bedroom. "Yes, I am."

CHAPTER TWELVE

After putting Ellen in her place, (something that was, in retrospect, not the best idea right after eating lunch), Gabe got back to work.

He plowed through the rest of the day and the night getting Sadie's second story edited and ready for publication, then hung out with Ellen until they were falling asleep on the couch together. They went to bed and the first half of the next day was more work.

He was prepared to keep going after having a quick lunch with Ellen, but his phone buzzed.

Gabe was just sitting down back at his desk when it happened. He pulled it out and checked it, found a message from Holly.

Hey sorry if this is weird but where do we stand on just hanging out one on one? Like if I wanted to go somewhere just with you?

Huh. Interesting.

Gabe got up and returned to the living room where Ellen was stretched out on the couch with her laptop.

"What's up? Forget something?" she asked.

"No. Just got a text from Holly. She wants to know if just me and her could hang out somewhere," he replied. As he spoke, he saw, just for the barest instant, a look of unhappiness pass across Ellen's face.

It was there and gone so fast he was almost sure he'd imagined it.

"Yeah, I'm fine with that," she replied.

"...are you sure?" he asked.

"Yeah. Why?"

"You just-for a second there, just a split second, you looked upset."

She opened her mouth, then paused. Finally, she let out a little sigh. "I just had a paranoid thought, is all. They come and go."

"Tell me about it," he said.

"I don't know if it's a great idea to give it voice..."

"Maybe, but if I can reassure you, I'd like to. You always reassure me, even when I know I'm being ridiculous...not that I think you're being ridiculous."

"No, I get it. Just-all right. The thing is, I know I'm not perfect, in that I can be wrong. And there is a part of me that wonders if I'm wrong about Holly. I don't think I am, but sometimes I do? There's a paranoid voice inside me telling me that she's trying to take you from me."

"Oh shit, babe," Gabe said. He moved over to her and sat down on the floor beside her, taking her hand. "I'm sorry."

"It's fine," she replied, giving him an awkward smile. "I know it's just a fleeting, paranoid thought and the thing is, I don't believe it. It's just...insecurities."

"If it truly came down to it, and Holly, for some reason, decided to give me an ultimatum, you or her, you'd win without question," he replied.

"No question, huh?"

"No question. No contest. Holly's great, but you're...you. You're my own personal goddess," he replied.

She sighed heavily and shook her head. "You...are too much sometimes. And honestly, that's what worries me, that you feel that way."

"Why does it worry you?" he asked.

"Core rule of putting someone on a pedestal: they will eventually let you down because they are just human. That rule magnifies if you actually start living with the person you put up on a pedestal. You clearly think I'm just fucking amazing, and that's going to wear off now that you've actually landed me and are fucking me regularly."

"I understand the point you're making, but I think you have to worry about that less than you think you do," he said.

"You'll have to explain that to me," she replied.

"Yes, I put you on a pedestal. Yes, you are still up there. Yes, I am adjusting to the reality of living with you and actually dating you. But, unless I'm missing something, unless you're holding some massive thing back, then I've seen behind the curtain and I'm still very happy with what I've found. You're an *amazing* girlfriend and person. And I love you. I'm going to keep loving you even if you aren't perfect. I'm going to love you when you're sick and when we fight and when you're being unreasonable," he replied.

She let out a strained laugh and then reached up and brushed at her eyes. "Fucking goddamnit I cry so much around you, you've gotta be sick of this by now."

"Given what you've gone through, I think a lot of crying is reasonable," he replied.

She laughed again and then grabbed his wrist and gave him a gentle tug. He took her meaning and laid out on the couch with her. She wrapped both her arms around him and held him tightly.

"Thank you," she whispered, "for reassuring me again, and again, because apparently I need it a lot."

"You're welcome, Ellen. I want to care for you."

"You are doing that *extremely* effectively, Gabe. Being able to be vulnerable around you is more valuable than just about everything else in my life. I feel like...I've been living with some awful illness for years, and I am *finally* getting the medicine. Now," she gave him a kiss, "go on and be with Holly."

"Are you sure? I will absolutely stay here and let her know I'm busy right now or even that you aren't comfortable with it," he replied.

"No! I mean, yes, I'm sure. Seriously, it was a fleeting insecurity. An intrusive thought. I wouldn't have gone this far with Holly and I wouldn't be angling to get her into our house on a more permanent basis if I seriously doubted her intentions or didn't trust her. And that girl needs you, Gabe. I mean, I do too, but she *really* needs you right now."

"Why do you say that?" he asked.

"Think about it: she's only ever had the one serious relationship and it went south. She was raised by awful parents who abused her. Her friends are treating her like shit. She hates her job. Jobs? I think I remember her saying she has two jobs. She *has* to see her budding relationship, casual though it maybe, with us as a beacon of hope and fun. She *loves* being with us, and she obviously has a huge crush on you. If she wants to treat you like a boyfriend, let her, is what I'm saying. Because she *needs* some emotional support right now," Ellen said.

"Yeah, that makes sense," he murmured. "But you're really sure?"

"I'm really sure. We have to watch out for each other, and you...are way too good of a guy to have suffered through what you did. I'm hesitant to use the word 'deserve', especially when it comes to sex and relationships, but honestly? You fucking deserve this. You deserve to have Holly gagging for your cock."

He laughed. "Wow, babe."

"I know what I said. Now, go be with her, whatever it is she wants to do. Be her friend, be her boyfriend, be her master, whatever it is she needs from you. That's a good woman, and she needs help right now, and I know you want to help her."

"All right...thanks Ellen. I love you," he said, kissing her again.

"I love you too, now go."

He chuckled. "All right."

Gabe got up off of her and grabbed his phone. He typed out a response: *Yeah, that'd be cool. Where do you want to go?*

She replied almost immediately. *Will you meet me at Willow Lake Park?*

He frowned and headed back into his office. That name sounded very vaguely familiar, but he wasn't sure where it even was. Typing it in, he saw that it was maybe eight minutes from his house. And it had an actual lake in it. Was this what he and Ellen had been discussing earlier? How many parks had lakes in the town?

Whatever, it didn't really matter. He put the information into his phone and shut down his laptop.

Yeah, I'll be there in ten minutes.

Okay, thanks! See you there!

...

As Gabe drove through the cold gray city, beneath skies that promised rain and, perhaps, snow, he felt strange.

It occurred to him, abruptly, that ever since Ellen

had reentered his life, he'd barely spent any time by himself, save for the time he spent in his office. If he went somewhere, it was almost always with her.

Not that it bothered him, if anything it was a welcome reprieve from the soul-sucking isolation.

But now that he was in the position that he was, being alone no longer hurt.

As he followed his phone's instructions to the park, Gabe was briefly but intensely struck by the utter surreality of the fact that he was driving to meet a beautiful redheaded woman, that he had slept with more than once now, while his girlfriend was relaxing in his home, knowing he was doing this. Although he doubted Holly was going to want to have sex at the park.

Well...

That was another hard striking thought: fucking a model-hot woman in his car was now actually on the table for him.

And that thought made him hesitate.

Things were extremely fun with Holly, and sex with her was amazing, but...everything Ellen had said about her rang true. Gabe was beginning to become of aware of just how much of a blind spot he had for attractive women.

In a world where beauty was everything, it was extremely difficult to believe that a young woman who was as hot as a movie star or a supermodel could be seriously suffering.

Only he knew that he shouldn't have difficulty with this fact.

As much as pretty privilege was a thing, as much as society tended to bend over backwards for attractive people–especially attractive women–he knew they could be as dismally miserable as anyone else.

If anything, he knew that they often might have more reason to be unhappy.

He'd read more than a few accounts of women who had been exceptionally attractive and had lost it for one reason or another, and had never been happier. Because now everyone wasn't fucking bugging them about sex twenty four seven.

And it was clear that Holly was suffering, much as she tried to hide it from them.

He definitely wanted to keep having sex with her, but he also knew that he needed to not approach every single encounter they had with a mindset of 'we are going to fuck soon'.

A few moments later, he found the park she'd indicated and saw her car. It was only one of just a few in the lot. He pulled up and parked next to her. She smiled warmly at him as they both got out of their cars.

"Hi!" she said brightly, hurrying over to him and hugging him.

"Hey, Holly," he replied, hugging her back, taking in her...everything. She felt wonderful against him, smelled wonderful. She was like a ray of soft, clean sunshine. "How are you?"

"Better now," she said, pulling back and smiling. She quickly lost the smile, though. "So...Ellen is cool with this, right? This isn't...weird?"

"I promise, Ellen is cool with this. We talked about it, she's fine with it being just you and more. Or just you and her, if that's what you want."

"Are you sure? I want to be *really* sure I'm not messing up your guys' relationship at all. I'd never live it down if I did…"

"We're positive, Holly," he said. "Trust me."

She slowly regained her smile. "I do...I really do."

"So, anything in specific you wanted to do or discuss?" he asked.

"Yes. Today is my short day at the cafe, but my long day at the other job, so my off time is in a different spot. And I wanted to get some time in with you. There's a cool spot I want you to visit with me because I've always seen it from a distance but I've never actually had the guts to go there by myself."

"All right," Gabe said, offering his hand, "show me."

She laughed merrily and took it, then began leading him deeper into the park.

CHAPTER THIRTEEN

Willow Lake Park was a very beautiful place.

The lake wasn't too big and probably was manmade, but it looked good and fairly natural. A flock of geese had come and settled on it. They were mostly bobbing gently on the water. One of them would occasionally let out a honk.

The lake was surrounded by a paved path and, beyond that, trees on three sides. There were a few areas of note along the path. A bathroom, a little picnic area with a gazebo, some benches to sit. There was almost no one around.

Even in the chill November air, it was pleasant to be there.

"I don't know if we every actually talked about it, but what's your other job?" Gabe asked.

"Oh, yeah, I guess I did never bring it up. Waitress, again, only at a bar and grill. I work three or four nights a week there, sometimes one long day. I make a lot more money, but it's even more intense than the cafe. A lot of running around, never getting a break. I've seriously considered taking up smoking just so I can have access to fucking smoke breaks, but...that still sounds incredibly stupid to me," she replied.

"Yeah, not the best choice," he agreed. "Sorry your jobs are so stressful."

"Well...it could be a lot worse."

"Yeah but it could definitely be better."

She laughed. "Yeah, I could be a writer. That has to be really nice."

"It is, but it's only working right now because we got *real* lucky. I pretty much put everything on the line to try and make this work. And it still might not," he replied.

"That kind of makes it cooler...sorry, I don't mean-it's gotta be scary, dealing with that, but it's, I dunno, romantic? Kind of like a story."

"It *is* pretty cool so far." A moment went by. "So, I've got a question."

"Ask away."

"Is there a specific reason you wanted just me? Ellen's not offended, I'm just curious."

"Well...a few reasons, I guess. The first and most practical one was I thought Ellen would be working. Second, I wanted to see what it was like to be with just you, I guess? I don't know why that's important or why I want to, but I do. And also..." She hesitated.

"What?" She didn't say anything. "Whatever it is, you can tell me."

"Okay. I guess, the third reason, is that I'm...kind of scared of Ellen."

"I can understand that," he said.

She looked immensely relieved. "Really? You don't think it's, like, insulting?"

"No, not at all. Ellen's an intimidating woman. And not just because she's tall and insanely beautiful. She's really got that aura of 'I have my shit together and I know exactly what I want'. I mean, I've been dating her and living with her for like three weeks now and she still intimidates me. But you don't have to worry. Ellen really likes you."

"I get that sense, it's just...there's this part of me that's so scared she's going to decide she hates me for having sex with you. Or you'll hate me for having sex with her. And, the thing is, I trust you both. I mostly believe you about the fact that you're cool with it. You *seem* cool with it when we're doing it. It's just...I don't know, I've read a lot of stories about couples who were into stuff like this, but then it blows up spectacularly because one of them wasn't *actually* okay with it..."

"I understand, Holly. The sense you're getting is the same I get: Ellen's cool with it. Obviously I am. The two of you together are like...man! The kind of sex people would pay *good* money to see."

She giggled. "I can't believe I've actually been filmed fucking in a threesome. Oh hey, there it is."

They were at the rear of the lake now, where a gentle incline led into a small forest. Through the trees, Gabe could see a big field and in the center was what looked like an abandoned factory or warehouse.

"You want to go in there?" he asked uncertainly.

"Yes! It looks so awesome...are you okay with that?" she asked.

He considered it. Technically speaking it was breaking and entering, but he doubted there were cops around, or anyone around who'd care, and the place did look pretty abandoned, like years, not months. That made it potentially dangerous though...

Fuck it, he thought.

Holly really wanted to do this, clearly, and he was trying to be braver. Sometimes that meant taking more adventurous risks.

"Let's go," he said.

She grinned and headed off.

"So, any particular reason you want to go here?" he asked as they began making their way through the trees.

"Yes! I fucking *love* abandoned places! They're so cool. I spend a lot of time just looking at abandoned porn online." She paused. "That sounds really weird now that I say it out loud. Like the word porn is just...ruined."

"I've heard differing arguments on whether or not the word porn should be specifically reserved for sexual acts, but I think it's fair to apply it to other things. And I agree with you, abandoned porn or derelict porn, it can be really cool."

"Yes! There's a strange beauty to it. I visit places like this when I can, take pictures of it. Just for fun. I know it's stupid, but I can't help it. Something about it just draws me. There's just something to it, something that speaks to my soul..." She paused, flushed a little. "Sorry, this has to be so lame to hear me gushing about this stuff."

"What? No! Don't think that," Gabe replied.

"You don't think it's dumb?"

"No, I don't, Holly. I agree with you about it, but even if I didn't...you care about it. You like it. Therefore it matters."

"That's really nice," she murmured. "But you don't have to care about something just because I do. I don't want to bore you or Ellen."

"I understand that, although in this case the interest isn't polite."

"Have you ever explored a place like this?"

"A few times, when I was a young teen and me and a few of my friends were out in a place like this. It was an old abandoned house, although they tore it down eventually," he replied.

They came suddenly out of the forest and into the clearing.

The sounds of the city seemed somehow faraway here, the hum of power and the honking almost muted, even compared to being in the park. The field was still a little overgrown, though it was clear that it was well on its way towards a winter death. There was trash around, some old garbage bags, torn up clothes, and, on the other side of the area, the rusted-out, skeletal remains of an ancient, long since stripped car.

"We have to be careful in there, if you actually want go in," Gabe murmured.

"I know. There could be people inside or it could be structurally unsound. I'll be careful," she replied.

"You've got guts, you know that?" he asked as they began walking across the field.

"Really?"

"Yes. As cool as I think that place is, I wouldn't go in alone either."

"Oh, well...I'll protect you," she said, grinning and blushing a little.

"Good. I'll have to think of some way to pay you back later," he replied, and she giggled and blushed more. "Oh, also, now that I'm thinking about it, there's something I wanted to go over with you related to that aspect of our relationship."

"Oh...did I do something weird last time we were having sex?" she asked, losing her smile again.

"No, no, nothing like that," he replied. "You did something *awesome* the last time we had sex. Several awesome things. But this doesn't have to do with that. So...Ellen and I have been afforded an, uh, opportunity. A sexual one. By a few friends of Ellen's."

"Oh, the redhead you showed me pics of?" she asked.

"No, that's Krystal...huh, it suddenly strikes me how unlikely it is that I now know *two* women couples where one person involved is interested in me," he murmured. "Anyway, this is Emily and Abby. Wait, didn't we show you the video of her sucking my dick and me eating her out?"

"Oh right, yeah. Okay. I remember. The dark-haired woman with tons of tats."

"Right. So, yes, they are a married couple and Ellen's friends. I guess mine now, too. But Emily wants to go all the way with me. Without protection. And given the fact that you are sexually involved with Ellen and I, we thought it would be ethical to inform you of this and let you weigh in on it."

"Wait, so...if I didn't want it to happen, I could say 'no', and you'd listen and not do it?" she asked.

"Well, we'd discuss it, try to figure out a solution that makes everyone happy," he replied.

"That's really nice. Also, I'm fine with it. I trust you and Ellen so I guess I trust you not to do something dumb." They came to a halt at the edge of the old structure. "Can I see her again?"

"Sure," he replied, pulling out his phone and calling up a picture of Emily that she'd sent him with her shirt off. "I, uh...all the pictures I have of her involve nudity."

"Oh my lord, she's *so* hot. I thought I was remembering her as hotter than she really was, but no. Those tattoos...wow, you're really lucky," she murmured, passing him back the phone.

"I am," he agreed. "You know...I imagine a threesome between you, me, and her would probably be in the cards."

"Really!? That'd be amazing!"

Gabe laughed. "So that's a yes then?"

"That's a strong yes. But I want you to handle all the, uh, details."

He studied her for a moment, contemplating. "You like being told what to do, don't you?"

"Yeah, I do. I don't know why, and it's never

really felt completely right...until I met you. For some reason, I *really* like it when you tell me to do things."

"Well, that's a fun coincidence," he replied, reaching out and trailing one finger slowly down her jawline. She shuddered at the contact, looking like she was relishing it. "Because I really enjoy telling you what to do."

"You can tell me to do whatever you want," Holly whispered.

"I will keep that in mind," he said, "but I imagine you're on a timeline. We should probably get into the building."

"Yes, I am, and yes, we should," Holly replied, sounding disappointed.

She pulled out her phone and took a picture of the front of the building, then walked up to the door and tried it. It opened, though loudly, the rusty squeal of the hinges echoing across the clearing. They paused and looked around, then walked inside.

Within, the atmosphere was immediately different, though in a way that was difficult to nail down.

It felt...heavy, though not necessarily in a dangerous sort of way. They had come into a long corridor, the floor of which was scattered with collapsed tiles from the ceiling, scraps of paper, old magazines, empty cans, and scrap metal.

Shafts of sunlight slanted across the hallway through a few open doors and motes of dust floated on the ultraviolet illumination.

"I wonder how old this place is," Holly whispered, slowly raising her phone. Gabe made way as she adjusted herself more to the center of the hallway, then she snapped a picture. "I bet this place was built in the thirties. Almost a hundred years of history. How many people have passed through here?...sorry, I'm rambling," she murmured.

"You aren't rambling," he replied. "Come on, let's poke around a little."

She smiled and they began walking down the corridor.

It was slow going, but it didn't bother Gabe at all. It felt like an experience he was going to remember for a long time. They stopped to look in each of the open doors, and each time Holly took a picture with her phone.

They found a few completely empty rooms, a bathroom covered in graffiti, a room packed with shelves that were all empty and dusty, and what might once have been a break room. All that was left to suggest this was a large foldout table that leaned heavily to one side and a handful of foldout chairs.

"All right," Holly said, "that's all I've got time for. Although..." She turned to look at him, smirking suddenly. They were in the old break room. "Maybe *you* could take a picture."

"Of you?" Gabe replied.

"If you wanted to…"

He pulled out his phone and fired up the camera function. "Okay...unzip your hoodie."

"Yes, sir," she murmured, pulling the zipper down slowly.

"Good. Now lift up your shirt."

She kept smiling, raising up the t-shirt she was wearing under the hoodie, exposing her smooth stomach and all that pale skin of hers.

"And your bra," he said when she revealed a white sports bra.

She was blushing badly now but she still looked excited. She pulled her bra up, freeing her big breasts.

"Like this?" she murmured softly.

"Exactly like that," he replied. Gabe snapped the picture and then sent it to Ellen.

"Can I put my tits away? It's cold," Holly said.

Gabe briefly toyed with the idea of telling her no, for some reason filled with the notion that she wanted him to, but she had work to get to and he didn't want to derail that. Much as they both wanted that.

"Yes, put them away."

Holly looked a little disappointed as she put her bra and shirt back into place, though she then seemed grateful as she zipped her hoodie back up and hugged herself.

"Come on, let's get out of here," he said, and they started heading back to the park.

CHAPTER FOURTEEN

"This is a really good picture, Holly," Gabe muttered as he studied her phone.

They stood back in the parking lot, in front of her car. He'd been curious to see what exactly it looked like through a camera lens, wondering how much different it would be compared to actually seeing it in real life.

"Thanks," Holly replied. "I really like photography."

"You've certainly got a hell of an eye for it," he replied, passing her phone back.

"Just wait til I put it through a few filters. I've got a bunch of these, actually. Not all abandoned stuff, but nature mostly. Anyway, um, thanks for that. That was a really special thing to me. And...can I come over tonight? I don't know if I'll have the energy for...fun things, but I can try."

"You can come over and spend the night even if we don't have sex," he replied.

"Are you sure it won't be weird? I don't want to crowd you guys."

"I'm sure. We really like having you around, Holly."

"Okay then, I'll come right over from work. Although I gotta get up tomorrow at like eight or so."

"That's fine, Holly."

She gave him a long kiss on the mouth and pulled away smiling. "Give that to Ellen too, okay?"

"I will. Good luck at work," he replied.

She sighed and looked suddenly tired. "Thanks. I'm gonna need it."

Holly got into her car and drove off. Gabe

watched her go, considering everything they'd talked about. She was showing many of the signs of someone who had been shut down for years, maybe even most of her life, whenever she got excited about something.

He had a lot of sympathy for that, because most of the time whenever he talked about writing, a lot of people seemed to default towards either telling him it was a dead dream or asking if he was going to write the next 'Great American Novel'.

There didn't seem to be much in between.

Eventually, he'd mostly stopped talking about it.

Gabe sighed softly and got behind the wheel of his car. There were times, and they were increasing, where it seemed like too many people had damage. Almost like everyone had damage. And he wondered, not for the first time, if it was possible to get through life without some kind of severe emotional and mental trauma.

Though at this point he actually wondered if it was possible to hit twenty without that.

As he started his car, he realized that Ellen hadn't responded. Frowning as that set off some kind of vague worry, he checked his phone to make sure he'd sent the photo. He had indeed, though she hadn't seen it.

Well...she was probably busy with something.

Only she was pretty much out of work, and he didn't see her away from her phone for too long. Gabe shook his head and put his phone away. He was being paranoid. But as he pulled out of the parking lot and began driving home, he couldn't shake the feeling that his worry was warranted.

...

When he got home, he found Ellen sitting on the sofa in the same position as he'd left her, but she was frowning deeply into her laptop.

"What's wrong?" he asked immediately.

"Nothing," she replied, setting the laptop aside. She sighed heavily. "Just something boring...and stupid. How'd your time with Holly go?"

"Well, I *did* send you a pic," he replied. "And don't dodge, what's wrong?"

Ellen grabbed her phone, still looking annoyed. "I just...have a responsibility I need to deal with that I literally completely forgot about, until I got an e-mail reminding me of it. It's dumb...ooh, wow. Nice. Wait, where the hell were you two? This looks like the set of a horror movie."

"Holly is into poking around abandoned buildings and there's one out behind a park. That's why she wanted me there. Also, are you cool with it if she spends the night?" he asked.

"Yeah, definitely...what abandoned building? Like what kind? Because some of those are really dangerous, also, it's illegal to actually go in there, even if I doubt they ever actually do anything about it or even notice," Ellen replied.

"It was like a factory or something, and I know. But seriously, what's wrong?"

She groaned, looking once more at Holly's wonderful breasts before setting the phone aside. "Okay, fine. When it occurred to me that I was going to be getting fired at some point in the near future, I made a doctor's appointment. I figured I should get whatever use out of my health insurance that I still could. And it's today. I completely fucking spaced it."

"Oh...why didn't they warn you, like, a week ago?"

"I was wondering the same thing. Apparently I either deleted the e-mail without realizing it or it got sent to my spam folder. But I have to be there in about an hour and I do not want to go."

"...is there something I'm missing? I mean, I get it, going to the doctor isn't much fun, but...? Is there some reason in particular you don't want to go?" he asked, sitting down on the couch with her as she drew her feet up to make room for him.

"Yes. And it's fucking stupid. I mean, I hate going to the doctor in general, I always have. But...promise you won't make fun of me."

"Of course I promise not to make fun of you," he replied.

"Sorry, it's kind of a reflex at this point...going to the doctor will mean knowing exactly how much weight I've put on. I know it's fucking stupid to worry about! I know it's not like it will actually change anything, it's just-seeing a number will make it real, and I've been not worrying about it for at least a week now, just not thinking about it and...this feels like such a dumb thing to worry about but I can't get it out of my head. I've always been sensitive to it because my extra height meant extra weight."

"I hate how much this bothers you," Gabe said. "But with the height–"

"I know," she interrupted, "I know that height changes things for weight. One fifty at five foot nine is *not* the same as one fifty at five foot one. It's just-it never seemed to matter. I feel like I've been raging against my body for most of my life and I hate it and I hate anything that reminds me of it and it's so frustrating because I was actually in great shape like three years ago. And I hate how worked up I get over it, and just...I don't know. I don't want to deal with it, but I have to."

"Do you want me to go with you?" he asked.

"Would you? Yes, I want that. It's not going to be any fun."

"Not everything has to be fun, babe. And I don't mind going with you."

"All right. Thank you. Um...lemme go get ready, then we can just do this and deal with it and get it out of the way."

Ellen sat up all the way, hesitated, then leaned over and gave him a kiss. She looked like she wanted to say something, but ended up just giving him a quick, awkward smile and getting to her feet. Gabe frowned as he watched her go. He'd rarely seen her this anxious over something.

But, whatever it was, however much it bothered her, whatever she needed from him, he intended to be there for her, however he could.

. . .

"Are you sure there isn't something more to this?" Gabe asked as they drove through the city.

"I mean, maybe," Ellen replied, staring out the window.

The clouds were grayer, darker, the promised rain that much closer.

"I'm willing to listen."

"I know, it's...usually when something bothers me like this it's because of one big thing, or maybe two or three big things, but I think in this case it's just a ton of little things. I think this might be a case where you might not fully understand what's going on. But basically...going to the doctor is different when you're a woman."

"I have heard that," he replied when she stopped talking and it became clear she was waiting for some kind of response.

She let out a soft, quiet sigh of what sounded like relief. "I've had to argue over so much petty bullshit that I keep expecting it, which isn't fair to you. Anytime I dare to opine that women have it harder in a difficult situation, any man listening will hop in with something. Either that I'm wrong, or the statistics are wrong, or I'm lying, or being dramatic, and then it usually circles around to how they have it worse somehow...sorry, I'm getting into a rant. Obviously this is a sore spot. My point is: thank you for not immediately arguing with me over stuff like this."

"You're welcome," he replied, unsure of what else to say.

"I think that's something you're going to have to put up with in this relationship for a while. Maybe forever. I've got a lot of built up anger and frustration and, in some cases, sheer fucking rage, and it's going to just keep coming out sometimes...anyway. You asked a question, and I'll do my best to answer it.

"Basically, I'm stressed out because of a history of just...being dismissed. Anything I go to the doctor for, it's basically blown off like it's no big deal, no matter how much pain I'm in. I almost fucking died of double pneumonia because they wanted to say I was being dramatic, it was just a cold. I just–" she stopped abruptly and heaved another sigh.

"I'm starting to rant again. This is a sensitive subject. It's kind of like you said about go online, ask men about their problems? Go online, ask women what shit they have to put up with that men just don't get and a *lot* of the stories will be 'medical professionals just do not take my pain seriously'."

"I've definitely heard that," Gabe replied. "And it's really fucking enraging. Being in pain is awful enough, but having people telling you you're being dramatic or even just outright faking? Fuck that. Fuck that into the ground. If there's anything I can do, let me know."

"I appreciate it, and at this point I'm just ranting. I've actually managed to find a doctor who listens and takes me seriously. It's just leftover trauma. I guess that and the fact that I'm staring down the barrel of the future now," she murmured.

"What do you mean?"

"Well, I'm going to be losing my health insurance soon, so I'll need to deal with *that*. But also my doctor has been sort of gently asking about me giving therapy a shot for two years now and I keep thinking 'I don't want to deal with that', but the more time goes on the more I wonder if I should at least give it a shot, and now that I've gotten with you and I'm slowly coming to realize that a lot of the shit I put up with and thought was normal actually wasn't, or at least *shouldn't* be...this is too much right now, let's talk about something else. What exactly happened with Holly?"

"We met at a park and she took me to an abandoned building because she didn't want to go alone and she has a thing for abandoned buildings. She's also *really* good at photography," he replied.

"Really?"

"Yes. I was there when she took some of the pictures and I saw the same thing that she photographed but...I don't know, there was something different in her pics."

Ellen smirked. "I told you: presentation is everything."

"Apparently," he replied.

"So how has this not come up before? I figured we would've heard about her love of photography at this point...or maybe not. Jesus, have we really only been with her for a few weeks?"

"Not even that," he said. "Like a week and a half, maybe."

"I'm not crazy, right? It feels like longer?"

"It does. It's...well, it kind of feels like how it felt with you and me," he said. "And it seems to be from both ends. She seems to be *really* wanting to be around us a lot. She was worried about spending the night tonight even though she might be too tired for sex."

"And what'd you tell her?" Ellen asked.

"That we are friends and it's cool if she spends the night regardless of whether or not sex happens."

"Mmm."

"What?" he asked. They were getting close to the clinic now. He kept an eye out for it as they rolled through the streets of the gray saturated city.

"It's just that it sounds like we're getting a lot closer to being in a relationship with her."

"We *are* in a relationship with her...or, I mean, right?"

"Yes, but I mean like a relationship like you and I have," Ellen replied.

There it was. Gabe pulled into the parking lot, parked, and killed the engine. He looked over at her intently. "So I really want to know: you are *actually* okay with it if Holly was living with us, and I was treating her the exact same way I am treating you?"

"Yes," Ellen said.

"You'd be okay with it if I was dating her in addition to you? In that I would have two girlfriends? I mean, you would have a girlfriend and a boyfriend in this scenario, given you'd be dating Holly and myself, but...I just want to be completely clear on this, because it feels really, really important that we're very clear and very on the same page. Because I want this to happen."

Ellen was quiet for a moment, staring at him, her expression growing more intent. If anything, more intense as well. She looked down at her hands in her lap suddenly. Gabe waited. He'd already gotten to know her well enough that he could read her 'I'm thinking very seriously about this' face immediately.

He was also very glad that he wasn't seeing her 'wait this is actually fucking awful' face.

"I've had a lot of time to think over the past few weeks, ever since you let me move in with you," Ellen said at last, her voice slow and measured. She kept staring at her hands, frowning in what looked like concentration.

"My life collapsed," she continued. "I lost a fiance. I lost my home. I lost my friends. I, more or less, lost my job. I left most of my things behind. I left probably thirty thousand dollars of stuff in that condo when I walked out. I walked away from my life, Gabe. And right now...I'm in a very strange place. Things that I've been sure about for twenty years or more, as in, things I was convinced were acid-etched in fucking titanium, are now either being questioned or I'm realizing are just wrong.

"And I've been figuring out what I want to do. I've been thinking about what really fucking *matters* to me. You and I are in love. We're tying our lives together. We aren't just dating, we aren't just sharing a house, we're building a home…" She looked at him now. "I mean, that's accurate, right? You would say that?"

"Yes, that's accurate. I would say that we are making a home together, and a life together," he replied.

She smiled and reached out and took his hand, squeezed it. "That's what matters to me, Gabe. A life together. A home together. A way that we can be together and we can live the way that we want to live, and we can help people, and do nice things, and just…live for ourselves and for each other. I ran in the fucking rat race for twenty motherfucking years. Twenty. *Years.* And my life collapsed in the span of a day.

"I mean, I'm not going to sit here and pretend that working hard and saving up didn't have some sort of payoff. I have a bank account with a fair amount of cash, I have decent credit, I have experience that I can turn into another job if I *really* need to…but fucking hell, was it worth it? I was almost never happy, I was never fucking *satisfied.* It always felt like everything I was doing was either pointless or aiding and abetting evil shitfucks suck the soul out of society.

"But this? *This?* Everything that you and I have done together over the past month, our time together, our time with Holly, our time with Em and Abby? That all feels *good,* and it feels like it finally fucking *means* something to me. With all that being said, I would say that yes, I'm very confident about my desire to have Holly be a part of our lives and our home. I feel a connection with her, like I do with you, and I want the home that we are making to be a...refuge. A place of good vibes and happiness and a place where people feel safe and welcome and comfortable."

"That's what I want, too," he murmured. Ellen seemed so intently focused on him, it was like the rest of the world didn't exist to her in that moment.

"I know, and that's just one of the reasons I love you so much. And this?" She nodded to the clinic, beyond the windshield. "I know you think this isn't that big a deal, you're coming along with me for moral support, but it *is* a big deal to me. No one else I've been with would bother with this shit. If I wanted to do something like this, nine times out of ten, I had to do it on my own. And I will do it on my own, because shit needs to get done, but it means *so* much to me that you came here with me for the sole reason that you know I want you to. I don't have to justify this shit to you, you just accept it, you just believe me, you just *care.*"

"I...do care," he said. "And...yeah, I didn't know it meant that much."

"It does. It all does. I'm sorry I'm so intense right now, it's just...I'm realizing what it means to actually have a *partner* in my life. Not a boyfriend or a fiance or even a husband, but a real, genuine, true-to-fucking-life *partner*. Because I've clearly never had that before. I've never had someone who would buy me soup in the middle of the night because I was sick, or who would help clean up vomit or piss if I got too sick or too drunk."

"Jesus Christ, what? Seriously?"

"Yes. God, I got drunk on some questionable wine at a party one night and my stomach was just-ugh. Bad. I ended up waking up in the middle of the night and just puked all over myself and the bed, and

Blake got pissed and I was crying and he told me to just fuck off and clean it up myself and he went to sleep in the guest bedroom."

"Holy fucking shit, Ellen, I'm so sorry that happened," he said, immediately pulling her into a hug.

"And that's another reason why I love you. You hear that and your reaction is this. I don't ever have to question that again, Gabe. I don't know if I can convey this enough, but I don't ever have to question: will he help me if I get sick? Will he take care of me? Will he clean it up if I throw up when I get the stomach flu? If I really, seriously need something from the store in the middle of the night, will he get up and get it for me? Would he help me shower if I broke my leg? I don't have to worry about that anymore because I trust that you'll help me no matter what."

"I will," he replied, hugging her more tightly. "I love you, I'd never just leave you to deal with something like that."

"And that is more comforting and reassuring than ten million dollars or a paid off condo or a really nice car or a vacation to Hawaii. Knowing that you will be there for me. And knowing that I will be there for you. And I know that you will be there for Holly, too. She's a good person, and I would love to have her in our home and our bed on a more permanent basis," Ellen said. She let out a little laugh as they parted, breaking up the tension. "I hope that answers the question."

"It really does," he replied.

She laughed again, then sighed heavily as she looked out the windshield again. "Come on, let's get this over with."

CHAPTER FIFTEEN

Being inside of a medical clinic gave Gabe flashbacks to the few times he'd had to visit such an establishment.

He hated being there. Immediately, upon stepping inside, he caught a smell of antiseptic, and it was like unlocking psychic damage instantaneously. He couldn't help but tense up at the feeling, his heartbeat picking up a bit, his breathing coming just a little faster.

He and Ellen waited in a short line, checked in and did the copay and insurance dance, then were admitted to another area of the clinic where they waited. He had to admit that it at least looked a lot more slick and upscale than anywhere he'd been.

"You seem really nervous," Ellen murmured as they sat down.

"I am. I almost died when I was nine. I fell down a steep driveway and scraped myself up pretty bad. My parents cleaned me up and I thought I was fine, I'd got cuts and scrapes before and it was no big deal, but then a few days later I was washing my hands and I saw this, like, red line on the inside of my arm?"

"That would be fucking terrifying."

"Yeah, although I was more just confused than anything else. I showed my mom and she got angry, like she accused me of drawing it on with a marker and started like vigorously trying to wash it off, which of course it wouldn't because it was under my fucking skin. This went on for half an hour before finally she took me to a doctor. Turns out I had some kind of blood poisoning...I think? I don't really remember what the actual problem was, just that it resulted in me being in the hospital for a few days with an IV plugged into my arm and feeling super shitty."

"Damn, I'm sorry, babe," she murmured.

"Yeah, it sucked, but, you know, it was forever ago. It sort of left an impression. Just...every time I come to a place like this, anywhere that smells like a hospital, it reminds me of that. Or it makes me think I'm going to get a shot. I'm one of those cowards that hates needles."

"I don't think that makes you a coward, Gabe. I mean, you still *get* the shots, right?" she asked.

"Yeah, as much as I fucking hate them."

"That's kind of the opposite of a coward. We don't get to choose what we're afraid of, but we *do* get to choose how we react to it," she said. "*I* will be the one getting a shot this time...unless you haven't gotten your flu shot yet?"

"Thankfully, I have. They give them out for free at the pharmacy near where I used to live and I figured one day back in October I might as well just go and make it happen, since I fucking *hate* the flu."

"Same, that's why I'm gonna get this done."

Not much later, Ellen got called, and then they had to apologize and inform them that, due to policy, he couldn't actually go into the room with her unless they were married or related. Ellen was annoyed but, given she just wanted to get this over with, went with the nurse back to the next area. Gabe found himself waiting still.

He pulled out his phone and saw that at some point he'd gotten a text.

It was from, of all people, Krystal, and he immediately felt guilty because he realized that they hadn't actually spoken for a while.

Are you ignoring me?

He stared at the message for a bit. It seemed like the kind of thing Krystal would send, based of the little he actually knew of her, but the real question was: was she being serious or playful?

Finally, he typed: *What if I am?*

It felt like playing with fire, especially given the fact that this was Ellen's best friend and she had told him there was a really good chance he might actually put his cock inside of Krystal if they ever met in real life, but apparently he liked playing with fire nowadays.

Ellen had definitely had a very big impact on him.

Krystal responded quickly: *If you were, I'd be annoyed. And then I would guess that I need to do something to get your attention.*

He felt his heart flutter a little at that. *Suppose you continued this line of thought, what exactly would 'getting my attention' look like?*

Gabe waited, staring at the screen, wondering exactly what kind of game he was playing with her. This felt so strange, though at least some of that was amplified by the deeply emotional heart-to-heart he and Ellen had engaged in barely twenty minutes ago in the car.

All his thoughts were derailed, hard, as Krystal responded.

A picture of her, obviously taken by someone else, he imagined her girlfriend, completely naked from the back.

Not only did she have some nice tattoos on her back, but she had probably the most amazing ass he'd ever seen on a woman who wasn't a porn star.

He immediately responded back: *Krystal, dear*

God, your ass is amazing.

She began typing back quickly: *I'm glad you approve. Also, I know fucking every chick says this but I actually mean it because I am in a monogamous relationship, mostly, but consider yourself fucking lucky because I don't send nudes to anyone.*

Gabe laughed softly. *I definitely feel lucky.*

Good. Now, I want the truth: did I hear right and you fucked Emily?

He thought about it for a moment and a quick mental check confirmed that yes, everyone involved in this was cool with Krystal knowing, and seeing.

Well, I fucked her in the mouth.

Immediately the ... appeared: *WHAT!? BULLSHIT! I CALL BULLSHIT SHE'S MARRIED NOW!*

He chuckled and uploaded a picture of that wonderful night. Emily looked especially good, topless and sucking him off, staring up at him with a surprisingly aggressive look on her face as they locked eyes.

HOLY FUCK DUDE! THAT'S AMAZING! GODDAMNIT!

Gabe typed more: *Why do you sound angry?*

The ... appeared again. Then disappeared. Appeared again. Disappeared again.

Finally, he got: *Can I call?*

Gabe fired off a quick text to Ellen, telling her about the situation, and apparently she was still waiting on the doctor because she responded quickly that she was fine with it. He got up and headed back outside, then leaned against the hood of his car.

Yeah, you can call.

A few seconds later his phone began to ring. He answered. "Hello, Krystal."

"Gabe!...wow, you have a nice voice," Krystal replied.

"So do you...so what's up?"

"FUCK! I'm frustrated! Do you have *any* idea how much I've wanted to fuck Ellen and Emily?! Two bisexual girls, who are both hot as *fuck,* that I've known since we were all in high school, and none of us ever went all the way! And now you're there doing both of them! How'd you get Abby to agree to that, she's so fucking straitlaced!"

"Wait, what gave you that impression? How well do you actually know Abby?" he asked.

"Not *that* well, but I mean, she's like a lawyer and shit!"

"Krystal, most lawyers are fucking freaks," he replied.

"Are you fucking with me?! Goddamnit, sometime this winter I'm going to come over there and fuck you into a goddamn coma!"

"And that...is a punishment?" he replied.

"Shut up!"

"All right, you're throwing a lot at me right now Krystal. This is the first time we're actually talking and I seriously can't tell if you're angry at me or not."

"I'm...frustrated! But mostly I'm happy. Obviously Ellen's over the fucking moon for you and you seem to be doing a lot of nice things for her and treating her right. Not like the other shitheads. Also, side note, if you fuck Ellen over I will seriously hunt you down and stab you. Understand?"

"Understood," he replied.

She laughed. "Well, that's good to get out of the way, at least. And that fucking redhead! You and Ellen aren't fucking with me, right? You're really fucking railing her?"

"I'm really railing her," he replied. "I'm probably going to rail Emily soon, too."

"GABE! YOU FUCK!" Krystal cried so loud he winced and had to hold the phone away from his head for moment.

"Krystal, you are *loud* and *weird*."

"Is that complaint? Or a compliment?" she replied.

"Compliment...mostly. It's really weird that this is the first thing we talk about."

"Oh whatever, you've seen my tits. And vagina. And ass, now. And-what? No, I'm not-ugh, fine! That was my girlfriend, she says I should dial it back. I guess I do come on a little strong."

"I'm not exactly complaining, though I am having a bit of a hard time keeping up. I'm not used to talking with ridiculously attractive women," he replied.

"What the fuck? Of course you are, you're dating Ellen and fucking that redheaded girl *and* Em apparently!"

"Yeah, I'm still not *used* to it," he replied. "So...how much as Ellen told you about me?"

"A lot," Krystal said. "Mostly it's just her gushing about how great you are. I know you're a writer and I am assuming she told you I am also a writer. Though not a very successful one." She paused. "Honestly, everything she says is just...nice shit you do for her. Normally all I'd used to hear from her was money, job, car make and model...I love Ellen to death but she very much had an obsession with materialism and I am *so* fucking glad you apparently broke her of it."

"Yeah, I...honestly, getting to know her as well as I have, I've really gotten the impression that she didn't so much like that stuff as assumed that she was supposed to like it. That not liking it and not chasing it was some kind of failure," he replied.

"That's kind of how I always felt about it, but whenever I tried to broach the subject with her, she'd get pissy...ugh, I hate talking about her like this behind her back."

"Same."

"Yeah but *you* are defending her...whatever. Can you get me a video of you just fucking nailing Emily? And also Ellen? And that little redhead of yours?"

"Jeez, you ask for a lot...what am I gonna get in return?" he replied.

"Hmm. What do you *want?*"

He glanced around, making sure he was still alone out there. It felt so fucking weird to talk about this stuff in public. "I want another picture of your pussy."

She laughed deviously. "You really like my pussy, huh?"

"Yep," he replied.

She snorted. "Well you have an appropriate reaction because my pussy looks fantastic."

"Man, you are...*really* cocky," he muttered.

"*Confident,* good sir," she replied. "After being told a thousand million times how fucking hot I am, yes, that tends to boost the confidence up. But, Gabe, I will have you know that I don't let it confuse me into thinking I'm better than anyone else simply because I won the genetic lottery and put a little work in. So, three sex vids for one pussy pic?"

"Uh-uh, one vid for the pic. I want something else for the rest," he replied.

"Oh-ho, bold. I can see why Ellen likes you. All right, what?"

"Two things, one for each video. First one: I want a reciprocal video. You and your girlfriend. Or, if she isn't comfortable with being filmed, you going solo."

"I can do that. I'll talk to Liz about it," she replied in a tone that for some reason made him imagine her casually examining her fingernails as she spoke. "And the second thing?"

"Tell me right now...are you serious about hooking up with me or just flirting?"

A pause from the other end. When she spoke again, she was more serious. "Liz and I are have broached the topic seriously. We've been monogamous since we started dating, but we've both always known that there may come a time when someone...special comes along. So...put it this way: if Liz gives me the green light, I absolutely intend to be all over that dick. And also Ellen. I would *kill* for a threesome with you two."

"Same, honestly," he replied, and she laughed. "Okay, that's pretty great to hear."

"It had better be. And I expect one of those vids *today* because I answered that question," Krystal replied.

"Yeah, yeah, you'll get it."

"Don't you fucking snark me!" she growled.

"What are you gonna do about it?" he replied.

"Oh you fucking-you are just like her! Always giving me shit!"

"To be honest, Krystal, you really seem to bring it out in us."

"Yeah, whatever. I gotta go. I've got annoying grownup things to do. I will most certainly be speaking with you later."

"Goodbye, Krystal."

"Bye, Gabe."

She hung up and he pulled his phone back, staring at it for what seemed like a long time.

For the first time, Gabe found himself not just marveling over the fact that he was speaking with yet another ridiculously attractive woman about having sex, but also beginning to wonder if he could actually handle this.

Finally, he slipped his phone in his pocket and headed back to the waiting room.

Only one way to find out.

…

It took almost another hour before Ellen emerged from the patient area, though Gabe wasn't really surprised, given how long it could take and how overtaxed the healthcare infrastructure was. If anything he'd expected to wait a lot longer.

He was trying to get a measure of her general mood as they checked out and headed for the car, but it was difficult. She seemed neutral. When they got into the car, he started it up, then waited for a bit.

"So...how are you doing?" he asked when she didn't say anything.

"I'm okay," she replied. "Just...thinking a lot. At a glance, I'm healthy. I had them draw some blood for some tests, make sure all my enzymes and whatnot are in order. I also finally agreed to let them consult with a therapist and set me up with an appointment, so...I'll be going to therapy sometime in the next few weeks, or maybe a little longer, the list is *quite* long these days."

"I'm glad," Gabe said, backing out of the space and beginning the drive home.

"That I'm going to therapy?"

"Yeah."

"Mmm."

"Were you hoping for a different reaction?"

"No, definitely not. It's clear at this point that I could really use it. I just...I'm seeing a lot now, about my life, that I have no fucking clue how I was so blind to it. For example, I've put on another eleven pounds since the last time I had a doctor's visit some six months ago. And that would have just fucking *ruined* my day in any other relationship. Because, well, for obvious reasons of 'weight going up is bad', but also I knew I couldn't let my significant other know about it.

"Because then they'd start in with whatever their version of 'I gotta get her to be more presentable arm candy' is, and I don't have to fucking worry about that with you. But also the therapy thing. I'm just remembering that every time it's come up they would always rail against it, and they even fucking told me why! It was always 'your therapist will get in your head and try to break us up', like, fucking hell, how did I miss that!? They *knew* they were shitty boyfriends!"

She stopped suddenly, staring down at her hands clenched into fists in her lap, and looked up and over at him. "Do I talk about my exes too much? That just occurred to me. Which is sad, because Holly asked the same fucking thing not that long ago so you'd think I would've thought of it then, but...do I?"

"I don't think so," he replied. "They did a lot of damage. It makes sense that you'd bring them up as much as you do."

"You don't really bring up yours. And it sounds like they did some shitty things, too," she said.

"Especially that last one."

"That's true." He considered it. "I don't know, I guess, for some reason, I don't like talking about them. It's probably got something to do with how we're wired. I know people have different ways of dealing with things, I imagine one of the more common ways is to talk about it, and another is to just not talk about it. But it's not like I'm over here thinking 'God shut the fuck up about your exes, I never talk about mine', you know?"

"That's a fair point," she murmured. "Does it really not bother you? What a mess I am?"

"I don't think you're a mess, Ellen. And even if I did, no, it doesn't bother me."

"Why?"

"Because...life fucking sucks. The common denominator of existence is pain. We all suffer. We do our best to try and mitigate the suffering, but in truth, given how absolutely fucked society is, given how normalized abject cruelty is, I think it's completely reasonable to be a mess. You can't help everyone, but at the very least you can help the people you love. And I love you. I want you to be happy, and I want to take care of you, and help you be less of a mess, if you feel like you are a mess," he replied.

"I have no fucking clue how three women let you get away from them," she muttered. "Because *fuck* are you a catch."

Gabe laughed awkwardly. "I could definitely say the same thing about you."

"You know, I don't believe in fate...but it's shit like this that does make me wonder. Were our relationships doomed to fail because we were always on the path towards each other?"

"I don't believe in fate either, but it's nice to think, at least," he replied.

She chuckled. "Yes, very much so. Oh! Also, just remembered, how was the conversation with Krystal?"

"Uh...you know, it was intense," he replied.

"Yeah, she's a fucking handful, right?"

"She really is."

"She wants videos of us fucking. And me and Holly fucking. And me and Emily. She's *mad* jealous of me, apparently," he replied.

"Ah. Yeah...I *do* feel a little bad. As I said before, Krystal's the one I got the farthest with and she used to gag over Em all the time, but Em was always with someone else and I know she wanted nothing more than a threeway between all of us and it never happened, and honestly I would've done it, I think, I was just...scared, if I'm going to go for brutal honesty."

They came to their house and he parked in the driveway. "Scared of what?"

"What it would mean, I guess, if I went all the way with a woman? Let alone two," Ellen replied. They got out and headed inside. "It's weird and I don't even-I can't even really articulate my concern, what I thought would happen. Maybe I just thought people would think less of me...I guess it doesn't matter anymore. So what are you getting out of her in return? Or is this charity porn?"

He laughed. "What the fuck? Charity porn?"

"I don't know what to call it, just giving it because she asked for it?"

"Three things."

"Wow! I feel like Krystal would hedge hard if this were anyone else. How the fuck did you get her to agree to that? She is one stubborn bitch usually," Ellen said, taking off her shoes and coat.

"I don't really know, I just asked? I mean I guess she was giving me shit, so I gave it right back to her, and that seemed to surprise her. She agreed to give me a nude picture, a video of either her going solo or her and her girlfriend having sex, and she gave me an honest answer to the question of if she was serious or not about fucking me."

Ellen raised her eyebrows. "What'd she say?"

"She said if she gets the green light from her girlfriend, she will be all over me...how does that make you feel?" he replied.

"Turned on," Ellen replied. "That would be amazing...well, you can send her one of us fucking and I know Holly is already cool with it. And Em already said she didn't care if we showed that video or pics to Krystal and Liz, it'll just be a question of how she feels about being filmed while actually fucking you."

"What's her girlfriend like?" he asked.

"A bit closer to your age and fit. Like, she works out a lot. She's a gym girl. She's got abs. So hot. She's also shy. I haven't actually met her, but Krystal has been telling me about her for a few years now and I've seen a lot of pictures of them on her social media."

"Hmm. Nice. You think *she'd* be into me?" he asked.

Ellen grinned. "Does your hunger know no bounds?"

"Not really."

She laughed. "I think the chances are a lot lower with Liz. She's never been with a guy as far as I know. I think their relationship might be like Em and

Abby's, but I don't know for sure. So you're into muscle girls as well as tall girls?"

"Duh," he replied.

"Good to know...all right, well, I want to fuck off for the rest of the day. How about you?"

"I could do some fucking off, but then I've got to get back to work. I wanna get that editing out of the way and I really want to get back to the stone age fucking."

"Perfect."

They shared a kiss and ended up getting settled on the couch to watch some cartoons.

CHAPTER SIXTEEN

Gabe sighed and stopped messing with his hair. "Goddamnit, Ellen."

"What?!" she called. "What is it this time, love!?"

"I can *hear* you smirking, do you know that?"

"You cannot! Stop lying!"

"Okay, come here and show me your face."

"...no."

"Why?"

"...I'm busy."

"Oh bullshit, get in here," he replied, turning around and leaning against the bathroom sink.

He heard her sighed heavily, then there was a pause, he thought he heard her mutter 'goddamnit', then she walked out of the bedroom. When she stepped in front of the bathroom door, he had to admit, she did an admirable job of keeping it together.

Gabe crossed his arms and stared hard at her.

She snorted and then smirked. "Fuck!"

"Knew it."

"Oh shut up! You don't even get to complain! I have set you up to fuck a *really* hot married woman that has basically zero chance of going wrong, so you're welcome," she replied immediately, crossing her arms as well.

"And that's why you enjoy this relationship so much. You're intimidating as hell and you've had to fight for everything..." He started walking towards her, out of the bathroom, into the hallway, and she started backing up. "But I can put you properly in your place, Ellen," he continued, speaking slowly, staring into her eyes, "and I can make you do things, and make you glad to do them, because we love each other, you know that I respect you, and I am one hundred percent the dom to your sub."

Ellen began to say something but she bumped into the wall and let out a soft, surprised gasp instead. She swallowed and cleared her throat.

"You have a good point," she murmured.

"Do I now?"

"Yes."

"Yes...?"

"Yes, sir," she said, blushing now.

"And, for the record," he replied, reaching out and slowly pulling open her robe, exposing her large breasts, "if I didn't have a date with your married friend, I would take your clothes off, drag you to the bedroom, bend you over the bed and fuck you until you screamed."

"...maybe we could push the date back," she murmured as he cupped her breasts.

"No," Gabe replied. "We're not doing that. You're just going to have to wait."

She growled and pulled her robe closed. "You'd better watch it with the teasing, or you're going to unleash that side of me again."

"Is that a promise?" he asked.

Her eyes flashed and her stance changed, Ellen drawing herself up to her full height, and Gabe could feel their entire dynamic change in an instant. "Go back to the bathroom so I can fix your hair before *I* take you to the bedroom and fuck *you* until you scream."

He laughed, just a little, and nodded. "Yes, ma'am."

She chuckled softly and followed him into the bathroom. He stood before the mirror and she began messing with his hair. "You remember to clip your nails? Put on deodorant?"

"Yes."

"Toenails? You washed your dick?" she asked.

He laughed. "Fuck's sake yes, love. I washed everything."

"Hey, Em's letting you fuck her raw, okay? And I'm sure she's going to put your dick in her mouth again. So I think it'd be kind to make sure you are clean as a whistle," she murmured, finishing up.

"I happen to agree, which was why I was so thorough," he replied. "You sure this isn't too messy?"

"She likes messy," Ellen replied, teasing his hair just a bit more. "I do too, for the record."

"Good for me, I guess," he said, studying himself in the mirror.

"Quite good for you. Okay..." She stepped back and turned him to face her, looking him over. "You look great. Come on."

They headed out into the living room and Gabe put his shoes on, the pulled on his hoodie.

"Just remember...put her at ease. Although I guess I don't need to tell you that, you just fucking *do* that automatically."

"Apparently I do," he agreed. "Don't worry. We've been texting and I think this is going to be fine."

Ellen adopted a different kind of smile and stared at him intently, almost like she was admiring a work of art. "I can't believe how far you've come this quickly," she murmured. "You were...shall we say, lacking in confidence when I walked back into your life. I thought it was going to last a lot longer, but here you are, proving me wrong."

He laughed. "Well, don't get too happy there. I'm still plenty insecure. It just helps that I know sex is almost certainly going to happen and there's actually a very small chance I can fuck this up bad enough that Emily would change her mind."

"Yeah, plus you know that even if you strike out with her, you have," she opened her robe, showing her long, naked, pale body off, "this to come home to."

"Yes...I do," he murmured.

She laughed and began rocking gently back and forth, making her huge breasts sway. "God, I can fucking hypnotize you."

"You actually can," he replied. "Your body is just...absolutely off-the-charts, absurd sex appeal to me."

She sighed and blushed and pulled her robe closed again. "Yeah okay."

"You get embarrassed *so* easily."

"I know! Now shut up and go on your date! Just text me when you're almost done and I'll meet you at their place with Holly."

"Sounds perfect." He gave her a hug and a kiss. "Love you, dear."

"Love you too, babe."

Gabe headed out. As he got in his car and began driving back to the bowling alley-arcade-mini-golf-course combination he'd taken Ellen and Holly to, he reflected on all that had happened. It had been about a week since he'd taken Ellen to the doctor's office, and it had been both a busy and extremely pleasant week.

Holly had spent the night every single night since she'd come that first one, and he was admittedly a little surprised by how quickly they seemed to settle into that. Usually Holly was gone before he woke up, but twice she was still there and both times they'd ended up fucking and *damn* if that wasn't a great way to start the day.

But she seemed so completely relaxed and at home whenever they got up and went about their morning routines. She pretty much just chilled with them, either hanging out with one or both of them or, if they were busy, usually relaxing in bed and doing her own thing.

It was never weird or awkward, it was almost like she was supposed to be there with them.

And that was a great feeling.

Gabe's mind drifted as he drove. Or really it felt more like bouncing, given he was hyped up with nervous energy. Despite how he felt in his head, despite what Ellen and Holly had both told him, he was still nervous about this.

He kept expecting this to go wrong in some massive, terrifying way.

Being in love with Ellen and dating and living with her, and having her love him back just as much, was certainly at the top of his hopes and dreams list. But there were others beyond that, and like a lot of people, yes, he very much wanted to be in a relationship where he also got to have sex with hot women *and* his girlfriend was enthusiastically involved.

It was just that he never actually thought he'd get to do it.

And even while he'd been fantasizing about it, Gabe knew in the back of his head that were he ever to actually live that dream, it would almost certainly come with its own difficulties.

Only so far it hadn't.

Everyone seemed happy and chill about the whole thing. No one had gotten angry or hurt, as far as he could tell, and that they were bringing Emily deeper into their little sexual circle (and intended to do the same with Krystal at some point in the future) only seemed to make everyone happier.

He knew he should stop being paranoid, but life had really hammered that into him.

As he found the bowling alley and drove to a parking spot, Gabe made a conscious effort to put it out of his mind. He was here to have fun with Emily, and put her at ease, get her more comfortable with him, and he was going to do that.

It had taken a bit longer than they'd originally anticipated because, surprise surprise, it was hard to coordinate things that involved five separate people. Given they'd had more time to think about it, he wasn't surprised that Emily had gotten a little more nervous. She'd reassured him more than once that she was still very much onboard with the encounter, she just wanted to ease into it more. And he could understand that.

Sex was fun and sex with someone you'd never done it with before was even more fun, but it was also a little intimidating.

He sent her a message that he was there, and she told him to meet her at the entrance.

Gabe got out and began walking across the lot. It was more packed this time than when he'd gone before, which seemed a little weird given it was a Tuesday evening. Maybe they had some kind of special deal on Tuesdays, or maybe that was just the way the dice had landed. Gabe shivered and quickened his pace as another cold wind gusted through the lot.

Winter was on approach and it was becoming more evident each day. They'd gotten a few abnormally warm days for November so far, but mostly it was cold and gray and sometimes it rained. Otherwise known as Gabe's favorite time of the year.

He realized, abruptly, that this would be his first winter with Ellen. His first winter in a home of his own, a real home of his own.

His first winter that he didn't have to wake up too early, dig his car out of the snow, and drive through a packed city just to piss away eight or nine hours at a job he hated.

There she was. Emily stood in the little entryway between rows of mostly glass doors, looking fairly calm and remarkably sexy in a pair of tight pink pants and a sleek pink hoodie, both of which showed off her lean, pleasantly proportioned body.

The smile she got when she saw him lit up her face and she opened the door for him.

"Hey, you," she said warmly.

"Hey. You look...amazing," Gabe replied.

She laughed awkwardly. "Abby thought it was a bit much, but, I dunno, I've always liked pink for whatever dumb reason. I haven't been on a date with anyone but Abby in years. I mean, obviously. But you know I wanted to dress a little more for myself. Usually when we go on dates I clean up and Abby dresses down. She likes the smart cut look and I like the trashy look, apparently...am I talking too much?"

"No, you aren't...I didn't think you'd be this nervous," Gabe replied.

"I'm not nervous!" She paused, pursed her lips, sighed. "Okay, I'm a little nervous. But I haven't been...I haven't done anything with a guy–barring what we did in the back of the car–in literal years!

Like over half a decade or so. And *never* with a guy Ellen was with, Christ."

"Still scared of pissing her off?" he asked.

"Yes! She's so fucking intimidating, I don't even know how you date her."

"I could say the same thing about Abby," he replied.

She laughed. "Okay, that's a fair point, I guess. I don't know how to describe it, but like...Abby's intimidation doesn't really work on me, not unless she's trying in a sexual way. I guess it's because I've seen her crying in the shower at three in the morning, drunk off her ass, mascara running, and then I have to hold her hair while she pukes and tries to get it all in the toilet. I guess...I saw Abby's human side and I've never really seen Ellen's?"

"I definitely have," he replied, "so I can understand it. But, I mean, she was acting pretty human over that first dinner we had."

"Yeah, but that's not...I don't know, the same? I've seen her like that before, though it was more honest and open than usual by far, but something...I don't know. I can't really describe it. Anyway, what do you want to do?" she asked.

"What do *you* want to do?" he replied.

She snorted and rolled her eyes. "That's how it's going to be, huh?"

"I'm just trying to be reasonable, Em."

"Oh sure you are. I hope Abby didn't call you and tell you to 'go easy on me' because she thinks I'm just a bag of nerves."

"She didn't, as a matter of fact. But if that's how it's going to be, let's hit the arcade," he said, going to push open the interior door.

"Wait," Emily replied, grabbing his wrist. "I'm

sorry, I'm not trying to be a bitch. I *am* kind of nervous. And I just get...snarky."

"It's fine, I understand," he said. "Are you down for the arcades?"

"Yes, actually, that sounds great."

"All right then."

He offered her his hand. She smiled and took it, lacing their fingers together.

They walked into the main receiving area and headed for the arcade section. It was definitely more packed than last time, but they managed to exchange a twenty for a lot of tokens and track down a game without having to wait too long.

And then the date was really on.

CHAPTER SEVENTEEN

"I actually used to be a gamer girl," Emily said, breaking the silence that had settled over them.

"In what capacity?" Gabe replied.

They were sitting together in the tiny restaurant section of the bowling alley. It was empty because people tended to want their food brought to the lanes, so they basically had it to themselves. The arcade had been a good, fun, simple time. They'd gone from cabinet to cabinet for almost an hour and a half, not really talking about much, just playing, vibing really.

"Used to play a bunch of games. I had a console and a shitty laptop. I was into horror games. I actually made a go of being a streamer about a decade ago." She paused, reconsidered. "Well, streamer is what we say now, but I didn't really stream, more just recorded myself and put it up on the internet."

"Seriously? What happened? You *had* to have gotten a following with how fucking hot and fun you are," he replied.

She laughed and shook her head, blushing a little bit. "I did, actually. I did it for about a year. Made some decent money. And then I gave it up. That's actually why I have the tattoo sleeves. I wanted a really different look after that. It was, um...a bad time. Way too much harassment."

"Oh. Shit, sorry," he murmured. "That would've been around...twenty fourteen. Ah, yeah."

"Yep," she replied.

The internet had always been a toxic place, at least for as long as he'd known about it, but there had been some kind of paradigm shift that year, a sort of flashpoint that seemed to solidify and magnify a lot of hatred.

Especially with regards to women and video games.

"I actually had like fifty thousand followers," she said, poking at her pizza slice. "Small peanuts nowadays and even back then I guess it wasn't crazy, but it was enough for me to quit my job. I thought I'd found, like, my thing. But I don't know, something about me just really drew out the psychopaths and assholes. I quit when someone emailed me a picture of my apartment complex they'd taken."

"Holy fucking shit," he muttered.

"Yeah. That was really scary. Guys online are fucking *insane*." She paused. "I mean, definitely some chicks are too, but it was basically always men who were coming after me. Either trying to fuck me or threatening to kill me, or worse, or both. I dunno, I've never really felt scared around a woman like I have around a man." She paused again. "Fuck, I'm killing the mood."

"It's fine," Gabe replied.

Emily gave him a measured look suddenly. "You don't feel like telling me 'not all men'?" Before he could reply she groaned and hid her face behind her hands. "*Fuck.* I'm being a bitch right now. I'm sorry."

"It's really fine, Em," he replied. "There's...very definitely a specific dynamic between men and women, on and offline, that is common enough it's a clearly a massive problem. You obviously had a lot of shitty guys fucking with you and it logically follows that you'd feel this way. And, to be fair, I've met more shitty guys than I have shitty women."

"Maybe women are just better at hiding it," she said, lowering her hands.

"Maybe. Men tend to be a lot more

straightforward. But, I don't know, I mean, this kind of thing is the whole reason I want to just...pull out, you know? I want to just fucking be by myself, with a handful of people that I actually trust, and that's my life."

"Same." A moment went by where neither of them said anything, just ate in silence. Finally, Emily sighed heavily. "I *did* fuck the mood up."

"Emily," Gabe said, and she looked up from her food at him, her expression vulnerable and a little anxious, "this isn't like a normal date. And I'll tell you what I told Ellen and Holly: I'd rather have a real conversation with real emotions, unhappy or not, than a meaningless filler conversation. We want to have sex with each other. That's going to be intimate. Intimacy can be uncomfortable for most people, and the only way to mitigate that is to get to know each other, be vulnerable around each other, feel like we're speaking our minds and being heard. I want you to feel comfortable. I'm not looking to say or do whatever it takes to nail you and then tell you to fuck off."

Emily stared at him for a long moment, looking almost startled. "Jesus fucking Christ, Ellen was right about you."

"What does that mean?"

"It's just-she told me you're like a goddamned grandmaster safe-cracker in terms of getting women to feel truly comfortable. And *fuck* if that wasn't effective. I believe you."

"I mean it's not like I'm lying," he replied, now himself a little uncomfortable.

"I know. I think you could probably fool me, but I doubt you could fool Abby and I *know* you couldn't fool Ellen. It's just...I was thinking that with that sort of power, you could absolutely be so effectively evil. Seducing women and using them and moving on."

"I don't want to be that kind of person."

"Which is good. Great, really. And ironically is what is leading you to being able to hook up with other women while your girlfriend watches." She had begun to smile but she lost it suddenly. "I've got a question that I want to ask you, but I'm afraid you might take it the wrong way, and I really don't want to insult you."

"I promise to try not to take it the wrong way," Gabe replied.

"Mmm..."

"No really, I want to hear it. You've got my curiosity going."

She laughed. "Fine. In some ways, I see a lot of myself and my relationship with Abby in you, and in your relationship with Ellen. Both Abby and Ellen were really high-powered, professional women who absolutely dominated and kicked ass in their field for, like, a decade. Abby gave it up, Ellen has basically done the same. And...I still worry I'm not enough for Abby. Or I'm not a good match for her. I'm a lot less worried now, especially now that we're well into being married, but it still bothers me..."

"And you want to know if I feel the same way and how I deal with it?" he asked. She nodded. "That's a fair question. Honestly I'm still wrestling with myself. Ellen seems...*so* fucking far out of my league it's ridiculous. So do you. So does Holly. So does Krystal–"

"Wait, you fucked Krystal?" Emily asked, sitting up.

"No, but we've been...talking. She has been very plain about the fact that she wants to jump me," he replied.

"Oh my God that fucking whore," she muttered, smirking.

"She said something similar about you."

"That fucking bitch! If I ever get my fucking hands on her again...whatever. Oh, I know that look. You're imagining what it would be like to have me and Krystal in a threesome, yeah?"

"Uh, yeah. One hundred percent. Tattooed goddess heaven," he replied.

She laughed and blushed worse. "Oh my God, shut the fuck up weirdo."

"I'm not weird. I actually think it's very normal and not weird to think that you are insanely hot tatted vision of beauty," he replied.

"Gabe! Shut up!" she growled.

"Am I embarrassing you?"

"Yes! And you know it! You're derailing the conversation, you prick."

"Okay, okay. We're on the same wavelength, is what I was saying. And I'm still grappling. But I think...most people like Ellen and Abby reach a certain point in their life where they realize that grinding hard on their career got them less satisfaction than they were hoping for. Much less, in some cases. And given the fact that they grinded away their most productive years, they feel at a loss, unsure of what to do. Whereas you and I, on the other hand, have been rolling around in the mud of 'I don't know what to do with my life' for years, many years, and so we have a lot more experience with knowing how to handle that feeling. So, in a way, the tables are turned."

"...it *did* kind of feel that way for a while," Emily murmured. "Abby seemed really lost for a few months. But I dunno, it still feels like there's this imbalance. She's so fucking put together and motivated, even after she stopped being insane about it, and I'm just...not. I half-ass so much and I finally got really lucky and found something I can half-ass and get a disproportionate return on. Sometimes she gets annoyed at how little effort I put into things, but she says it's fine..." she heaved a sigh.

Gabe thought about it for a moment. "People can be really different. These differences can be no big deal or utter incompatibilities. We can be willing to overlook them or just let them bother us and put up with it...Abby doesn't strike me as the kind of person to just put up with something from a partner. And, if it helps, from what I've seen in how you two are around each other, you've got a good, loving relationship, and she is extremely into you."

Emily laughed awkwardly, pursed her lips, played the remains of her food for a bit. She couldn't seem to meet his eyes. "Thanks," she said finally. "It does help, actually. I'm just realizing right now that, uh, I'm still a little awkward about being real with men. Or maybe it's just with anyone who isn't Abby at this point. I haven't really opened up to anyone for a long time."

"I understand. I also wanted to say...if you don't feel comfortable with this, we don't have to go ahead. And this is *not* me trying to get out of the encounter, because to be completely clear: I *desperately* want to sleep with you."

She laughed loudly, breaking into a wide grin. "Wow, desperately, huh?"

"Yep."

"Well, that's good to know. And I'm comfortable with this. Mostly. I trust that Abby is comfortable with letting you fucking rail me raw, and I know I am. It's just...Ellen still intimidates me. I trust her, to be clear, that she's cool with this, it's sort of a reflex at this point. So I'm happy with this whole thing happening. Even happier now after this, to be honest. But yeah, you *do* make a good point about the relationships...all right, you've officially made me feel better. So thanks for that. I will try *extra* hard when we're fucking."

"Appreciated. What does that look like exactly?" he asked.

She smirked. "I guess you'll just have to find out. Now, tell me about this girl of yours. This redheaded little fuck-slave you have."

Gabe glanced around, wanting to reconfirm that no one was in earshot. "*Wow,* Em. That seems a little, um…"

"Insensitive? Why? Because she's a woman? Guys can be fuck-slaves, too. And from what I've heard she sounds like she'd be really happy to be called that to her face."

"She...yeah. Probably. I'm still getting used to all this. You have to remember that I had like three girlfriends before Ellen came along and A) fucked me better than anyone else in my entire life, and B) let me fuck other women. But yeah, Holly is...shy, and nervous, but definitely getting to be less so. She's wicked hot, she's young and inexperienced, and she is learning that she *really* enjoys being dominated. I grabbed her wrists while we were fucking and she just like squirted immediately."

"So hot," Emily whispered.

"Yep. It's a lot like living a porn, in all the best ways."

"Which is what tonight's gonna be like," she

murmured, and he felt her brush his legs with her foot under the table.

"Man, you jumped straight from insecure to horny pretty fast."

She laughed. "There was some time between those two things." Emily chewed on her lip for a moment, staring at him from across the table. "Can we go back to my place? Because I am *feeling* it." She lifted her foot suddenly and placed it against his crotch, then grinned fiercely. "And so are you, apparently."

"Uh, yeah. I mean you're...you," he replied.

She chuckled. "I am me. So is that a yes?"

"That's a yes," he replied.

"Okay." She stood up quickly and when he did as well, she grabbed him and kissed him firmly on the mouth. "I'm heading back now, I need to get a little ready. So, I'll see you there?"

"You will see me there," he agreed.

Her grin widened and she began walking away. Gabe watched her go for a moment. Her ass looked ridiculously good in the pants she was wearing. He shook his head and got to work clearing off the table of their leftovers.

This definitely felt like another too good to be true situation.

CHAPTER EIGHTEEN

Gabe tried not to speed as he drove to Emily's and Abby's house.

He'd spoken with Ellen briefly on the phone. She was already at Abby's place with Holly, and was very happy to hear their date night had gone well. And they were very ready to watch him have sex with Emily.

And so now he was horny enough that it was difficult to focus properly.

Somehow, though, he managed to make it to their very nice house, park in the driveway, and bang on the front door.

"Holy shit, Gabe, you scared us," Abby said when she answered the door.

"Yeah, I thought it was the police knocking," Emily called from somewhere deeper in the house.

"Sorry. I'm...excited," he replied, taking off his hoodie and shoes.

"So are we," Abby said. "I have no clue what you said to Emily but it apparently fucking worked. She came back her and she couldn't wait to doll up for you like the submissive little whore she is."

"I fucking heard that!" Emily called.

"I know!" Abby replied.

"You know you're a hard sub, Em!" Ellen called from elsewhere in the house.

"All of you can fucking eat me!" Emily yelled back.

"Everyone here would!" Gabe called.

She didn't seem to know what to say to that, and he heard everyone else laugh.

"Come on," Abby said, "let's get you upstairs

before she pops from sheer anticipation. That means you too, girls!"

"Coming!" Ellen replied.

"For the record," Abby said, "Em's safeword is pineapple, and she likes to be slapped. On the face."

"Noted," Gabe murmured.

As they moved deeper into the house, they were joined by Ellen and Holly. Ellen seemed relaxed and Holly seemed both anxious and excited, favoring him with a smile when they saw each other. Abby led him upstairs, her hand in his, and then down a corridor to a door at the end. Every open door he saw seemed to let on a nice room.

A nicely furnished office.

A finely polished bathroom.

A little well-stocked library and reading area.

"Fuck's sake you have a nice house," he muttered as she took him into their bedroom.

"Thank you. We worked hard for it," Abby replied. "And now, may I present my wife, who got an idea of what you might like from Ellen and decided to do something nice for you."

"Nicer than letting me fuck her?" he asked, then stopped as he laid eyes on Emily, who was stretched out on a very large bed like a model posing for a photoshoot. "Holy fuck."

"Yeah, holy fuck," Ellen muttered.

"Wow," Holly whispered.

Emily was laying on her side, head propped up by her hand, one knee raised, exposing a smooth and beautiful pussy. She was naked save for a black choker collar and a pair of fishnet stockings pulled up to her upper thighs.

"I'm seeing Ellen thinks I like goth girls," he murmured, noticing she'd tossed on a dash of makeup.

Ellen scoffed. "Give me a break, 'thinks'? *Look* at you, you're captivated."

"I used to go goth but I stopped...mostly."

"I like goth girls, too," Abby murmured with a smirk.

"I see you doing your 'research'. Half the time it's goths, the other half it's either naked middle-aged MILFs or naked pregnant chicks," Ellen said.

"You like pregnant chicks?" Emily asked, her smirking confidence faltering a bit.

"Yeah," Gabe said, glad that Ellen had given him that opening, because he had still been trying to figure out how to naturally work that into their encounter. "I really like pregnant ladies."

"You looking to get my wife pregnant?" Abby asked, walking over to a camera mounted on a tripod aimed at the bed. "Because, you know, I can't."

The effect on Emily was immediate. He saw her tensing up and reddening in the face, losing all of her confident self-possession in an instant and beginning to chew on her lower lip. She even started breathing more heavily.

"Would you like that, Emily?" Gabe asked, taking his shirt off and unbuttoning his jeans. "You want me to knock you up?"

"Yes," she managed, then cleared her throat.

"I think you might have a breeding kink, Em," Gabe replied.

"Look at her," Ellen said, "that's no kink, that's a full on fetish. She is fucking *gagging* to get knocked up. And luckily for her, you have a similar fetish."

"I can't help it," Emily replied as Gabe dropped his jeans and began sliding down his boxers. "Also, it's been quite a while since I've done this, so, um...go slow."

"I will," he replied, climbing onto the bed with her.

"I can assure you, I have vetted him thoroughly," Ellen murmured.

"Everyone take a seat, we're officially recording this magic," Abby said.

Gabe tried to start slow, but as soon as he got closer to her it became very clear that Emily wanted to take it fast. She grabbed him and pulled him close, kissing him firmly on the mouth, then taking one hand and bringing it to her bare breast.

"What the fuck happened to 'go slow'?" he asked when she let him come up for air.

"They smashed my 'horny' button," Emily replied. "And *Abby* wouldn't fuck me last night."

"I would have if you'd pressed even a little and you know it," Abby replied, rolling her eyes. "I wanted to prime you for tonight and you let me."

"Oh shut up," Emily growled.

"I think she needs to be put in her place, Gabe," Abby said. "She's been a mouthy little bitch all day long to me, knowing I wouldn't be putting her in her place. And she thought you'd be a pushover."

"Is that right?" Gabe asked.

"She's lying!" Emily snapped, blushing worse than ever.

"Oh ho did *you* fuck up," Ellen murmured.

"Oh give me a break, he's dating you for God's sake and—"

Gabe reached up and grabbed one of her wrists, then pressed it down into the mattress. With his other hand, he gripped her jaw and turned her head so that she was looking directly into his eyes.

"And what, Emily?" he asked, his face barely

two inches from hers.

Emily seemed lost for words, staring into his eyes.

"Come on Emily, I want to hear the rest of that sentence," he said.

"Holy shit, look at her," Holly whispered.

"That's her 'oh fuck I've made a *huge* miscalculation' face," Abby said, grinning broadly.

"Is Abby right, Emily? Have you been bad today? Do you need to be put in your place?"

"Yes," she whispered, never breaking eye contact.

"I thought so. Spread your legs," he replied.

He let go of her as he felt her shifting, then slipped his hand down between her thighs. She gasped as he ran his fingertip between her lips, finding her hot and wet, and then made contact with her clit. She moaned loudly as he began to rub it. He resumed kissing her and he noticed she was immediately a lot less aggressive.

If anything, it felt like she was inviting him to be more aggressive.

He could do that.

She cried out as he began rubbing her clit harder and faster, shoving his tongue into her mouth. She was soon moaning wildly, pressing her hips up in time with his fingering, and then she actually screamed as he slipped a finger inside of her.

He fingered her for a bit longer, then gripped her chin. "Emily, did I say you could make noise?"

Gabe kept watching for some sign that she wasn't into it, that he was coming on too strong or, what he most worried about, that he sounded stupid. He'd been into this kind of thing in a vague sort of way for a while now, but had never really explored it before Ellen because he found it hard to imagine a woman taking him seriously.

But Emily was basically gagging for it, inviting him more than ever with her body language.

"I-I'm sorry," she managed, panting now, "I can't help it."

He stopped fingering her and shifted. "If that's the case, put your mouth to use."

A look of petulance came onto her face. "Come on, I'm not done yet–"

He slapped her.

Not very hard, and even though Abby had explicitly told him she liked it, he still felt like he was taking a calculated risk. For a few seconds she simply stared at him in shock, blushing and panting heavily.

Then she whispered, "Yes, sir."

"Oh my God that was amazing," Holly murmured as Gabe laid back and Emily sat up and began shifting into place.

"Do as your told, Em," Abby murmured, taking a drink from a wineglass. "If you don't, I'll have to get involved, and then no one will be happy."

"Literally *everyone* will be happy if you get involved," Gabe replied, and Ellen laughed loudly.

"He's right," she murmured.

"Just fuck my wife," Abby replied, blushing herself a little now.

"Gladly," he replied as Emily slipped his cock into her mouth.

He put a hand over the back of her head and began guiding her a little forcefully. She let out a muffled moan and let him have his way with her. He simply guided her for a bit, letting her suck him off, her head bobbing up and down. Then he gave in to his urge, shifted her so that she was laying on her side and he was laying on his, then he grabbed her head and started fucking her mouth, jamming his cock into her throat.

She moaned louder and he waited for her to somehow try to and stop him if this wasn't a thing she was into, but it very quickly became obvious she was into it. He kept fucking her mouth until he could no longer stand not fucking her pussy and pulled out of her.

"Hands and knees," he said.

"Okay," she panted, coughing. "I forgot to take my birth control today, so...don't forget to pull out."

For just a second, he thought she was being serious. But immediately following that thought, he remembered being told, more than once, that she had gotten her tubes tied years and years ago. She couldn't get pregnant.

Huh.

So...

She wasn't just into being bred, she was into being bred against her will. He glanced briefly at the other three women in the room and found all of them smiling broadly at him, staring at the two of them with wide eyes. Ellen and Holly both had wineglasses as well now, sipping from them occasionally.

For an instant he was struck by the sheer insanity that this was actually his life in this moment.

"Okay," he said as he got behind Emily, who was now on her hands and knees.

She definitely had a really nice ass.

She also had a tattoo of a black rose on her right cheek.

"Do you promise you'll remember?" she asked, looking back over her shoulder at him. Her face conveyed mostly anxiety but he could see absolute lust bleeding through. She was already sweating a little.

"Yeah, whatever," he replied, getting up against her and rubbing his erection against her hot, wet opening.

"That's not a promise," she muttered petulantly as she shivered. "I need–"

"God, shut the fuck *up,* Emily," he replied and penetrated her.

She cried out as he gripped her hips and started working his way into her, inching in deeper and deeper each time he pushed forward, finding her absurdly wet. For a moment he became utterly enraptured by the sensation of being inside of her for the first time, having her on her hands and knees like this, naked and sweaty and absolutely seductively beautiful.

Emily moaned, long and loud, as he finished getting into her and then started stroking smoothly, settling into a good rhythm. He could hear her moaning and panting, could hear the sound of their skin slapping together. The faint hum of the camera, the heavy breathing of the other three women watching this happen.

Gabe kept at it for as long as he could manage, but Emily's pussy was even better than he had anticipated. He knew he was going to blow, and soon.

Might as well be a good one.

"All right, Em, you're gonna lay down now," he said.

"Why?" she asked.

He slapped her ass, hard. "Now!"

"Okay!"

She laid down flat on her stomach. Gabe considered his position briefly and though he was sorely tempted to lay flat against and hold her down that way, he had the sense that Emily could get really...wild, especially when she was coming, and she seemed close to it. And if he laid down against her, there was a decent chance she might pop him in the face with the back of her head as she was thrashing around.

Getting a black eye or even a broken nose due to wild sex was a fun thought, but he didn't want to suffer through that and he knew she'd feel terrible.

So he did the next best thing.

Gabe got up against her, resting on his knees, and slid back into her. She moaned loudly, then shifted as he gripped both her hands and pressed them into the small of her back.

"What are you doing?" she asked.

"What do you think I'm doing?" he replied.

"I don't know," she said, shifting a little. "I can't move too well."

"That's the idea, Emily."

"Why?"

He put his other hand on the side of her head, pressing it down into the pillow. Then he started fucking her again, faster, making her cry out.

"Because I'm going to breed you like the fuckslut you are," he growled at her.

"What!? No!" she cried, but he felt a primal response from her body as soon as he'd said that. She shuddered hard and she was soon even wetter inside. "Please! Abby!"

"She isn't going to help you," Gabe replied.

"I warned you about being bad, Emily," Abby said.

"Please!" she cried, but already she was losing it.

Before he knew it she began to orgasm. She

made a strange sound deep in her throat and she spasmed so hard she legitimately almost threw him off. Then she started crying out in pure sexual release as her inner muscles began twitching and fluttering wildly.

Gabe heard himself groaning in raw rapture as he began fucking her harder and faster. Before he knew it, he was coming, too. His seed burst out of him in a hard, intense contraction. He felt his entire self become completely smothered in the utter ecstasy of orgasming inside of a married woman while her wife watched.

He heard, faintly, Ellen and Holly and Abby cheering as they both shared a perfect union of orgasmic bliss and he emptied himself into her, pumping her pussy full of his seed in fast, hard spurts that send shockwaves of pleasure racing through him.

And then it was over, and he was left panting and sweaty atop her.

"Mmm...Gabe," Emily murmured. "Gabe...need to breathe."

"Oh, sorry," he replied, breathing heavily as well.

He let go of her and pulled out of her at the same time, then flopped over onto his back, his sweat-slicked chest heaving as he caught his breath.

"Oh fuck that was intense," he groaned.

"Fucking Christ yes it was," Ellen said.

"Are you okay, Emily?" Gabe asked.

"Oh yes. I'm fine," she murmured dreamily. "I'm in Heaven right now. Although I know my pussy is going to be sore soon. I didn't expect you to go *that* hard."

"I couldn't help it. Whew, fuck," he panted.

He heard footsteps getting closer and suddenly Abby appeared beside them, holding the camera in front of her smirking face with one hand, the other still holding her wineglass.

"So, did you have a good time with the love of my life?" she asked, smirking.

"The best," he replied, raising a thumb, then running a hand across his forehead. "Jesus, I worked up an actual sweat."

"Yep," Ellen agreed, coming to stand beside Abby. "How about you, Em? How did you enjoy getting fuckin railed by the love of *my* life?"

"It was amazing," she replied. "Ugh, I forgot how hard impregnation play hits me."

"I didn't expect it to go in the direction it did," Gabe murmured.

"Sorry if I kinda dropped that on you but oh my fucking *God,* did you fucking nail it. That was an insane orgasm. Or two...three. I lost count." She shuddered as a post-orgasmic tremor ran through her. "Oh God, that was so good. But...ew. Oh man, I can feel your stuff in me. You came *so* much."

"It's leaking," Holly murmured.

"Yep, I can feel it. Need a shower," Emily replied.

"Press your thighs together and don't fucking move you filthy whore," Abby said, setting the camera down and walking off quickly. "You are *not* getting that shit on the carpet, definitely not in the bed if it can be helped."

"Ugh, fine."

"So that wasn't too much, right?" Gabe asked.

"Oh no, that was perfect. That was just right. I had hoped it would go there but I didn't realize you'd be so good at it. Ellen said you were a natural and I didn't quite believe her," Emily replied.

"Thanks," Ellen said.

"Well...look at him! Gabe, you're great and I like you a lot, you just...don't *look* like a dom, you know?"

"He is," Holly murmured.

"Clearly," Abby said, coming back with a hand-towel.

"I wouldn't mind some aftercare, though," Emily said.

"Oh. Uh...I wouldn't be stepping on toes, would I?" Gabe asked uncertainly.

"Traditionally," Abby replied as she worked the soft towel carefully into place, "the one doing the domination provides the aftercare. I think it's only fair that you do it. Honestly, I'd have a bigger problem with it if you *didn't* give her aftercare."

"Okay, cool then," Gabe replied, getting up.

"Come on," Emily said, carefully getting to her feet. "Let's take a shower. My shower is fucking awesome."

CHAPTER NINETEEN

"Are you all right, babe?" Ellen murmured.

"What? Yeah...mostly," Gabe replied, then yawned.

"Mostly, huh?"

They were sitting together in their living room and had decided to watch an episode of a cartoon they were going through before joining Holly in bed. Emily's shower had indeed been awesome. It was large with two showerheads and giving her aftercare in there had felt incredibly intimate. After they'd dried and dressed, everyone had sat around in their living room and talked. Mostly about sex-adjacent things.

Ellen had needed to stick around long enough to sober up, given she needed to drive Holly and her car back home. Though Holly could have done it, as she hadn't been drinking something alcoholic. Eventually they'd said their goodbyes, Gabe had thanked Emily and Abby more than once for what they'd done for him, and then he'd driven home, alone in his own car. He had felt strange the whole drive, and not in a good way.

Ellen nudged him. "Come on, babe, what's up? I *know* you had fun tonight."

He shifted uncomfortably. "I feel...weird. About what happened."

"Oh." Ellen lost her smile and turned to face him more. "Was it the roughness? The slap? I know that can be weird at first..."

"No, it wasn't that. I mean, I feel a *little* weird about that but not that weird. Clearly she was into it and clearly I did a good job."

"A *really* good job," Ellen agreed.

"It's more...I feel...guilty. Kind of like how I felt about Holly after we fucked for the first time, only more intense. Now I know how *she* feels. I'm guilty and scared. I'm scared you're going to decide you actually hated what happened and scared Abby's going to hate me, and I also feel kind of like...I cheated on you?"

"Oh, Gabe," she whispered, and hugged him. "I'm sorry, love. I understand. Sort of. I felt a little strange about getting with Holly, too, but I was able to brush it off pretty easily. I'm not mad. Abby's not mad, I promise."

"You're sure?"

She nodded. "Uh-huh. You know how me and her slipped off for a while?"

"Yeah."

"I asked her very candidly how she felt about it, and she told me honestly that she felt fine. She thought it was hot as hell. She's happy. And I believe her."

"Well...that's good," he murmured, looking down slowly.

"Sweetheart?"

He looked back over at her. "Yeah?"

Ellen had a very warm, loving smile on her face. She laid a hand against his cheek. "I value this relationship more than I do anything else. I wouldn't have let you sleep with Emily if I seriously thought there was any real chance it might jeopardize what we have. Or what Emily and Abby have. I love you.

"And...it might sound a little ridiculous, but honestly? I'm fucking *thrilled* to be on this sexual journey with you. And I do mean *with you*. I used to hate that I kept chickening out of doing any sexual exploration in my other relationships, but looking back at it now? Oh my God, I am *so* grateful that I listened to myself and waited. Because I was waiting for this, I was waiting for *you,* Gabe. And the fact that you and I get to explore all this together is absurdly meaningful to me."

Gabe laughed softly, feeling an intense, almost overwhelming emotional pressure somewhere deep inside himself.

"I love you, Ellen," he said softly, placing his hand over the back of hers.

Her smile broadened. "And I love you too, Gabe. More than I've ever loved anyone in my entire life. It's so trite because everyone said this, but you are *genuinely* the best thing that's ever happened to me."

He kissed her. "I can, in absolute truth, say the same thing."

They stared at each other for a moment, then Ellen's smile changed a little and she shot a quick glance back towards the bedroom. "I don't mean to ruin the moment," she whispered, "but I am also *so* glad we get to go on the sex journey with Holly, too."

"Oh yeah, big time," he agreed.

"And, can I just say, for the record, that all of our emotions aside, from a pure horny perspective: you can *fuck.* Tonight? *So* fucking hot."

"Thank you very much, babe," he replied, chuckling. "And, for the horny record, I still *really* want a threesome with you and Emily. And also Emily and Holly."

"If you hadn't so thoroughly *demolished* her vagina, I'm sure Emily would have jumped in bed with you and one of us tonight."

"I couldn't help it."

"Apparently. You were just fucking *hammering*

her...come on, let's go bed. You have to be tired."

"I am," he replied, yawning. They stood up and he paused. "A lot of things happened tonight...Abby *did* invite us to a party that's in a few days, right?"

"Yes."

"Killer." He took her hand. "Let's get some sleep."

. . .

Holly wanted something.

Gabe could read her like a book by now, and she'd woken up wanting something. He'd thought it was sex at first, but then they'd had sex and she still had that air of 'I really want to ask you for something but I don't actually want to ask' some people telegraphed.

A shared look with Ellen at one point indicated she could tell as well.

They waited as they went through their morning together, but as noon approached she still hadn't said anything. They knew she had to go somewhere around noon, and it was a bit of a lazy Wednesday for both him and her. Ellen because her work was throwing even less work her way and Gabe because he was trying to be better about giving himself time between long bouts of writing.

Finally, as Holly was gathering her things into her purse and then pulling on her shoes, Gabe decided to offer her a path forward.

"So, Holly..." he said, and she looked up.

"Yeah?"

"Anything on your mind?"

Both he and Ellen were staring at her now, him leaning against the couch, Ellen stretched out on it.

Holly looked back at them, for a moment apparently utterly thunderstruck.

"How the fuck could you tell!?" she demanded finally.

He laughed. "Just...something in the way you're moving, your expression, your tone of voice," he replied. "Whatever it is, you can ask. We won't get mad at you for asking."

"It's...petty."

"Holly, I *love* being petty...to the right people. And I know, not the best trait, and I'm trying to prune it down, and I *have,* but sometimes being petty is good for the soul," Ellen said.

"I don't know about that," Gabe murmured.

"Come on, spill," Ellen said, sitting up.

Holly laughed awkwardly. "All right, all right. I'm headed to the mall food court for a lunch date with my two friends. They still think I'm lying. I was wondering if maybe you could...make an appearance? Prove them wrong?" She sighed. "It's petty."

"No, fuck that," Ellen replied, getting to her feet. "Fuck that noise, we're going to help you out."

"Really?"

"Yes. Gabe?"

"Yeah, I'm down for that."

"You don't have to if you think it's weird or dumb…"

"We're going to because we want to...and because I imagine Gabe would *love* to prove that he absolutely fucking railed you and you *loved* it," Ellen replied with a smirk.

"Well, both those things *are* true," Holly murmured.

"Go on, get to your friends. Gabe and I will show up in a bit and 'run into you', and we will absolutely confirm it however it needs to be confirmed," Ellen replied.

"Yep," Gabe agreed.

"Thank you!" She paused. "What if they ask if we're dating?"

"What would you like us to say?" Gabe replied.

"...yes?"

"Then yes it will be," Ellen said.

Holly brightened noticeably at that. "Thank you!" she repeated, hurrying over and hugging and kissing both of them. She checked her phone. "Shit, I'm going to be late. I'll see you there! Thanks again!" she said as she hurried out the door.

"She's really fucking cute," Ellen murmured.

"She is," Gabe agreed.

"Come on, let's wash up."

"Oh, you want to look nice for this confirmation?" He paused. "Confrontation?"

"If it needs to be, and yes," Ellen replied, walking to the bedroom.

"Well..." Gabe paused as he followed her, his eyes going down to her broad ass, and everything seemed to jolt right out of his head.

There was just something about the shape her ass made under that robe she wore...

"No, dear," Ellen said.

"No dear what?" he replied.

"I know that trailing off. You're looking at my ass and you're thinking to yourself 'maybe we have time to bang out a doggystyle quickie' and we absolutely do not."

"You don't *know* that's what I was thinking," he said as they came into the bedroom.

"Oh don't I? What were you thinking then?" she asked, turning around and staring down at him.

Looking up into her bright, fierce eyes killed any ability he had to lie. He sighed. She smirked. "That's what I thought. Now, come on. Get ready. Put on something nice."

...

"This feels kinda weird," Gabe murmured as they drove through the city in Ellen's car.

They had agreed to take hers as it was a much nicer car and although he thought that didn't really matter, she had pointed out that it would help put him in a certain mindset. And damn if she wasn't right. There *was* something about being in Ellen's crisp, clean car that seemed to focus him.

"Good weird or bad weird?" Ellen replied.

"I guess good. I normally don't really seek out confrontation."

"And that's not a bad policy, but I think that it's a good thing to be able to handle confrontation when it comes your way. You'd be *shocked* how many people just...back down if you resist even a bit. But yes, it's smart, not seeking it out."

"So then this isn't smart by your own admission?"

"It's...practice," she said.

"I think you just want to show off Holly, and maybe mark your territory a little."

"Okay maybe I do! And her friends can fuck off! I'm *defending* Holly. And so are you."

"Fair point. That's enough justification."

Ellen was silent for a few minutes before saying, "She wants us to say we're dating."

Gabe shot a glance at her. She was positively beaming. "That she did."

"You can't tell me you're still uncertain about how much she wants this to be a full time thing between the three of us, Gabe."

"Okay, no, I can't," he agreed. "At this point it's obvious even to me that she wants to be our girlfriend. And, clearly, I am very happy with the prospect. Now we just need to determine if it's a good idea or not."

"I think it is," Ellen replied. "We could do so much for her. And you know us. You know we'll take good care of her. Help her."

"I do, but I also wonder if she'll just go along with whatever we say because she's young and insecure *and* into being submissive. And I think that when you're still figuring out what submissive means and you're very early into learning that and you suddenly find yourself in a relationship with someone you *really* want to submit to, it might be very easy to confuse submission as a kink with submission as a way of life."

"...okay wow, that's...yeah, that's a very good point," she murmured. "And perhaps I am a little biased here, but I think you and I are observant enough to notice if that's what's happening."

"Probably," he agreed after considering it. "But all that aside, I still need to talk to Sadie."

"You need to talk to her about spreading her legs for you," Ellen murmured with a smirk.

"That...would be great. I'm still not convinced she's into me."

"Gabe! She has you writing *porn* of *her and you* and she admitted openly that she *masturbated to the porn fan fiction you wrote of you and her!* Come on!"

"Maybe I'd be reading too much into it," he replied.

"Holy fucking-are you shitting me!? God, no wonder guys miss so many fucking signals," she muttered.

"Hey, to be fair, women also hate the fact that they can't smile most men's direction without the men assuming they want to fuck or date."

"That's not missing, that's misinterpreting. Two very different things. And fine, fair. Oh hey, there's the turn, don't miss it."

"I'm not going to miss it."

Ellen's smirk broadened. "Am I annoying you?"

"No."

"I think I am."

"Okay, *now* you are annoying me."

"What are you going to do about it?" she asked. He sighed heavily and said nothing as he turned into the vast mall parking lot and found a space.

"Nothing. Now, let's go and help out Holly you fucking...woman I love," he muttered.

"Oh don't hold back on my account, dearest," Ellen replied, smirking worse than ever now. "Come on, tell me what I am."

"Fine!" He whirled in the seat the face her. "Get out of the car you fucking bitch."

She leaned in, the quality of her smirk changing just a little, and somehow she became so much more daunting. "I'm going to make you eat those words the next time we're in bed."

"I'm going to make you eat my fucking dick and choke on it the next time we're in bed," he replied without breaking eye contact.

Something flashed in her eyes. "Prove it."

"Oh I will. Now let's go."

CHAPTER TWENTY

Gabe felt several things as they crossed the threshold into the mall's food court.

He was anxious, he was nervous, he was horny and a little frustrated thanks to Ellen, but mostly...

He felt pretty confident and good about this. Whether or not that was a good thing was open to debate, but it wasn't like they were doing anything cruel, or even mean. They were just proving their friend right by telling the truth.

And if Holly wanted to rub it in their faces, well...

They didn't seem like great friends.

Gabe glanced at Ellen as they walked slowly in. She had dressed up nice and looked rather sharp in her business attire. She had a button-down long-sleeve shirt that had the top two buttons undone and the pale gray slacks she wore to go with it showed off her lower half so very nicely.

And she'd worn heels.

Nothing extravagant, they added an inch, but God, he could really tell. He'd asked if she was sure she wanted to walk around the mall in heels and she'd said she had been meaning to buy new shoes for a while, and this would properly motivate her.

Couldn't argue with that, and he didn't want to miss the chance to see her in heels.

Even an inch seemed to add three to her.

She was definitely turning heads.

"There she is," Ellen murmured, adjusting their course and moving among the tables.

Holly sat at one such table with her two friends. Holly had her back to them, so they could see the looks on her friends faces as they approached. Both of them were staring at Ellen in what seemed to be open shock.

"Holly!" Ellen said brightly as they approached. "I knew it was you."

"Oh wow, hi!" she replied, and Gabe was a little surprised by how authentic she sounded.

She was a good actress. It made her inability to hide or fake basically anything around them a little strange, but even as he considered it, he thought of trying to hide something from Ellen. He didn't consider himself a great actor, but he absolutely fumbled around her.

It would make sense that Holly would, too.

Holly stood up and embraced each of them, making a point to kiss both of them on the mouth.

"Destiny, Kaitlyn, this is the couple I'm with," Holly said, turning back around to face them.

"Hi," one of them murmured quietly.

"Hello," Ellen said, leaning forward just a little and no doubt showing off her impressive cleavage. "Am I to understand that you thought we were fake?"

"I...Destiny thought she was, uh, making you up," the blonde murmured.

"Fuck you," Destiny hissed.

They looked petrified. Gabe had to admit, it was kind of gratifying to see.

"As you can see," Holly said, "they are most definitely real."

"And you are...um...both dating her? Like, she's your girlfriend?" Kaitlyn asked.

"Yes," Gabe replied. "She is our girlfriend. We are dating her."

"And, in case it wasn't abundantly clear, also fucking her," Ellen said, slowly straightening back up. "Good to meet you both."

"Uh...you too," Destiny replied softly.

"Well, we're having a shopping day at the mall," Ellen said. "If it wouldn't interfere with your plans, we would love you to join us, Holly."

Holly was practically a ray of sunshine by that point. "Destiny, you have work in like five minutes right?"

"Yeah."

"All right. Well, I'm gonna bow out then and hang out with my girlfriend and my boyfriend. Later!" she said, quickly gathering up the remains of her meal.

"...later," Kaitlyn said.

Holly threw everything away and then joined them. They walked away from the food court area, heading into one of the massive corridors that snaked through the mall.

"That was amazing!" Holly whispered loudly. "Did you see their faces?!"

"Oh yeah, totally blown away," Gabe agreed.

"Thank you so much! Also, Ellen, oh my God, you look *so* amazing." She looked up at her as they walked. "You're *so* tall! Are you wearing–" She looked down. "You are!"

Ellen laughed. "Yep, I am. Though it won't last for long. We're hitting the shoe store. And we are actually making a day of this, we'd be extremely happy if you joined us."

"I...mmm. I can for an hour..."

"Come on...you can call in," Ellen replied.

"I could..."

"God, we're a terrible influence on you," Gabe muttered.

"Oh whatever," Ellen said. "Holly needs, and

deserves, a break. And we're already here and there's so many cool stores we could hit up, so…"

Holly was chewing on her lower lip, staring at the two of them. They all stopped off to the side.

"If you say no, we won't be mad, Holly," Gabe said.

Ellen sighed. "Yes, this is true. To be clear: making the responsible choice is completely fine. But if you want my honest opinion, I think you could do with another day off."

She groaned and leaned back against the nearest wall. "I know. I feel the exact same way…okay, fuck it. I'm going to call in." She pulled out her phone. "Which, luckily for me, in this job at least, means I can do it as a text."

"Lucky," Gabe said.

"Yeah." She finished up and then put her phone away. "All right, you've both officially convinced me."

"Great! Come on, let's get the shoes out of the way first," Ellen said.

They started walking again, and before long, Holly made an unhappy sound.

"What's wrong?" Gabe asked.

"It's just that I'm realizing it's getting harder and harder to go into my jobs all of a sudden. And it keeps getting worse. I just…*do not* fucking want to go. I mean I've never really wanted to but there wasn't much resistance before? Now it's like, every day I get up to go, it's like I have to break through a concrete wall first…"

"I know why," Ellen said.

"You do? Of course you do, you're a genius," she murmured.

"Well…be careful not to confuse different kinds

of intelligences," Ellen replied. "Just because I'm fantastic with numbers doesn't mean I'm fantastic with emotional intelligence or other fields. Those credits don't necessarily transfer. I just happen to know the why of this."

"I'd love to hear it."

"Okay, although it does require some guesswork on my part. I'm guessing that, for most of the time you had those jobs, you didn't necessarily want to be home, right?"

"Yeah I guess that's true," Holly replied after considering it. "I mean I'd rather be home in my apartment but I also know that there's not really much of anything waiting for me there."

"Exactly. *Now,* on the other hand, you have another home you *really* want to go to, and so you *really* don't want to leave," Ellen replied. "You miss us."

"That actually makes a lot of sense and also seems super obvious. How did I not realize that?"

"We all have bizarrely powerful blind spots for ourselves," Gabe said.

"Yeah, exactly that," Ellen agreed.

"...so what do I do? I need both my jobs."

"Do you?" Ellen asked.

Holly opened her mouth, then slowly closed it. Considered further. "Well...maybe not. Maybe I could dump one of them...I dunno. I still owe a lot of money...did we talk about that?"

"You mentioned college debt at one point," Gabe replied.

She sighed heavily. "Yeah. There's still...a lot. And some on my car, too. Credit cards, of course. Everything's so goddamned motherfucking expensive now."

"Yes, it is," Ellen replied.

She looked like she was seriously contemplating something, and from a glance at Gabe he suddenly knew she was considering popping the question of moving in, but he simply gave his head a tiny shake when she made eye contact with him. For some reason, it didn't feel like the right time. She simply gave a tiny nod in return, acquiescing.

"Are you sure I'm not cutting into something? You don't have work responsibilities?" Holly asked suddenly.

"I've done my work for the day," Ellen replied.

"And my work is...flexible. Part of the joy of being an independent writer, or it's *supposed* to be, anyway, is being able to put writing off when real life things come up. Either positive or negative. And this is a positive thing, so I am glad to put off writing about stone age people having sex."

"I really want to read that one," Holly said.

"It's getting there," Gabe replied. "I'll let you know as soon as it's ready."

"I appreciate it. It's so wild to be with a guy who writes erotica. I've read, uh, spicy romance before and I always wonder what the writer is really like. I mean, you know, behind closed doors. You never really know. But now I know!"

"And?" Ellen asked.

"And what?" Holly replied.

"What's he like behind closed doors?"

"Oh. Um...I mean, you know," she murmured.

Ellen laughed. "Maybe I'd like to hear it out loud."

"He's...*really* good at sex."

Gabe laughed awkwardly. "That's a way to say it, I guess."

"Am I embarrassing you two?" Ellen asked.

"Kinda," Holly murmured.

"Yes, but you know that," Gabe said.

"Mmm. Come on, there's the shoe place."

Gabe found himself focusing on Ellen as she led them inside. He found her so...interesting.

He had been aware of dom-sub culture for a while now, but up until fairly recently he didn't have much more than a very basic grasp of it. In truth, he didn't really completely understand half of it. He understood the obvious benefits of assuming a dominant role, but he couldn't fully comprehend why anyone would want to be submissive.

In the end, he'd surmised that ultimately it was just a thing you got or you didn't. And you didn't really get much choice in the matter. And that it was a lot more nuanced than a lot of people cared to admit or acknowledge.

Clearly, Ellen didn't want to just be told what to do by everyone all the time.

Very clearly she enjoyed being in control of certain situations. But also quite obviously she enjoyed fucking with him so that he'd fuck with her back. The problem though was determining the exact type of fucking around she was doing.

Because she wasn't just a straight up sub.

And it was even more complicated because Holly, who *was* a straight up submissive type, was submissive in just about everything when it came to him and Ellen. And that wasn't necessarily a good thing. But it also didn't have to be a bad thing, either.

Submission was trust, he had learned. Deep trust.

She was trusting that they wouldn't take advantage of her.

But what complicated it was that while Holly

was fairly cut and dry, Ellen was a sub *and* a dom. So was she fucking with him to get him to fuck with her back so that he could put her in her place, or was she just...sharpening her claws?

At least they had the social safe word.

"All right," Ellen said as she looked around the interior for a moment, "why don't you two stay here and flirt and I'll be back when I've got my shoes?"

"Fine by me," Gabe replied, taking a seat in one of the few chairs clustered near the entrance for apparently this exact reason.

"Okay," Holly said, sitting beside him. They both watched her stalk away into the store, like she was on a mission. "Ellen is...fierce."

"Very," he agreed. "It's been interesting, learning her different moods."

"I bet," she murmured. "Is Ellen a, um...brat? Is that the right word? Someone who likes to argue with their, uh, dom, so that they'll be, you know, put in their place?"

"That is the right word," he replied, "and surprisingly no, she isn't. Not *all* the time, at least. I was just thinking about this actually. Sometimes she wants that, but sometimes not."

"That makes sense, I think." She paused. "Do you *want* a brat girlfriend?"

"Yes."

She laughed. "Wow you didn't even have to think about it."

"I used to think no, God, what a nightmare that would be to put up with. But now that I've actually got that relationship type going on with Ellen some of the time...yeah, if it was with the right person that I could trust, I'd actually love to be with a chick like that."

"You like punishing, huh?" she murmured.

He glanced over at her. She was blushing a little now. "I guess I do...how about you? You looking to get punished?"

She laughed awkwardly, blushing worse now. "I mean...yeah. I don't think I have it in me to be a brat, though. I'm too much of a pushover. I don't have the attitude for it. I want you to just...do things, you know? Just tell me what to do. I don't really know why, and it's weird because I've never felt this way before? Well, not quite. I mean, I'd rather just sort of go with the flow, but with you and Ellen, especially with you, it's the first time I've actually really liked being told what to do. And I mean outside of, you know, the bedroom, too."

"I have to admit I like the dynamic," he said, taking her hand.

Her smile became warmer and she leaned against him, resting her head on his shoulder. "I do, too. Although, is this like...a bad idea? I mean Ellen is your girlfriend, like your main girlfriend in public? It isn't weird that I'm...all up on you?"

"We don't care if it's weird," Gabe replied. "And if you're comfortable with it, then so are we."

"Okay. I'm still getting used to this whole thing, although I'm surprised by how comfortable I am. We've been...together for barely a few weeks but it already feels like it's been months. Or is that just from my end?"

"No, that's not just from your end. You fit very nicely into our lives and it's something Ellen and I both feel too, that you fit so well it feels like you've been here for a long time," he replied.

"That's so good to hear. I keep worrying I'm sort of just wedging myself into your lives."

Gabe shifted and slipped an arm around her midriff. "You aren't wedging yourself into our lives, Holly. We're inviting you in, and you are agreeing to the invite." He hesitated as a thought occurred to him. "I think a lot of people have made you feel unwelcome."

"...maybe," she murmured. "But not you and Ellen."

"It's okay. I wasn't looking for reassurance...I want to remind you that the thing we agreed to in the very beginning, about being very open and honest with each other? That thing still stands. And it always will. I really mean it when I say that I don't want you to hide your discomfort from me or Ellen. If you're upset or annoyed or angry or hurt, tell us. Tell us at home, tell us during sex, pull one of us off to the side and tell us if we're at a party or in public. We always want to hear."

She shifted and wrapped both her arms around him, squeezing him. "Thank you," she whispered. "And I'll try. I have a hard time with speaking up. I don't want to make a fuss."

"I truly understand," Gabe replied, hugging her back. "But I'd look at it one of two ways, whichever works better for you. You speaking up for yourself isn't making a fuss or, if it's easier, Ellen and I would like you to make a fuss if it will help you feel better. Regardless, too many people keep quiet and hide their suffering for the sake of others. It's not a *terrible* idea, but it's too common."

"Okay," she murmured.

"You two look cute."

They both looked over to see Ellen approaching, holding a box.

"Find what you were looking for?" Gabe asked.

"I think so," she replied, stepping up to them and presenting the box, opening it up to show what was inside. A relatively simple pair of dark gray sneakers.

"Seems a little...underwhelming," he said, looking at them. "Compared to most of the stuff you own. Not that I'm complaining."

"Exactly," Ellen replied. "I'm tired of dressing to the goddamned nines all the time. I like to have that option available, but it is no longer my default. My default is fucking *comfy*. So...do they have your approval?"

Gabe almost said 'yes' without thinking about it, and then he almost said 'why do you need that?'. It struck him as an odd question, and when he looked up at her face, he saw the tiniest hint of a smile. For just an instant he considered telling her no, to go find something else, largely to see what she would do, but he wanted to move on from the shoe store.

"I approve," he replied simply.

Ellen looked just the tiniest bit disappointed as she closed the box. "Good," she said, "let's get a move on, then. There's a whole mall to see."

CHAPTER TWENTY ONE

Holly looked at the camera Ellen was presenting her, and a curious mixture of amazement and horror passed across her features.

"What?" she murmured, taking it slowly. "Ellen, no. I-this is *way* too expensive!"

"I can afford it right now, Holly, and I want to give it to you," Ellen replied.

"But it's five hundred dollars! And that's only because it's on sale!"

"I know, Holly," Ellen replied patiently, "but I'm serious. I genuinely want to buy this for you and I want you to take it and use it."

"Why?" she asked, slowly looking up.

"Because you love photography. And because you are my friend."

Holly looked back down at the digital camera grasped firmly in her delicate, pale hands, then looked over at Gabe.

"You'll get no help from me, Holly. I think you should have it, too," he said.

"I don't know...it feels so weird, accepting a gift like this. It's *so* expensive..."

"Listen Holly, I'm not going to try and make you accept it. If you genuinely do not want to, we can put it back and that will be fine. But if you want the camera, then I *want* to give it to you. And I can, and I will if you let me," Ellen replied.

"I'd use it, but...normally when people want to give crazy gifts like this related to something creative...I don't know, there's this expectation..."

"Holly, what you do with it is your business," Ellen replied.

"...all right." She handed Gabe the camera carefully, then hugged Ellen tightly. "Thank you. A lot. So much. This is probably the best and nicest thing anyone has ever gotten for me."

Ellen smiled and kissed the top of her head. "I'm just glad I can make you happy, Holly, and support your passion."

"I feel like I don't have enough words to say thank you," she murmured.

"I understand how you feel. That's how I am around Gabe sometimes when he's *way* too nice and patient with me." Holly laughed softly. "But it's fine. You have successfully conveyed your gratefulness."

"Okay."

Ellen accepted the camera from Gabe and they all headed for the checkout area to buy it.

They were just about finished with their mall day. It had been a good one. Gabe wasn't normally one to hang out at the mall for hours on end. The times he did go were usually just to hang out at the arcade, buy something specific, or eat at a food stall he was particularly craving. Mall court food wasn't all that great, but sometimes it was bizarrely amazing.

They'd swung by a bookstore after the shoes, spending almost an hour and a half perusing the aisles and checking out the books, old and new. After that they'd poked through a string of stores that had caught their interest. Among them were a board game shop, a video gaming store, and a cookware place since Ellen apparently wanted to do 'at least two' responsible things while they were there, and he was evidently seriously lacking in spatulas.

As they headed out of the photography store, Ellen abruptly stopped.

"Oh my God."

"What?" Gabe asked.

"I just had a lightbulb moment."

She was staring at the store directly across from the one they'd just come out of. A lingerie shop.

"What kind of lightbulb?" he asked.

"I've been trying to figure out how to make the cover art for Tall Blonde. And I couldn't really find anything. Tall, thick blondes apparently just don't model all that much. But all of a sudden this idea just popped into my head, and it's admittedly a frightening one for me...what if we buy sexy clothes for me and I pose and Holly photographs? I mean, it'd be perfect, right? Or am I missing something obvious?"

"No...that'd be pretty perfect. Plus the win-win of you buying hot lingerie," Gabe replied.

"Can I have some too? I will so wear it for you," Holly asked.

"Yes," both he and Ellen replied at the same time.

"Come on," Ellen said, striding across the large hall and into the lingerie shop.

Gabe had never actually been into one, mostly because he always felt like he'd be seen as some weird pervert as a guy coming alone into such a shop. Maybe that was a ridiculous fear, but then the world was increasingly becoming a ridiculous place.

Now that he was actually here...it didn't seem all that impressive. Then again, he *was* in a mall. He'd for some reason had an idea of attractive women walking around in the lingerie, modeling it live, but...was that even a real thing?

He wasn't sure where he'd gotten the idea from, but even if it was, there was no way a simple outlet shop in a mall would get that kind of treatment.

As they began moving down the aisles, looking at what was on offer, Gabe could tell Ellen was slowly losing her confidence.

He reached out suddenly and took her hand. "Hey," he murmured, stepping closer and then having to stand on his toes to get closer to her ear, "goddess," he whispered.

She turned to look at him, an awkward smile on her face, a small blush coming to her cheeks.

"Own it," he said.

Her smile grew firmer, more confident, and she nodded.

"You're right," she replied.

She gave him a kiss and then began moving through the store again with more purpose. They spent a while sorting through at least a few dozen different sets of lingerie, and while Ellen definitely had a few ideas of her own in mind, she ultimately would ask Gabe what he thought. And usually he was happy to go along with whatever she was getting.

Because Ellen looked sexy in everything she wore.

Though he did make a special request for black fishnet stockings.

Something about that...

"Should I be investing in a choker collar? Em seemed to *really* get you going with that," Ellen murmured with a smirk as they finished gathering everything they were going to buy.

"I mean...I sure wouldn't say no," he replied.

"Mmm...I just had a really kinky thought," Holly said quietly.

"Please share," Ellen replied immediately.

"Maybe if you get more girlfriends, we can all wear chokers and like...I dunno," she murmured, blushing really bad now, "maybe we could wear, like, little tags that say something like Gabe's Girls."

"Holly, you absolute *freak*," Ellen whispered, sounding absolutely delighted.

"Am I crazy for wanting that?"

"No, you're fucking awesome for wanting that," Ellen replied.

"...no comment," Gabe murmured.

"Oh like you wouldn't fucking *love* having three or more girlfriends sucking and fucking your fat cock every day, wearing 'Gabe's Girls' on their sexy goth choker collars," Ellen murmured.

"I mean *duh*," he replied. "It just feels…"

"It feels uncomfortable because you are aware of power dynamics but at a certain point, my love, you are going to have to face the fact that not only are you a dom, but you are a very effective one, and you are going to have girls who want to sub to you. *That* is something worth embracing."

"You aren't gonna get jealous of these other girls?" he asked.

"I won't," Ellen replied with a casual shrug.

"Holly?"

"No, I don't think so," she murmured.

"I'm positive there's a website somewhere on the internet that sells customizable chokers like that," Ellen said. "We should so fucking do this."

"Well…I'm cool with it if you are," Gabe replied.

"Mmm," Ellen murmured.

"What?" he asked.

"Just…I feel like a decision regarding choker collars bearing your name should be made with a bit more…hmm, firmness?"

Gabe crossed his arms and stared at her. She looked back with something like challenge in her gaze.

"We'll buy the collars when I'm ready," he replied.

Her smile broadened just a little more. "Good," she murmured.

"Finish up, it's time to go home," he said.

"Yes, sir," Ellen replied with a demure smile.

. . .

"I'm a little less confident about this now," Ellen said from behind the bedroom door.

"I'm positive you look ridiculously hot," Gabe replied.

"Okay, see, I believe you. I believe that you and Holly are going to drool over me. But what about your readers?"

"Anyone who shows up to read Tall, Blonde, and Beautiful is showing up for a really tall, thick goddess like yourself," he said.

"I get that, too, but...a lot of people have an image in their head of what that looks like, and the reality of the what that looks like might be very disappointing..."

"Ellen, we won't do this if you don't want to, but I don't care if this loses me readers, I want to do it," he said.

A long pause. "Okay...come in."

His hand was already on the doorknob and he had it open before she'd finished speaking. Holly was right beside him, almost trembling with eagerness.

They both stopped one step into the bedroom and stared.

Ellen stood in the center of the room, wearing nothing but a pair of black lacy panties, a black bra that showcased her huge breasts, and black fishnet stockings.

"Holy crap," Holly muttered.

"I'm taking it that this is a good look of stunned silence and not a bad one?" Ellen asked.

"Good doesn't start to cut it," Gabe replied. "You look...can we put the photoshoot off for, like, five minutes?"

Ellen laughed. "*No*, babe," she said firmly. "I'm not getting all mussed up after I went through all this cleaning and primping and dressing. After. So, Holly, do you think you can make me look good with your new camera?"

"Dear God *yes*," Holly replied, walking into the room and immediately beginning to adjust the settings on the new digital camera they'd bought her. "Although, um, Gabe, can you go out there and grab that lamp and bring it in here? Lighting is *everything*. Ugh, should've remembered that and maybe bought some at the mall..."

"I'm sure we'll manage," Gabe replied as he headed back out into the living room. He came back a moment later with the lamp and, listening to Holly, placed it and plugged it in.

"Okay, um...I'll need to-can I just, you know, guide you?" Holly asked.

"Guide away, sweetheart," Ellen replied, making Holly giggle.

"Okay, cool. If you could...well, wait. Hold on. Gabe, this is *your* work. I think you should probably adjust her first, to strike the pose that makes the most sense to you? And then I can make further adjustments?"

"Sounds perfect," he replied, thinking back to the first story. "Given it's the first in the series, it should probably be pretty striking...hands on your hips. Okay, good. Stand up straight, all the way. Right foot forward. Turn your body just a little to the left. Okay, perfect. Holly?"

"All right," she murmured, stepping a bit farther from Ellen, then a bit more.

She adjusted her camera again and then put it to her eye. Hesitated. Shifted around a little. Hesitated further. For a moment she looked stymied, then suddenly she said "Oh!" and dropped down on one knee.

She snapped the picture and got up, then checked the image and smiled.

"Well?" Ellen asked after a bit.

"It's amazing, and that's even without tweaking it," Holly replied, passing the camera to Gabe.

"Whoa. Holy shit," he muttered.

"Come on, let me see," Ellen said.

He studied it a few seconds longer, then passed the camera to Ellen.

"Oh. Wow. Damn, Holly, you seriously do have an eye for this. I'm not even sure...how did you actually do this? I feel like I couldn't do this."

"I don't really know," Holly replied. "I just...know? I mean, like I said I've done research online, took a class in high school, but I've always just kinda known?"

"I guess if you've got it...Gabe, you've got a funny look on your face," Ellen said, and Holly turned to look at him.

"What? Oh, I was just thinking...it's obvious at this point that there are people who are just amazing at certain things. Holly for example. Put a camera in her hands and she can take professional looking pics immediately. She didn't necessarily learn that, the seed of that talent was always there, right?"

"That tracks," Ellen said.

"Yeah. I was good with a camera even when I was still pretty young," Holly replied.

"Okay, so...where the fuck did that seed come from?" he asked.

"Some people are just good at stuff," Ellen replied after a moment.

"Yeah, but there's always a reason for it. And the reason is usually: evolution. We evolved that trait because it was useful. But here's the kicker: evolution takes, like, hundreds of thousands of years. Or at least tens of thousands. Or, at the *very* least, thousands. It's a slow, gradual process. Meaning that the evolutionary seed necessary to be good at photography has existed for *way* longer than cameras have existed. Or even painting. Cameras are barely two hundred years old, the oldest cave painting is, what, forty thousand?"

"I think they found one at some point that's closer to sixty thousand now," Ellen said.

"Right. I don't know, it just strikes me as so fucking bizarre that apparently you could put a camera in a caveman's hand and, after teaching him the basics, he could produce something roughly the same level of quality provided he had that same seed. It seems really bizarre," he replied.

"I guess it does," Holly said.

Ellen fell deep into thought for a moment. "I think the seed comes from the ability to accurately judge distance for throwing something, which was important for hunting for quite a while. Either that or the ability to quickly study a given environment for predators."

"That tracks," Gabe said. "It's kind of like how

humans are obsessed with jewelry because it's a side effect of humans learning to seek out fresh water, which the sun glints off of. Or maybe because it reminds us of fire, like the sparks? Our brains have been taught 'water and fire equals good' and so it rewards us when we see it, to train us to seek it out, and the glint from jewelry is close enough that it sparks a similar response."

"...how the fuck did I never put that together?" Ellen muttered. "Is that real?"

"I mean I think so. It's at least my theory for why practically every civilization has some bizarre obsession with shiny rocks and why it's a multi-billion dollar industry," he replied. Gabe paused for a moment. "It just struck me how absolutely crazy this is. We're talking about shiny rocks and cavemen and evolution while taking lingerie pics to help provide covers for my erotica..."

"And we're going to fuck soon," Ellen said, grinning.

"I'm guessing good weird," Holly murmured, adjusting her camera again.

"Very, very good weird. This is the kind of shit I dreamed of. Honestly, I can't really convey how amazing this is, having you two this deeply and enthusiastically involved in my writing is beyond anything I ever realistically hoped for," he replied.

"Good," Ellen said. "Now, shall I change or do we want another?"

"You should change, this one is good," Gabe replied.

Ellen laughed and rolled her eyes. "You just want to see me naked."

"...duh? Of course I do."

"Same," Holly said.

Ellen laughed again and started taking off her bra.

CHAPTER TWENTY TWO

Gabe sensed that someone was outside his office just before there was a light tap at the door.

"Come in," he said, spinning around in his chair.

The door was pushed open and he found a very nervous Holly standing there, wearing one of his t-shirts. He felt a twinge of sympathy for her. Holly defaulted to anxious so often.

"What's up?" he asked. "Can't sleep?"

"No...are you really busy?" she replied, not quite meeting his eyes.

"Not if it's for you."

She smiled and shifted awkwardly in place. "Uh...I want to talk about something. It's kinda serious."

"All right." He stood up and walked over to her, then took her hand and walked with her into the living room.

It was dark now, past midnight, and he'd wanted to get some more writing done. Yesterday had been fun, the lingerie shoot going on for a while, and ultimately be derailed by a threesome that both Gabe and Holly initiated because they couldn't contain themselves with Ellen looking that fantastic. And, luckily, Holly only had a short shift at the cafe the following day, so they'd spent most of it just hanging out and fucking around.

They sat together on the big couch, lit mostly by the soft light of the moon and the streetlights spilling in through the window around the edges of the curtain behind them.

He looked at her and waited. He'd known something like this was coming. Holly was many things, but subtle was not one of them. She wore her heart on her sleeve and didn't seem to be able to do anything but that.

"Holly," he murmured when it became clear she was struggling, he took her hand, "whatever it is, trust that I won't yell at you, or blow you off, or make you leave. Trust that if you're taking a leap of faith, even if the answer is 'no', I'll still be there to catch you."

She smiled and something seemed to resolve behind her eyes, like some battle she'd been waging internally had abruptly come to an end.

"Okay...you're right. I do trust you. I mean I sleep beside you almost every night now and I let you fuck me raw pretty much every day. Doesn't get much more trusting than that," she murmured. She paused, then took a deep breath and let it out slowly. "Okay, so...I've talked about this with Ellen already, and she kind of told me 'yes', but also gently guided me towards you. But basically...I want this to be official. I want to for real be dating you and Ellen, and I want to move in with you."

She stopped speaking abruptly, looking like she wanted to throw a lot more out, probably to try and justify it, but was sitting on that impulse. She regarded him with wide eyes, her lips pressed tightly together.

"And you spoke to Ellen about it already?" Gabe asked, trying to consider everything here.

"Yes. And she said...basically yes, but it's up to you?"

He chuckled softly. "All right then. We've been discussing the possibility of making this official and having you move in with us for a bit now. Pretty much from the beginning, when we began pursuing you, it wasn't really with the intent for it to be causal.

We both really like you. We both want to date you, live with you, be with you. But I think there's a few things we'll have to cover so that you're completely in the know about what a relationship with us would mean."

"I'm listening," she replied, excited as well as anxious now.

"The very first thing is that I need to talk with my landlady about this. This is technically her house that she's renting to us. Now, I'd be willing to move somewhere else if she puts her foot down and says no, but I don't think she will. I think she'll be cool with it. But I want you to know about that."

"Okay."

"Next thing. Finances. We're going to try and be smart about it, but...Ellen's leaving her job soon and I have no idea how long I might be a struggling writer. We're obviously in a great spot right now, but that might not always be true...I guess what I'm saying is, dating us means dating people who will legitimately try to be financially responsible, but ultimately put more emphasis on comfort and sanity instead of a mad grind to get more money."

"I'm totally cool with that," Holly replied. "At this point, I like you both so much, I don't care if we lived out of a broken down van."

"Wow...okay. That's appreciated. Final thing. Um." He hesitated, considering it. "Well, I guess there isn't a great way to put this, and I don't want to lie to you, so I will just come out with it: there is a *very* good chance I'm going to have sex with other women besides you and Ellen in the future, but I would not be comfortable with you being with another guy. I know that's not fair–"

"I don't care," Holly interrupted. "I'm fine with

that. To be completely honest..." She hesitated, blushing now. "This feels weird to say, but I actually really like the idea of this relationship. Like...I like the idea of dating you while you're dating or fucking other women. I mean I like to watch, but I also like to know it's happening...? I have no idea why. I talked about it with Ellen briefly and she said it makes sense that there's something hot about being with a guy who can, and does, get other women into bed...and I also don't want any other guys. I just want you. I mean, more than just sexually. Romantically, too. Just...I'm very happy with the arrangement."

"Oh. Well...great," he replied. He chuckled, relieved. "That was definitely going out on my own limb."

"Yeah, I imagine that wouldn't go well with a lot of women, but...for some reason it works really well with me. So...is that a yes?"

"That is a yes. Still need to check with my landlady and I would like to have one serious talk with Ellen about it, just to double-check, because this is a big change, but yes. You are basically invited into our house, and our relationship. You are my girlfriend, Holly," Gabe replied.

Her smile grew broader and she was blushing fiercely now, breathing more heavily. "Your girlfriend would like to be put to use..." she murmured.

"Would she now?" he asked.

"Yes..."

"Well." Gabe reached forward and lifted up the t-shirt a little. Holly was chewing on her lower lip again and she shifted her legs, opening then a little, revealing that she wore no panties beneath the shirt. He looked at her bare pussy for a second, then kept lifting it, revealing her big breasts.

"You little slut," he murmured.

"What are you going to do to me?" she whispered.

He pulled the t-shirt off of her, then shifted and put a hand over the back of her neck. Unzipping his jeans, he pulled her head down into his lap. She took his meaning immediately, quickly pulling his erection out of his boxers and putting it in her mouth.

"That's a good girl," he whispered as she began sucking him off, bobbing her head smoothly, coating his cock in her saliva. "Suck it like the little whore you are, Holly."

She murmured something that was lost completely given her mouth was full. He kept his hand on the back of her head, guiding her up and down, and then pushed.

"Take it," he said, pushing up and getting his dick into her throat. "Swallow."

She swallowed and a hot, wet burst of pleasure hit him. "Again, Holly."

She swallowed again and another pulse of bliss hit him. He kept her there for a moment longer, then released her. She came up, coughing a few times and wiping her mouth on the back of her hand.

"Now what, master?" she whispered, panting now.

"Fuck me until I come inside of you," he replied, settling back into the sofa a bit more.

"Yes, master," she replied demurely, standing up and settling her big, pale ass in his lap.

Reaching between them, she grasped his erection and got lower until she penetrated herself with it. She gasped and then moaned quietly as she began fucking herself with it. She placed her hands on his knees to steady herself and then got to it, riding his dick faster, taking it all the way into herself.

"Are you a whore, Holly?" he asked.

"Yes," she whispered, panting now.

"Say it."

"I'm a whore," she moaned quietly.

"That's right. Come on, keep going. Faster, Holly."

"I'll be loud…" she panted.

"I guess you'll just have to try extra hard to keep your mouth shut, won't you? Don't backtalk me, Holly."

"I'm sorry…" she moaned, then cried out as he grasped her hips and began bouncing her more roughly on his cock.

The session didn't last much longer.

She rode him until he grasped her hips even more firmly and pulled her down hard into his lap, and then he began releasing his seed into her, filling her up with hard, furious spurts that left her gasping and moaning.

When it was over, she was sitting in his lap, laying against him, his softening cock still inside of her, his arms around her. She was holding his hands, getting her breath back.

"Gabe?" she murmured.

"Yes, Holly?" he replied.

"You know that saying, 'when you know, you know'?"

"Yes."

"I know something right now, and I want to tell you something, but I'm worried it will freak you out…but you keep telling me to be braver and say what's on my mind. So I'm going to tell you. Gabe…I love you," she murmured.

Gabe felt his heart flutter hard in his chest and his stomach did a hard roll, but he knew what to say without even hesitating.

"I love you too, Holly."

He felt as much as heard her exhale sharply. "Really?" she whispered after a moment of silence.

"Really. I didn't fully realize it until you told me just now but...you're right. When you know, you know. And I know."

"...will Ellen be mad?" she murmured.

"No," he replied. "Ellen and I have been talking about the kind of life and the kind of home we want to build together, and that home involves loving relationships. And I think Ellen loves you, too. But that's something you need to discuss with her."

"You're right." She laughed. "Ah God...I'm in love. And I'm *loved*. That feels-it feels amazing."

"It really does," he agreed.

She yawned suddenly. "Oh wow, I'm very tired all of a sudden. I should sleep...I have work tomorrow, and we have things to do...ugh."

"What?"

"You'll have to see my apartment, because I know you're going to want to help me move and...it's so messy. Is there any way I can talk you into just letting me handle the apartment stuff?"

"No dice," he replied. She sighed. "Holly...we won't judge you for it. Whatever it is, we'll tackle it together. All right?"

"All right," she murmured, then yawned again. "I gotta wash up."

"Yep," he agreed.

"Are you-are you still inside of me?" she asked.

"A little," he replied. "You know what?" He turned her around so that she was sitting sideways, then got her arms under her and stood up. She let out a little cry of surprise as he began carrying her across the living towards the bathroom.

"Oh my goodness!" she whispered. "That's...not what I expected. But it's nice. I've never been carried like this."

"I can't realistically do it with Ellen, but I can with you," he replied as he got her to the shower and let her get to her feet. He turned on the water, making sure to turn the showerhead away from her naked body so the cold water wouldn't hit her before it heated up.

"I appreciate it," she replied, then giggled. "I feel amazing right now."

"Same," he said. "Now, I need to go grab my pants because I stepped out of them. You wash up and get to bed."

"Yes, sir," she replied.

Gabe leaned in and kissed her on the lips. "I love you," he whispered.

She shuddered and closed her eyes for a second, her smile growing. "I love you, too," she murmured.

He closed the shower curtain and headed out of the bathroom.

CHAPTER TWENTY THREE

Gabe opened his eyes to the very soft sound of rain hitting his house, the almost silent murmur of lo-fi music, and quiet respiration beside him.

For a moment he laid there in bed and simply enjoyed the ambience. Then, knowing that there were things he needed to do, very important things, he checked the time on his phone. It was almost ten o'clock, meaning Holly would be up before too long because she had to get to work.

Careful not to disturb Holly, Gabe got up and headed for the bathroom. He pissed and brushed his teeth, then walked out to the living room, where he found Ellen in her usual spot, stretched out on the couch in her robe.

"Hey, you," she said, grinning. "I heard you two fucking last night."

"Yeah...we need to talk," Gabe replied, coming and sitting.

"Oh? What about?" she asked with the air of someone who was in on a secret.

He chuckled. "So. Holly and I had a talk last night. She wants to move in and be our girlfriend for real. She said you pointed her towards me...is there a specific reason?"

Ellen slowly lost her smirk and instead became thoughtful. She set aside her laptop and sat up fully. "So...yes. There was a reason. I was hoping to kind of give you another gentle nudge towards stepping up and being...the head of the household. Our relationship is a nuanced thing, and it always will be. And obviously I want you to consult with me on big decisions. But at the end of the day...I've had my fill of being in charge.

"Maybe that will change in the future. Probably it will. But for now? Yes, I want input on where we're going, but I want you to be the captain of this particular ship, Gabe. Because I trust you, and I believe in you. I know that I can hand control over to you, and you won't go mad with power. You'll never try to actually *control* me. And I'm also doing it because I think you want it. I think you want to be in charge...or am I wrong?"

Gabe looked at her for a long moment, then away, out the window behind the couch, contemplating the question.

On the surface, of course he would like to be in control of his relationships, of his household. But deeper than that, he knew what that meant. Control wasn't just control, it was responsibility. That was the biggest thing those 'alpha' douchebags never seemed to grasp. Being in control wasn't just a free pass to do whatever the fuck you wanted with no consequences, living only for yourself.

Being in charge meant taking care of people, making sure that everyone had what they needed, what they wanted, making sure everyone was safe and able to live their lives.

And...

She was right.

He'd been stepping up more recently, making decisions, and it always felt good, if a little nerve-wracking.

"You're not wrong," he said finally, looking back to her. "You're very right."

She got that little cocky smirk on her face. "Knew it."

"I need to talk with Sadie about this, and we're

going to help her move her stuff, wrap up her affairs, get everything in order...there's one other thing," he said.

"What?"

"...Holly told me she loved me last night."

Ellen looked a little surprised, but not that surprised. "What did you say to her?"

"That I love her, too...how do you feel about that?" he asked, a little cautiously.

"Great," Ellen replied. "That was always where this was going. I'm...a little surprised it got there so quickly, but then again, I'm not. I mean, you're you. You're amazing, despite how you feel about it. You're the real deal, Gabe, and Holly knows that. Recognizes it. And is responding to it...I imagine you told her that you're going to be banging other chicks?"

"Yes. And she's *really* happy to pretty much keep on going like we are. It still feels weird, me telling her and you that you aren't allowed to sleep with other guys, but..."

"It's a boundary you are choosing to place," Ellen said. "And I know that if either Holly or myself wasn't interested in accepting that boundary, you would let us walk away from the relationship, amicably, if painfully. We all have boundaries and conditions, Gabe, and that's okay. We're comfortable with it, and honestly, I'm pretty happy with the idea that you are the last man I'll ever have sex with for the rest of my life."

"Seriously?" he asked.

"Really. Truly. When I tell you that you're the best fuck I've ever had, I don't just mean that in the obvious way. You actually fucking *listen* to me. Yes, you're skilled. Yes, you've got a nice cock. Yes, you can fuck very well. But with you...it doesn't feel like I'm basically just a sextoy." She laughed and rolled her eyes. "Even if, sometimes, that's exactly how I want you to use me. God, even *I* don't understand my wants and needs sometimes. All I know is, this is great, and I'll be happy to fuck you, and Holly, and Emily, and hopefully Krystal...maybe Abby and Liz, too. Mmm...Abby's such a hot little piece of ass..."

"She really is," he agreed. "I would kill to be in a threesome with you and her. Or even just to fuck her."

"Well...she *did* say she's ninety eighty percent lesbian..." Ellen murmured.

"You think there's a chance?"

"I think there's a chance. But Abby will let you know if she's interested." She giggled suddenly. "Ah, you and Holly love each other. Did you say it during sex?"

"No, after actually."

"Oh my. I'm happy. I could see it in the way she looks at you...I should tell her I love her, too. I thought we should probably wait for her to say it, and now she has!"

"I think that would be the best thing in the whole world for her to wake up to," Gabe said.

"You are absolutely right," Ellen replied, getting up.

He watched her go, briefly tempted to join her, but this should be a moment between the two of them. He and Holly had gotten their intimate moment together. He instead grabbed his phone from where he'd set it on the coffee table and fired up his texts.

Hey Sadie, I was hoping to talk with you about something important.

He shot that off after some consideration. He'd

wanted to just come right out and ask it, but something told him not to.

He only had to wait about thirty seconds for a response: *If you aren't busy, I wouldn't mind meeting in person to discuss whatever it is.*

Gabe thought about that, then replied: *Yeah, I can do that. Where?*

After a moment an address appeared, followed by: *It's a little restaurant I frequent. We could have lunch together.*

He began typing a response: *Sounds good. I'll be there soon.*

...

Ellen and Holly had teased him mercilessly about the fact that he was driving off to see Sadie.

Now, as he drove through the rain-slicked city, (it was cold and gray, but the rain was little more than a light mist for now), he found himself contemplating the reality of actually hooking up with Sadie.

At this point, he was mostly convinced that Ellen was right, she wanted to fuck him.

But he was reluctant to make such an assumption wholeheartedly. It was entirely possible that she didn't. It was also possible that she was flirting and maybe teasing a little, but didn't intend to go all the way, which...

Well, that would suck, but it wasn't like he minded flirting with her.

Ellen had said that the mature woman was playing the long game with him, and he wondered if she was right.

He also wondered if she knew something he didn't. They *had* had that private conversation the last, and only, time that they'd met face to face. But he couldn't shake the feeling that it was just wishful thinking. He'd always been attracted to noticeably older women and Sadie had the double-threat of being both noticeably older than him *and* banging hot.

He had to admit, that second erotica request was extremely suggestive.

And the fact that she'd admitted to masturbating to it.

That seemed like a big tell, but again, she could just be flirting.

On the other hand, after the past few weeks, he was a lot more willing to lean into a flirtatious situation than before.

The last thing Ellen had told him was that if Sadie jumped him, let her. Just try to get pictures if she would let him.

And Holly had enthusiastically agreed.

As he found the little restaurant she'd told him to go to, it abruptly occurred to Gabe that there was at least a semi-realistic chance of him going home with a fifty year old woman and fucking her brains out.

For all his doubt, it did actually feel at least within the realm of possibility.

He tried to maintain his focus as he parked in the mostly empty lot and got out. As he did, another of the car doors opened up and Sadie stepped out of her own vehicle. She smiled at him, a little tentatively, and they met by the front door.

Gabe held it open for her.

"Thank you," she murmured. "It's good to see you again."

"Definitely good to see you," he replied.

The restaurant turned out to be a pizza place. They walked to the front counter and ended up agreeing to split a simple pepperoni pizza, got their drinks, and headed back to a booth tucked away in the corner.

Sadie offered to pay and he accepted it graciously, which seemed to please her.

"So, what's this important event?" she asked.

"How would you feel about another person moving into the house?" he asked.

She paused to consider it, taking a long drink from her soda. "I would probably agree, based on our interactions and my level of trust with you so far. But I would like to meet her."

"All right." He paused. "...how did you know that the person in question is a her?"

Sadie smiled a small smile. "I was guessing," she admitted, "but I also know what kind of man you are."

"And what kind of man is that?" he asked, genuinely curious now.

"The kind of man who is rather popular with women. In a very specific way."

He leaned forward, even more curious now. "What about me says that, exactly?"

"I'm not entirely sure," Sadie replied. "Something about the way you were with Ellen. Something about the way you are with...me. Something about the way you write."

"Is the way I am with you...unseemly?" he asked.

"No," Sadie replied, then seemed to reconsider. "Well, put it this way: if it *is* unseemly, I don't care. I like it."

"Good to know."

"So, who is this girl?"

"Her name is Holly," Gabe replied, pulling out his phone and scrolling through his pictures. "She's a...um, we met at a cafe she works at. Uh. Mmm…"

"Having some trouble?" Sadie asked, grinning more now.

"It's just that none of the pictures I have of her are...PG-13 or less," he muttered.

"If she's okay with that, so am I," Sadie replied with an easy shrug.

Gabe glanced up at her, then looked back down at his phone and found the most recent picture of her posing with her tits out in the abandoned building. Holly had already told him he had blanket permission to show her nude pics to any lady he thought was trustworthy and wanted to see.

"Okay, you asked for it," he replied, turning the phone around.

Sadie's eyes went wide as she took the phone from his hand and brought it closer to her face. "Good. *Lord.* Gabe. She is a *heartstopper.*"

"Uh, yeah. Yes. Yes, she is," he agreed with an awkward chuckle.

Sadie stared at the phone for a bit longer before passing it back. "I take it you and her are an item now?"

"Yes. Well, me and her and Ellen. We're dating now. As of last night. And she...could use the support. We still don't know all the details but she's working herself to death trying to keep up with bills and debt, and she's an *amazing* photographer. Shit, here, look at this," Gabe said, calling up the first photo they'd taken of Ellen in lingerie.

He'd had Holly send it to him. He turned the phone around to show her.

"Oh my," Sadie whispered. "That's...wow. That's an amazing photograph. And not just because Ellen is spectacularly beautiful...hmm. I don't suppose you have a...non-PG-13 photo of Ellen?"

He laughed softly and began scrolling again. "I do. Several, actually. And she's also okay with you being shown...here's a great one."

He passed her the phone and she began blushing again. It showed Ellen posing naked on the bed with her legs spread and the most seductive smile he'd ever seen on her.

"That woman...is intimidatingly attractive," she murmured. She slowly reached out. "Can you zoom in-oops. I accidentally-oh my."

She passed him back the phone and he saw that it was a picture of his dick in Ellen's pussy, and he immediately felt blood rushing to his face.

"Ah, wow. Jeez. And now my landlady has seen my cock," he muttered, turning his screen off and putting his phone away.

"Is that such a bad thing?" Sadie replied.

"Well...I guess not. I mean if it was an experience you liked..."

"It was an experience I liked," she said. She was smiling but she looked uncertain, like she felt she was on shaky ground. She cleared her throat and shifted in her seat, took another drink. "So, um, how have things been?"

"Great, honestly," he replied. "That picture of Ellen, uh, the non-nude one, is one of a series that Holly took. Ellen is making new cover art for my series, Tall, Blonde, and Beautiful. The final one is finished and ready to go, and I'm working on a new series. Stone age era."

"Oh wow. That's...certainly very unusual and inspired," she said. "I would love to read that."

"First episode is almost done. I'm actually experimenting with somewhat longer form this time.

The shorter form is already starting to feel kind of restrictive and I'm beginning to suspect that one longer title will earn more than two or even three shorter ones. At least in terms of these lengths...are you sure this isn't boring?" he asked.

"No. God no. I told you, I'm a patron of the arts, Gabe. I love hearing about this. Tell me."

"Well...all right."

He started telling her about his idea for the stone age story, the little bit of research he'd done, the characters. He didn't want to give away too much, but that transitioned into how he got ideas for his other stories, and how he planned them out, and his general process. The pizza came at some point and he tore through it.

Sadie had told him that it was a very high quality pizza place and as soon as he'd had the first bite, he knew she was right.

The pizza was amazing.

"Whew, okay...um...I've probably taken up enough of your time," Gabe said as a lull in the conversation came about naturally and he realized that not only was all the pizza gone, and had been for a bit, but they'd been here for over an hour.

Sadie, however, didn't seem bored in the slightest.

"I'm happy being here, Gabe," Sadie replied. "I'm a fifty year old woman who's basically retired, divorced, and most of my friends have spread out across the country. I have a lot of time nowadays. This has been very nice."

"Oh...well okay then, cool. Uh...you wanna come over and meet Holly? Maybe check up on the house? See what we did with the place?" he suggested.

"I would love that," she replied.

"Okay, awesome. Lemme just text Ellen...although shit, Holly might be at work by now. I guess we'll find out," he said, pulling out his phone.

He fired off a text to Ellen, and quickly got a response saying that she was thrilled at the idea of Sadie coming by and Holly was still there, as she'd found someone to cover her shift for the day because she was having a *really* hard time working up the strength to go into her shitty job.

"Perfect," he said as they got out of the booth and headed for the exit, "she's still there."

"Sounds great. I'll meet you there?" Sadie replied.

"Yep. Also...thanks. For being so reasonable and letting this happen."

"You're welcome, Gabe. I spent enough time having to tell people no or dash people's dreams. I like saying yes nowadays if I can help it."

"...what was your job?" he asked.

She sighed softly. "Loan officer, basically. People came to me desperately needing loans, and I had to determine if they got them. A lot of people who really needed the money...I couldn't give it to them. My job wouldn't let me."

"Oh...wow, shit. I'm sorry, Sadie. That had to be awful."

She nodded. "Yes, it was. I'm so grateful to be out of it now." She regained her smile. "I'll see you there."

"See you there," Gabe replied.

They got into their respective vehicles and began making their way back home.

CHAPTER TWENTY FOUR

It was definitely different now, being around Sadie.

The fullness of the shift didn't truly occur to Gabe until he was walking up to the front door with her. He found himself worrying a little, wondering if he or Ellen or Holly was going to say something to offend or upset her. This was, potentially, a break-point. He had meant what he said, that he would choose Holly over this house.

But it would complicate things.

They walked inside and found Ellen and Holly dressed and on the couch. The place had been cleaned up, too, he noticed. They must have done it in a hurry. Both women stood up as they came inside and Sadie took off her shoes.

"Hello, Sadie," Ellen said.

"Ellen, hello," Sadie replied.

Gabe paused. Something about that exchange seemed off. He tried furiously to parse what exactly it was for a few seconds as Sadie took off her jacket and hung it, and her purse, on the coat rack, and finally he decided that Ellen was speaking to Sadie like she knew some sort of secret of hers, and was pleased about it.

And Sadie responded as if that were true.

It was amazing how much tone and expression could convey.

Holly seemed oblivious and nervously polite.

"You must be Holly," Sadie said, regaining her mature confidence rather quickly.

"Yes. Hi. It's nice to meet you," Holly replied.

Sadie laughed softly. "It's nice to meet you too.

And regardless of what these two have told you, you don't have to be nervous around me."

"I can't help it," Holly said after a moment. "It's just...how I am."

"Well, I can understand that at least." Sadie took a seat on the loveseat while Gabe sat between Ellen and Holly on the sofa as they regained their own seats. "I also have come to understand that you wish to live here as well?"

"Yes," Holly murmured. "I would like that very much."

"*I* have come to understand that you've seen us all naked now," Ellen said with a tiny smirk.

Gabe looked at her. She didn't look at him, her gaze fixed entirely on Sadie. He looked to the older woman. She was blushing ever so slightly now and looked a bit awkward, but otherwise composed herself admirably.

"Ah. Gabe mentioned that. I was hoping he would have mentioned it after I'd left. It's an...awkward position to be in," she murmured.

"It doesn't have to be," Ellen replied. "Permission was granted by everyone involved."

"I suppose that's true. Although I myself am not bisexual at all, I would like to say that both of you are marvelously beautiful women."

"Thank you. You are too, you know," Ellen replied.

Sadie cleared her throat and shifted in her seat. "Thank you," she murmured. "So, Holly, tell me about yourself, if you wouldn't mind. What do you care about?"

"Oh. Um. Hmm." She shifted around uncomfortably in her seat, suddenly the center of attention. "Well, photography mostly. And nature.

And abandoned places. And Gabe and Ellen. I also really like reading and watching horror movies."

"Interesting. May I see some of your photographs?" Sadie asked.

"Oh yeah, sure," she murmured, reaching forward and picking up her phone off the coffee table. She navigated it for a moment, then passed it to Sadie. "It's open to the collection. I think those are my best."

"Goodness," Sadie murmured as she stared at the first image on the screen.

They waited as she studied the phone, occasionally swiping on to the next one. She looked genuinely impressed. After several moments, she passed the phone back.

"You are very talented," she said.

"You really think so?" Holly replied uncertainly.

"Oh yes. I dabbled in photography myself for a time. In truth, I thought perhaps I could make a go of it as a career about five years ago. I was all right after some practice, but I learned I just didn't have an eye for it. I spent some time around others trying to do the same, obviously, and I took a few classes. One of the teachers was a woman about my age who had been in the business for twenty years. She was excellent. She had photographs in big time magazines. Copies of several of her best hung on the walls of the classroom, they were breathtaking. Your present skill is at least approaching hers. You seem to be a natural," Sadie said.

"Oh...wow," she murmured. "I...don't know how to feel about that."

"It takes time to figure that out," Sadie said. "It's important to do, though. What do you *want* to do?"

"Well..." She chuckled awkwardly, looking

around. "Man, I didn't know I'd be put on the spot like this."

"I apologize, I don't mean to make you uncomfortable, but I also have come to learn that people sometimes, often even, need just a little push if they're to speak the truth. And speaking the truth is important, even if only to yourself. And to be clear now: I am comfortable with you moving in. So far, I trust Gabe and Ellen, and they have done nothing to betray that trust or make me question it in the slightest, so if they want you in their house and their bed, they must trust you."

Sadie fell silent, but they could tell she wasn't finished speaking. She looked like she was concentrating, perhaps searching for the right words, and they all waited patiently. Whatever it was, it seemed important to her.

"I'm fifty years old, Holly. Over twice your age. Almost twice Gabe's age. My twenties were a lifetime ago. Hell, my thirties were too. I have passions, things I care about, but I put them aside for my career and my marriage. Both are gone now, and what's left? I'm not going to tell you that your life is over once you hit forty five, but...certain aspects of it are. Not because society says so, not because I think they should be, but simply because they are. Because that is how life works. My life is not joyless now, but...the joy does not come nearly so easily as it did at your age.

"I know some of that is a function of who I am as a person. I've never been the happiest of women. But I also know that some of it is simply a function of being human. Who knows? You seem like a cheerful sort, Holly, and perhaps you will hold onto that to your dying day, many decades from now, ideally.

Perhaps you will be a happy-go-lucky eighty six year old. I truly wish that to be the case. But you can't count on that. And so my point is this: use it while you've got it. And the sooner you can begin seriously investigating and investing in your passion, or passions, the better. We're on a deadline and none of us has any idea when our number might be up."

It was quiet for a long moment when she stopped speaking.

Sadie sighed softly and then chuckled ruefully. "Sorry, I didn't mean to get grim. It's sort of second nature for me. I've always been a brooding, grim sort of woman. But at this point I don't see much point in not speaking truthfully about most things."

"Agreed," Ellen replied almost immediately.

"So, what you mean is, you missed your chance to follow your passion at a younger age, and I'm pretty young, so I should not make the same mistake?" Holly asked.

"Exactly. But it's more than that. Knowing your passion is a gift, Holly. There are a *lot* of people out there who have no idea what they want to do with their lives, or have been pressured into doing something they don't care about or actively hate, or are so clouded by society's expectations that they simply follow what they think they should," Sadie said.

"She's right," Ellen said.

"Yep," Gabe agreed immediately.

"I *do* really care about photography, I know that at least," Holly murmured after a moment. "But...I worry about how to pursue it. Part of me wants to go after it, take it seriously, make it my job. But another part of me is afraid of that and just wants to make it my hobby, something I do for fun in my spare time.

What if I can't handle having it as a job? What if having it as a job makes me hate doing it?"

"This is why I wanted to do this, Holly," Sadie replied. "Why I wanted to be a patron of the arts. If you live in an environment where you don't need to aggressively pursue money simply to keep your head above water, it takes the pressure off and not only allows you to actually *live your fucking life,* but to figure these kinds of things out. Despite what everyone says, you don't have to monetize your passion. You can experiment, try things out. Maybe it can be a hobby most of the time, and once or twice a week you take on a paid job? Just as a suggestion."

"That...is a good idea," she murmured. Then she shifted around uncomfortably again, an awkward expression coming onto her face. "I still feel weird about living off of someone else's money." She paused, glanced at Gabe and then Ellen, her frown deepening. "Except that I *don't* feel the same way if I imagine living off of Gabe and Ellen's money...I don't know why that is."

"Because that's what our society is set up for you to do, Holly," Sadie said. "You are an attractive young woman. It's not nearly as bad as it was when I was your age, and it's far, far better than it was when my own mother was your age, but society still largely expects, or perhaps hopes is a better word for it, hopes that a woman in your position will find a man, get married, and settle into being a housewife and stay at home mother, entirely dependent on your husband for income."

"Is it bad that part of me likes that idea?" Holly murmured.

"No," Sadie replied, "because on some level, and depending on who you are, it's a very appealing idea.

You can just live your life and have someone else take the guesswork out of living? Some people have the personality type to take charge, make decisions, and love it every single day. Most of us do not have that. Why do you think so many people just...go along with things? Well, that's actually a far more complicated situation, but I think a not insignificant portion of the population would enjoy doing their own thing while having their life taken care of by someone who knew what they were doing and had their best interests in mind."

"And that's where reality shatters the illusion," Ellen muttered.

"Yes," Sadie agreed, grim again. "Because most people who take charge do not know what they are doing, and do not have your best interests in mind. And power tends to corrupt. But I would not be in charge of your life, Holly. I just expect a few things from you. Really, I just expect you not to ruin my property or do anything illegal or particularly dangerous here. It would be Gabe who you would be surrendering to, and Gabe is a good man."

"You think he's incorruptible?" Ellen asked with only the smallest smile.

"No one is incorruptible," Sadie replied with a surprising gravity. "But certainly some are far harder to corrupt than others. I imagine you've always found the idea appealing, Holly, of surrendering. But I imagine you find the idea of surrendering to Gabe far more appealing because you trust him, because something in you recognizes that he is a good man, a caretaker, and who doesn't want to be taken care of? That isn't to say the relationship would be entirely one-sided. You bring your own things to the table..."

She hesitated and seemed to reconsider

something, then she straightened up a little. "It occurs to me that I've gotten *way* too familiar with you all, especially you, Holly, given that this is our first meeting," she murmured.

"I don't mind," Holly replied.

"Yeah, you successfully read the room, Sadie. You wouldn't have gotten comfortable like that if we didn't like it," Gabe said. "Also thank you, for what you said about me."

She smiled a little tentatively, seeming to relax again. "You're welcome." She cleared her throat. "Well, I believe I've said most of what I wanted to say. I am okay with Holly moving in here. The terms and conditions of our lease remain intact."

"Oh yeah?" Gabe asked, surprised by how brash he felt in the moment. "You going to ask Holly to send the occasionally nude photo commission like you ask me for erotica?" He noticed both Holly and Ellen looked interestedly between him and Sadie as he said that.

"I, well...that is to say...I would not ask for anything that anyone is uncomfortable with providing," she murmured, blushing now.

Ellen laughed very softly, looking infinitely amused.

"Look, if you want nude pics or a video of Gabe fucking railing Holly while I make her eat my pussy, I'm sure we can hook you up," Ellen said.

Sadie's eyes widened a little and she blushed a lot worse.

"Wow, babe," Gabe said.

"What?" Ellen replied with a smirk and an easy shrug.

"You have *no* fucking subtlety," he muttered.

Sadie cleared her throat. "I will...think on it. And

let you know," she managed. "And, ah, if that is all, I would like to have a word with Holly...alone."

"Oh...mmm, why?" Holly replied.

"I just want to talk with you about something privately. It isn't bad," Sadie replied.

"Don't worry, sweetie," Ellen said, patting Holly's leg reassuringly, "it isn't bad."

"You know what it is?" Holly asked.

"Yep, we had the same talk," Ellen replied.

"Then why–" Holly paused and glanced at Gabe, putting two and two together. "So...it's about Gabe?"

"Apparently," Gabe replied. "No idea what it is, though. Ellen assures me it's in my best interest."

"It is," both Ellen and Sadie said at the same time.

"Well, okay," Holly replied, looking more curious than anything else now.

"Come along love," Ellen said, standing up.

Gabe sighed and followed her. They walked back to the bedroom and closed the door.

"You really won't tell me?" he asked after a moment.

Ellen smiled and sat down on the bed. "I really won't. But you know that I love you with all my heart and soul, Gabe. I would tell you if there was any danger or even unpleasantness of any kind involved. As I said before, it's personal. Although I have a growing suspicion that you know what it is."

"I can't be sure," was all he would say.

Because he did have his hopes.

Ellen just smiled. Despite how he felt about it, Gabe made no attempt to listen in. Instead he walked over to the dresser and fiddled with his music station for a bit.

"By the way," Ellen said, and her voice was

surprisingly sheepish, "I texted Abby because I realized that I was kind of fuzzy on when that party we're supposed to go to actually was and...it's tonight."

He turned to face her. "Tonight, huh?"

"Yes. Sorry. I was...distracted."

He chuckled. "Yeah, so was I. Think we have time to help Holly move and make the party?"

"Oh no, definitely not," she replied. "I mean, we can grab some essentials and make a dent, but from what I've gathered, Holly has a very messy apartment. Which is kind of surprising, given how good she is about being neat and clean over here, but also not surprising, because the girl is clearly suffering from depression. And I'm going to need your help on that."

"Help how?" he asked.

"We've got a closing window of time, I think, before helping her gets harder. One of the biggest problems with depression is actually getting the momentum going to haul yourself up out of it. Even with people who care helping, it's still hard. We need to get her a doctor's appointment and get her started on some antidepressants. We have to figure out her insurance and she's not going to want to do it, and it's already going to be an uphill battle because our healthcare infrastructure is a fucking nightmare in general..."

"I'll help however I can," he replied.

She smiled. "We both really appreciate it." Ellen looked at him speculatively for a moment. "Sadie's right, you know."

"About?"

"You. You're a caretaker. And something in us recognizes that, and responds strongly to it. I just hope I'm up to the task of taking care of you back," she murmured.

"Why do you doubt that?" he asked.

"I am...selfish by nature. I don't know that it's always been that way, but I was taught to be selfish. Not directly...well, most of the time. But some lessons are written between the lines. I was taught that people are going to fuck you over no matter what, so you'd better fuck them over first. Clearly, this isn't true for some people. Clearly, it isn't true for you. I trust you, but I know I'm going to have to be careful to make sure that I keep an eye on you, make sure I'm not neglecting you. Or Holly."

"I'll let you know if I feel neglected," he said after a moment.

"I think you will...but sometimes I worry you're too polite to speak up for yourself. Or you're still too intimidated by me."

"I clearly am not too intimidated by you at this point."

She smirked. "I love you dear, but telling me to drop to my knees and suck you dry is not the same as telling me you feel neglected."

"...okay, fair point. But I will make an effort."

They both looked over as they heard someone getting closer, then a gentle knock at the door. Gabe opened it to find Sadie.

"I'm finished speaking with Holly," she uttered, then peered past him into the room beyond. "So this is where the magic happens," she murmured.

"Oh yes. Though at this point I believe it's happened in every room in the house," Ellen said.

"...even that tiny laundry closet?" Sadie asked.

Gabe chuckled. "Uh...yeah. I realized that while the dryer wasn't really a great height for sex, it *was* the perfect height for me to sit on and Ellen to be able to kneel down and give me head."

"Interesting," Sadie said quietly, blushing again. "Well, I've spoken with Holly. If there's nothing else, I will take my leave."

"Nothing I can think of," Gabe said.

They followed her back out to the living room, where they found Holly sitting on the sofa, a small, strange smile on her face. She was blushing. She looked at Gabe and blushed worse, then looked at Ellen, her smile growing a little.

"Don't be afraid to ask for something," Ellen said as Sadie gathered her things.

"I will give it some serious consideration," she replied diplomatically. "Farewell."

"Farewell, Sadie," Gabe said.

They watched her go to her car, then closed the door. He looked at the two women in his life for a long moment, curiosity temporary rising severely. He considered if he really could get them to tell him what the fuck it was Sadie was speaking with them about so privately. But the urge passed and he knew he shouldn't seriously try to pressure them into it.

"All right," he said, fixating on Holly, "let's see this apartment of yours."

CHAPTER TWENTY FIVE

"Okay," Holly said as they came to stand before her apartment door, "I'm really, seriously asking you to *please* not give me shit for my place. I know how bad it is. And...if at all possible, I would like to do this on my own."

"Holly," Gabe replied, honestly kind of surprised and actually worried at this point, "we aren't going to give you shit for it. And this isn't something you should do on your own. We're together now. We obviously still have separate lives of our own, but we want to help you."

Holly sighed softly. "I don't want to do it on my own," she muttered. "I don't want to do it at all."

"But it has to be done," Ellen said, a hand on her back, "and since you don't want to do it alone, you should let us help."

"I know, I know," she muttered. Finally, she put the key to the lock and opened the door up.

Her apartment was small, he realized. Actually, it was barely bigger than the studio apartment that Gabe himself had lived in briefly. And as she flipped on the lights, he quickly saw the full scope of why she was so reluctant to show them.

There was a lot of stuff scattered around. Clothes, trash, dishes, books, food containers, some magazines, and a lot of other random items. The sink was overloaded with dirty dishes, the two trash cans he saw were piled high with trash. The bathroom door was open and through it he could see a dirty shower and a stained mirror.

Holly stood in the middle of it, facing away from them. Abruptly she began to cry.

"Oh sweetheart," Ellen said, walking over quickly and hugging her.

"I'm sorry!" she cried, hugging herself tightly and letting Ellen wrap her arms around her. "Every time I try to get started I just...I can't. I don't know why. It just feels impossible. And the few times I do clean up it just gets like this again and everything feels so fucking pointless..."

"Shh," Ellen replied.

They stood there for a moment, none of them moving, Holly crying quietly as Ellen held her. Then Gabe walked over and put his hands on her hips from behind, letting her know that he was there. She continued for a moment longer, then slowed, then stopped.

"I'm sorry," she murmured finally, "this has to be annoying."

"It's not annoying, Holly," Ellen said.

"My ex hated it when I cried," she muttered.

"So did mine," Ellen said. She looked at Gabe suddenly. "How about you?"

He laughed darkly. "I never got that far."

"You've never cried in front of your girlfriend?" Holly murmured, pulling her head back from Ellen's chest and wiping at her eyes.

"No. Call it a survival instinct."

"I...don't understand."

"Men don't cry in front of their girlfriends or they lose them," he replied.

Holly looked dismayed. "What? Why?"

Ellen sighed heavily. "There are, frankly, too many women out there who view men crying or, fuck, even admitting to depression, anxiety, fear, whatever, as weakness. It sounds ridiculous but I *have* encountered it. I know of more than a few guys who got broken up with after their girlfriend begged and begged for them to open up emotionally, and they finally did."

"What the fuck? Why?" Holly asked, sniffing and growing more angry. "Why even bother if they're just going to break up? Were they just looking for an excuse?"

"I think the cold reality of the situation," Gabe replied, "is that they *think* they want it, but once they actually get it, they find that it tarnishes their view." He sighed. "But this isn't really the time to talk about that particular wrinkle in modern dating. Are you okay, Holly?"

He glanced briefly at Ellen, curious why she'd even brought it up, but there was an oddly knowing look on her face.

Holly sniffed and nodded. "Yeah, I'm okay. I hate being here and I hate it now more than ever. But...I'm okay now. It feels better, with you two here, and knowing I can leave. Like actually leave and live somewhere else."

"You will be free," Ellen said.

Holly smiled, and the penny dropped. So she'd brought it up to help derail Holly's downward emotional spiral. It seemed to have worked.

"I'm ready to start," she murmured. "How long do we have? There's a party tonight?"

"Yes," Ellen replied. "We've got about..." She checked her phone. "I'd say three hours here before we should head back and start getting ready."

"Plenty of time," Holly said. "And I've actually got a lot of cleaning supplies. I kept meaning to do this seriously, and I got far enough that I bought it, just..." She trailed off, looking over the messy desolation of her apartment.

"We'll make it work," Ellen said. "How about you start sorting through this stuff, figure out what you want to keep and what you're comfortable getting rid of? Gabe and I will start getting rid of the trash and deal with the dishes."

"All right," Holly replied.

And so they set to work.

...

They spent all three hours cleaning, and would have continued had Ellen's alarm not gone off.

Gabe expected it to be boring but necessary work, only it wasn't. Fun wasn't really the word, but after a bit, he ferreted that word out, and it was: satisfying. The work was satisfying, and he knew it was more so because he was doing it to help Holly.

He loved her.

That he was in love with Ellen was something that was obvious to him. He had begun the process of falling in love with Ellen years ago, in that break room, talking with her about everything that crossed their minds. It had grown in her absence, and yes, he had indeed put her up on a pedestal. He thought of her the same way most people thought of movie stars.

But it was clearly evening out...probably.

It was, admittedly, hard to tell.

That he loved Holly, though...

He didn't question it, because it felt not all that different from how he felt about Ellen. It more surprised him than anything. That he liked Holly was no surprise. That he was in lust with her was no surprise either. That he wanted to date her and live with her? Same thing.

That he loved her? After two weeks?

That was the surprising part. He heard stories all the time of people falling in love very, very quickly, but had often written those off as lust. And he still believed that, in most cases, he was right. People often mistook the honeymoon period for love.

Somehow, though, he knew he was right about Holly.

Or perhaps he was just deluding himself.

But even then, even if what they were feeling was just the honeymoon phase, well...he still believed that Holly was a great fit for them. He would have welcomed her into their home and their life even if he wasn't in love with her.

And so he worked happily to clean up her apartment. He washed and ran a load of dishes in her tiny dishwasher, then took to cleaning out the fridge. It was a nasty business, a lot of things had expired in there, and when he ran the garbage bag he'd filled up down to the dumpster, he was extremely grateful. About the time he finished cleaning the fridge, (and he did a great job, as far as he was concerned), the dishwasher was finished.

He unloaded and reloaded it, then set to cleaning the counters and the sink.

Ellen and Holly made very good headway on the rest of the apartment. They cleaned up all the trash, and got through two loads of laundry. Holly seemed to be in a clean slate sort of mood, as she threw out or agreed to donate a great deal of stuff.

By the time they were done, she had filled her backpack with clothes and books, and claimed that load represented probably ninety percent of what she was actually going to take with her.

They went home, showered and prepared for a fancy party and changed into nice clothes. Gabe kept trying to tease either Ellen or Holly into having sex with him during the process, because they did have enough time for a roll in bed, but neither would engage with him. They both had that look, the look of a woman who was preparing to spring something on her significant other, and was looking forward to it with immense, joyous anticipation.

Gabe somehow managed not to comment on it, though he really, really wanted to.

"So...either I forgot or I never asked, but what actually are we doing?" Holly asked.

They were in Ellen's nice car now, Holly in the back, Gabe driving, Ellen beside him.

"We're celebrating a divorce," Ellen replied.

"Oh. Wow," Holly murmured.

"Yes. Potentially touchy subject but I think it'll be a mostly relaxed affair. The host of the party is a woman named Isabella. She's a surgeon and a bit older than all of us. Somewhere in her mid forties, I think," Ellen explained.

"Is this going to be like...a rich person party?" Holly asked.

"Not quite? I mean, I imagine her house is going to be big and nice. And yes, there's going to be a group of well off people there. Lawyers, doctors, a few scientists, I think. But Abby's social circle is...not usual. I know for a fact there's going to be a personal trainer, that author you were speaking with at the other party, Gabe, a grocer, a pharmacist, and a random assortment of other people. Abby tends to make friends with people who don't really discriminate in most cases," Ellen replied.

"How'd she meet a surgeon?" Gabe asked.

"Her husband—ex now—was a lawyer at Abby's law firm. I imagine he invited her to one of their parties a few years back to try and nail her. But when it became obvious she was a lesbian he lost interest and Abby pretty quickly lost any interest in being his friend. However, she got along with the guy's wife like a house on fire. At least this is what Emily tells me. But don't worry, you two, it's not going to be weird. No one's going to be looking down their noses at you as they guffaw over 'the poors'," Ellen replied.

"I don't think I've ever heard anyone actually say the word guffaw out loud," Gabe said. He paused. "It sounds so fucking stupid out loud."

"Yeah, it does," Ellen agreed after considering it. Then she smirked and looked out the window.

"Okay, so, I can't hold it in any longer. What the fuck are you smirking about?" he asked.

"I have no idea what you're talking about," Ellen replied without looking at him.

Gabe glanced in the rearview mirror. Holly was smirking, too. Well, hers was closer to a smile, she was too sweet to really smirk. "You two are both in on it...you can't lie to me Holly, what's going on?"

"Uh...I don't know...what you mean," she murmured awkwardly, looking down at her shoes abruptly.

"We're going to a party, love of my life, and that's all you need to know, Gabe," Ellen replied sweetly but firmly.

"Uh-huh."

"You trust me, obviously."

"Obviously."

"So you trust that if anything *is* going on–not to say that there is–then it's something that's happening with your best interests taken into consideration."

Gabe sighed heavily after a long moment. "You and your fucking secrets."

"I keep almost *zero* secrets from you, and the ones that I do, you know about them," Ellen replied. "Don't pretend you're annoyed." He sighed but said nothing else. Ellen simply smiled a bit wider. "Now, Holly, I know you've got anxiety problems, so if you want, just stay near me, okay? I'll keep you safe."

"Thank you," she murmured.

"Always, sweetheart. You *are* my girlfriend now. And Gabe's girlfriend...you must be really happy, dear. Two girlfriends?"

"I mean obviously," he replied. "Why wouldn't I be?"

"Just take care that you don't take us for granted," she said.

"I genuinely don't see that happening."

"Which is why you need to take care. It's the problems you don't think you'll face that do the most damage."

"...okay, that's a fair point."

A moment of silence passed.

"I hope it won't be weird, with Emily and Abby," Gabe said. "Now that I've...done all that I have with Em."

"It'll be fine," Ellen replied. "Okay, we're almost there."

CHAPTER TWENTY SIX

As Gabe parked by the curb in front of the house in question, he immediately felt his confidence slip a notch.

He thought that Abby and Emily had had a really big house, but theirs was small compared to this one. It was closer to what he thought of as a mansion. It was huge and at three stories looked ridiculously large for what was supposed to be just a house.

And there were about twenty cars parked either along the side of the road or in the huge driveway.

"Fuck me," Gabe muttered as he stared up at the brightly lit house.

"It's a bit bigger than I was led to believe," Ellen murmured.

"That looks like a movie set," Holly whispered. "I definitely don't belong here."

"Now dear, none of that," Ellen said. "Come on, let's go have some fun."

Gabe tried to reach for that confidence he'd been building over the past several weeks as he got out of the car and began walking across the lawn with Ellen and Holly. Surprisingly, he found it, though it wasn't as powerful as he'd hoped.

Still though, he felt a long way from where he had been when he'd moved into that crappy little studio apartment.

Good lord, was that just a month ago?

It felt like last year.

He noticed Holly was sticking close to him and he took her hand, slipping a sidelong glance her way. She caught his eye and smiled shyly, squeezing his hand.

"I actually kind of wish I had that choker with your name on it now," she murmured.

"Seriously?" he asked.

"Yeah. I...don't know. I guess I'm thinking about, you know, if people hit on me. It'd be nice if I had something that...tied me to you?"

"She wants you mark your territory," Ellen said. "I do too, actually."

"Hopefully not literally," Gabe replied.

"No, I can't say I'm into being peed on. But...I'd do it if you asked me," Holly murmured.

"Hmm. Well...interesting to know. But I'm not into that either, so I think we're good there," Gabe replied. He paused. "Wait."

They both stopped as well, almost to the door now.

"What?" Ellen asked.

"I got an idea." He reached into his pocket and pulled out a slim black sharpie. "I *can* mark you...if you want."

Holly's eyes actually seem to light up and she broke into a broad grin. "Yes, do it," she replied immediately, stepping closer and raising her chin, exposing her throat.

"Why do you have a sharpie?" Ellen asked.

"Habit, I guess. Not really sure why I started," he replied. Gabe popped the top off and stepped up to Holly. He wrote **GABE'S GIRL** at the base of her throat, just above where her collarbones met. She gasped softly and fidgeted as he did this. He finished by drawing a circle around the words.

Then he turned to Ellen.

"Your turn," he said.

"Oh is it?" she asked, amused. "Will you make me?"

"No," he replied.

"Maybe you should," she said demurely.

Gabe stared up at her for a long moment. "...lean forward, Ellen."

"Yes, sir," she whispered, leaning forward.

Gabe looked down her shirtfront at her enormous breasts, then wrote the same thing in the same spot. She made no noise, but she shivered a few times.

"There," he said, "now everyone will know."

"How will everyone know who Gabe is though?" Holly murmured.

"It's not about that, it's about them knowing that you're *mine*," Gabe replied, reaching out and running a finger slowly along her jawline. "Aren't you?"

"Yes," she whispered.

"Yes what?"

"Yes, sir."

"Maybe I should take you two somewhere private and make you blow me," he said.

"That's a thought," Ellen said, smirking. "I guess we'll see how the night plays out, won't we?"

"I guess we will," he agreed.

They resumed walking towards the enormous house, and damn if Holly didn't have more of a spring her in step. She seemed actually more confident, or at least calmer. Gabe wasn't sure what to make of that, but he could at least tell she was happier now, and so he just accepted it. He certainly felt happier.

They rang the doorbell, which was one of those long, drawn-out series of tones that fancy houses all seemed to have, at least in the movies. He could hear people talking inside, and then after a long moment, the front door opened up to show an attractive, middle-aged woman with shoulder-length dark brown hair and smooth olive skin.

"Hello," she said warmly. "You *have* to be Ellen. Which would make you Gabe and Holly."

"Correct on all three accounts," Ellen said.

"I'm Isabella, welcome to my home, and thank you for coming," she replied.

Gabe saw her eyes flick so very briefly to Ellen's and then Holly's necks, and then she stepped back to make room for them.

"Thank you for having us," he said as they came inside.

Something was off. He realized that immediately and puzzled over it as he got out of his shoes and his hoodie. It didn't feel *bad*, whatever it was. Gabe was realizing, the more time he spent around Ellen and Abby and women like them, older and high-powered and used to being in charge, that he did indeed have skills related to picking up on things.

In some way that had somehow been conveyed through little more than tone and body language, Gabe had the impression that Isabella was opening a door for him. A rather specific door. A door that granted access to a room of flirtation.

He had no idea how he knew this, and if he didn't feel it so strongly, he would have immediately passed it out of hand, because the notion that a middle-aged woman who was staggeringly attractive *and* successful *and* intelligent (if surgeons weren't very intelligent then who the fuck was?), would be coming onto him felt ridiculous.

Or, more specifically, wanting him to come onto her.

Let alone in front of both of his girlfriends.

But...

She *was* a very close friend of Abby's, it seemed,

and Abby and Ellen had been speaking a great deal just recently. And they all knew he was coming to this party. And Ellen and Holly had both been acting just a little weird on the way here…

Gabe took a calculated risk.

"I understand you're celebrating a divorce."

He sensed all three of them react to that, Holly less subtly than the others. But they did react. If he didn't have such a strong suspicion, he definitely wouldn't have said that, because it felt extremely presumptuous to broach what, for all he might know, was a very sensitive topic.

Gabe looked more directly at Isabella as he finished speaking. Her eyes were very, very blue and they seemed to sparkle with something like excitement.

She stuck a finger in her wineglass, swirling the wine within around for a moment. "You understand correctly," she said, her tone almost neutral.

She brought her finger out, stuck it in her mouth, and sucked on it as she slowly withdrew it.

Before he could respond, she spoke again. "I'm afraid I need to go continue a conversation I was having. There's food and drinks in the kitchen, a firepit out back, and board games in the basement. Have fun!"

"Thank you, we will," he replied.

She smiled and then walked away.

Was she swinging her hips?

He watched her disappear out of the foyer and deeper into the house, and thought yes, she seemed to be swinging them more than would be natural. She was wearing a sleek black dress that was doing a whole hell of a lot to show off her gently padded frame.

"Gabe, what was that!?" Ellen whispered, a huge smile on her face.

"What?" he replied.

"Don't fucking 'what' me!" she snapped. "That was like a precision shot from a mile away. That was like...'taking the fucking Coriolis Effect into account' precise."

"The *what?*" Holly asked.

"It's a sniper and pilot thing, your perception gets a little screwed up-it doesn't matter. Did I really?" he asked.

"Yes! I saw that. Do-do you *know?*" she asked suddenly.

"Know what?" he replied.

Ellen stared at him for a long moment, then sighed. "This is getting out of hand."

"What is?"

"Your ability to outmaneuver me."

"Am I?"

She stared at him even harder. "I *actually* cannot tell if you're fucking with me right now. Holy shit."

"Are you getting turned on?" he asked.

"It looks that way," Holly murmured.

"Fuck's sake, let's just go find Em and Abby," Ellen growled.

Hmm. That wasn't exactly a confirmation, but obviously *something* was up. Were they seriously trying to hook him up with Isabella? That would be beyond amazing, she looked like an Italian supermodel who had only recently retired. Not because she was losing her looks, but because she was beginning to show her age, and standards were fucking ridiculous.

Ellen led them deeper into the house. As they passed out of the entryway and into an expansive living room, Gabe saw about a dozen people gathered in small groups, scattered across the large room, most of them with wineglasses in their hands, chatting calmly. The far back wall was mostly glass and it let on a huge backyard beyond a large wooden deck.

There were more people out there, either standing on the deck or sitting around a bonfire that was deeper in the yard.

Everyone turned and gave Ellen a lingering look. She ignored them as she scanned the room and spied Abby and Emily sitting on a couch not far from a large fireplace. They both smiled when they saw her, and Ellen led Gabe and Holly over.

"You made it," Abby said. "And...oh my God, Ellen. Really?"

"What?" Ellen replied.

"What's that say...oh wow," Emily said, then giggled. "I can't believe you let him write that on you, Ellen."

"Oh shut up, both of you," Ellen replied, blushing. Gabe glanced at her. She actually seemed off balance, socially speaking, which he rarely saw. "I don't have to defend my choices."

"Not at all," Emily replied. "I'm just...surprised, is all. How's it going?"

Ellen seemed to relax after a moment. "Fine," she said. "How about you two?"

"I'm still sore," Emily said, shooting a look at Gabe, who shifted awkwardly.

"We're fine," Abby said, rolling her eyes. "You three look sharp."

"Thank you. So do you," Gabe replied.

"Shut up," Emily muttered, taking a drink from the glass she held.

"Now that you've been inside her, she's all weird

about you," Abby said with a smirk.

"Shut *up,*" Emily hissed.

"You wanna hang out? Talk for a bit?" Gabe asked.

Emily looked up at him for a moment, then glanced briefly at Abby, then sighed softly and got to her feet. "I would, actually, yes."

"Go on, you two," Abby said.

"Yeah, I'm sure you'd like slip off with him for a little fun," Ellen said.

"You know what? Maybe I will-oh my lord."

"What?" Gabe asked, turning as he saw her staring back the way they'd come. "Holy mother of God," he whispered.

"Whoa," Holly murmured.

"What the fuck's going on?" Abby asked, standing up.

They were all staring at what seemed to be a new arrival, a woman in her mid to late twenties who was not simply stunningly beautiful but was also gothed out hardcore. She was speaking with Isabella at the threshold between the main entryway and the living room.

She wore a simple black dress and fishnet stockings up all four limbs. She had on a black choker collar. Her hair was as jet black as her clothes, chin-length, down and framing a face that was ice white. She had on black lipstick and a lot of mascara.

"Fuck me she's hot," Abby whispered.

"Anyone know her?" Ellen asked.

"Nope," Abby murmured, and everyone else said the same. A long moment of silence passed. Abby sat back down.

"Stop staring or you'll freak her out," she murmured.

"Right," Ellen said, turning away.

"Gabe, you *have* to hit on her," Holly whispered harshly. They all looked at her. "What!? I mean, right?"

"Just surprised you're the one saying it," Ellen replied with a smirk. "But you are one hundred percent correct, Holly. Gabe needs to hit on her."

"Why is this my responsibility?" he muttered.

"You don't *want to?*" Emily asked.

"Of course I want to, she's just...*way* out of my league," he replied. "I'd absolutely fuck up."

"First of all you're wrong," Emily said. "Second of all, you probably wouldn't fuck it up."

"But Gabe does need to slow play it," Ellen murmured. "And he needs a...an ace in the hole."

"Uh, what were you thinking?" he replied.

Her smirk broadened. "Don't worry, I've already got one lined up."

Gabe noticed every other woman there smile when she said that, though none of them were looking at him when they did it. "Does *everyone* know what's going on but me?"

Ellen looked at him suddenly and closely, then laughed softly. "Apparently. Go on, go with Emily, walk around, see the place, mingle."

Gabe looked at her, then at Holly, then sighed. "All right." He leaned forward and kissed Ellen, then Holly. "Love you two." He turned to Emily and raised one arm. "Come on."

She looked at him, then his arm, then giggled. "What the fuck, dude?"

"Oh shut it," he replied.

She snorted and then looped her arm through his. "Lead on, sir knight."

Holly laughed, too.

Gabe sighed heavily. "All this fucking sass I'm forced to endure."

"Yeah, forced," Ellen replied, rolling her eyes. "What an unutterable burden."

He and Emily walked away.

CHAPTER TWENTY SEVEN

They moved elsewhere in the house, eventually ending up in the kitchen.

"Holy crap," Gabe muttered as they looked around.

"Yep," Emily replied. "You thought me and Abby were well off. No way, not compared to this. Surgeon plus lawyer times twenty years equals a *fuckload* of money. Although I get why she's selling it all."

"Really?" he asked as they made their way over to one of the two counter islands in the middle of the expansive kitchen.

"Yep. I know Isabella kind of well. We've gotten drunk together and shared stories that we wouldn't tell most people. I know her and Abby are very close. I'd honestly have been a bit more concerned if I didn't know for a fact that she was straight."

Gabe gave her a sidelong glance as they investigated the food that was on offer. There was a lot of it, a great deal of variety, and it all looked very high quality. They each grabbed a plate and began grabbing an assortment of food.

"I mean this with no disrespect at all, but...how to put this...your insecurity level is not proportionate to your physical attractiveness," he said.

She scoffed. "Yeah, well, I was cheated on."

"Oh. God. Sorry," he muttered.

"It's fine, you didn't know. Let's just say...there's a lot more to relationships than being hot."

"Yeah, I know that, it's just–"

"It's just that who the fuck would cheat on me? I

actually know exactly how you feel. I know I'm hot, but it didn't really matter. Hot just gets your foot in the door. It's not enough for the basis of an actual relationship. I thought the *exact* same goddamned thing about Ellen. Who in their right mind would cheat on her? She's the whole package. Ridiculously attractive, smart, funny, kind, confident, fun, sexy...and yet? More than once. But as for me? This probably shouldn't be much of a surprise but before Abby came around my love life was one tragedy after another."

"Seriously?"

"Yeah. I'm...if you haven't picked up on it yet, Gabe, I'm kind of a mess. And a lot of that is my fault. I'm...what I imagine a goblin girl would be like, you know? Very wild, very crazy, poor impulse control. Fun to hook up with, fun to date for a while, not exactly marriage material, though."

"So...are you saying, uh...did *you* ever...?"

She sighed and looked away.

"Oh," he murmured.

"I didn't cheat," she said firmly, looking back at him. "But...I did blow up at least two relationships over some horny shit. I always had a rule: I'd break up before I'd cheat. And, well, that's exactly what I did. Broke up with my present boyfriend, well, once boyfriend, once girlfriend, because someone who made me feel *way* hornier started hitting on me and I knew I wouldn't be able to say no. I'm very ashamed of myself, so you don't have to rub it in," she muttered.

"I...wasn't going to," he replied.

She sighed. "Right. Because you're so nice." A long pause went by as they sat down at one of the few small tables lined up in front of a window looking onto a side yard. "Sorry, that was mean."

"Is it going to be weird between us now that we've...you know?" he asked.

"No," she replied. "I'm sorry, I'm bitchy right now. I'm grateful to be here, it's just that this shit all makes me insecure."

"Why?"

"Oh my God, come on, Gabe. You know why," she replied.

"I wanted to give you an opportunity to tell me," he said. "And maybe I got it wrong."

"You're too reasonable for your own good," she muttered. "But fine. I'm a trashy party girl. *Former,* I may add, but that's my past, and kind of my present. I mean I sure toned it down. Now that I'm in my thirties, I wanna just chill. But I mean look at me. Just a glance can tell you I'm trashy. And I never really fit into this kind of scene, this is Abby's scene. I'm not made for upper class. Fuck, I'm not even made for middle class."

"You don't look trashy, Emily," Gabe replied. "You look...exotic."

She stared at him over the table, an assemblage of cheese, meat, and cracker halfway to her mouth. Finally, she put it back down. "...don't take this the wrong way, but there's a part of me that's really convinced you're being nice to me because you want to fuck me."

"I *do* want that, but that's not the only reason," he replied.

"I know."

"Is that not on the table anymore? I'm okay with it if it isn't."

She twisted her lips, seeming to consider it. "So...Abby would prefer that it not become a habit, and I'm inclined to agree with her. It was fun, but...if it goes on too often, I think it might complicate things. But we would rather treat it as a...rare and infrequent delicacy?"

"Very, very happy with that," Gabe replied.

She smiled. "I really appreciate that. I'm glad that, despite the fact that we're hooking up, it doesn't seem to be overshadowing or defining our entire friendship. Hookup culture is...many things, but typically speaking, it is not conducive to friendship. 'Friends with benefits' usually just means 'I can fuck you and you expect nothing from me'. For a lot of guys, at least. And don't get me wrong, girls too, it's just...rarer among women. But anyway, my point is, I'm glad it didn't get weird or unpleasant for anyone involved."

"Same," he agreed.

"I think..." Emily trailed off as she glanced to the side and her eyes seemed to glaze over a little bit and her mouth hang open. He followed her gaze. Through one of the doors that led into the kitchen, they could now see the goth girl.

She was talking with another party goer, a guy in a business suit. Well, she was more being talked at by him.

She looked bored and vaguely irritated.

"Good fucking God, Gabe, that is such a hot woman," Emily whispered finally. "You *need* to hit that."

"I think you are just *way* overestimating my abilities," he replied.

"Gabe." Emily looked back at him. "You landed Ellen. You landed Holly. You landed *me*. You've got Krystal gagging for your cock. Congrats, by the by, about Holly."

"You heard, huh?"

"Yes. She's a little sweetheart and I want her. The next time you and I do hook up, I want her there, involved. I want her eating my pussy," she murmured quietly, looking around. "While you fucking ram her from the back."

"I want that, too. And will happily provide it. However, you're still overestimating. Ellen was a *very* unique case. Holly happened also because of Ellen, she did most of the flirtation. Krystal...is also a unique situation, and Ellen's fault."

"And me?" she asked, leaning forward and raising an eyebrow.

"You were horny for a guy, I was apparently attractive enough and safe enough that you could put me to use," he replied.

"Uh-huh. You're pretty fucking cute, and you're confident. Or, you should be, at least. Also, Gabe, listen to me, okay? This is important: that girl is looking for a guy just like you."

"What?" He stole another glance at the goth chick. She looked more annoyed now, and the guy talking to her either didn't notice or didn't care that he was striking out. Gabe wondered vaguely why she was still talking with him.

The goth chick suddenly looked at him. They locked eyes for just one instant, and then Gabe looked away, back to Emily.

"She looked right at you," she murmured.

"Yep," he replied. "And I don't know…"

"Okay, so, do you not want her? Because you seem like you do…"

"Of course I want her. I just don't think I can land her. She's ridiculously fucking hot. And she has the air of a woman who *knows* just how fucking hot she is."

"She might not think so. That could be projection on our part. Or maybe she thinks the same thing about you. We don't know why she's here but I think you have a pretty decent shot. You're a writer and she looks like she might be into that," Emily replied.

"Okay, okay. I'll do it. But...I need time. I also need you to tell me what's going on."

"What...do you mean?" she replied, looking down at her plate.

"You all have obviously got something going on. You're planning something. What is it?"

"No idea what you're talking about."

He stared hard at her. She kept looking down at her plate. He sighed. "So that's how it's going to be, huh?"

"I'm afraid so," Emily replied, smirking now.

"Fine. Just...finish up and then accompany me. I need to do some reconnaissance."

"Ooh, big word."

"Shut up."

She looked up abruptly. "Why don't you make me?"

"*Please* do not tempt me."

Emily smirked and went back to eating.

...

Gabe doubted more than an hour passed, but it felt like much longer.

With Emily's, and later Abby's and then Holly's help, he wandered the party, mingling and just generally hanging out, all the while scoping out the mystery woman.

It felt strange and kind of creepy to do, and he

was prepared to break off at a moment's notice, but he caught her eye more than once over the course of that hour. And she never looked annoyed or angry or afraid.

She looked…

Intrigued.

Maybe he really did have a shot.

This was the thought he found himself clinging to when the opportunity finally arose. He wasn't sure how he knew, but at some point he caught her eye again and something seemed to pass between them. More than that, she suddenly looked resolved, like she had just come to a decision. What he felt was that she was going to talk to him.

So he took the opportunity to wrap up his conversation, (he had been speaking with Margo, the woman from the party in the forest who'd been chatting him up about his books, as she was more than happy to do it again), and then made his way into a library/reading area. It was empty of people and it made perfect sense why he'd go in there.

He made sure the goth woman saw him walk in there.

He tried to stay confident, and was again surprised to find that his stomach wasn't boiling. Well, okay, it wasn't boiling *that* much. He was still pretty nervous. This was a *wicked* hot woman, and a goth girl to boot.

As much as he had a thing for tall women and redheads and tattooed women…

He *really* had a thing for goth girls.

Gabe examined some of the books for a moment. There were hundreds upon hundreds of them. Enough time passed that he wondered if he was wrong, that she hadn't decided to talk to him, and just as he was beginning to reassess how to handle this or if maybe he should give it up, he suddenly heard the faintest sound of someone entering the room behind him.

Still, for a few seconds, nothing happened, no statement was forthcoming.

Gabe glanced without moving his head too much at a window not far from him, pretending to look at another book. He could see that it was indeed her. She was lingering in the doorway, just looking at him. Her expression was hard to read.

Finally, deciding he should probably give her more of an opening, he turned around, pretending he hadn't noticed her yet, then stopped as they locked eyes.

"Hi," he said.

"Hey," she replied. "Sorry if I startled you."

"It's fine," he said.

Another awkward moment passed. Up close, she was staggeringly attractive. Her cleavage was also even more impressive when viewed from the front. In fact, it was almost gratuitous. He wondered, suddenly, if she'd done that on purpose, to see who would look.

"I was talking to one of the others and I heard that you're an author?" she asked finally.

"I am," he replied. "Well, self-published author with not a whole lot on the market right now. But I'd call myself that."

"Would it be imposing to ask you about it? I'm...curious."

"No, not at all," he said, gesturing to one of the comfortable seats in the library. "I'm Gabe."

"Chloe," she said, sitting down across from him as he took the other seat. She seemed pretty in control of herself, but there was a vague, or perhaps well-hidden, undercurrent of social anxiety.

"What do you want to know?" he asked.

"What kind of books do you write?"

He smiled a little awkwardly, he couldn't help it. This was always the weird part, no matter how he felt about it. "I write erotica."

Now came the moment of truth. How would she react to that? It clearly caught her off guard, but after a brief pause, the smallest hint of a smile touched the corners of her mouth. "Really? That's...interesting."

"Is it?"

She laughed softly. "Yes. Normally people try to frame it as romance or maybe spicy romance, I've heard that one a lot."

He shrugged. "No point in hiding it. I'm not ashamed and I have no one to hide it from for fear of getting fired."

"Oh. So...you're your own boss? It's going that well?" she asked.

He laughed. "Well, heh, let's not get ahead of ourselves there. I'm in some pretty unique circumstances that...really lowers the bar for what might be called success," he said.

"Okay. What exactly does that mean?"

"I'm living in a house for three hundred dollars a month," he replied. "I found a really unique scenario. Or, in other words, I got extremely lucky."

"How the hell did you manage that?" she replied.

"Found someone who has money, is a kind person, and wants to be a patron of the arts."

She laughed, then hesitated, slowly losing her smile. "Wait, you're serious? You're not fucking with me?"

"I'm not fucking with you."

"That's insane. And...amazing." Chloe shifted in

her chair, pursing her lips as she seemed to study him. Gabe had to admit, he was having a hard time getting a reading on how the conversation was going. "So what exactly do you write? Like, what kind of erotica?"

"Well I haven't had a whole lot of time to get going, honestly. I've barely got over a dozen short works right now. I really just started back in August or so–"

"Wait, hold on. You started taking writing seriously barely a few months ago and you're already paying your bills with it?"

Gabe chuckled. She reminded him of Ellen in a way, she was pretty brash, but with Ellen's...refinement? Tempering of it, maybe.

"Yes, but like I said: luck."

"It can't *all* be luck, you've got to be pretty decent at it." She smiled a little. "So come on, what'd you write about?"

"Well..."

Gabe lost track of time for a while there, telling her about what he'd written so far, mostly because she kept asking questions. Not that he at all minded answering them. The longer they went on talking, the more he began to find himself believing that maybe she was into him. It still seemed pretty unlikely, but Ellen, Holly, Emily, even Krystal had been telling him over the past month of ways to tell a woman was into you.

"What about you?" he asked when he ran out of things to say.

"What about me?" Chloe replied. She seemed a lot more relaxed now at least.

"What creative thing are you into?"

She shifted slightly, her smile getting just a tiny

bit bigger. "Why do you assume I've got a creative thing I'm into?"

"First off: everyone has something creative they're into. Secondly: no one asks me this much about my craft unless they have a lot of personal interest invested in their own creative endeavor," he replied.

She snorted. "Your *craft?*" He stared at her. She lost her smile and cleared her throat. "Uh. Sorry." She opened her mouth, then hesitated and looked back towards the library's exit. "I'm thirsty, you wanna get something to drink?"

"Sure," he replied.

They both got up and headed back to the kitchen. He saw Emily deeper in the living room, talking with Abby. He couldn't see Ellen or Holly anywhere. Emily gave him a desperately inquisitive look. He shrugged. She bared her teeth at him, looking wildly frustrated, and it was hard not to laugh.

He and Chloe ended up in the kitchen. They got some sodas and sat exactly where he and Emily had been sitting.

"Well?" he asked.

"Oh, right," she replied. "Me. Uh, well, I'm not that interesting."

"You know everyone says that? Although I guess it makes sense to say if you don't want to sound like you're full of yourself. But interest, like beauty, is definitely in the eye of the beholder."

Chloe paused before responding, giving him a slightly recalculating look, then subtly adjusted herself, then leaned forward not so subtly.

It took a surprising amount of willpower not to look down at her pale breasts, which were now almost falling out of her midnight black dress. He wasn't sure he'd call the past hour flirtatious, though he'd made what he hoped were a few subtle passes at her. Either this was her deciding to respond to this latest one, or she was finally picking up on it.

Ellen had told him at some point that men didn't have an exclusive reign over missing obvious signs.

"All right then," Chloe said, sounding a little amused now. "Me. I like goth stuff, obviously. I working a boring-ass job as a barista that I hate with all my dark little heart but allows me to pay for my crappy little apartment."

"Really? As a barista? You must be amazing at it."

She laughed and rolled her eyes. "No, I'm really not. It's mostly tips because, well," she looked down at her considerable chest.

"Ah." Gabe took another calculated risk. "I can see why."

She paused, just for a moment, then smiled a little more. "Yes, quite. It's annoying but we all have gifts and apparently my gift is big tits."

"Among other things."

"I...what's that mean?"

"Clearly you have a gift for the goth look. I'm guessing you did all this yourself."

She paused again, then chuckled. Was she blushing? "Yes, I'm a one woman show. And...thank you. But, uh, anyway. I'm a streamer. Or, well, I'm trying to be, anyway."

"What kind of games? Do you have a theme?" he asked.

"Horror," she replied, then rolled her eyes. "I know, it's dumb but it seemed to go well with the whole goth look."

"It's not dumb," he said. "There's a lot of really

good horror games out there...do you know Emily?"

"No. I actually hardly know anyone here. I was coming here with a friend of mine who knows...someone else here that I don't know, but she ditched at the last second and *didn't* tell me until I was basically here. So I figured fuck it, why not?"

"That sucks, but at least you're here...so, Emily, she's the dark-haired woman with the tattoo sleeves. She used to be a streamer a while ago, you might want to chat her up about that."

"Oh, right, her. I saw you with her for a while. I thought you two were together, from the way she was with you, but...she's got a wedding ring and you don't."

"Ah. Yes. Uh, we're not...together."

"You sort of hesitated there," she said, sounding interested.

He chuckled and cleared his throat. "We're friends."

"Friends. Hmm. How about *you?* What are you doing here? Actually," she said, sitting up suddenly, "maybe you can tell me: who the hell is that blonde woman? The *really* tall one? She looks like a fucking supermodel and she seems kind of out of place here..."

He laughed. "Uh, yeah. Her name's Ellen, she..."

Gabe hesitated as he sensed someone coming up behind him. Turning, he saw Isabella on approach. He'd noticed her throughout the night, watching him, sometimes talking with Ellen, sometimes talking with Abby, often one of them talking quietly about something while they both stared at him.

"Hello. I'm sorry to interrupt," Isabella said, then she leaned in and put her lips very close to Gabe's ear, "but will you please follow me?...upstairs?" she whispered.

"Of course," Gabe replied, standing up. "Chloe, uh...I'll be back when I can. The hostess needs to see me about something."

Chloe looked confused and a little annoyed. "Right," she said after a moment, "well, I'll be here."

Gabe nodded and began following Isabella out of the kitchen.

CHAPTER TWENTY EIGHT

Whatever the thing they'd been keeping from him was, it was happening.

That much was obvious.

"So...what exactly is going on?" Gabe asked as they headed upstairs. "I know something is, you and Ellen have been giggling at me all night."

Isabella glanced back over her shoulder, smiling. "Ellen was right about you," she murmured as she led him farther upstairs, past the second story and up to the third. "You've very direct."

"She really brings that out in me," he replied.

"I appreciate that. Honestly, you have no idea how *much* I appreciate that after twenty fucking years of passive-aggressive bullsh–" She stopped herself as they reached the third floor. "No. I'm not doing this. Not talking about this. Sorry. It was a rough divorce."

"I understand, and I'm sorry, that sounds awful," Gabe replied.

She turned fully to favor him with a smile. "They said they wouldn't tell you and that this would be a surprise, and I would be the one who got to spring it on you. And I feel confident in how it will go, but before we go along with it, I wanted to have an honest and open conversation about it."

"I'm listening."

"As you know, I'm celebrating my divorce. And that means many things. But one thing that it means, one thing I began speaking with Abby about, which led me to Ellen, which led me to *you,* is that, obviously, I would very much like to have sex with...well, someone new. Obviously someone I'm attracted to, someone who's safe, someone who's attracted to me...but I want to be completely sure that we're on the same page. I saw the way you were looking at me, more than once, but looking and fucking are two very different things..."

"Ah," Gabe replied, sure that he was blushing now. "I thought something like this might be happening. Honestly, I'd hoped." He looked her up and down. "I had *really* hoped. And you can rest assured that I am *deeply* sexually attracted to you and will be extremely grateful for the opportunity to sleep with you. Provided Ellen and Holly sign off on it definitively."

Her smile widened. "I'm very glad to hear that. In that case, please follow me. They're waiting for us."

Isabella led him down the hall to one door in particular and opened it up. He walked in behind her, finding a lavish bedroom. Ellen and Holly were both seated on a small loveseat together across the room. Both of them were smiling broadly.

"Happy early birthday," Ellen said, looking exquisitely satisfied with herself.

"Wait, when is your birthday?" Holly asked.

"Later, dearest," Ellen whispered.

"Oh. Right. Sorry. Just-ignore me."

"So when you were asking if I *know,* love of my life, you meant, did I *know* whether or not you were hooking me up with a ridiculously attractive, recently divorced cougar?" he asked.

"Exactly...did you?" Ellen asked.

"Ridiculously attractive?" Isabella murmured.

"Ridiculously," he agreed. "And no, I didn't know."

"Wait, so...you just seriously pulled that off on the fly?" Ellen asked.

"Apparently," he replied.

Ellen began to reply, hesitated, then composed herself. "All right...we're invisible now. Just do your thing."

"I almost feel bad," Isabella said as she began taking her dress off. "You were absolutely hitting it off with Chloe."

"That goth woman!?" Ellen asked, almost leaping out of her seat. "Really!?"

"I mean, I hope so," Gabe replied.

"What? Honey, no. I saw her when I was coming in to get you. That girl was *into* you, handsome. Whatever you were doing, it was working," Isabella said.

"Oh my God," Ellen whispered. "I...mmm! Fuck! Okay, you two have fun...maybe I should go down there and...fuck! Wow, this is quite the rock and the hard place. I want to watch you two have sex but I also don't want to let her get away...fuck!"

"Relax, babe," Gabe said as he took off his shirt.

"How can you be so calm!?" she cried.

"Because, as I've said many times, she's out of my league."

"Gabe...not to sound arrogant, but you're about to have sex with me, while your two extremely beautiful girlfriends watch," Isabella said.

"Very good point *oh wow,*" he said as she pushed her dress and panties down in one smooth motion, revealing her nude body.

"What?" she asked, looking a little more uncertain.

"You are...so very attractive. Good lord," he muttered.

"Yep," Ellen said. Holly made a noise of affirmation.

"Oh. Well...thank you," she murmured. "You should take your clothes off, too."

"Right."

Gabe finished getting undressed and quickly stood as naked as she was before him. Isabella looked him up and down, studying him for a bit before walking forward and taking his hand. He let her lead him up onto her large, lavish bed. As he climbed onto it, Gabe thought he could sense something off about the situation.

He looked at Isabella closely as they settled into place among the silken blankets and soft pillows. She looked seductive, mature, and...nervous. Before he could consider it further, she kissed him hard on the mouth, grabbing one of his hands and bringing it to her breast. As they began making out, Gabe immediately felt that sense of something being off again, only much stronger now.

After a moment he pulled back.

"What? Is something wrong?" Isabella asked a little breathlessly.

"Uh...I was gonna ask you the same thing," he replied.

She stared at him for a drawn out moment, then began slowly chewing on her lower lip. The moment seemed to expand uncomfortably.

"I...need a minute," she said finally.

"All right," Gabe replied.

"I'll, uh, be right back."

He watched as she got up off the bed and hurried over to a bathroom. She disappeared behind a closed door. Gabe rolled over and looked at Ellen and Holly.

"Oops," Ellen murmured.

"What exactly was that?" Gabe replied.

"I was worried about this."

"She did seem really nervous sometimes," Holly murmured.

"So did I fuck up or…?" Gabe asked, sitting up.

"No, babe. This isn't anything you did," Ellen replied. "Let's just...see what she has to say."

Gabe glanced at the closed door again, then laid on his back, staring at the ceiling.

"Be real with me, Gabe. Were you hitting it off with the goth chick? What's her name?"

"Chloe," he said.

"Mmm...Chloe. Nice. So? Well?"

"It *did* feel like we were getting along pretty well. I want to introduce her to Emily."

"Oh?"

Gabe laughed. "Okay, this feels kind of weird, coming from me, especially in *this* situation, but...maybe you think about sex too much, Ellen," Gabe said.

She was silent for a moment, then she let out a huff of annoyance. "I think I have a good reason, and I think I'm making you and Holly pretty happy in the process."

"Extremely," Holly said.

"Yes," he agreed, "that's not in question. I want her to talk with Emily because she wants to be a streamer. She's into horror games."

"Oh. That also makes sense," Ellen replied.

They looked over as the door opened up. Isabella came back out, looking regretful. "So...I'm going to be completely honest. I'm not up to this. And it sounds really trite but, it's not you, it's me."

"I understand," Gabe replied.

"I'm sorry. To all of you. I didn't give you wonderful ladies a show."

"We don't want you doing anything you're not

comfortable with," Gabe said.

Isabella still looked embarrassed and guilty, but that seemed to at least ease the burden of those emotions. She sighed heavily and then walked over to where a large black robe hung. Grabbing it, she pulled it on.

"I very much appreciate your reaction," she said as she walked back over and sat down on the bed, facing the three of them. "I know a lot of people who I imagine would react very poorly to coming this close to sex and then suddenly being denied..." She sighed softly.

"Do you want to talk about it?" he asked.

"Honestly I'm too embarrassed right now...but again, I appreciate the offer."

"I get it," he replied.

She looked at him in a speculative and still kind of guilty way, then slowly looked over at Ellen and Holly. "So...I have a very selfish and frankly humiliating request, but I've come this far, so I might as well just ask."

"We're listening," Gabe replied.

"I am...a vain person. I've worked hard to cultivate my reputation. I let a few subtle hints drop that I was going to be celebrating my divorce more directly, and tonight. By doing this. And obviously I'm not ready. But...would two of you be willing to have very noisy sex right now? I imagine either Ellen or Holly would be muffled but loud enough to let people know that someone's having sex up here..." She looked away suddenly, blushing. "This is embarrassing."

"I'd be down to fuck," Ellen said.

"Obviously I would be," Gabe said.

"Are you sure? I know this is just stupid fucking

ego stroking but–"

"Isabella," Ellen said, standing up smoothly and walking over. "We obviously don't know each other that well, but based on everything I've heard from you so far...I get it. Ego is a fickle thing at the best of times. It sounds like you've been through the wringer. And as a woman who has also been put through the goddamned wringer, and a woman who has been fucking Gabe for a month now, I feel uniquely positioned to tell you that I very much understand why you would want people to believe that you took Gabe upstairs and pounced on his cock like the ferocious cougar you are."

Isabella let out an awkward, breathy laugh and stood up, blushing fiercely. "I...obviously am not a cougar," she murmured. "But...thank you."

"Just because you're having a bad night doesn't mean you aren't a cougar," Gabe said as Ellen quickly began taking her clothes off.

"Cougars fuck younger guys though, which I have never done."

"Do you intend to in the future?" Ellen asked.

"Yes. Really, if you all are still comfortable with it, I absolutely intend to go through with this at a future date," Isabella replied.

"Then there you go," Ellen said, pulling her panties down.

"Well...I don't really know what to say other than 'thank you'. Uh...is it-would it still be all right if I watched? I've never actually seen people having sex before in the flesh."

"Watch away," Gabe replied as Ellen climbed onto the bed and then pushed him down.

"Yep," she agreed, grinning fiercely down at him, "I am going to fuck your goddamned brains out."

...

Thirty minutes later Gabe was pulling his clothes back on.

Ellen had been quite loud, and he had no doubt that everyone downstairs had heard her. He was feeling very good about the whole thing. Holly had left first, after they'd all agreed to leave one by one. Isabella didn't want it to be *too* obvious, though Gabe thought that particular desire was off the table after Ellen's performance and he'd honestly been kind of hoping to walk down the stairs at least alongside Isabella.

Even if it hadn't happened, he was happy to collaborate in maintaining the illusion that they'd fucked like animals.

Isabella had just left as well, leaving him and Ellen alone. They'd had a quick shower and were now pulling their clothes back on.

"Don't get too cocky now," Ellen murmured as she adjusted her bra.

"What?" he replied. "Are you serious?"

"Yes," she said in a tone that brooked no playful response. He looked at her. "This was fun, but I think it would be nice practice in...maintaining a sense of subtlety."

"Any particular reason I should do that?" he asked.

"A very good reason. A certain amount of confidence is greatly appreciated and rather attractive. A certain amount of cockiness—a *much* smaller amount, I must point out—is also attractive. To me, at least. But, and I don't want you to take this the wrong way, you *really* need to keep an eye on it."

He continued looking at her for a moment before speaking. "You're afraid I'm going to turn into Blake."

She bit her lower lip and looked down for a moment. "If I was seriously afraid of that, the relationship would be different. Very different," she replied, slowly looking back up at him. "I'm sorry, I'm not trying to insult you or say that I don't trust you–"

"It's okay, Ellen," he replied, finishing pulling his clothes into place and then walking over to her. He took one of her hands. "It's a reasonable concern, and you're right. It's something to keep an eye on." He chuckled suddenly. "I must admit, it's getting harder because I am now dating you *and* Holly, and I have somehow hooked up with Emily. And I came very close to sleeping with Isabella, which, Jesus Christ, how did you swing that?"

Ellen laughed. "I didn't really have to. Isabella has been looking for this to happen since she got her divorce and naturally she brought it up to Abby and, well, Abby happened to know an attractive man in his twenties who was safe and fun to sleep with, so naturally she forwarded your name."

"That was ridiculously nice," he muttered. "You think Isabella was disappointed when she actually met me?"

"What?! How can you even ask that!? You saw her with the whole finger sucking thing. That was her immediate reaction to you! Gabe I love you with all my heart but you are going to give me fucking whiplash with this whole 'very confident-no confidence' thing you do."

Gabe considered a response to that before finally

settling on: "...it's been a difficult life. That tends to fuck with your confidence."

Ellen's smile changed from something beguiling to something more comforting and she hugged him tightly. "I know, babe. It's why I have trouble talking about this kind of stuff with you. I don't want you to think I'm attacking you. You're actually doing really well, I'm just...paranoid."

"Understandable," he replied. A moment passed. "You should probably let me get back downstairs before I give into temptation, lift up your shirt, and start sucking on your tits."

"*Gabe!*" she hissed, releasing him.

"I'm just being honest...wow, you're really blushing."

"Shut up! I'm not blushing."

"You so are, don't tell me you can't feel that."

She sighed heavily and shook her head. "Whatever. Just...go downstairs and keep chatting up Chloe."

"Ah. Chloe. Right. I should really get back to her," Gabe replied. He shared a kiss with Ellen. "I love you. And thank you for trying to hook me up with a ridiculously hot cougar."

"You're welcome, and don't worry, it'll happen."

"You seem really confident about that," he replied.

"I am. She's into you, it's just too early. Now go around and strut your stuff. Just a little. Not too much."

He rolled his eyes. "All right."

They shared one more kiss and then he headed for the stairs.

CHAPTER TWENTY NINE

Gabe wasn't sure how to feel as he went back downstairs.

His natural assumption was that he'd feel great about everyone thinking he'd just nailed the woman hosting the party, and certainly he did feel that, but as he actually came back downstairs and he caught several people looking at him, he found that it was much more of a mixed bag than he thought it would be.

Surprisingly, Chloe was actually still waiting for him, and that made him feel bad. He hadn't meant to be gone that long.

The moment he entered the kitchen again she locked eyes with him, and she stared at him with a flat, surprisingly intimidating stare the whole way over. He sat down across from her, staring back, and for a moment neither of them said anything.

"So...what was that about?" she asked.

"Uh, Isabella wanted to talk to me about something," he replied.

"Uh-huh." She shifted in her chair, keep an admirable poker face. "You were gone for like half an hour."

"I ran into someone else on the way back and got asked about my writing," he lied with a surprising ease.

It didn't really seem to work on Chloe, though. She looked vaguely annoyed, but also vaguely intrigued. "Okay, level with me, man: did you fuck Isabella up there? Obviously *someone* was getting laid."

Gabe was stymied for just a moment, then finally

came back with: "A gentleman never tells."

Chloe continued staring at him. Finally, she seemed to give it up. "All right, whatever. So you were telling me about the tall blonde? Her name is Ellen? You know her?"

"Ah. Yes. Ellen. I do know her. She's close friends with Emily, the tattooed woman we were talking about earlier, and Emily is married to Abby, the mousy blonde with eyes of steel, who is very good friends with Isabella. And also Ellen and I are dating."

Chloe began to respond but for the first time since they had begun speaking, she looked lost. More than that, she looked like he'd just pulled the rug out from under her.

"You *prick!*" she said finally, her voice low but sharp. "You didn't think to mention this earlier!?"

"I...hadn't got to it yet," he replied, immediately becoming more uncomfortable. "I'm sorry, I didn't mean to freak you out, it just...didn't seem relevant yet."

"*Relevant!* Gabe. Are you shitting me? We have *obviously* been flirting for the past hour. It didn't occur to you to mention that you're dating a fucking statuesque blonde Amazon woman!? You don't think that's a little manipulative?"

"I was going to tell you before anything happened, if anything was going to happen," Gabe replied. She pursed her lips and continued staring at him, leaning back in her chair suddenly and crossing her arms. He sighed softly. "Okay, look. I'm sorry I pissed you off, but level with me: would you have bothered flirting with me if I said 'oh, before we begin, I'm in an open relationship with that blonde goddess over there and also that cute little redhead'?

Or would you have just said 'fuck it, I'm out' before you had a chance to even figure out whether or not I was worth pursuing?"

Chloe stared at him for a long time in silence. She still had a very excellent poker face, but he could tell she was thinking hard about what he had to say. He was still worried, though. Gabe knew that, at a certain point, his relationship...shenanigans, for want of a better word, would ultimately lead him into some sort of socially awkward situation.

He just hadn't expected it to be so soon.

Slowly, Chloe seemed to relax, though she kept her defensive posture. "Did they know?" she asked finally.

"That we were flirting? Yes. And both of them will be happy to back that up. If anything, they both pushed me to hit on you, since we're throwing caution to the wind and just being straight up brutally honest at this point. Not that I really *needed* pushing."

He waited. Chloe continued staring.

After what felt like far too long, heading dangerously close into the territory of her possibly just saying 'fuck it' and storming off, she uncrossed her arms.

"I suppose you have a point," she admitted, though it sounded like pulling teeth. "I probably would have said fuck it and gone elsewhere. But why the fuck are you chatting me up if you've got Ellen and that redhead *and* you apparently fucked Isabella? Or is it really just as simple as guys can't say no to more pussy?"

"...that's kind of hostile," he murmured.

"I'm in a hostile kind of mood," she replied, but she did relax slightly more. Interesting.

"Fair," Gabe said. "But do I have a point about

why I...withheld certain information?"

She kept staring at him, then sighed. "Yes. You do. I concede the point."

"I appreciate it," he said. "And, just so we're completely clear, I didn't hit on you just because I was horny or just because my girlfriends wanted me to or to get you into a three, or four, way."

"Good, because that's not on the table. I'm not into chicks," Chloe replied.

Hmm. That was potentially going to be a hiccup in...whatever the fuck this was.

So far, just about all of their conversations about potential sexual adventures involved something for both him and them. Then again...they *were* both very much pushing him to hook up with Sadie, with or without them. Although on the other hand, maybe there was some kind of tell that Ellen had picked up on that Sadie was bisexual.

"So," he said finally, "where does that leave us?"

"I'm still trying to decide," Chloe replied. "I was...enjoying our flirting. I have to admit that your girlfriend freaks me out."

"Which one?"

"Oh gee, I wonder! Is it the cute little redhead who looks barely old enough to drink and like she'd never hurt a fly, or is the fucking six foot six blonde who looks like a mixture between a goddess of war and a sex demon?" she replied.

He chuckled. "Okay, I just thought I'd ask. I mean, Holly intimidates *me,* or at least she did."

"Why?"

"Because she is as attractive as she is. I mean you intimidated the shit out of me. You still do."

"...are you an actor, then?"

"What?"

"I couldn't tell that you're intimidated, and I normally can. Or are you rich? A porn star?"

"What-why are you asking these questions?"

"You really gonna sit there and tell me with a straight face that you pulled *those two* with your winning personality?" Chloe replied.

"That strikes me as kind of rude," Gabe said. "And as a matter of fact, yes, I did. I'm a not-quite-starving artist writer who got very lucky."

Chloe stared at him. "Are you fucking with me right now?"

"No. Although if this is how the conversation is going to go, I'm not sure anything's going to work out between you and me," Gabe said, pushing back his chair.

"Wait," Chloe said, sitting up. "I-you're right. I'm sorry. Like I said, I'm in a hostile kind of mood. It's been a painfully long...month, year? I've been in a bad mood for a very long time, and you seriously caught me off guard with all this stuff, and when that happens, I tend to...lash out and clam up. Especially when it comes to strange men who make me feel...funny. I've been betrayed before. More than once. So...sorry I'm being a bitch."

Gabe felt that sense of unreality sweeping over him again, but it was coming on much, much stronger than before.

He had never, not once, in his entire life, had a woman try to smooth things over for what seemed to be the hope of getting into his pants. And he had *certainly* never had a woman this attractive talk to him like this before. It felt...impossible.

All the others he'd been with so far had been operating from a position of power. Ellen, Holly, Emily, Krystal, Isabella, even Sadie, they all knew (or had to know) that *obviously* he would have sex with them if they offered.

How did Chloe not realize that?

He realized at once that he was flashing back to his and Emily's date night.

This was another blind spot, it had to be, the evidence was right there in front of him. But this woman, Chloe, who was absurdly attractive, confident, and had every reason to be, had every appearance of fumbling to keep him from walking away from her.

Gabe wasn't even sure if it had been a bluff on his part, but in a flash, he realized it wasn't.

How the hell had this happened? It felt like some sort of impossible role reversal.

If anything he felt sort of like he was walking a tightrope, and he had to handle this carefully. He was willing to walk if that's what she wanted, but he also very much wanted to be with her. Even if it was just a one night stand.

Chloe was attractive in a way that Ellen and Holly weren't. He knew a lot of it had to do with her goth allure, but it was something more than that. She had...a harder, sharper edge to her attractiveness. She was almost daunting, like a lethal snake with beautiful patterning.

"I accept your apology," Gabe replied, relaxing back into his chair. "And I get it. And, for the record, I am very much in love with my girlfriends."

He could tell Chloe wanted to refute that in some way, a sour look of bitterness briefly flashing across her face, but she didn't give voice to it.

"That's fair," she said instead.

Another moment of uncomfortable silence passed.

"So, again, where exactly does this leave us?" Gabe asked finally.

Chloe shifted uncomfortably in her chair. She looked less willing to budge now, though he wasn't really sure what that meant. If she wasn't into him, why not just walk away? But she had to be into him, or maybe she just wanted something from him, but their back-and-forth had felt pretty authentic.

"If you could get me to say yes to anything, what would you ask me to do?" she asked finally.

"Whew, man, that's quite the question to dump in this particular situation," he muttered. Chloe remained steadfast, staring at him with her makeup-ringed eyes. He decided to stick to his policy of honesty. "Provided the yes is authentic, I'd ask you to come to my place and have sex with me while my girlfriends watch."

She raised an eyebrow. "That's very honest."

"It's served me well so far."

"Hmm. If you could get me to 'authentically' say yes to anything, you wouldn't push me into a threesome with one of your girls?"

"No, you said you weren't into women."

"In my experience, that has not stopped a lot of men from trying past what I would consider the point of reason." She was silent for a few seconds. "So, you want to sleep with me then."

"Uh, yeah. Who the fuck *wouldn't?* Look at you," he replied.

She began to respond, then seemed to stumble verbally. Holy shit, was she blushing? Chloe cleared her throat. "Well, I appreciate that," she said, her voice low. "And I appreciate your honesty. I'll say now that sex isn't on the table for tonight. I'm...just not there yet. But I don't want to walk away, uh, empty-handed. So...I would maybe like to go somewhere a little more private in the house and make out, if you'd be open to that."

"I would be extremely open to that," Gabe replied, feeling his heart beating harder and faster. "But," he said as they both stood up, "I believe it would only be responsible if I introduced you to Ellen and Holly first."

She sighed softly. "Yes, that *would* be responsible."

"Nervous?" he asked as he began leading her out of the kitchen.

"Uh, hello? Fuck yes I'm nervous. One of your girlfriends looks like a supermodel CEO hybrid who eats corporations for brunch and the other looks like a fucking porn star." She paused. "Not in a bad way, I just meant–"

"I know," he replied. "And she does. But she's really sweet."

"Which one is really sweet? I'm *trying* not to make assumptions..."

"Clearly. Who do you think? Ellen is nice but she's tough as nails."

They came into the living room where they found Ellen and Holly off in one corner, talking with Emily. Abby was out on the back deck now, talking with Isabella and another woman, both Abby and the other woman looking scandalized and loving it as Isabella described something to them. No doubt what was her fictitious version of their encounter.

He still wasn't sure how to feel about that.

Emily said something and nodded as they approached, and both Ellen and Holly turned to look as Gabe approached with Chloe.

Ellen smiled broadly, in a predatory kind of way,

as she saw them.

"Ladies," Gabe said as they stepped up, "this is Chloe."

"Hello Chloe. I'm Ellen. This is Holly, our girlfriend. And this is our friend Emily."

"Hi. Um, hello everyone," Chloe replied, doing an admirable job of keeping a straight face and not showing her anxiety too much.

"So...did you fuck my boyfriend yet?" Ellen asked, smirking and swirling her wine around in its glass.

Chloe's eyes widened and she lost all her composure, blushing terribly. "No," she managed, then cleared her throat. "I didn't do that."

"Ease off the pedal there, dear," Gabe said.

Ellen sighed. "Fine, I will." Something in her seemed to shift, something that wasn't obviously visible, but abruptly, her presence wasn't quite so overwhelming. She seemed much more at ease suddenly, and her smirk became a more friendly smile. "I don't bite, Chloe."

"Okay," she murmured, then straightened up a little.

"Chloe and I have been flirting and she...would like to take me for a very mild test drive."

"That's one way of putting it," Chloe said awkwardly.

"All right, that's fine, right Holly?" Ellen asked.

Holly nodded happily. "Yes, that's completely fine with me."

"What does test drive mean, though?" Ellen asked. "Test drive like...swapping oral?"

"Whew! I was thinking more like, uh...making out? Maybe some groping?" Chloe replied.

"Whatever you're comfortable with," Gabe said.

"I'm *so* not used to talking about this," Chloe muttered. "Especially not talking about what I'm trying to do with a guy to his *girlfriend*." She paused. "Girl*friends*."

"It takes some getting used to," Holly murmured.

"Yep," Ellen agreed. "But if you aren't comfortable with it and want to walk away, we won't take it personally."

"Appreciate that," Chloe said, then cleared her throat again. "I want to do this, though. I definitely want to do this. Although," she looked around, "I would like it somewhere private."

"I know a place," Abby said, approaching their group. Apparently she'd decided to come in and join them.

"You should probably show them, I don't want to...impose," Ellen said.

"This way, lovebirds," Abby replied, walking away and curling a finger at them over her shoulder.

CHAPTER THIRTY

He glanced once at Chloe, who looked a little uncertain, and he offered her his hand.

She looked at him, then at his hand, then muttered '*fuck it*' and took it. Gabe wasn't sure if that was the reaction he was hoping for, but he understood that she was in a weird position. They followed Abby, hand in hand, and she took them back to the stairway he'd walked up after Isabella not all that long ago.

They went up to the second story and Abby walked unerringly to one of the closed doors. Opening it up, she revealed a sparsely furnished spare bedroom.

"Would you like me to stay around, for peace of mind?" Abby asked.

"I..." Chloe hesitated and glanced at Gabe. "That doesn't offend you?"

"No," he replied.

"Why not?"

"I mean it's not like you know me all that well, I could understand why you would be nervous and how it might be comforting to have another woman nearby to watch your back."

"He's very reasonable and kind," Abby said.

"You trust him?" Chloe replied.

"He fucked my wife, I trust him."

"...okay then. I appreciate the offer but I'll be fine."

Abby nodded. "Have fun."

She slipped away. They lingered for a moment in the hallway, then Gabe let Chloe lead him into the room.

"Door closed?" he asked.

"Yes," she replied.

He closed the door and walked over to the bed. Sat down on its edge. Chloe lingered for a moment, looking at him closely. She seemed suddenly more vulnerable, but there was also a firm steel in her gaze, and beneath that, what seemed to be a lot of lust and longing.

"This is weird," she murmured finally, sitting down next to him.

"Like I said, we can stop whenever you want," he replied.

The steel in her gaze suddenly became harder. "Why do you keep saying that?" she asked. "Do you not want to but you are for...some reason?"

"No," he replied. "I'm saying it because if there is one thing that I've been beaten over the head with, again and again, it's that men pressuring women into sex stuff is *really* common. And I never want to do that. I'm apparently weird for thinking so, but I only want to do sexy things with women who are very into me."

"...okay, that's fair," she said. Chloe seemed to take a moment to collect herself, then abruptly turned to look at him. "I'm just going to apologize for being so...weird. I know I'm kind of all over the place right now. It's been a long dry spell that followed a series of bad breakups. And there's just something about you...that makes me trust you, which kind of freaks me out, but also turns me on? But understand: I want to do this."

Before he could reply, she kissed him.

It squarely kicked every thought in his head out and pinned him to that moment in time and her lips and her next to him and her taste and everything wonderful about her.

The kiss went on for what felt like quite a while, and then she slowly pulled back.

"Okay wow," she whispered. "That was-yeah. I was wondering if it would be good but I didn't realize it was going to be that good."

"You wanna stretch out? Much more comfortable making out position," Gabe replied.

She chuckled. "Uh...yeah. Yes. Let's do that."

They both hurried to lay down facing each other near the middle of the bed and quickly resumed kissing. She put her tongue in his mouth and he moved his forward to meet it. She tasted vaguely sweet, and the fact that she tasted different from every other woman he'd been kissing recently sent a strange but potent surge of lust rushing through his body.

As their tongues danced together, Gabe laid a hand across her breast. He went cautiously at first, some part of him still trying to be aware of her body language. Something was just the slightest bit off, but he genuinely couldn't parse what that was. She seemed not just happy but enthusiastic, and that was already starting to elevate to something closer to desperation the more they kissed.

At some point he found his hand going up to the strap on her dress and he began to push it down over her shoulder, and then he made himself pause.

"Is this okay?" he asked.

"What?" Chloe replied, breathing heavily, distracted. He tugged at her strap a little. "Oh...yeah. That's fine. Here, lemme just..."

She broke away and maneuvered her arm through the strap, then did the same with her other arm, then began tugging the front of the dress down over her considerable chest. Abruptly she stopped and grinned, then turned to face him.

He took the opportunity eagerly, pulling it down and exposing her breasts. They tumbled out, big and bare and so very pale.

"Holy shit," he whispered.

She laughed. "Yeah, I know."

Then they were kissing again and his hand was on one of those huge tits. He felt a shudder of raw, powerful lust pulse through his body as he massaged her breast.

"Jeez, that good, huh?" she murmured, her lips so close they brushed his as she spoke.

"Better," he replied, and kissed her again, pushing his tongue into her mouth.

Chloe moaned and invited him closer with her body. He was resting against her now, groping her bare breast, feeling her tongue twisting and twining with his own, tasting her wonderful taste. After another long bout of kissing, he pulled back and looked down at her bare breasts.

"Can I suck?" he asked.

"Yes, *please*," she replied, grinning and laying back. "My nipples are sensitive in the best way."

That was all the invitation he needed. Gabe lowered himself and licked across one bare breast. She gasped, then moaned as his tongue circled her nipple once, twice, three times, and then he was sucking on it. Chloe moaned louder. His hand, almost by habit, rested on her thigh, then began to creep up her dress.

He was almost up to her hip before he realized what he was doing.

"You know, I could go a bit further," he said, and she gasped as he ran a fingertip slowly over her pussy, hidden behind her panties.

"Lemme see your fingers," she replied after a

moment. He pulled his hand out of her dress and showed her. "Man, your fingernails are clean and clipped-oh, of course they are. I'm sure you finger-fuck your girlfriends all the time."

"I do," he replied.

"Take my panties off," she replied.

"Yes, ma'am," he said, and she laughed.

As he got down and reached up under her dress, his fingers finding the hem of her panties and pulling them slowly down over her fishnet-clad legs, she looked down at her breasts.

"Impressive though they are, I imagine you're used to bigger. Ellen's look absolutely massive," she murmured.

"Let's not talk about Ellen," he replied, taking her black panties off and tossing them aside.

"Why?"

"I don't want you comparing yourself to other girls, and I don't want you to think that I am either," he replied.

"Oh. That's...sweet."

"Well there's enough meanness in the world...fuck's sake you have a nice vagina," he muttered as he rucked up her dress.

She laughed loudly, like it had caught her off guard. "What!? I don't think I've ever heard those words before."

"They are very true," he replied. "That is one clean shave."

"Well I thought maybe I might get some action tonight," she murmured, shifting awkwardly as he studied her pussy. "And everyone seems to like shaved now, so...can you stop looking at it?"

"Yeah," he replied, then hesitated as a look of what he swore was disappointment and irritation crossed her face.

Was she expecting him to say no? Argue with her?

Whatever.

He laid back down beside her and resumed sucking on her breast, her other one this time, and she gasped, then moaned as he began running his fingertips along her inner thighs. Firmly enough as not to tickle, but lightly enough to feel good. He drifted them across her thighs, back and forth, then over her pussy, getting her used to his touch.

When he touched her clit, he got an extremely strong response from her.

Chloe moaned loudly, her hips bucking as he began to pleasure her, and she quickly began panting harder. Gabe kept going, excited lusty desire roaring through him. She felt wet, wonderfully wet. His fingertip described small, firm circles on her clit and he could feel her trembling against him.

"Oh my fucking *God,* Gabe!" she cried.

"You like that, huh?" he murmured, then licked across one of her nipples.

She let out a blissful cry. "Yes!"

"Can I go inside?" he asked.

"Fuck's sake-*yes!*"

He could again read some odd sense of exasperation but he couldn't quite figure it out. She still seemed into it, so he slipped a finger inside of her. Good lord was she hot and *slick* inside. Chloe moaned even more loudly as he began fucking her with his finger.

"Kiss me…" she moaned as he kept going.

Gabe stopped sucking on her tits and shifted back up, locking lips with her again. She aggressively shoved her tongue into his mouth and as he pushed a second finger into her and began pressing up, hard and fast, she let out a shriek.

Within a few seconds he'd brought her to climax.

He expected a gush of feminine juices to escape her, like Ellen or Holly, but there wasn't much. He could feel her inner muscles fluttering and clenching wildly, though, and her hips bucked furiously as he kept fingering her.

At some point her hand came down and pushed his away. He stopped pleasuring her and she fell back, gasping for breath, no longer kissing him, staring at the ceiling with wide eyes.

"I feel bad," was the first thing she said.

"Really?" he replied. "Because it does *not* seem like it."

She chuckled weakly. "No, not-I mean, that felt *amazing*. I feel bad because you just gave me a fucking killer orgasm and I didn't give you one. I wasn't intending to but I also didn't know if you were gonna go that far for me...mmm, do you have anything? Any, you know, STIs?"

"No," he replied. "I'm fairly confident in that."

"Same," she said. "Actually I know I don't...fuck."

"Don't do anything you aren't comfortable with."

"I *am* comfortable with it, is the thing." She sighed heavily and shook her head.

"Okay are you mad at me or something? Because I feel like I've done a *really* good job—"

"You have! And I'm...frustrated!"

"Why?"

"It's stupid."

"Tell me anyway," he replied. Something in her seemed to react to that.

"I want you to stop being so damned nice! I

want...to argue with you. Or you to argue with me. But not for real?"

He stared at her for a moment, then laughed as everything abruptly fell into place. "Oh."

"Oh *what?* Don't laugh at me," she replied abruptly, and he couldn't tell if the suddenly petulance in her voice was genuine or not.

"I'm not," he replied. "I just put together what was off about this whole thing. You kept acting just a little weird. You're a fucking brat."

Something flashed in her eyes, but she looked more than a little embarrassed. "Yes," she mumbled, looking away from him.

"And you want me to be the...counter to your brattiness."

She sighed, blushing badly now. "Yes," she mumbled.

"Thought so."

"I don't want to go all the way," she said, still not meeting his eyes, "but I wouldn't be against...swallowing."

"Just so we're completely clear—"

"Stop being so nice!" she snapped, looking directly at him now.

Gabe put a hand over her mouth. "Shut the fuck up, Chloe," he replied, his tone even but firm, and her eyes widened a little. "Don't interrupt me."

"Or what?" she managed behind his hand.

He clamped it tighter. "Or you'll be punished. But I'm not going to stop being nice until we're absolutely clear. You're all right to get fucked in the mouth and to let me come down your throat?"

He released her. "Yes," she said, breathing heavily again.

This felt like dangerous territory but Gabe

couldn't deny that he was enjoying being thrown into it wildly. And what were the odds?! It hadn't been all that long ago that he'd been talking with Holly about dating a bratty girl.

And now that he'd had practice…

"You," he said, grabbing her dress and tugging it down, "have been a sassy, backtalking little bitch to me all night."

"Stop!" she hissed as he tugged her dress down.

"Shut your mouth, Chloe," he replied.

"Make me," she growled.

He got her dress off and tossed it away, rendering her completely naked save for her socks and her fishnet stockings.

"You're on thin ice, girl," he muttered, keeping his voice low. *That* was all he needed, someone to overhear their little roleplay and assume the worst.

"Don't call me girl," she snapped back.

"Get down on your knees...girl."

"You fucker. Make me-oh!" she cried as he grasped her wrist and pulled her to the edge of the bed.

This still felt wildly reckless but he no longer cared. He wanted nothing more than to push her down onto her knees and force her to suck him dry. He got her off the bed and pushed her down onto her knees.

A thought stopped him and he reached into his pocket as she began undoing his jeans. He pulled out his phone.

She froze. "I don't want any pics taken."

"Don't worry, I'm not going to," he replied as called up his text chain with Ellen and began sending her a message.

"I'm being serious right now," Chloe said. "I'm-ugh, fuck. We should've-safeword! I'm being serious."

"Chloe," he said, turning the phone around to shower her mid-message, "I'm being serious, too. I wouldn't take your picture without your consent. I'm texting Ellen about this to make double sure. So get my dick out and start with your huge tits."

"Okay. Um...un-safeword." He laughed and resumed texting. "Don't fucking laugh at me!"

"Shut the fuck up, Chloe," he replied, gripping her hair by the roots and giving it a little tug.

She gasped and began breathing heavily again. "You fucking bastard," she whispered.

"Get to work, you mouthy little bitch."

She stared at him at him, her jaw set, her expression defiant, then she got back to work digging him out of his pants.

He texted his question to Ellen. Holding onto the phone, he watched as Chloe finished getting his erection out. She stared at it for a moment, then up at him, then scowled and spit into her hand.

"Don't give me that face," he said.

"What are you gonna do about it?" she shot back immediately.

"Keep pushing, Chloe. See what happens."

Something again flashed in her eyes, and she looked like she wanted to say more, but then probably thought better of it because this was their first time together and she wasn't willing to go all the way.

She wrapped her hand around his erection and began massaging it, muttering something quietly under her breath.

"What was that?"

"Nothing," she said.

"Uh-huh."

She kept at it until his cock was coated in a thin

layer of her saliva, then brought her huge breasts up and pressed them together, his erection between then. He leaned back a little, resting on the heels of his palms, as she began sliding them up and down.

Dear fucking lord were her tits huge and soft and hot and smooth. They felt pretty damn good and the sight of her was setting his lust on fire.

His phone chimed. He checked the text from Ellen: *Yeah you can get head from her but if you fuck her you have to use a condom. And I have one for you to use. I was gonna have you use it for Isabella.*

He began texting back quickly: *No sex but she's giving me a tit-job.*

"Who is that?" she murmured.

"My girlfriend," he replied.

"What!? You said you were single!" she growled.

For a moment he was caught completely off guard, but he recovered almost immediately. Unsafeword. Right.

"So I lied. Deal with it," he replied.

Ellen responded quickly: *So fucking hot. She has huge tits. How is she?*

"You fucker!" she snapped, but she didn't stop with her big breasts.

He sent one more reply: *She's a bad girl gagging for punishment, apparently.*

Gabe tossed the phone aside.

"I'll tell her," Chloe said, smirking darkly, looking very pleased with herself suddenly. "I'll tell her everything. I'll tell her we fucked without protection and–"

He slapped her in the side of her head. Not hard, but enough that she felt it. She stared at him in open shock.

"You'll do as you're told, you little whore," he replied, and then he grabbed her head and pushed his cock into her mouth.

Chloe let go of her tits as he gripped her head tightly and began fucking her in the mouth. The pleasure was immediate and immense, flowing into him as he made good use of her hot, wet mouth. After a bit of forcibly sliding her lips up and down his cock, he let go and leaned back again.

"Finish it," he said.

She glared at him with what looked like real anger, his dick still between her lips, and then she began bobbing her head. She wrapped two fingers and a thumb around his shaft and began using it in tandem with her lips.

The pleasure magnified greatly. Gabe groaned and shuddered hard as she worked his cock.

Chloe managed to get him off fast like that. He was coming into her mouth inside of thirty seconds. He groaned loudly, falling onto his back as he began shooting his load down her throat. She moaned and kept sucking, swallowing occasionally as he pumped his seed into her mouth. It was a moment of absolute ecstasy.

And then it was over, ebbing away slowly as she finished sucking him dry, and she took his dick out of her mouth.

For a long moment of silence, he laid there on his back, staring at the ceiling, feeling what he imagined she had been feeling after she had come.

"Holy shit I can't believe I did that," she whispered. "I barely know you...I've never done something like this before."

"But you've always wanted to," Gabe replied.

"...yes."

"Well, if it's any consolation, I took a bigger risk than you did."

"What? How!?"

"I have other women backing me up. I just have your own word."

"Okay...fair. But you're kind of a tramp," she murmured.

He laughed. "*Tramp?*"

"I mean, you have two girlfriends, you fucked that tatted chick, you fucked Isabella—"

"Hey, I never said that."

"You didn't have to, she screamed it loud enough for everyone to hear," Chloe replied dryly.

"You're being a little rude," Gabe said, sitting up.

She sighed, crossing her arms. "Yes, I suppose I am. But I feel like I bought myself a little rudeness after I drained your cock down my throat."

"Hey, that was after I gave you one hell an orgasm," he replied.

She sighed again, more heavily. "Yes, *fine.* I'll reel it in. I'm a brat but I'm also kind of bitchy in general." She smiled suddenly. "You are *really* into it, aren't you?"

"Is it that obvious?"

She laughed. "Yes, it's very obvious. Also, you're *really* good at it. To be honest, I thought, uh…" She looked away suddenly.

"Uh *what?*" he replied. "And put my dick away."

"Oh yes, *sir,*" she said, rolling her eyes as she put his cock away.

"I wasn't too rough, was I?" he asked as she zipped him up.

"No, I'm not some fucking delicate flower. Jesus fucking Christ," she muttered.

"Hey! I'm trying to be nice, Chloe."

She looked up at him, abashed. "Sorry," she murmured. "It's hard to turn off."

"I can understand that," he replied. "Now, would you like to come down from everything we just did? Grab some food or something, sit on the back deck, just chill and chat?"

"You sure it won't be...weird?"

"I'm sure," he replied.

"...yeah, I'd like that. A lot. Lemme just get my dress and panties back on."

CHAPTER THIRTY ONE

"So do you feel like a playboy or a baller or whatever the fuck word means 'super cool badass dude' nowadays?" Chloe asked as they walked down the stairs together.

"I mean yeah, kinda," he replied.

"*Kinda?* Fuck's sake dude, what would it take? You walk in here with *two* girlfriends who you *literally* marked for everyone to see as basically your fucking property, and *then* you went upstairs and fucked the shit out of the crazy attractive hostess, whether you actually did it or not, people believe you did, and *now* you are coming downstairs with a big titty goth girl and people think *we* fucked. I was pretty loud," she said.

"Well, when you put it that way, lemme just make sure my swagger is in check," he muttered.

"Oh my fucking God, you are so weird," Chloe replied.

Ellen, Holly, Abby, Emily, and Isabella were all standing together in the living room. They all stared at him and Chloe as they walked by, all of them smiling big.

"Later," he mouthed to them.

Ellen rolled her eyes but nodded. Emily whispered something in Holly's ear and she blushed and giggled. Gabe sighed, they were going to be giving him shit about this for days, if not weeks. Not that he was in a position to complain at all.

He'd just gotten blown by a self-admitted big-titty goth girl.

It was a thing that most men aspired to.

And he'd actually fucking picked her up at a

party, mostly by himself...right? He was positive that Ellen and Holly and the others had *some* influence on the situation, propping him up in their way that they did. What Holly had told him, about liking being with a guy who could get other women into bed, that had to be rare, but not *that* rare.

Chloe must have it, or she would've iced him out the moment she thought he'd gone off to fuck Isabella or had two girlfriends.

They stopped in the kitchen and she grabbed some pizza.

"You want some hot chocolate?" he asked when he saw some had been made in their absence.

"Yeah," she replied. He began pouring her a cup. "I can get it myself."

Gabe sighed softly and looked at her. "I know you can get it yourself, Chloe, I'm trying to be nice to you."

"...oh. Sorry," she murmured, blushing again. "Thanks."

"You're welcome," he replied as he passed her the mug.

He poured one for himself and then they headed outside. It was dark and cold now, but not bitterly so. They'd stopped to pull on their hoodies and shoes before heading out and now were fairly comfortable as they found a pair of deck chairs off to one side and sat down beside each other.

For a long moment, neither of them spoke.

"So, Gabe..." She hesitated, then fell silent.

"I'm listening," he replied.

"I want to try and just put aside all my...sass, and bitchiness, and all that, and just talk to you like, I don't know, a normal person. Just...talk about things. I'm a weird place right now," she said, and she sounded like it.

She almost sounded a little lost.

"I'm okay with this," he replied. "And I don't know if it helps, but you can take what I say at face value, and you can trust me. I know how vulnerable you feel right now. And I'm not looking to take advantage of you."

"What *are* you looking for?" she replied suddenly.

"Friendship? Sex? To engage with your brattiness more."

She chuckled. "You really liked that, huh?"

"Hard yes."

"I think you may find it a tad more grating the more you experience it," she murmured.

"No way. I want to make sweet, angry arguments with you all night long, until the sun rises," he replied.

She laughed again in that way, that unexpected burst of laughter when something truly funny unexpectedly slips past all your defenses and punches you right in the funny bone. "You...are so weird...but in a good way," she murmured as her laughter died down.

"So are you," he replied.

"You sure your girlfriends won't get jealous if we hang out more? If we have sex? I'm not saying that's on the table...even though I want it to be."

"They will be *thrilled* if you and I fuck. They're going to want to watch, though," he replied.

"I've never been watched before," she murmured. "I mean, I guess I should be a bit more open to the idea, given what I want to do, but also, being watched by strangers electronically playing video games and being watched by people actually in the room while I'm butt naked and getting pounded and punished are two extremely different things."

"Yeah," he agreed. Another awkward moment passed. "So...I feel like we never actually got down to why you're here, at this party. What you were looking for. I mean, you said you were looking for some action? I don't know, I just get the impression that you didn't come to this party casually."

"You're good at reading people," Chloe replied. "I...am in a weird place right now. What could be called an ugly place. I came here because...I wanted to stop thinking. I just wanted to turn my brain off. But I can't even do that. I'm sure you saw that guy chatting me up earlier?"

"Yeah. You looked...bored. And annoyed."

"Understatement of the century," she growled. "I know some people can't tell when they're boring or annoying the shit out of someone but fucking hell, that guy could do it for the Olympics. I'm not trying to be a bitch...it just comes very naturally to me, apparently." Chloe was silent for a long moment after that, looking out at the dark, cold backyard. Finally, she sighed softly. "I'm kind of reluctant to go into detail about my problems because I want you to maintain the illusion that I'm cool."

"Unless you're about to tell me that you cheat on all your boyfriends or rip off old people by way of scam calling or some other really shitty thing, I'm not going to think you're not cool. I'm a lot less judgmental than you apparently think I am," he replied.

She looked at him closely, like she was actually studying him to try and catch him in a lie. Finally she gave a little shrug. "Okay, yeah, fine. You've been really nice so far. I came to the party looking for, you know, a hookup, because that's what I thought I wanted. Or what I thought I should want. And I mean I *do* want it, but also I'm really nervous about it? I've been single for a year. And some of that was definitely because I wanted to be, but at some point I realized *no one* was hitting on me.

"Well, I mean...okay, hitting on me in a way that wasn't completely stupid? I mean every douchebag hits on baristas, no matter how obvious you make it. I could be wearing a fucking big, garish wedding ring on my finger and they'd still try to get my number *while I am working*. But no one was more, I don't know, authentically hitting on me? If that makes sense? Just really, really lazy 'hey baby wanna fuck?' levels of 'flirtation', if you can even call it that..."

She sighed heavily and got to her feet suddenly. She seemed more agitated.

"And I don't even know. I'm just frustrated. Like...besides my job, I don't really go out much, so I guess it makes sense why I wouldn't get hit on? I don't really put myself out there, and I've had a few people tell me I'm really unapproachable." Chloe stopped suddenly and looked at him directly. "Am I? Am I unapproachable?"

"Well...I'm not a great person to ask about that," he replied.

"How? How can you possibly not be a person to ask about that? You are dating two fucking tens, you nailed Emily which, my God, she is *beautiful.* And then you fucked–"

"Let me just stop you there," Gabe said. He thought she was working herself into a really pissed off state and imagined it wouldn't be happy for *any* of them if she managed it. "You obviously are looking at my situation like all these women are orbiting around me. Like they came to me. And I could lie to you and tell you that's the way it is.

"But I don't want to. Ellen and I were a really unique situation, we knew each other years ago, then reconnected under incredibly unique circumstances and clicked hard and fast. Ellen decided we should both go after Holly and it worked well. Ellen already knew Abby and Emily, and they all decided it'd be great if Emily hooked up with me. I didn't really make any of that happen. So...what I'm saying is we're a lot closer than you'd think. In truth, I'm stupefied by your beauty."

"Oh come *on,*" she replied, rolling her eyes.

"I'm being serious right now. I am intimidated by your beauty and I also, before dating Ellen, did *not* have a lot of luck with women. Like...at all. My natural inclination, were I to see you in the wild, would be that you are *waaaaay* out of my league, so don't even bother approaching. Given what we just did, you are apparently not out of my league. I'd say someone like Ellen or Abby would be a far better judge of how approachable you are," he replied.

Chloe crossed her arms, scrutinizing him again with her stern, mascaraed gaze. "There's a part of me, a really powerful part, that feels like you're fucking with me...but I can tell you're telling the truth. Which is so goddamned weird. You are...*very* attractive. I mean did you have some kind of a glow up recently? Ugh," she rolled her eyes, "I fucking hate that phrase."

"I don't really think I look different than before Ellen," he replied.

"That's weird. What changed? Because obviously something changed."

He shrugged. "I don't know? Ellen says I'm

more confident. But we're getting off track. So you were coming here to figure out if you were approachable or not?"

"Yes? No? Fuck, I don't know," she muttered, sitting back down suddenly. "I'm a mess, to be honest." She looked at him again abruptly. "Do you actually like me? Or do I just make you horny?"

"I like you, yeah," he replied.

"Why?"

"You seem cool. The conversation we had? It felt good. It felt like a connection, it was nice. You're into horror games, you're into books enough to talk with a writer for an hour, you know how to hold up your end of a conversation, you weren't pulling out your phone every fucking five minutes. I'll be honest: I've got a full-blown crush on you."

She gave him a wild, wide-eyed look, and then started laughing hard once more. "How the fuck do you keep making me laugh like this!?" she asked when she'd finished, wiping at one of her eyes carefully. "A *crush?!* Are you for real?"

"I'm for real," he replied. "Are you laughing at me?"

"I...I don't even know," she replied. "Not really, but kind of? I'm half-convinced you're trying to make me laugh. And it's working. And after everything I've gone through...I could use it, so thank you."

"You're welcome."

She slowly lost her smile, then looked out at the backyard again for a long moment. Gabe waited. She seemed like she had a lot on her mind.

Finally, she exhaled softly. "This is *not* what I had in mind when I showed up tonight, but...damn if I'm not really, really enjoying myself. More than I have in a long time."

"That's good," he replied. "So...I honestly feel *really* off-kilter right now, but I'm gonna ask this anyway: you wanna go back to my place?"

Chloe gave him a measured look, then let out a groan, hiding her face behind her hands.

"Oops," he murmured. "Sorry."

"No!" she replied, pulling her head back up. "No, it isn't you. I am actually *sorely* tempted to go back to your house and just...sass you into *destroying* me. But you aren't the only one feeling off-kilter. I can't tell if it'd be a really stupid decision or not. Maybe if you were single, but...Ellen and Holly sort of throw a wrench in everything. I'm not saying it's off the table, it's more just...I feel too weird tonight. But in a week? A few days, even? I'll have a better idea, I think."

"That's fair," he replied.

"You're disappointed."

"Well obviously."

She laughed. "I'll take the compliment. Um." She looked around for a moment, then checked her phone. "Jeez, time really flies. Okay, uh...something is telling me I should at least try to talk with Ellen for a bit. I'm not sure *why* I'm thinking this, but I am. Also, we should exchange numbers."

"Good idea on both accounts," Gabe replied, pulling out his phone.

"You really think so?" Chloe asked.

"Yes. She was telling the truth earlier: she won't bite...I know she seems incredibly intimidating, and not just because she's six foot five, but Ellen's actually very kind and thoughtful. And intelligent. I think you and her could have a nice talk."

"...yeah, all right."

They exchanged numbers, finished off their hot chocolate, and then headed inside. He brought Chloe over to Ellen, and the two of them walked off to somewhere more private and he was left standing with Holly, Emily, and Abby.

"So…" Emily said, smirking. "You slut."

"What?!" Gabe replied, turning to look at her swiftly.

"Did I stutter?"

"How am I a slut?"

"You fucked two women at this party," Emily replied, then took a drink from her wineglass.

"I–" Gabe paused, looked around, lowered his voice. "I fucked my *girlfriend* and I fucked Chloe in the mouth, not full on sex."

"You fucked two women," Emily replied, rolling her eyes. "In the mouth, in the vag, whatever. You engaged in sexual acts."

"Fine, are you giving me shit for it?"

"No, not at all. Bravo, is what I'm saying. Everyone thinks you railed Isabella," she murmured.

"Yep, and she's one hot, hot, *hot* lady," Abby said.

"Wait, so, you knew?"

"That you didn't fuck her? Yeah. I know Ellen's voice. And I figured she'd be too shy. She's just not ready to jump in bed with a hot young stranger. And, Gabe," Abby reached out and touched his arm, "I wanted to also say bravo for not trying to pressure her into sex even after she took off all her clothes and tried to jump you."

"Thanks," he murmured. "Wait, how'd you know the specifics?"

"I asked Ellen for the truth while you were with Chloe. Congrats on that, by the way. I am *very* jealous," Abby replied.

"Well, if it helps, I'm positive you could jump

her if she was into girls," he replied.

"So she isn't into girls?" Emily asked, immediately pouting. "Fuck."

"Told you," Abby murmured.

"Yeah, she confirmed that. She's...a bit of a mess right now. But I like her. And she seems to like me, apparently. So...we parted on good and hopeful terms."

"Hopeful?" Holly asked.

"She might come over and fuck. Also...she's a brat."

Holly's eyes widened. "Oh my God, that's so awesome. I want to see you two going at it."

"You mean going at it as in arguing or fucking?"

"Both."

He chuckled. "Well, hopefully I'll get the opportunity...so now what?"

"Now we chill in the library and talk about whatever comes to mind," Emily replied.

"Sounds good to me," Gabe replied, glancing at Ellen and Chloe. "I imagine they'll be busy for a little while."

"That girl does look a little lost," Abby murmured. "And Ellen is definitely a woman who can help a lost girl."

They began to head for the library.

CHAPTER THIRTY TWO

"So what did you two actually talk about last night?" Gabe asked, then grunted as he reached awkwardly into the lower cabinet in Holly's kitchen.

"Her feelings, mostly," Ellen replied. "And she wanted to be very, *very* sure that I wasn't going to rip her throat out with my teeth for 'sucking my man dry'."

He chuckled. "Ah. Yeah, she was worried about that. I have to say, you are a very intimidating girlfriend."

"You are," Holly said from elsewhere in the apartment.

"I'm mostly okay with this," Ellen replied. "I want to make sure that...only the right women get to my man."

"Is she a right woman?" Gabe asked.

"I think so," Ellen replied. "What are you doing?"

"There's a can of something back here," he muttered. "*Way* back there…"

"I'm positive she'll at least fuck you once," Ellen said.

"I want her for more," Gabe replied.

"Oh really?" Ellen asked.

"Yep. I want to date her."

"Goodness, you've only had me for a month, and Holly for less than that," Ellen murmured.

"Are you saying I shouldn't?"

"I'm not saying that at all."

"Well, I think-*oh fuck me!*" he screamed, jerking backwards as a spider crawled down over the edge of the countertop his face was right in front of.

"What!? Oh shit! Get it!" Ellen yelled.

"What's going on!?" Holly cried.

"Spider!" Gabe snapped, backing up across the kitchen and bumping into Ellen.

"Get me something flat!" Ellen said.

"No! Wait! I'll get it!" Holly called.

Before either of them could act, she appeared with a cup and a piece of paper. She masterfully and unflinchingly worked the spider into the cup and sealed the top with the paper, holding it firmly in place, then began heading for the front door.

"Uh, could someone get this for me? I can get the downstairs door with my shoulder," she said.

"I got it," Ellen said.

"Thanks."

Gabe watched as she opened the front door and Holly disappeared out it.

"Are you all right?" Ellen asked.

"Yeah. Just-goddamn! That scared the absolute fuck out of me. I *hate* spiders."

"Me too," she murmured. "Apparently Holly isn't bothered by them at all."

"Apparently."

Holly returned a moment later. "Okay, I let her go outside."

"You didn't hesitate at all," Gabe murmured, finally getting back to his feet.

"Oh, yeah. Spiders don't freak me out. I don't know why. Bugs don't bug me. Wasps do, though. I hate wasps. And snakes scare the shit out of me."

"You got lucky there, given how common spiders are and how common snakes aren't," Ellen murmured.

"I didn't get the can," Gabe said, looking back down at the darkened cabinet.

"Here, let me get it, I've got longer arms," Ellen said, taking his place.

"All right. Fuck, I hate spiders," he muttered, shuddering. He walked out of the kitchen and took a look around.

They'd made a lot of progress today.

After the party, they'd headed home, all of them sleepy and in a good mood. Gabe had an idea that something would happen once they got home, but for once all three of them were too tired for it. So they'd curled up together beneath the blankets and fallen asleep promptly.

Holly had work the following day, but it was her evening job so she had most of the day free. When they'd gotten up the next morning, Ellen had initially planned to go over to Holly's apartment alone to continue working on it, but both Gabe and especially Holly felt weird about that, not wanting to let her do all the work solo.

And so here they were, almost done now.

They'd gotten the biggest, most annoying part out of the way just an hour ago. Holly had agreed to donate all her furniture. They had briefly considered moving at least some of it over, but none of them actually wanted any of it.

In the end, Ellen had set up a donation service to come by with a truck to haul it away and see if they could put it to use. They had hauled her bed, dresser, desk, tiny sofa, coffee table, TV, and a small assortment of other little pieces of furniture away.

The apartment seemed much, much emptier now.

The trash was cleaned up, the laundry was finished, almost three quarters of it thrown away or given away as well. Holly had been tackling the bathroom, insisting that it be her responsibility given how gross she'd let it get.

"So, before we got derailed by that...how would you two feel about it? If I seriously romantically pursued Chloe?" Gabe asked.

"I'd be so very okay with it," Holly replied.

"She's not into women, unfortunately."

"I know," Holly said. "But that's fine. She seems fun, but also sad, and like she doesn't deserve to be sad? And being with the two of you made me *so* much happier, so I imagine that being with Gabe will make Chloe a lot happier, too. Or, well, I hope so."

"I'm okay with it, provided you do your due diligence," Ellen said.

"What, in your mind, does that look like?" he asked.

"Checking for red flags, ensuring that she's actually down for a relationship with a guy who is already dating two other women *and* will be likely occasionally be banging other women as well. Making sure that we all get along and she doesn't upset the vibes or atmosphere of our home," Ellen replied.

"I can do that," he replied.

Ellen smirked. "I think you just want regular access to hot goth pussy."

"...that's also possible," he murmured.

"Well, like I said, I trust you with this, and I'm okay with it...what actually is this?" Ellen muttered now that she'd successfully extracted the can. "Hmm, pork and beans. Still within its expiration date. I can fry this up with some bacon and eggs tonight or tomorrow." She got back to her feet. "Are we almost done?"

"I think so. I'm basically done with the bathroom," Holly replied.

"Lemme see," Gabe said. He walked over and looked in. "Jesus Christ, Holly."

"What?" she asked, sounding vaguely worried.

"This is fucking sparkling. It looks almost brand new. Goddamn, you can fucking *clean*."

She broke into a grin. "Thank you."

"I think that's almost everything," Ellen murmured as she checked it out. "We washed the windows, dealt with any stains on the walls. Everything has been moved out of the apartment now. The trash has been taken out. All that's left is vacuuming, I believe."

"That adds up," Holly said.

"Yeah, I can't think of anything else," Gabe agreed.

"Perfect. We can vacuum and begone. I'll do it," Ellen said, and set to work.

The next ten minutes passed quickly as Ellen dumped a light dusting of nice-smelling carpet deodorant everywhere, then vacuumed everything up. They double checked everything one more time, peered in all the cabinets, looked in the medicine cabinet, investigated beneath the sinks. In the end, they stood together by the front door, looking over a very clean apartment.

"I bet I still don't get the security deposit back," Holly murmured.

"We'll see about that," Ellen replied.

Twenty minutes later, they were getting into Ellen's car, a very satisfied Ellen sitting behind the wheel and turning over the engine.

"Man, you *are* intimidating," Gabe muttered.

"Told you I could do it," Ellen replied.

All it had taken to scare the landlord into at the very least giving her a genuine investigation of the apartment and a real chance at returning the deposit were a few very legal-sounding sentences from Ellen. He imagined that her great height and sharp professionalism, which she could pull out at the drop of a hat, had a lot to do with it too.

"Okay," Ellen said, losing her smile and glancing in the rearview at Holly, "there's just one more thing we need to discuss. In all our moving, unless I missed it, we never saw your birth certificate or social security card."

"Oh, well...I don't have them," Holly replied, as if that should have been obvious.

"Why not?" Ellen asked.

"I didn't think I'd need them...?" Holly replied, quickly growing uncertain. Ellen turned around in her seat and looked at her. "I'm sorry," Holly whispered.

Ellen hesitated, then seemed to take a moment to dial it back. "It's fine, Holly," she said. "I'm not angry, but...you really, *really* want to have your birth certificate and your social security card. They're very important. You might go your whole life without ever actually needing them, but they're the kind of thing where if you *do* need them, you *really* need them. And they're a big pain in the ass to get replaced. Where are they?"

Now she was blushing unhappily and not meeting Ellen's gaze anymore. "...with my parents. I'm really sorry. I didn't know I needed them."

"It's okay, Holly," Ellen replied. She faced forward again and fell into a contemplative silence.

"How difficult would it be to just...go over there and get them?" Gabe asked.

She sighed and groaned. "It'd be...a real pain in the ass. We aren't on good terms, although they *want* to be. Sort of. In their own way. I mean really, what they want is an obedient little daughter who does everything they say and gets married to a good Christian man and is already pregnant. God, they'd flip *so* hard if they knew I was dating a guy *and* a girl, *and* we live together without being married or even engaged, let alone after just a few weeks."

Everyone was silent for a long moment.

"What if…" Ellen murmured, slowly raising her head, "you were just dating Gabe?"

"Are you saying you want to break up with me?" Holly asked.

"*What?* Holly, *no*. Honey, you aren't in trouble. I'm not angry with you, seriously. I want to help you." She turned back around in the seat and reached back, taking Holly's hand. "This is okay. We can fix this."

"Okay...what do you mean just Gabe?" she asked, relaxing.

"I mean...okay, you know where your parents live still, right?" Holly nodded. "And you know where your social security card and your birth certificate would be?"

"Yeah. They should be in my room still. In my closet." She patted her purse. "My mom gave me a little lockbox to keep my important stuff in and I've still got the key for it. There's not really anything else in there, I think, besides those things. Maybe some cash, but not much. But it's not like I can just pop over and grab it. They had the locks changed since I last moved and I never got the new key. And I'm not gonna risk breaking in. I'd have to actually talk to them…"

"Are you okay with lying to them?" Ellen asked.

"Yes," Holly replied after giving it a little consideration.

"Perfect. So. This is the plan: you call up your parents and tell them Gabe is your fiance. Naturally, they'll want to meet him. Arrange a meeting at their place. You two get inside, you find an opportunity to slip away and grab your shit, and then get out as soon as you can," Ellen said.

"That could work...Gabe?" she asked.

"I'd be down. This is important and...I have to admit, I'm curious to meet your parents. In a morbid kind of way," he replied.

"Perfect," Ellen said, grinning now. "Let's get home and work out the details."

...

Barely two hours passed before they had the entire plan locked down.

It came together surprisingly well and quickly, but Gabe knew that sometimes things just worked out. Although he was admittedly nervous about the whole thing. Meeting his girlfriend's parents had always been awkward, because they had always been disappointed in him. He could just tell, read it in their expressions, the soft sigh, the slight glazing of the eyes, the defeated slump of the shoulders when they finally met him.

Holly had texted her parents about it, Ellen coaching her slightly on how to approach it. They hadn't actually spoken in any real capacity in nearly a year. But her mother had responded almost immediately, evidently overjoyed to learn about her engagement and saying that they were having a family get together Sunday, which was tomorrow, and they would be so thrilled for her to finally come back home and for her to introduce her new fiance to the whole family.

She had also already asked if Holly was pregnant.

"So, Holly, are you feeling good about this whole thing?" Ellen asked.

"I do, I think. Mostly," she murmured. "But...there's something I want to ask for." She hesitated, then rolled her eyes. "No, it's stupid. It's ridiculous."

"No, ask for it," Gabe said.

"No, I couldn't..." she murmured.

"Holly," Gabe said, a firm tone in his voice.

She began chewing on her lip, a slow smile spreading across her face. "Okay," she murmured. "If I have to..." She tilted her head down, twisting her foot along the floor, slowly looking up at him.

"You have to," Gabe replied.

Her smile widened a little more and she began to blush. "Okay." She grew more serious. "I want...you to propose to me. I know, it's ridiculous. And I know it wouldn't be a real proposal! But I mean, we need a ring anyway, right? So if we've gotta get a ring, I figured maybe, even a fake proposal would just-it would feel really good...it's stupid."

"I'll do it," Gabe said.

"Really!?"

"Yes."

She looked up at Ellen. "Would it be weird?"

"No, I think it would be incredibly sweet," Ellen replied. "But...I want it, too."

"You want me to propose to both of you?" Gabe asked.

"Separately. And, yes, a fake proposal. We...well, weddings can wait for quite a while."

"All right then. What kind of a timeline am I

looking at for this?" he asked.

"Let's say a month," Ellen replied.

Holly was grinning more broadly than ever and seemed to be having trouble standing still. "You guys make me so happy!" she cried.

Before Gabe could respond, she rushed over and hugged him, then kissed him firmly on the mouth. After a moment, she released him and did the same thing with Ellen.

"Well, we really like you, Holly," she murmured, making her giggle.

She began to say something else, then hesitated and checked her phone. She sighed heavily. "Goddamnit! I'm going to be late if I don't leave now...fuck. Okay, I have to go. Love you both!"

She gave each of them a quick kiss, grabbed her things, and then was gone a moment later.

"I really want her to quit her jobs," Ellen murmured.

"I do, too. But is it the best idea?" Gabe replied.

She sighed. "Maybe. It depends on how things play out. Anyway...come on. Let's go ring shopping!"

CHAPTER THIRTY THREE

"This feels kinda weird," Gabe murmured as they drove through the darkened city.

"I get that," Ellen said. "But it's fun, right?"

"Yeah, actually." Gabe looked out as Ellen drove along. She'd been in a driving mood just recently. It was dark out, but this late into November that was to be expected...

Gabe thought about that. Late. Into November...

"Oh shit."

"What?" Ellen asked.

"I just realized, we missed Thanksgiving, didn't we?" he replied.

"I guess so. Yeah, it would've been two days ago. Why does that matter?"

"I don't know, I just thought...you know, it's a holiday. Our first Thanksgiving together. As a couple...throuple? What the fuck is the word for three people dating?"

"I don't know. Does it matter? I didn't get the impression you really cared about that kind of stuff."

"I mean I don't, but if *you* or Holly cares, then I care."

"That's sweet but I'll be completely honest, Gabe: fuck Thanksgiving."

He glanced at her. She was deadly serious. "Wow."

"I know, it's weird, but I hate Thanksgiving. When I was growing up it was a responsibility. First it was a responsibility to go over to my aunt's and uncle's place and pretend we had more money than we did and that we were more upper class than we really were. And then later it was the same thing, only now I was expected to cook my fucking ass off.

"It was never fun, it was always a responsibility. Always stiff conversation, afraid of saying the wrong thing. And that never stopped. Everyone I was ever with, it was always the same. Showing me off, trying to pretend we were more successful and had more money than we really did. Lying, lying, lying. Always the stiff atmosphere and no one really wants to be there...fuck."

"Jeez, babe. Sorry."

"It's not your fault, you didn't know. And...I mean, I'm not against a little celebration if you or if Holly really wants to. Just, you know, I'm *not* busting ass cooking a massive fucking turkey dinner again. Ever, if I can manage it. I've got fucking Thanksgiving PTSD. Christmas, too, but I'm a lot more willing to give ground on that...maybe. Ugh, Valentine's Day, too, but I *am* willing to give a lot of ground on that one. Valentine's Day was made for fucking and I love fucking you."

"Looking forward to that," Gabe murmured.

She chuckled. "You have no idea...okay, there it is."

Ellen pulled into the parking lot of a row of buildings that all looked more upscale than he was used to.

"Okay, we're not going over more than two hundred bucks a pop for these rings. I know it's a fake proposal but it *is* representative of our bond, I think. Also, I have to admit I know what kind of people Holly's parents are and it'll piss them off if she doesn't have a ring with a big fat diamond on it. And I want to piss them off...I just realized we've never talked much about your parents."

He sighed as they got out of the car. "It's

depressing. What's there to say? More or less like yours. Worked me half to death from when I was sixteen, took most of my paycheck as 'rent', kept me from going to college so they could keep on with the exploitation. They both drank the cash away."

"I'm sorry, honey. We don't have to talk about it," Ellen murmured.

"Appreciated," he replied.

They walked into a fancy looking jeweler's shop and immediately Gabe felt out of his depth. Everywhere he looked there were shiny rings, earrings, necklaces, and an assortment of other jewelry he didn't quite recognize.

He was afraid to move for fear of breaking something ridiculously expensive.

Ellen seemed a lot more at home, though, as she walked right in and kept on going without hesitating. He moved to follow her.

"What kind of ring do you want?" she asked.

"I don't know...something simple. Just a metal band. Titanium? That appeals for some reason," he replied.

"Not a bad idea," she replied.

"Oh fuck," he muttered as they kept hunting around.

"What?"

"I just realized I have no idea what her ring size is."

"Oh, don't worry about that. Her ring finger is about the size of my pinky, so that'll be fine. Mmm. What to get her, though..."

"An emerald," he replied.

Ellen looked at him. "You say that with a lot of confidence."

"Green's her favorite color and I'm almost

positive I've heard her talking about emeralds before in a positive way," he replied.

Ellen kept staring at him. "What's my favorite color?"

"Blue."

She blinked. "Did I tell you that?"

"Yeah, a while ago."

"I feel like a bad girlfriend now. I don't know your favorite color."

"Don't feel bad. People remember different things," he replied.

"...so what is it?"

"Yellow."

"...I still feel bad."

"It's really okay, honey. I don't even know if it ever came up."

"Well, all right," she murmured.

"What about this one?" he asked, studying a ring marked as titanium. It had what looked like gold threaded back and forth across the band. "Not quite yellow, but I like gold, too."

Ellen leaned forward, looking closely at it. "It's a hundred bucks," she murmured. "If you want it, I'd totally buy it."

"Yeah, I'm down for it."

"Perfect. One down. Let's see what else we can find..."

It was a strange experience, and a bit of pain, as they had to have someone come and take out the ring from behind glass each time they wanted to see it. But he supposed it made enough sense. They were expensive and you couldn't really trust the general public to just come in and have relatively free access to expensive jewelry.

They poked around for a while, and once they

had found Holly's ring, one that Ellen ultimately insisted he have final say on, she gave him a little push back the way they'd come.

"What?" he asked.

"Find my ring now," she replied.

"...without you?"

"Yeah. Of course. It's meant to be a surprise."

"But you're the one paying for it."

"I know, Gabe. Come on, do I need to explain this?"

"No, no, I got it," he replied.

"Thank you, babe."

Gabe headed back. He'd actually seen one that had caught his eye. He felt that old serpent of fear trying to uncoil, the fear that said: *she's testing you, she already saw the one she wants and now you'd better pick it or she'll rage.*

Gabe shook his head. Ellen wasn't like that, he knew that now, trusted that, but his own natural insecurity, combined with her generally intense nature, fed into that worry. He was very grateful that he was able to push his anxieties aside with increasing ease.

Living a life of anxiety was a very miserable existence.

He spent about five minutes looking back over the rings in the price range that Ellen had indicated, to see if any others jumped out at him. But none did. He called the person over, had them take the ring out so he could study it closer, and then had them put it in one of those little boxes so that Ellen wouldn't see it.

The person behind the register was obviously a little confused by the couple purchasing three rings, and Ellen very specifically wasn't looking at one of them, but they managed to make the purchases without being seriously questioned.

As they got back into the car and began heading home, Gabe decided to again broach a topic that had been weighing heavily on his mind since last night.

"So I want to talk seriously about Chloe," he said.

"I feel like we did, but I'm listening," Ellen replied.

He paused as he considered it. "I'm having a hard time getting my head around it. I guess, just, I'll ask one more time: you're okay with it if I genuinely and seriously pursue Chloe romantically?"

"Yes," she said.

"As in: go on dates with her, have unprotected sex with her, fall in love with her, move her in with us, treat her like you and Holly."

"Yes, I'm okay with that."

"Mmm."

"You aren't happy with that?"

"Of course I'm happy with that, it's just...different."

"I know." He glanced briefly at her. "You won't have my help this time."

He chuckled softly. "Yeah, that's definitely some of it. Although I won't be *completely* solo. Obviously you reassured her last night."

"I did. She's...rough around the edges, but it seems like she's been through a lot. You two would make a great couple, though."

"You think so?"

"I do. That's my gut instinct, anyway. She's a wild girl, but she's also grimly responsible. I see a lot of myself in her, only she's smarter than I am."

"You think?"

"Oh yeah. She's been single for a year by choice,

that alone is smarter than me. I...do not handle being single well. And now that I've flung myself into the heavenly abyss that is our relationship for the rest of my life, I won't have to worry about that ever again, ideally. She needs a man...who isn't afraid of her, but also respects her. It's surprisingly difficult to get those two things in just the right alignment. And you have both."

"I'm kind of afraid of her," Gabe replied.

She laughed. "I know, so is Holly. But you were kind of afraid of me, and look where we are now. I think once you slap her around a little bit, blow a huge load in her pussy, and actually spend some more time with her, go on a few real dates, that fear with evaporate."

"You have such a way with words," he murmured.

"I'm just being honest."

A few moments went by. "I'll admit, I'm having a hard time getting used to this idea."

"Kind of like a dog chasing cars. You finally got the car, now you aren't sure what to do with it," she murmured.

"Yeah honestly. But...if you're serious about this, I want to stop being so hesitant then. I want to actually do this. Actually pursue her. Because I *am* extremely attracted to her, and I do feel something, a connection between us that's not all that dissimilar from how I feel about you and me, or me and Holly."

"Then do it," Ellen replied. "Just...see if you can talk her into letting me watch."

He laughed. "She didn't seem terribly averse to the idea...all right, I'll think more on this. However I feel about it, I know I don't want to rush her. Are you all right with it if I spend the rest of the night writing?

I think I'm on the home stretch of finishing up By the Hearthfire's Light."

"I'm fine with that and I still *love* that name," Ellen replied.

"You sure it's not too...I dunno, cheesy?"

"No. Trust me. It perfectly straddles the line between romantic and erotic, but it doesn't come off as stupid. And I'm fucking dying to read the whole thing. So yes, please, write away."

Gabe just grinned and kept on driving.

...

"I'm going to die of anticipation," Holly complained as Gabe led her back through the woods behind their home.

"You will be fine," he replied.

"How much longer?!"

"I don't know, Holly, but not much. I had to get a little creative finding this place," he replied.

"I'm so excited!" she whispered harshly.

He laughed and kept on going.

Today was the big day. Last night had been exhausting but satisfying. He'd marathoned finishing off By the Hearthfire's Light and then tossed it to Ellen. When Holly had come home, he and her had spent about an hour finishing getting her all settled into her new home.

They were going to have to buy another dresser, he could tell that, even after Holly had dumped like eighty percent of her clothes. He knew she'd want to buy more. But there had been something profoundly special about it.

Making more space for her, giving her a drawer to herself, and then adding her handful of little things to his and Ellen's atop the dresser. She had a little painted gray cat figurine made of clay that she'd sculpted herself back in high school, a single framed photograph that she had taken, printed out, and had framed, as it was what she considered her first 'real' photo, about a dozen novels, some simple jewelry, and a couple of other knickknacks that she'd picked up over the course of her life.

And now his bathroom was positively overflowing with stuff. He'd rarely needed more than some clippers, a toothbrush, toothpaste, a razor, some shaving cream, and deodorant, but now he had two women living with him, women who both were image conscious and also smarter about hygiene and upkeep than he was.

Not that he was complaining at all.

But it had felt so...romantic, and unifying, helping her get settled into his place.

Into their place.

And she fit like she was born to it.

"Holly...I was kinda curious about something," he said.

"Ask me anything," she replied as they walked on through the forest, following a very rough path through the dead trees, the discarded vegetation crunching underfoot.

"Don't take this wrong, but...does it ever freak you out, how much you love me? Or Ellen?"

"No," she replied.

"Why not? Again, I'm not complaining, I'm just curious."

"I know, and I get it. My whole life...has always felt off. Sometimes a lot, sometimes a little. When I finally went on my own, I slowly began to realize that a lot of the times where the off-ness seemed less, it wasn't really, it was more just that I got used to something shitty. And, I don't know, Gabe. A lot of women end up discovering they're happier alone, but I'm not. I just know I'm not. I was so fucking lonely and miserable in my apartment. I need to live with people, but people like you and Ellen, obviously. And...well, let's just say that loving you and loving Ellen feels as natural and comfortable as dozing beneath a warm, soft blanket on a rainy day. Loving you two is easy, and it just feels right. You are the answer to the question that is my life."

"...wow," he murmured.

"I know. It's intense. It's a lot of responsibility to put on someone. But...you seem like you're into it," she said.

"I am," he replied. "And I feel the same way. You and Ellen just...click, you just fit with me. It's like this was supposed to happen. Being with you feels as natural as writing. And I love you so much."

She giggled and shivered. "I love you too. So, so much. You make me feel insane sometimes, but in a good way."

Gabe could see it now, what he had spent the rest of last night hunting down, after writing and after sending Holly off to bed. He was trying to hide how tired he was. He hadn't gotten much sleep. He had to stay up late to get the details and then wake up early to make this work. It was just past nine in the morning now and the day was tolerably chilly.

"Oh my God...is that what I think it is?" Holly whispered.

"Yes," he replied, "it is an abandoned house. And we are going to go inside *after* we poke around for a bit, and be extremely careful. And you're going to take some pictures."

"Thank you so much!" she replied, hugging him tightly and kissing him firmly on the mouth.

Before he could properly respond, she let go and hurried forward. Gabe sighed softly and chuckled. Holly was very brave for how timid she was. Gabe made sure to pay close attention to the yard that they stepped out into.

He'd been stymied at first on how to handle this, because he knew that he wanted to give Holly the gift of an abandoned building. Finally, it had occurred to him to check the satellite maps of his area. His house was up against a forest and usually there should be *some* kind of abandoned structures in such an environment.

Sure enough, he'd encountered an old house that was only accessible via a gravel road that was perhaps a five minute walk from his backyard. He'd investigated it as much as he could but now that he was actually standing here, he was grateful to see that it looked even more abandoned than it had in the imaging he'd been able to find.

"I wonder who lived here," Holly murmured as they began making a slow circle of the house, carefully peering in through the windows.

"Maybe someone who was rich in, like, the forties," Gabe replied, looking up at the house.

It definitely looked pretty old, and it had that vague forties or fifties era style to it. Though obviously it had been added onto. But he imagined that no one had lived there for probably twenty years, maybe longer. And he doubted anyone had actually been to the place in a decade or more. Some of the windows were broken, and those that remained intact were pretty dusty and dirty.

Any looks inside showed mostly barren rooms

with a few pieces of old, time-decayed furniture within. They made a complete circuit of the outside and arrived back at the front door. Cautiously, he tried it as Holly adjusted her camera. It was unlocked.

Gabe pushed the door slowly open. It creaked loudly.

"All right, remember, very careful," he murmured. "Don't touch anything. Take some pictures, soak in the ambience, and then we should go. We have to be at your parent's place by noon."

"That's like three hours away," she murmured.

"I know, I just like to have too much time rather than too little," he replied.

"Okay, fair enough. I'm ready."

He led her inside, keeping Ellen's can of mace in one hand as he did. He seriously doubted they'd run into anyone here and he wasn't prepared to immediately escalate to macing them in the face, but it was nice to have the option.

They came into a dusty living room absent of all furniture. There was some trash on the floor but otherwise the room was vacant. He couldn't see any footprints of any kind in the dust, so that was a good sign at least. Holly raised her camera and snapped a photo.

They moved on.

Time passed as the two of them moved silently through the house. They investigated an ancient bathroom with a claw-foot tub. A tiny closet that had an old broom and an uncomfortably large spider with a web up near the ceiling. What might have been a bedroom, though now all that remained was a chair and a table and the rusted, skeletal remains of a bed frame.

Finally there was a kitchen, most of the cabinet

doors open, drawers pulled out, and here one of the windows had been broken. Rain had gotten in and done a lot of water damage over the years.

Gabe wondered who had lived here, how many, what they'd done. What the walls of this house had seen, what it stood in silent testament to.

It looked like it could go either way. Maybe a loving a family had lived here for generations before finally moving on, or maybe awful, twisted misery and abuse had been endured. It was uncomfortable how those two things were just as likely.

Hell, if anything, the abuse was more likely, given his own life experience and what he'd seen so far.

Gabe could feel the weight of the ringbox in his pocket.

It was almost time.

They spent about half an hour moving through the old house slowly, Holly pausing to take pictures every now and then. Though she took less than he thought she might. She seemed to think long and hard about it each time.

Finally, they ended up back in the living room. He could tell she was tempted to investigate the other floors of the house, but thankfully she didn't push for that. Even with his newfound confidence, Gabe didn't think he could muster the courage to investigate the basement of a house like this. It felt too much like a horror movie.

"Holly…" Gabe said as they began making their way back home, outside again now.

"Yeah?" she replied, slowly turning back to face him.

He reached into his pocket and dropped down one knee as he pulled out the ringbox. She inhaled sharply and her eyes went wide. She seemed to freeze in place as she finished fully turning to face him. Gabe brought the box forth and cracked it open, presenting the ring with the thin silver band and the small, very green emerald mounted on it to her.

"Will you marry me?"

She let out a little shriek and actually dived onto him. "*YES!*" she cried as he let out his own shout of surprise, just barely managing to snap the box shut and keep it in hand instead of losing the ring on the ground.

Holly laughed wildly as she kissed him repeatedly, now laying atop him in the cold, overgrown yard.

"Yes! I will!" she cried again.

Gabe wasn't even sure what to say as she trembled in excitement, her eyes wet and wide. She kissed him several more times and then finally seemed to get control of herself. She laughed again and then got up.

"Oh, I'm sorry. I didn't mean-I was just so excited!" she said, offering him a hand.

He laughed softly and took it, letting her help him up. "I'm glad, Holly."

"I know it's not real but it *felt* real! Oh my God, did you drop the ring!?"

"No, it's right here," he replied, opening the box again and showing her.

She immediately took it and slipped it onto the ring finger of her left hand, then raised it high, staring at it with a massive smile. Gabe had to admit, there *was* something magic about it, about this specific interaction.

"Well it's not really fake," he said as he pulled his own ringbox out and opened it up. "I *do* love you and I *am* asking you to be with me."

"I know, and it's so wonderful-let me see yours!"

"Here, babe," he said, showing her.

She took the ring and studied it, still grinning madly. "Can I put it on you?"

"Yeah." He presented his hand to her and she slipped it onto his proper finger.

"Oh fuck I'm going to cry," she whispered, wiping at her eyes. "I'm so happy."

"You know, Holly, we *could* have a ceremony at some point. It's not going to be official in the eyes of the government but who gives a fuck? We could have a wedding ceremony, maybe in Em's and Abby's backyard? You could wear a dress if you wanted, and Ellen, too. One of our friends could ask us if we commit to loving each other…"

"*Could we really do that!?*" she cried in sheer jubilation.

Gabe laughed. "Yes, but *please* don't be screaming out here."

"I'm sorry," she said as they began making their way back again. "I'm just so excited! Oh my goodness, this is amazing! That would be so wonderful! I can get a wedding dress...but it would be so expensive…"

"Who cares? If you want a nice wedding dress then why not?" he replied.

"You'd really do all that for me?"

"Of course I would. I know Ellen would, too."

She giggled again, staring at her ring still. "It really is beautiful," she whispered. "I love it. It's...I don't know, would you be mad if I said it was minimalist?"

"No."

"Good, because I like minimalism. It's...simple

yet elegant. Sleek. I fucking love it. What does Ellen's look like?"

"I can show you, but you have to promise not to tell her at all. I want to surprise her with it just like I surprised you."

"I promise, but wasn't she there when you bought it?"

"Yes, but she purposefully didn't look at it."

"Oh, okay then. Yes, I promise. But I want to see it!"

"Come on, I'll show you when we get back, then we have to start getting ready."

CHAPTER THIRTY FOUR

"So...what exactly can I expect here?" Gabe asked as he drove his car through the city.

He'd been tempted to take Ellen's, to make a better impression, but remembered that he wasn't there to make a good impression.

If anything, he was there to make a bad one.

Though he had to make sure he didn't lean too far in that direction. He didn't want to make it obvious.

"So, my parents will be there. Almost certainly my older sister will be there. She's a bitch. I've got two aunts and uncles, and both couples have a kid, so two cousins. My cousins are okay. Well, one of them I feel bad for, the other...I mean, I feel bad for him, it's just that he's kind of a shit sometimes so it's harder to feel bad for him. One aunt-uncle pair are both pretty money obsessed and are socially religious, my other pair are, like, really religious, like my parents. Worse than my parents, I think. My grandparents are dead, so they won't be there, thank God. All the grown ups there will look down on you, so...sorry."

"Hey, I don't care," Gabe replied.

"Really?"

"Fucking hell yeah, I'm bulletproof."

She laughed. "Really? I mean I'm glad you feel that, but I know you struggle with this kind of thing. I don't think you should, I think you're the greatest man ever, but I also know *you* think I'm a fucking supermodel and I...just do not think that, so obviously I can conceptually understand what you're going through. But if you've stopped doing that, then awesome?"

"It's a little complicated. I still have anxiety and I still have self-worth issues, but it feels like it's getting better. I know it's not healthy but it is what is, but dating you and Ellen obviously was a massive shot of self esteem. Getting away from my soul-destroying job helped a lot. Actually starting to write and make something of myself that way has helped a lot. Having my own place and living with people I *want* to live with helped big time.

"But specifically with relation to this current situation? I guess...consider how you feel when you think you're being judged by a random person. You don't really know who they are or what they do. Everyone can't be an asshole, so maybe their judgment has some weight. But with your family? Fuck them, they *are* assholes! I don't give a *fuck* what they think about me because their opinion isn't worth shit! And I don't even have to convince myself of that, I can tell that I honestly just believe it. And yeah, maybe that's fucked up, but your family can fuck off for how they treated you."

Holly laughed. "Okay then," she said. "And...you know, you're right. I kinda feel the same way. I mean I feel like they're always going to have some sort of sway over me, but it's down to almost nothing right now. My mom could call me a slutty failure and I wouldn't give a shit. And I know exactly how you feel: I have you and Ellen. I don't know if I feel bulletproof, but certainly this is the best I've ever felt going to see them."

"Okay, what's the actual plan?" Gabe asked.

"We'll get in there and sort of play it by ear," Holly replied, and the tone she adopted was one he'd never quite heard before, except, he realized, when she was talking about photography. And abruptly he knew why that was: she was an expert on her family just like she was an expert on photography. Though with her family it was a necessity of survival. "They'll bullshit for about, I dunno, half an hour to an hour, and then lunch will happen, although we're cutting it a little closer, so maybe sooner than half an hour. I find the opening, I get it, we leave. I want out as soon as possible."

"So what, you look for an opening, slip away while I distract, then come back once you have it?" he asked.

"I'm *so* tempted to walk out with middle fingers and the 'fuck yous' flying, but I had no idea I needed this stuff, and there might be other things I need in the future? So I don't want to burn that bridge if I don't have to. So...how about this? Once I actually have it, I'll come find you and say 'work called me in'. That's the tell that we can get the fuck out."

"Sounds good to me," Gabe said. "Oh, one thing I want you to remember. This is important."

"I'm listening."

"Make sure to actually open the lockbox and visually confirm your social security card and birth certificate are there, and that they are *yours,* then re-lock it. Also, how big is it? Can it fit in your purse?"

"Yep."

"Perfect. Make sure they don't see it. Bury it a little, make sure no corners are sticking out or anything. You have no idea what they might be looking at or when," he said.

"I will remember all of this...you are really one for details, you know that?" she murmured.

"I am, but...don't get too attached to that notion. I can totally miss things. If you have an idea or a thought that you think I missed, please never be afraid to tell me." He paused. "Actually, just a standing statement right now: please never be afraid to tell me anything ever. Same with Ellen."

"I'm trying," she said.

"We appreciate it. I know it's not easy to just snap out of that, but we're here for you. Always."

"Always?" she murmured.

"*Always,* Holly. I don't care if it's four in the morning, if I'm writing, sleeping, having sex with another woman, taking a dump, whatever. You need me, you tell me."

"...really?"

"Yes. Really."

"Jeez. That's really intense," she murmured.

"It's like I told you, that wasn't really a fake proposal," Gabe said.

"Yeah...you're right. And that wasn't a fake acceptance, either," she replied, regaining her smile. "At least I'm not going to have to fake how in love I am with you."

"Yes. That part, at least, will be easy."

Ten minutes later, they pulled up on the curb in front of a two-story house in a middling part of town. Not a gated community by any stretch of the imagination, but he imagined no one impoverished was within a few city blocks.

Five other cars were already there.

"One more thing," Holly said as he put the car in park.

"Yeah?"

"I imagine you're going to feel the need to defend me. Strongly." She paused. "Very strongly. Don't. I know you love me and it's going to make you really mad, the things they'll have to say about me, but...just keep the peace."

"...all right," he said.

"Thank you."

Gabe sighed softly. Great.

Despite his bulletproof feeling, Gabe *was* nervous. Mostly, he didn't want to fuck this up. He reassured himself with the knowledge that, absolute worst case scenario, there were ways of getting these scraps of paper via other means.

Okay, Gabe thought to himself as he and Holly got out of the car, *I can do this.*

They held hands as they walked up to the front door. Holly rang the doorbell. He could hear people talking inside. Actually, he heard some people arguing loudly. It took a moment to finally stop and then the front door opened up. Gabe found himself looking at an older version of Holly, presumably her mother.

"Holly! Finally!" she declared.

"Hi mom," Holly replied. "We're here."

"Yes you are. I was beginning to wonder what it was going to take to get you to come home or even just answer my calls. I was really considering faking cancer just to scare you into coming home and being a good daughter for a bit there," she said.

"Yeah that would've been just great, mom," Holly muttered.

Her mom laughed and looked at Gabe now. "You must be Gabe. I imagine you've had your work cut out for you with this one. Always with the excuses and the lazy days and not taking care of herself like a woman should for her man."

Gabe was stuck for a response. He almost said: *I'm not even in the door yet.* Instead, he cleared his throat and tried to relax his muscles. "It's nice to meet you ma'am," he lied, "and it's been pretty smooth sailing with Holly so far, I'd say."

She laughed and took a drink from what looked to be a margarita. "Well that's good. I imagine her last boyfriend got a lot of the work done for you."

"Mom," Holly said.

"Oops! Probably not kosher to talk about that to you. Please, come in! Meet the family," she said, making way.

Gabe resisted the overwhelming impulse to in some capacity show his disgust and stepped inside with Holly.

He believed her that it was bad, but he didn't quite realize it was going to be *this* bad.

It had been thirty fucking seconds.

They took off their hoodies and hung them up.

"Holly...why don't you have a proper coat by now?" her mother groused, touching the hoodie. "These are so...unseemly. People are going to think you're poor."

"I *am* poor," Holly replied.

"I know but the average person doesn't need to *know* that...well, anyway. Come along. Let's introduce your fiance to the rest of the family," she said, walking away deeper into the house without looking to see if they were following.

Gabe shared a glance with Holly, who looked at once both irritated and embarrassed.

He whispered "I love you" and she regained her smile.

They walked through the living room, through a short hallway, and into a big dining room. Somewhere nearby he could hear that sounds of a football game on TV. Gabe realized that he was tensing up again and it was getting worse now. For a moment, he had no idea why that might be beyond the fact that he was walking deeper into the house.

But as he saw the three people setting the table in the dining room, heard the sound of presumably her aunts talking in the kitchen, it occurred to him why he was tensing up.

This was the exact same atmosphere he'd grown up in. Or, more specifically, the one he'd been subjected to during family get togethers.

"Look who showed up," her mom said.

"Wow, Holly," one of the people in the room, who *had* to be her older sister, said, "you couldn't even dress up after like a year and a half?"

"I *am* dressed up," Holly growled.

Yep, definitely her sister.

She rolled her eyes. "Come *on,* Holly, this is dressed up for you?"

"Yes, Mary."

Gabe took another glance at Holly, unsure if he was missing something. She was wearing a black dress that, while it did not show off her wonderful body as much as some of the things she wore around him did, it did look very good on her. Although it was possible that he was so enraptured by her he had lost all perspective.

Holly would look good to him even if she was wearing a garbage bag.

It was also possible her sister was being a huge bitch.

Gabe glanced quickly at Holly's mom out of the corner of his eye, wondering if she'd chastise her older sister, but if anything she looked oddly satisfied by the display. Which was worrying on a number of levels.

"I guess when you try to carve your own path

without any real plan at all and *insist* on doing it yourself, it makes sense that you'd have no money," she murmured. Mary looked suddenly at him. "Speaking of which, hi. What do you do for a living?"

"I'm a writer," Gabe replied.

He could actually sense the atmosphere in the room change, and for the worse, the moment the words left his mouth. He saw Mary and her mother share a glance that so successfully conveyed 'my God can you believe what a fucking loser she hitched herself to?' he could almost hear the words. Holly's mother turned to him.

"Gabe, would you be a dear and help the women in the kitchen?" she asked.

A few responses came to mind, but he simply nodded. "Yes, I can do that."

"I'll help, too," Holly murmured.

"No, Holly, dear, let me see that ring, and tell me all the things you've been keeping me in the dark about since you refuse to answer my messages," her mother replied.

Holly sighed softly and Gabe gave her a quick look, then headed through the door across the room where the sounds of the kitchen were coming from. He came in and found a pair of women who also vaguely resembled Holly. Her aunts. One was noticeably younger than her mother, one was a bit older. They seemed to be arguing quietly but heatedly about something as they finished assembling what looked to be Thanksgiving lunch.

They both stopped, however, as he came in.

"Who are you?" her older aunt asked.

"Holly's fiance," Gabe replied.

"Oh." She sounded distinctly disappointed, which he actually wasn't sure how to take. "Well, if you're here to help, start taking these out to the table."

"Why would he be here to help?" his younger aunt muttered. "You can go watch football with the guys across the hall there."

"I don't mind," Gabe replied, taking what looked to be a green bean casserole and shifting it out to the dining room.

He at least knew how to feel about being asked. It was an insult.

He knew how households like this were arranged, socially speaking. In families like these, there were basically two levels to the hierarchy: men, and women and children. And women and children had their own class of work, also known as most of the housework.

And he didn't take it as an insult because he thought doing what had once largely been referred to as 'women's work' was beneath him, but because they did.

Holly had told him more than one story about how her parents operated, and she'd heard her dad brag, not state, but specifically brag, that he'd never once changed a diaper in his life, because only women and pussy-whipped pussies changed diapers.

His exact words, apparently.

So Gabe had operated under no illusions about what it might be like when he'd walked in, but this was worse than he'd expected.

As he came back into the dining room, he saw her mother and her sister grilling her about the engagement ring. He heard 'God it looks cheap, Holly', and wasn't sure if he'd ever felt such a potent and overwhelming mixture of rage and astonishment before.

After delivering three more dishes, he returned to discover a middle-aged man standing at the kitchen's threshold. He stared at Gabe closely for a few seconds. Gabe paused and stared back, waiting. This was probably Holly's father.

"You Holly's fiance?" he asked.

"I am," Gabe replied.

He stared at him a few seconds longer. He seemed distinctly unwelcoming. Finally, he nodded off to his left. "Step outside with me for a minute."

"All right."

Great.

Gabe headed out onto a deck, only briefly considering heading back to grab his hoodie, as it had gotten colder since their time in the forest as a cloudbank had rolled in over the city. Her father pulled out a cigarette and lit up.

"What's your name?" he asked.

"Gabe."

"Hmm." Another uncomfortable pause. "It seems funny to me that I'm only just now meeting you."

Gabe hesitated. He could tell the man was trying to make a point right away, but he couldn't for the life of him think of what that might be beyond the most obvious interpretation.

"Well...Holly didn't talk about you much," he settled on saying.

"Traditionally speaking, when a man asks a woman to be his wife, he first asks her father's permission," he replied.

Oh. That's what this was about.

Gabe considered and rejected several responses. He genuinely did not trust the man not to take a swing at him if he heard the wrong thing. And he wasn't looking for a fight, though he was surprised by how calm he felt given that Ellen had practiced a couple of simple self defense techniques with him over the past month.

"Holly led me to believe that her relationship with you was...complicated," he replied finally.

Her father shook his head, then turned more fully to face Gabe just as he was exhaling a large cloud of smoke. It hit Gabe right in the face. He managed not to react, though it was a near thing as the urge to cough was, for a few seconds, overwhelming.

"Complicated," he repeated disdainfully. "I imagine she's been lying to you, saying we were bad parents. Too strict, too mean, too much responsibility. Everything's fucking 'abuse' now." He rolled his eyes. "If Holly had been a boy I'd've whupped her ass from sun up to sundown for all the mouth she gave me growing up. She's lucky she got away with what she did."

I need to get out of here, Gabe found himself thinking desperately, *or I'm going to do something really, really stupid.*

"Well, I hope you have a better time getting her to obey like a good girl should than her last boyfriend did. And if you ever hear her talking about pictures or photography, stamp that idea out right away. She got it in her head that it would be a good idea. Oh, and she might've already given you some bullshit about being depressed. Don't let her use it to be lazy."

Gabe realized something as he genuinely struggled to keep his hands from clenching into fists. His stomach was already boiling madly as his heart thundered in his chest. *He actually thinks he's doing me a favor.*

In a way, maybe he was.

If there was ever even the tiniest room for doubt

that it wasn't as bad as Holly had laid it out to be, hiding somewhere deep in the shadows of his mind, this was utterly and effectively destroying it. Gabe had never really been a violent person. He'd never been in a fight. He'd never actually struck anyone in anger.

Except for Blake, of course.

That little altercation of theirs was as close as he'd ever come to a fight.

But he now found himself actually have to stamp out the urge, like a fire that wouldn't go out, to punch this man squarely in the face for everything he had done to Holly.

"I'll keep it in mind," was what he ended up saying.

Her father took a few more puffs on the cigarette, then stubbed it out on the deck's railing. "Right. Well, I'll want to talk with you again, but lunch is ready."

Gabe said nothing, just nodded and focused on at the very least relaxing any obvious physical signs of the rage that was boiling through his body. They came back inside and found there to be a general move to the dining room now. He didn't see Holly anywhere though.

"Hey, you're back, Greg," Mary said. "Holly wouldn't really give an answer. What kind of books do you write?"

Gabe considered, and again rejected, a few responses, including correcting her. "Romance," he said.

Just about everyone but Holly was in the dining room now and they all stared at him as a deeply uncomfortable hush came across them.

"That's a joke," one of Holly's uncles said finally. "Right?"

"Nope," Gabe replied.

"Romance like...chick flicks but books?" her other uncle asked.

"That's not how I would describe them," Gabe said.

He heard footsteps getting closer and they all looked over as Holly came back into the dining room. "Hey, uh...work just called me in," she said.

"Are you serious?" her father asked.

"Yes."

"And you didn't tell them you were busy?" her mom asked. "With *family?*"

"Well, as you and Mary are so fond of pointing out, I'm *poor*. So I need the money. So…"

"I'll drive you there, babe," Gabe replied, already walking towards her.

"You could stick around, Holly can drive herself," her father said.

"Probably not the best idea," Gabe replied firmly. Before anyone could ask him to elaborate on that, he turned briefly to face them and lied. "It was nice to meet you all."

"I'll see you later everyone," Holly murmured, and they left the room.

CHAPTER THIRTY FIVE

"Tell me you got everything," Gabe said as he started up the car.

"I got it," she replied. "Are you okay?"

"No."

He made sure no cars were coming, resisted the urge to peel out, and hit the road, making his way as fast as he legally could home.

"What happened while I was gone?" she murmured.

"I don't want to talk about it."

"...I'm sorry," she said quietly. "I feel really bad now."

Gabe forced himself to relax. "I'm not mad at you, Holly. I'm mad *for* you. Your family...I don't want to tell you what to do when it comes to the big things, but you should really cut them off. Just cold cut them, flat out."

"What *happened?*" she asked.

He sighed. "Your dad pulled me out onto the back deck. Gave me shit for not asking his permission to marry you first, then warned me about you 'faking depression as an excuse for being lazy' and that if you brought up photography at all, crush your dream about it immediately because it was nonsense."

Holly's nervous frown immediately deepened into one far worse. "Yeah," she muttered, looking down at her feet, "that sounds like him...honestly, everything that happened, that was just the tip of the iceberg. Imagine that, but ten times worse, and just about every day. They were always on my ass about something...you seem *really* upset."

"I am," Gabe replied. "But it's fine. We got what

we came for. That's what matters."

"Yeah..." She shifted uncomfortably. "About cutting them off...I'm mostly with you. I mean, I basically did. I'm like ninety percent of the way there. But...that last ten percent. I don't know. It's like there's something inside me keeping me from completely doing it, you know? In my head, I know it's gotta be the right thing to do, I mean now more than ever. But..." She sighed and shook her head.

"I get it," Gabe replied. "They're your family. Shitty as they are, we're hardwired genetically to give a lot of leeway with family. Especially parents."

"It's like I can't let go, not completely...no matter how much I want to," she muttered. She looked over at him suddenly, like she'd had a lightbulb moment. "Tell me to do it."

"...are you serious?"

"Yes."

"All right. Cut off your family. Completely."

"Okay," she replied.

Silence filled the car as they kept driving.

"...just like that?" he asked. "It was that easy?"

Holly twisted her lips in consideration. "I...guess so? I'm kind of waiting for that usual doubt and uncertainty to creep back in, but it isn't. I actually feel good about it. I think...I think that to get that last ten percent, I needed someone I really, really trust to tell me to do it. It's like it feels different, it feels easier to do, if it's for you."

Gabe wasn't comfortable with all the specifics of this arrangement, but if it would help her, then so be it. It wasn't like he was going to be taking advantage of her or cutting her off from everyone in her life, like most other assholes who pulled the 'I don't want you talking to other people anymore' thing. He caught himself thinking *it's for her own good*, and *damn* did that sound bad, but that had to be true some of the time, right?

It authentically *was* for her own good. The good of the relationship too.

He still didn't feel great about it, but dear *lord* were her parents fucked. He tried to stop hearing her father talking to him as he drove back home but the memory wouldn't stop replaying. And by the time he actually pulled into the driveway, he felt almost ill with anger.

"You're still angry," Holly murmured as they got out.

"I'll be okay," Gabe replied.

She seemed not to know what to say in response to that, so they walked back into the house in silence.

"Hey, you're back! How'd it-oh my God, what happened? Gabe, you look...*furious,*" Ellen said, going from happy to concerned as she got up off the couch.

Gabe was considering how and what to say when, very abruptly, an ancient reflex began to warn him that something very, very bad was coming his way. He sprinted out of the room, crashed through the door to the bathroom, and just barely managed to get the toilet seat up as he dropped to his knees and vomited.

He could hear Holly and Ellen asking after him, worried, frightened even, but he was too lost in the horror of throwing up to actually hear them, let alone respond. He threw up his light breakfast, so thankfully there wasn't much in his stomach, but holy fuck was it awful. That godforsaken taste, the acid burn up his throat and into his nostrils.

He coughed harshly, spitting several times as he

finished dry heaving. Gabe flushed the toilet, spent a few moments more spitting out everything he could, then flushed again, groaned, and got to his feet. Ellen and Holly were in the doorway, looking deeply worried.

He held up a finger and shuffled over to the sink, then quickly rinsed and spat a few times with some mouthwash. Making little gestures, he got them to get out of the way after he washed his face off, then went to the kitchen and wiped at his mouth with a papertowel.

"Fuck," he said.

"What happened?!" Ellen asked.

"Holly's family made me so angry I vomited, apparently," he replied. He sighed and shook his head. "I don't want to talk about it. The important thing is: we got what we went in there for and Holly is going to just cut them out of the picture completely."

"Did they give you shit for being a romance writer?" Ellen murmured after a second.

"I mean they did, but honestly? I could've taken that. Trust me, it wasn't how they treated me. I mean that sucked, but again, I can handle it. It's just- whatever. Let's just, uh, relax for a while? Enjoy a nice quiet Sunday?"

"...all right," Ellen said, though it was clear she badly wanted to talk about it.

"I'm sorry about my family," Holly murmured awkwardly.

He walked over to her and hugged her tightly, kissed the top of her head. "Holly, it isn't your fault in the slightest. You are a very, very good person and I love you so much. And I will protect you, and take care of you."

"Thank you," she murmured into his chest. "I love you too, Gabe. And I feel safe with you."

He continued hugging her.

. . .

"Hey...can we talk?" Ellen asked quietly as she stepped into his office.

It had been a few hours, and Gabe had been getting whatever work he could done after trying, and failing, to relax. Mostly the work was planning for the next By the Hearthfire's Light installment.

"Yeah," he replied, turning around to face her. "Where's Holly?"

"She's still in bed. She's got her headphones on, all curled up with her laptop, watching something and just relaxing."

"Decompressing," he muttered.

Ellen shut the door. "What happened that made you fucking *vomit?*"

He sighed softly. "Her family was all pretty shitty to her, and just...so blatantly. But honestly, it was her father. He pulled me out back, gave me some shit for not asking 'his permission' to marry Holly, which again, whatever, I can shrug that off. But then he was telling me I was going to have to make sure to watch out for her 'faking depression' and that I'd have to crush her stupid photography dreams."

"What the *fuck?!*" Ellen snarled.

"Yeah, and even that I could've just...whatever, dealt with. But what really set me of is...he told me that if Holly had been a boy growing up, he would have beat the shit out of her constantly. And that she's lucky she got away with the punishments they did give her."

Ellen froze up. "What does *that* mean? Did-were they hitting her?"

"I don't know," Gabe replied. "I just knew I had to get out of there before *I* hit someone. And I don't want to talk with Holly about it, because she's never brought it up before. What if she repressed that shit? You really wanna bring that back up? I don't even know the protocol for repressed memories, but...fuck, I don't know, this is too much. I mean, I will do everything I can, but...I don't know if I can hear Holly tell me that her father beat her and *not* get arrested."

"I understand," Ellen said, her voice low. "I *really* understand. And you're right. There are some things that...we just aren't equipped to handle. This is exactly why I want to get her into therapy. Why I want all of us to, honestly. And, speaking of that...I think it's time we had a real talk about where we're planning on going with our lives now that Holly is all in."

Gabe nodded, getting to his feet. "Yeah, let's do that. I'm having no luck getting any work done right now."

"Hey," Ellen murmured, reaching out and taking his hand as he began to head for the door. "You did good today."

He chuckled ruefully. "You weren't there, you can't really know that."

"I know that you got what you went in there for, and I know that Holly is currently smiling in the next room, cozied up with her comfort show, instead of crying her eyes out...take the compliment," she murmured.

Gabe found himself resisting, just for a moment, but relaxed. She had a point. "Thanks," he said.

She smiled and kissed him, then took his hand and began walking out of his office. As they came into the bedroom, Holly looked up, then paused what she was watching and pulled off the headphones.

"What's up? You've got that 'we need to talk' look on your faces," she said.

"We do, but it's nothing bad," Ellen replied.

Holly smiled, then looked to the window as the wind, which had been blowing loudly for most of the night, seemed to moan and howl. "God, listen to that," she whispered. "I love it."

"Really? It doesn't freak you out?" Ellen asked as she made room on the bed and then sat down on it cross-legged.

"No. I mean, it used to, but now it's just...it makes me glad I'm inside and warm and with you," she replied.

"Same, honestly," Gabe said as he sat beside Ellen.

"Okay, what's up?" Holly asked, sitting up more.

"Before we began dating you, Ellen and I sat down and had a real talk about where we want to go with our lives. And now that you are a part of our lives, we want to have a similar talk," Gabe replied.

"Oh wow...big topic," she murmured.

"Yep," Ellen agreed. "I'm almost certain I'm going to get fired this upcoming week. That's kind of what I've been waiting for. And then, after that, I want to...fucking relax. For a while. I'm also going to be getting more into digital art and design." She looked back to Gabe.

"Right, so. Our goal is to live together and go our own way, apart from society as much as can be managed. Meaning we live here, in this house, chasing our dreams, and not working jobs that make us want to die. It means that we will be pursuing a life of happiness over a life of endless grinding for money...inasmuch as we can in this nightmare world."

"Okay...I like that. But does that mean you want me to quit my jobs?" she asked.

"Yes," Gabe replied. "Mostly for your mental, and physical, health. You have obviously been working yourself to the bone, and they are *not* paying you enough for that, and even if they were, I imagine that waitressing isn't what you were envisioning as your lifelong career path."

"No, it wasn't," she murmured. "But...do you really think it'd be smart to quit both? Don't get me wrong, I want to. I *really* want to. But the idea scares the shit out of me...although admittedly less than before we met."

"We don't want you doing anything you aren't comfortable with, Holly," Gabe replied. "But you live here now, and we aren't going to kick you out. Not even if your income drops to zero. We love you. A lot."

"That means...more than I can say," she murmured. "It's kind of unbelievable...but I *do* believe you. And I love you both too, so much." She paused. "What would I do then? I'd have so much free time…"

"Well, ideally you'd figure out what you want to do with your life. But you'd enjoy yourself. Relax. Catch up on your shows. Go on dates with us. Learn things. And, well, dive headlong into the world of photography. Or walk in and wade around in the shallow end of the pool. You obviously love taking pictures, and you're obviously very good at it. But it's like Sadie said: investigate, find out for yourself how much you want to invest."

"I don't know if there's going to be any money in it…" she said, looking down at her hands.

"Holly," Gabe said, and she looked up at him silently. "How can I put this? I know it's going to take some getting used to, but I want you to believe that there are more ways to contribute to a relationship, and to a household, than money. There are many different kinds of contributions."

She smirked suddenly, leaning forward, showing off her considerable breasts. "I can think of a way to contribute that would make you really happy."

Gabe chuckled. "Well…you sure aren't wrong," he replied, then he had stop himself from reaching out and pulling up her shirt so that he could suck on her tits.

"Focus, dear," Ellen murmured, a smile in her voice.

"Yeah, I know. So, Holly, how about you quit one of your jobs?"

"I'll do one better," she said. "I'll quit my stupid evening job, even though it makes more money, and I'll switch to part time on my other job, since the cafe is like…two blocks away. And then I can reassess later and see if quitting my job actually makes real sense. But…okay, so, I have debt. As in, *real* debt that's crazy. I still owe four grand on my car and I've got like…ugh, twenty grand in college debt still."

"Join the club," Gabe muttered.

"We can work on that, actually," Ellen said. "As you know, my specialty is finances. I've been researching a website that…well, in short it allows you to allow them to purchase your debts, combine them into a single debt, and pay it off at a more reasonable rate. It's looking like I could enable them, with your permission obviously, to purchase your debts and fold all three of our debts into a single monthly bill that we can just aggressively throw money at until it's gone."

"That would be cool," Holly said. She thought about it for a moment. "This almost seems too good to be true...but I mean obviously I would fucking *love* to live here with you guys, and maybe Chloe if Gabe can get into her pants and her heart–"

"Believe me honey, he's most of the way there on both accounts," Ellen murmured.

Holly giggled. "Good. But yeah, live here with everyone and *not* work jobs that make me want to die and get therapy and kill my debt and just fuck around and figure out photography more...if that could be my life, I'd be happy forever. But it sounds impossible."

"There's some obstacles in our way, but thanks to Sadie's immense kindness and my own fat bank account, which will likely get fatter once they fire me, most of those obstacles are gone. Besides...you were already talking about this all earlier, framing it a certain way. You remember that?"

"What, where I was talking about Gabe taking care of me and me basically being a housewife?" she asked.

"Yes. Lots of women do it. Why can't you?"

"I…" She trailed off, then laughed loudly. "You know what's fucking nuts? This is *literally* what my parents wanted me to do, only without the baby and the actual marriage. They wanted me to just quit my job, give up on my dreams–also without *that* part, thank fuck–and just be a good little submissive housewife for a good Christian man. I mean, it's not *exactly* the same, but…" She laughed again.

"I actually know how you feel," Ellen said.

"Really?"

"Yes. I had basically the exact same thought when I started wanting to submit to Gabe and let him make decisions for me and help him fuck other women...I thought, 'wow, this is *exactly* what my exes wanted me to do'."

"Huh...what does that mean? There's a part of me that feels bad, like I'm betraying the women of the world by just...giving in and being a submissive housewife."

"You aren't though," Ellen replied. "*We* aren't. We're living the lives we want to live. We aren't aiming for these lives because we think we're supposed to, we aren't being submissive because it's what men in our lives have told us to do. We're doing this because we *want to*, Holly. That makes all the difference. Plus, Gabe's never going to take advantage of us or abuse us. He loves us too much and he's too kind of a man for that."

"Both very true things," he murmured, making both of them giggle. "Okay, so, we're agreed then on a course of action? Holly quits one job, reduces another to part time, and starts actually enjoying her life and investigating photography?"

"Fine by me," Holly replied.

"Perfect. Anything else?"

"Two things," Ellen said. "Well, three. First thing, I want the two of you to spend some real time with me sometime this week figuring out your debt. Second thing, Holly: you have depression. You have several of the signs, and I know you feel just great right now, but we need to handle it, because it's going to come back unless you deal with it."

"Oh...how?" she murmured.

"Therapy and an evaluation. Also some blood

work," Ellen replied.

"Ugh. Blood work? I fucking hate needles."

"Me too but it has to be done. We need to see if you have any low levels. You might have chronic low vitamin d or iron or dopamine...a lot of stuff can cause depression and sometimes it can be fixed with something as simple as a supplement. My point is, you have to let us help you take care of this, and that means going to see the doctor, and going to see a therapist, and probably starting on some antidepressants."

Holly heaved a long, weary sigh. "You're right. I know you're right. I just don't want to deal with it. But I will."

"That's another thing, we also need to figure out health insurance. So, I'll get this sorted for you, Holly. But, final thing, and it's the fun one. Best for last. I'm basically done with the cover art! That means we can actually fucking launch after a bit more rearranging! And we should totally have a party!"

"Seriously?" Gabe asked.

"Yes! A little one. I made a little pass at Abby about that. She said she and Em would be thrilled to have a little get together at their place for us, celebrating your writing. We can invite Sadie, and Chloe...maybe Margo? Although that might be weird."

"Who's Margo again?" Holly asked.

"She's that writer Gabe talks to sometimes, at Abby's and Em's parties. She was giving you the 'fuck me' eye at least once," Ellen replied.

"...you sure? Because I did *not* get that vibe from her," Gabe asked.

"I'm positive," Ellen said firmly. "Trust me. You down to fuck her? She's cute."

"Yeah she is, and yeah I am," Gabe replied. "Just...okay. So, small party at Abby's and Em's place. When?" he asked.

"Friday?" Ellen suggested.

He nodded. "Yeah, all right. Friday. This Friday. I'll...talk to Chloe."

"I bet she fucks you at the party," Ellen murmured.

"Bet me what?" he asked.

Ellen turned more to face him, an eyebrow raised. "Are you challenging me?"

"Maybe I am."

"All right, fucker. Loser has to orally pleasure the winner, to orgasm, in a public place."

"*What!?* In public!?" he cried.

"I mean like in a bathroom or changing room or something," Ellen replied. "Obviously I'm not gonna just drop to my knees in the middle of a restaurant."

"So you foresee yourself losing this little contest? Well, that makes sense...I accept."

She leaned forward. "You're. Fucking. On."

"You get *way* too intense about this," Holly whispered.

"I take bets seriously," Ellen replied.

"So wait, why would you want to lose?" Holly asked. "I mean Ellen using her mouth on you is great and everything, but fucking Chloe..."

"I view it as a win-win situation," Gabe replied with a shrug. "Now, if there's nothing else..."

"Ah-ah!" Ellen said, grabbing him and pushing him onto his back beside Holly. "You earned yourself a fucking, mister."

Gabe put his hands behind his head. "Well, be my guest."

CHAPTER THIRTY SIX

"Oh shit, it's official!"

Gabe poked his head out of the bathroom as he heard Ellen call that out. "What is?"

"I'm getting fired!"

"I don't think I've ever heard anyone say that so happily," Holly murmured sleepily as she wandered out of the bedroom. "Are you done in there?"

"Yep, you can have it," Gabe replied as he hung the towel up and stepped out.

She giggled. "You're naked."

"So are you."

"Yeah but it's funny when guys are naked, it's mostly just hot or weird when girls are," Holly said.

"It can definitely be weird when guys are naked but...actually yeah, almost every time there's been male nudity in a movie, it's a comedic scene. Anyway, go shower," he replied, patting her bare ass as she walked into the bathroom.

Gabe found Ellen sitting up on the couch, a big grin on her face.

"So they fired you?" he asked.

"Not yet," she replied, setting her laptop down on the coffee table and standing up. "But they sent a message written in bureaucratic boilerplate and a bit of legalese and I know how to read both of them. They want me to come in now for a meeting about 'my future at the company'. Or lack thereof. This is the part where we negotiate about how much they're willing to pay me to not try to fuck them over in court. Which, you know, I'd feel worse about, except...well fuck them. They're a blood-sucking, soul-crushing accounting firm that fucks people out of money while lining their pockets and low-level torturing *and* underpaying as many people as they can."

"No argument from me," Gabe replied.

She grew more serious as she looked at him. "I have a stupid request."

"I doubt it's stupid and I'm all ears."

"Will you come with me? You'll have to wait in the lobby, and I don't know how long this will take...this is definitely a stupid request," she muttered.

"I'll go," Gabe replied.

"Seriously? You don't have to. And you don't have to feel bad if you don't, choosing to stay home is absolutely a reasonable choice."

"I understand that, but I want to go because it'll make you feel better," he replied. "And I happen to love you a lot."

She laughed and rolled her eyes, blushing. "...yes, you do. And I love you too," she murmured. Then she sighed. "Fuck, you still make me feel like a fucking schoolgirl with a crush and I have no idea how you do that."

He shrugged. "Me either."

"Whatever. Come on, let's tell Holly and then go."

...

"Wow...this place is big," Gabe muttered as he looked up at the huge office building.

"Yep. I hate it," Ellen replied. "Come on, it's freezing."

Gabe joined her in heading into the large lobby. It was indeed very cold outside, somewhere in the high or maybe mid thirties, and the gray skies seemed to still be promising as-yet-delivered snow. He loved the rain, but he still wasn't sure how to feel about snow.

Well, he supposed it was all right, so long as he didn't have to drive anywhere in it.

Stepping into the lobby, all the sounds of the city cut off abruptly, and he was left with a quiet hush. All he could hear was a very faint murmur of conversation and the hum of heating and lights.

"All right, find somewhere and sit, and...thank you, for coming with me," Ellen said.

"You're welcome, babe. Kick ass," Gabe replied.

She grinned broadly. "I will."

They shared a kiss and then Gabe found a relatively comfortable armchair that gave him a nice view out the glass-fronted wall that looked back out onto the parking lot and street beyond. Gabe felt his phone buzz as he got a text message. He quickly pulled his phone out. Given the fact that the likelihood of a woman sending him nudes had increased exponentially over the past month, he was now a lot more eager to check his phone.

As it was, he had indeed received a message from an attractive woman. But it wasn't a nude pic she'd sent.

It was from Chloe.

Hey man, so uh, I had a weekend to think it over.

Gabe paused, but no … was forthcoming. He waited for a moment, then decided to press on: *And?*

Not much, but at least it was a response.

After a long moment, she responded: *And I don't regret what we did.*

Another long pause.

Do you? Are your girlfriends mad?

He chuckled, considering all they'd spoken of

related to Chloe over the weekend. *No on both accounts. We're all still very happy.*

A briefer pause this time before she fired back: *So what now?*

Gabe considered his response only for a little bit before just throwing it out there: *I'm still extremely into you. I want to date you.*

Great. That really *was* just throwing it all out there. He probably should've not gone for the throat like that, but he wasn't sure how else to put it.

Wow man, that's a lot. But I sat with it for a moment, and no bad feeling ever came, so I guess I'm cool with that. At least to try. I think? How do you want to go forward?

Gabe began replying, surprised by how well she'd responded. *There's a party at Abby and Emily's place this Friday to celebrate something related to my writing. It's going to be small. I want you there.*

A pause. It became a longer pause. He began to worry.

Finally: *Okay, I can do that. I just have one question for now: can I be bitchy at you over text and you um respond back to me appropriately?*

He relaxed, then chuckled. After everything that had happened yesterday, this felt so good. He quickly replied. *Yeah, all right.*

She barely waited more than a second before responding: *Good. Fuckface.*

He quickly responded: *Don't start with me.*

Fucking make me she fired back immediately.

He was thinking of a reply when a picture appeared. It was her in what looked like a coffee shop storeroom. She was smirking, pulling down the front of her shirt and apron over it, exposing a lot of her breasts. He looked closer and realized the hand doing the pulling had its middle finger up.

Good lord was she hot.

He quickly texted back: *You fucking BITCH. You keep it up and you'll regret it.*

Her response was almost instant: *Prove it.*

Gabe felt actual frustration beginning to mount as he went back and forth with her. They went on like that for another few minutes before abruptly she had to go. Probably back to work. He played on his phone for a bit and then, on a whim, he did something he normally wouldn't to someone who he was not dating.

He opened up his and Sadie's text chain and typed: *I just thought I'd remind you that I think you're very beautiful.*

He felt a small burst of panic just after he hit the send button, wondering if that was stupid. His and Sadie's relationship was strange. At this point it was clear that making sexual or even romantic statements were on the table...well, kind of clear. It seemed clear that she was enjoying herself, at least. But things still felt ill-defined.

Sadie seemed like she enjoyed just about every statement he'd ever made to her, especially spicier things, but how far did she want that to go? How much was too much? What were her sore spots? And then there was the awful suspicion that she was just humoring him and actually found him very unattractive and wished he would stop.

That one, admittedly, was easier to push away. He wasn't *that* bad at reading people, and he was positive Ellen, Holly, or both would have said something by now.

Gabe's phone buzzed. He checked it.

Thank you for that. I mean that both

authentically and sarcastically, because I'm out to lunch with a few friends, and that got me blushing and flustered, and I may have let drop that I have what we used to call a 'gentleman caller'. And they are very intrigued and somewhat jealous now.

Hmm. Gabe considered that for a moment, then decided to push farther. It felt like the right time.

I'm happy to read that. I liked our time together at the pizza place, so if you ever want to hang out like that again, let me know. I have a flexible schedule and I would be very happy to let you know how attractive you are in person.

A pause, then the three dots appeared and disappeared several times.

Finally: *I think that might make your girlfriends jealous.*

He chuckled softly. *They don't get jealous. Also, since we're talking, I should tell you now: I'm setting up a small party related to my writing at a friend's house Friday. I'd like you to be there.*

This time her response seemed a lot less hesitant: *I would like to be there.*

He began to respond, then reconsidered it and added more: *Awesome, I'll send you the details once we have everything finalized. Also, fair warning, there is a very, very good chance that it will turn into me having sex with someone there at the party so...I guess keep that in mind?*

Another pause. *I see. Will this be viewing optional?*

Almost certainly.

Then I would like to come. The … appeared again almost immediately. *That was probably not the best phrasing.*

Gabe laughed. *I don't know, after you told me*

what you did after reading my stories I think it's fine.

Another pause in the texting, this one lasting almost two minutes. Finally, she said: *I will be there.*

That was probably about as far as they were going to get in this particular exchange, so he told her he'd be glad to see her there, thanked her again for being a patron of the arts, and left it at that. From there, he just kept waiting, looking out the window, then checking things on his phone again. At some point he realized that almost an hour had gone by.

It was about then that he heard a door open elsewhere in the lobby and glanced up from his phone.

And locked eyes with an unfortunately familiar figure.

Blake.

Right...he worked here.

Blake had been heading somewhere but he had frozen the moment they saw each other. The moment stretched out uncomfortably, and then Gabe tensed as he began walking over, his strides quick.

Well, this was going to be interesting.

Gabe considered getting to his feet. It seemed to be the smart thing to do, but was Blake stupid enough to attack him in the lobby of his actual workplace? He could actually see the cameras.

Ultimately, he decided to remain seated, if only because it would no doubt piss someone like Blake off. The tacit message would be: *You aren't threatening enough for me to feel the need to defend myself.*

Probably not true, Blake was obviously in better shape, although apparently Gabe was quicker than he was. Then again, that had likely been a fluke.

"What the fuck are you doing here?" Blake

asked, his voice low.

"Moral support for Ellen," Gabe replied.

"She's here?" He looked around. Gabe was pleased to note that he actually looked just the tiniest bit nervous.

"She is."

Blake returned his gaze to Gabe and something changed after a few seconds. He probably was thinking that he needed to 'establish and maintain social dominance' or whatever stupid fucking bullshit the alpha internet bros of today were feeding him.

"What the fuck does she even see in you? Like, Christ, how old are you?" he asked.

"Twenty six," Gabe replied.

"You're a fucking simp, you've gotta be. She got tired of a real man challenging her and putting her in her place, so she decided to play on easy with a beta simp ten years younger," he said.

Gabe considered how to respond to that for a moment and settled on: "Good lord, no wonder you're so fucking miserable."

Blake's eye twitched. "I never said I was miserable."

"You didn't have to say it."

He took another step closer. "Don't think for a goddamned second that just because you got lucky and sucker punched me like a little bitch that I can't beat you into a fucking coma."

"Maybe," Gabe replied, "but you and I both know you're afraid of Ellen, because you know that you wouldn't survive intact if she really decided to go after you."

Blake's eyes narrowed and Gabe could tell immediately he'd struck a nerve. So that was a thing that bothered him: he actually *was* afraid of Ellen.

Which had to just rip him up inside, because Ellen was a woman, and in Blake's world, a man being afraid of a woman was among the lowest of the low. Which was a depressing thought on a number of levels.

Whatever Blake was going to say next was interrupted as a door opened elsewhere in the lobby and, on the heels of that sound, came another. That of Ellen speaking a single word.

"Blake."

They both looked over immediately. Her voice was calm and low, but it carried very well on the still air of the lobby.

"What are you doing, Blake?" Ellen asked as she approached quickly, her long legs consuming the distance with ease.

"Talking to your fucking simp," he growled.

"You're still such a fucking moron," she said, coming to stand beside them.

Gabe noticed Blake take a small step back.

"Are you finished, babe?" he asked.

"Yes, love, I'm done. We can go," Ellen replied.

Gabe stood up and took her hand. He again considered several different things to say to Blake, but in the end, he simply began leading Ellen away, towards the front door. They left without saying a word. A moment later, they were in the car.

"What did he say to you?" Ellen asked as they began driving home.

"He puzzled over what you see in me, and reassured me that what happened at the condo was a fluke and he could easily put me in a coma," Gabe replied.

"You don't seem particularly upset by that," she said after a moment.

"I'm not. I don't really know why...he's scared of you."

"I always suspected that. But what makes you so sure?"

"He asked if you were around, and when I confirmed that you were, he got nervous. And I told him that he might be able to knock me out, but he wouldn't survive you if he did. He looked just a little afraid when I mentioned that."

Ellen laughed darkly. "Yes, he would *not* survive. At least his balls wouldn't. I've got a little switchblade in my purse and I'd gladly use it to carve his junk up." She lost her grim smile suddenly. "God, I can't believe I ever was with him. I don't even understand how it happened, now. I mean he's not that different. I guess...I was being shitty, thinking it was a fine attitude to have so long as he didn't turn it on me...ugh, that sounds so fucking awful. How are you not more disappointed in me?"

Gabe let out a long breath as he thought about it. "If I've learned anything, it's that relationships and the human condition are both very complicated subjects, and the weirdest things make sense in the proper context. Not that they're *right,* just that they make sense...from the inside. If you ever met my final girlfriend before you, well...we could compare notes on dating the wrongest of the wrong people."

She laughed softly. "I'm kinda interested, actually. I bet I'd scare the shit out of her."

"You would but she responds to fear very aggressively so you might *actually* have to knock her out or something. She is absolutely one of those psycho chicks who will throw down with another woman in the street or at the grocery store if she's in a bad enough mood."

"If you survived what was it, nine months? If you survived that long with her, it explains why you're able to handle me."

"You're pretty easy to handle," Gabe replied.

Ellen pursed her lips. "I'm not sure how to take that."

"Don't give me that, you know *exactly* how to take it given how often you take it."

She grinned and flicked a glance at him. "What got into *you?*"

"While I was waiting, I invited Sadie to our party on Friday and let her know it would almost certainly turn into me having sex with someone and she could watch if she wanted. Chloe also let me know that she feels good about what happened and then proceeded to argue with me over the phone."

"Holy shit, no wonder you're in such a mood," she murmured. "You think Chloe will be down to fuck this Friday?"

"I really hope so...now, what happened in there?" he asked.

"I want Holly to be there when I talk about it but it was good," she replied.

"Fair enough. I'm just glad it's over with...it *is* over with, right?"

"Oh yeah, it's so fucking over with."

As they headed home, it began to snow. Nothing intense, just a dusting of flakes coming down. It was brutally cold, though, so they hurried inside.

"It's snowing!" Holly called as she heard them coming in.

"Indeed it is," Gabe replied.

She came into the living room, grinning at them. "I'm really happy. No work today and I officially quit my other job while you guys were out...how'd *your* quitting, or um, firing, go?"

"Pretty well, all things considered," Ellen replied, getting out of her coat and shoes and sitting down on the couch. "I am officially fired. And I managed to get a really decent severance package. And they're going to wait to take me off of the company health insurance until the first of next year. In return for agreeing not to pursue them, legally speaking, which I could tell they were quite worried about, much as they tried to hide it, I am getting a twenty five thousand dollar severance package and I am being 'laid off'."

"Holy fuck, that's a lot of money," Holly whispered.

"Yep, although not nearly as much as you'd think. That's not even a good down payment for a house anymore. But it doesn't matter as much to us. The point is that after taxes, I'm sitting on about thirty grand altogether."

"Fuck," Gabe murmured.

"Yes, and so we should discuss what we're going to do with that. I definitely want to sock a fair amount of it away, but I also want to know if there's anything we want? Something we need or want? And by 'we' I also mean individually, too. Like...Gabe, would you like a new laptop?"

"Jesus Christ yes," he replied. "I would like a new laptop."

"Okay then. We can go shopping, although it'll be a bit. Both because I want to wait for prices to drop a bit, because we still want to be responsible with this money and Christmas is right around the corner. But also I gotta get the finances sorted. Holly?"

"Uh...honestly I'm pretty happy," Holly replied.

"I like my laptop, I like my phone, that camera you got me was really the last thing I seriously wanted...although I wouldn't mind having a bookshelf all to myself and books."

"We can absolutely make that happen," Ellen said.

"I have a thought," Gabe said.

"Listening," Ellen replied.

"So...I'm going to be banking on the assumption that even if Chloe doesn't work out, we're going to end up with another woman over here to spend the night at least every once in a while. That bed is about big enough for us all, but..."

"Oh my God *yes,*" Ellen replied. "That was going to be *my* thing. I want a California king bed. It's gonna be huge and we'll need to rearrange a little but I'm so tired of the bed not being long enough for my giant ass body."

"What do we do with the old bed? It's still really new," Gabe asked.

"Not sure. I'd like to hold onto it if we can find a place to store it, because here there just isn't enough room. But...well, I wouldn't mind living in a bigger house, eventually. I imagine we can save up. And if Chloe *does* get serious, then...I mean it's gonna get crowded."

"Yeah," Holly murmured. "I wonder if it'd weird her out to sleep in a bed with two naked women."

"Probably it'd at least take some getting used to," Ellen replied. "Okay, so. If that's everything...let's fucking celebrate."

"How?" Holly asked, clearly eager.

They both looked to Gabe. He looked back. "Well...we could treat it like a snow day. Get wrapped up and comfy together on the couch after making a bunch of snacks, and then...we each select one movie that we really want the other two to see to watch and marathon them?"

"That sounds amazing," Holly replied.

"I'm very down for this, I'll get started on snacks," Ellen agreed, heading to the kitchen.

"I'll bring the blankets in," Holly said.

Gabe watched the two women in his life head off elsewhere into the house and felt an overwhelming sense of comfort and security and love. Around him, the frigid wind shrieked and howled, and he agreed with Holly immensely: it was good to be inside with people you loved, taking it easy and hiding away from the cold.

He fired up his console and began preparing the movies.

CHAPTER THIRTY SEVEN

"Someone's getting laid tonight..." Ellen murmured.

"I mean obviously," Gabe replied.

"I mean by Chloe," she said.

"And I meant that if I strike out with Chloe, I'll still have you to fuck."

"Someone's getting cocky," Ellen said, crossing her arms and shifting in the passenger's seat as he drove them through the city. "What if I decide I'd rather not fuck you tonight?"

Gabe reached over and patted her thigh. "That's adorable that you think you could keep yourself from gagging to be fucked by me for even one night."

"Holy shit, I think she's choking you to death in her mind right now," Holly said from the back seat in the silence that followed.

"Keep pushing, handsome," Ellen said finally, grinning broadly at him.

Gabe simply smiled and kept driving.

She had been fucking with him all day long and at some point he'd begun to push back, and then at some point after that he'd really started to lay it on thick.

"Gabe, if you don't calm down you're going to be all...uh, dommed out before you even get to Chloe," Holly murmured.

"Ohhhhh fuck, I hadn't even considered that," Ellen groaned.

"Wait so you've seriously been bitching at me...what, instinctively?" Gabe asked.

"*Yes,* fucker! You...bring it out in me."

"Okay be honest: have you been hoping to get

put in your place or are you looking to sharpen your claws and stretch your own dom muscle?" he asked.

"I...am not sure," she admitted.

"Oh my God."

"What?! Shut up!" Ellen snapped, blushing. "I just...am in a mood."

"Clearly," Holly murmured.

"*You* shut your little whore mouth," Ellen growled, whirling around in her seat to stare at Holly.

"Yes, ma'am," Holly whispered.

"You gonna have a problem with another woman giving me shit?" Gabe asked.

"No," Ellen replied. She paused. "Wait was that an authentic question or are you fucking with me? I mean the answer is no both ways."

"...I'm not sure," he admitted. "Goddamnit, you've got me just being sarcastic as fuck without even thinking about it now."

"Yeah that's a problem," Ellen murmured. "Okay, okay, I'll calm down. We'll all calm down." She quickly regained her mischievous smile, though. "I have to admit, I'm very curious to see another woman arguing with you."

"It's fun to watch," Holly said.

"You both are weird," Gabe muttered.

"Oh like you aren't?" Ellen shot back. "You're the one who loves arguing with us so much."

"Okay, that's fair," he replied. "...I'm nervous about tonight."

"I know, but try not to be," Ellen said. "It's going to be a small get together, with people you've met already, at a place you've already been."

"Yeah, and that's great, and appreciated, it's just...it's going to be *about* me and it's a lot harder to blend into the background in a smaller group and when I'm the reason they're there. Plus, with one exception, every other person there is going to be a woman I've slept with or might possibly sleep with."

"Why would that be bad?" Holly asked. "Also...I'm guessing the exception is Abby?"

"Margo."

"But Abby's a lesbian."

"Ellen seems to think it's on the table."

Holly leaned forward. "Did I miss something?"

"Let's just say that Abby has pointed out that she's not *completely* lesbian. She said that she's a bisexual who is basically a lesbian, because there have been some men who've made her...feel a specific way."

"And Gabe is one of those men?" Holly asked.

"She implied," Ellen answered. "And...I dunno, I think she's really thinking about it. And obviously if she asked, Gabe would jump on her in a heartbeat."

"She's a very attractive woman," he replied.

"Oh yeah, I get that."

"Why do you not think Margo is on the table?" Holly asked.

"I'm just not getting any vibes from her." Gabe turned on Abby's and Em's street and parked in front of their house. He looked out the window for a moment. It seemed like everyone else was already here. He sighed softly.

"You seem really unhappy for a horny man about to walk into a house full of women who would probably fuck him," Ellen said.

"I'm not *unhappy,* I'm *nervous.* This just feels too good to be true. I'm really waiting for the other shoe to drop. Just...don't get me wrong, I very much appreciate this. A lot. There's just a part of me that's very anxious I'm missing something important,"

Gabe replied.

"I understand that, sweetheart," Ellen said. "But I want you to do me a favor."

"I'm listening."

"I want you to try as hard as you can to just put that aside, and try to let yourself enjoy this. Because even if there's something you're missing, even if there's some weird disaster waiting in the wings, hovering just out of sight, you know that Holly and I have your back, and you know that you can trust Emily and Abby at this point."

Gabe nodded slowly. "You're right." He took a deep breath, let it out slowly, then unbuckled his seatbelt. "Let's go have fun."

"That's the spirit," Holly said.

They got out of the car and began making their way up the front lawn. Emily answered the door when he knocked, and the moment she saw him she grinned wildly and opened up the red robe she was wearing, revealing her very naked, very beautiful body beneath.

"Congrats!" she said, then cried out as a cold gust of wind hit her. "Oh fuck me it's cold!"

Ellen laughed. "You fucking dumbass, it's almost December, of course it's cold."

"Fuck off, bitch!" Emily snapped back, pulling the robe closed again. "I thought you all would appreciate it. Get the fuck in here."

"Oh we appreciate it dearly," Ellen said.

"Yep," Gabe agreed as they walked in and began taking off their coats and shoes. "I think we just didn't expect it."

"God, I did," Ellen muttered. "What part of trashy party girl did you misunderstand?"

"Bitch," Emily began, turning to face her, "you'd

better–"

"What?" Ellen asked, stepping up to Emily so that there was barely a few inches of space between them, staring directly down into her eyes. "What had I better do, Emily? Please enlighten me."

Gabe watched with great interest as Emily froze up, staring with wide eyes at Ellen.

"That's what I thought," Ellen said with a smirk. "You're lucky this is my boyfriend's party or I'd drag you upstairs and break you over my knee with one of those hard paddles I know Abby's got squirreled away somewhere."

Emily was blushing badly now. Finally, she said, "Why did you never talk to me like that before? Because dear *lord* would I have fucking jumped you."

"Combination of not wanting to fuck up the friendship and always being busy. Also a tad of denial thrown in," Ellen replied. "And hey, we're here now, aren't we? Threesomes with my hot boyfriend are very much on the table. And my hot girlfriend."

"Yes…" Emily murmured, looking at Gabe, then at Holly, then back to Gabe. "But we should at the very least get to the living room. Your girl is nervous."

"My girl?"

"Chloe. We've been chatting a lot about streaming and gaming since she showed up, she's actually very cool and nice, but I can't tell she's intimidated by the company. Also Sadie is nervous and I don't know why, she has ice queen matriarch written all over her. She and Abby have been talking."

"Is Margo here?" Ellen asked.

"No, unfortunately she had to duck out at the last minute, some family thing. Abby also did a pass at

Isabella but she's trying to figure out moving and all that. Plus I think Gabe still intimidates her a little."

"How did you come to *that* conclusion?" Gabe asked.

"Oh come on, Gabe. You've got Ellen and Holly wrapped around your finger and you fucked me and you're half her age."

"I thought getting older made you *more* confident."

"...it *really* depends."

"Yep," Ellen said.

She led them into their expansive living room where he found Chloe, Abby, and Sadie. It was so very bizarre, but in a great way, to see these people together.

"There you fucking are," Chloe said the moment she locked eyes with him. "You sure took your sweet time getting here."

Gabe stared at her. So did everyone else. He considered walking over to her, then decided against it. "Chloe...come over here."

"Why should I?" she replied.

"You know exactly why you should, now get *over* here."

She muttered something as she walked over, looking as petulant and bitchy as ever. It was amazing, how quickly she could apparently just cut through everything else and push his horny button *and* his dom button at the same time, and so effectively. She was dressed about the same as she was last time, so she looked amazing.

"Okay, *what?*" she asked, annoyed, as she came to stand before him.

Gabe stepped up to her and then grabbed her chin and turned her head with a little more force than was necessary, then put his lips to her ear. "You are going to shut your fucking mouth and behave, Chloe, do you understand me?"

She opened her mouth to respond, then began blushing fiercely. She cleared her throat. "I will consider it," she said finally.

"No, you'll do it," Gabe replied.

He still didn't fully understand everything about the brat/dom dynamic, but he could tell that he understood it on an intuitive level, or at least he and Chloe clicked together very well, because he always seemed to know what to say with her.

Her eyes flashed in that way they did when he'd said precisely the right thing, like she was not just excited but absolutely *thrilled* to rise to the challenge he had just issued.

"Or what?"

Gabe leaned in again. "Or I won't fuck you tonight," he replied, his voice lower than ever.

She stared at him, opened her mouth, hesitated, swallowed. "You wouldn't."

"Oh I would. So you behave yourself, Chloe." She sneered at him as he began to pull back, then something occurred to him and leaned forward again. "On a more serious note, we need a safeword."

She sighed softly. "I'm liable to forget it, so can it just be safeword?" He snorted. "Don't fucking laugh at me!"

"You are in such a mood tonight," he replied. "Safeword it is."

Gabe still felt incredibly weird talking with her like this, it seemed entirely too familiar with a woman he'd met physically one time and had just a single sexual encounter with. But they'd been play fighting all week long over the phone.

"Thank you," she whispered.

"Yep. Now, be on your best behavior you little bitch."

She growled at him, regaining her glare as he stepped back.

Gabe realized that he hadn't actually greeted Sadie yet and turned his attention to her. He opened his mouth greet her and then stopped as he actually saw her.

"Sadie. Good. *Lord,*" he whispered.

"What?" she replied.

"That dress...is amazing."

"It really is, fucking god*damn* Sadie," Ellen said.

She didn't seem to know what to say in response. "Thank you," she said finally. "You all look quite nice."

She had on a spaghetti strap, low-cut red dress that seemed to frame and accentuate her physique in a lot of very good ways.

"I told her that's a very nice dress," Abby murmured.

"Well...it's appreciated. But I'm not here to steal the spotlight. This is about you, Gabe. I was hoping to hear about all the things that were happening, the specifics of why we're celebrating. I know you launched a new series but I was led to believe there's more," she replied.

"Right," Gabe said, walking over and sitting down on one of the large couches in the room. "Well, I have finally launched my new series, By the Hearthfire's Light. Caveman erotica. It's going to be a trilogy. That's been great to write, but really I'm celebrating how Ellen and Holly helped me completely overhaul my...well, everything really. New editing, new formatting, new covers, new website and social media presence."

"I just pointed out a few errors," Holly said as they all sat down as well. "Ellen did ninety nine percent of the work between the two of us."

"What?! You took the pictures!" Ellen cried.

"Oh. Right. But still, you did most of the work."

"You worked hard on it, Holly, you should be proud, and I am extremely grateful," Gabe replied.

"I believe I heard that Sadie had you write a few...smut pieces?" Abby asked, looking deeply amused.

Gabe looked at Sadie, who was blushing a little. She smiled a small smile. "I did," she said. "Part of being a patron of the arts is getting to enjoy them a lot more...intimately, I believe."

"Oh hell yeah," Emily said. "I'd do the exact same thing in your position. Shit...I might ask Gabe to write me some smut. I am, in my own way, a patron of the arts."

"Right," Abby said.

"Hey! Giving pussy, *unprotected* pussy, I might add, to a cute writer is absolutely being a patron of the arts," Emily snapped.

"She's right," Gabe agreed.

"Then I, too, am a patron of the arts, because you would not be getting said pussy without my permission," Abby said, smiling her own small smile as she took a sip from her wineglass.

"And you also have my deep gratitude for letting me fuck your wife," Gabe replied and she chuckled.

"To answer your question: yes, part of my agreement with Gabe was that I would, on occasion, ask for a custom short erotic story," Sadie replied. "So far he's done a very good job fulfilling my requests."

"Interesting," Abby murmured.

"It's been fun and-for the love of *God* Chloe, will you sit *still?*" he asked, looking over at her. She had ended up, with some subtle, nonverbal communication, managing to wedge herself between him and Ellen.

"Why don't you make me?" she replied sweetly.

Gabe felt himself stiffening with sexual frustration as she stared at him with that fucking smirk on her face. She was ridiculously beautiful right now and that just made the whole situation more frustrating. He realized that Sadie was looking at him with a slightly concerned expression.

"Oh, right," he muttered, returning his attention to her. "Just so you don't feel uncomfortable, we aren't actually fighting. Chloe is…"

"Your latest romantic pursuit?" Abby asked.

"Yes," Gabe replied. "I was going to say she's a fucking brat. She likes to bitch so that she can be put in her place. We met at a party a week ago and really hit it off."

"Apparently," Emily murmured, laughing softly.

"I'm getting it from all fucking sides now," Gabe said, glaring at her.

"Don't even pretend you're annoyed," Emily replied.

"That certainly explains it," Sadie said, relaxing. "I had a friend once and for a long time I really questioned her relationship. Her and her husband were always fighting, but it never seemed very serious and she always seemed just the faintest bit amused by it, so I didn't dig too deep. Finally, one day, she said the arguing was core to their relationship, they thrived off of it, but none of it was real. It was play fighting."

"Exactly that," Chloe said. "I've *always* wanted something like that. My relationships before have been...not great. It *always* goes wrong. Always. The fake fighting becomes real fighting and, I don't know, something breaks. It's ruined at some point."

"So *are* you two dating?" Emily asked.

"No," Chloe replied, looking embarrassed. "We're, uh...I mean, we're, you know, still getting to know each other." She looked at Gabe. "Right?"

"Yeah, I'd say that's accurate."

"Hmm," Sadie murmured.

"What?" Gabe asked.

"It's just...I figure it would be a complex situation. I feel like this level of...sassy banter, well, it would require a lot of trust and understanding. How do you know you aren't *really* pissing each other off?"

"We've got a safeword for that," Chloe replied. "Gabe suggested it." She froze up. "Um, I wasn't saying it. I mean, like, I wasn't using the safeword-fuck."

Gabe started laughing.

"Wait...what's your safeword?" Abby asked.

Gabe laughed louder and Chloe groaned.

"Go ahead, Chloe. Tell her. Tell her what you settled on," Gabe said.

"Fuck you," she growled.

"Go on," he said, nudging her by bumping her with his hip.

Chloe groaned again and hid her eyes behind her hand. "My safeword is...safeword."

They all laughed.

"Oh my God, that's amazing!" Emily said.

"That's...a little...hazardous, maybe," Abby said.

"No, it's-I just forget shit like that!"

"I believe that I can parse whether or not she's actually saying it," Gabe replied.

"You *are* weirdly good at reading me so far," Chloe said.

"He's very, very good at reading people," Ellen said.

"Yeah, that's true," Emily agreed. "I'd trust him."

"Interesting," Sadie said. "And I'd say I agree. Your ability to read women seems very on point...although admittedly my bar in that particular field might be too low after twenty plus years of marriage to a man who was rather lacking in that field."

"You should probably talk with my friend Isabella," Abby said. "She *just* got out of a marriage like that."

"I'm always open for new friends nowadays," Sadie replied.

"Oh!" Emily said, sitting up abruptly. "*Just* remembered: we have weed! Who wants to toke toke with me? No pressure."

"I *do* have to drive home later..." Sadie murmured.

"Again, no pressure," Emily said as she got to her feet, "but the night is still young, girlfriend! Plus, worst case scenario, you can crash here. We have a few extra beds. Also, the weed isn't *that* strong."

"I'm down," Chloe said.

"So same," Ellen agreed.

"I wanna try a little," Holly said.

"Well...all right, yeah. It's been too long since I've had a really good, relaxing time," she replied.

"I'll be right back!" Emily declared and raced off.

"She's very excited about this," Gabe said.

"Em loves getting high with friends. It reminds her of the best parts of the old days...so Sadie, how long has it been since you've indulged?" Abby replied.

"In weed? Lord...fifteen years, but it's rarely been in my life. I was more of a wine girl. Can't believe I actually lived to see the legalization of weed. At least in my state," she replied.

"Fifty isn't old," Abby said.

Sadie laughed. "Well, I was less referring to my age and more referring to the sheer unlikelihood of it being legalized. But...well, how about we see how you feel about it in twenty years. I sure *feel* damn old some mornings."

"Got it!" Emily called, hurrying back. She returned with a handful of thinly rolled joints, a pipe, and a few lighters. She quickly passed the joints out and the lighters out and then plopped back down beside Abby, who took the pipe and began lighting up.

"Let the fun begin," Ellen murmured, then started coughing harshly. "Oh shit! Fuck, it's been too long since I've smoked!" she groaned as she passed the lighter to Gabe.

"Think it's been a while for everyone but Em," Gabe said.

"Fuck you, writer boy!" Emily snapped, which made both Abby and Holly start giggling.

"As tempting as that is, I want to hear some embarrassing stories about Ellen," Gabe replied.

"Oh fucking hell no!" Ellen replied immediately.

"Hmm...let me see what I can remember," Emily replied with a broad grin.

Gabe settled in after taking a few puffs. This was

definitely going to be a good night.

CHAPTER THIRTY EIGHT

Chloe was definitely getting far more comfortable as time went on.

Gabe realized this as, after about two hours of conversation and a lot of laughter, she ended up in his lap and was fucking with him a lot more.

She'd sort of gone through phases of teasing him as they'd started out listening to Emily and Ellen swap increasingly unlikely sounding stories about each other, making her little comments or squirming around against him, bumping him, poking him, and then easing back. Ellen and Holly both seemed greatly amused by it.

They'd continued talking for a time. The weed was gone by now and Gabe was still feeling a little pleasantly toasty.

"*I* have a story I want to hear," Emily said after the latest conversation had come to a natural lull.

"What story?" Ellen asked.

"I want to hear about the first time you and Gabe fucked. How did that actually go down?"

"I admit I'm quite curious about that myself," Sadie murmured. She seemed to have settled calmly into a role as pleasantly stoned observer, not offering a lot over the past hour beyond laughter and good vibes. Holly, too, she hadn't said very much, just looked pleased as could be to be there.

"All right," Ellen said. "Gabe?"

"No, I want to hear *you* tell it. I want your perspective," he replied.

She laughed. "Okay, fine. So, first sex. Well, the tension had been building for *years* by the time we finally got there."

"Years?" Chloe asked.

"Yes. In the story I told of how we met, I said we were then split apart for several years, but what I failed to mention is that I had continued longing for and lusting after Gabe the entire time between those two points. To be honest, I fully expected him to try and jump me the very first night. I mean, I was kind of banking on it because I crawled into his bed."

"You were crying and miserable half that night. It hardly seemed appropriate," he replied.

"I know, and I appreciate it, but I definitely wouldn't have rejected you. Anyway. That night I had a positively *amazing* fuck dream about him. It was so intense it was actually a wet dream. After that...I couldn't stop thinking about him fucking pounding me. So I started, you know, trying to give him the hints as we spent the next day together."

"Did he miss them? All of them? Every last one?" Emily asked.

"Gee, thanks, Em," Gabe replied, rolling his eyes.

"You *are* a bit of a dumbass," Chloe murmured.

"You are fucking *pushing* it, you little goth slut," he growled at as he squeezed her thigh, and she let out a surprised little shriek.

Ellen just laughed. "Surprisingly, no. He latched onto it pretty quick. I was pretty worried I might have to escalated hard and just jump him given our...history. I love you, sweetheart, but you're rather tentative."

"I have good reason to be," Gabe replied.

"Clearly he's not anymore," Sadie murmured.

"Yes, I'm glad we've broken him of that habit," Ellen replied. "Anyway, we went shopping and when we got back he offered a massage and I thought *yes, the old massage offer, this is it!* He took his sweet time about it, though."

"What was the actual first outright sexual thing he did?" Emily asked, leaning in a little.

"Grabbed my tits," she replied.

Several of the women laughed.

"Subtle, Gabe," Abby said.

"Oh don't give him shit for it, I had to basically lead him in by the nose after a certain point. I had to not just open the door and ring the dinner bell, I had to prop it open and then set up a few big neon signs more or less saying 'free pussy'," Ellen replied, giggling.

"Okay, hey," Gabe said from beneath Chloe, who looked like she was enjoying herself greatly, "I have heard too many stories, all right? Stories of women doing *the most obvious* shit in the world that seems like they're screaming it through a megaphone that they are down to fuck...and then it turns out no, they aren't, actually."

"Well that just sounds cruel," Emily replied. "A lot of those stories, about girls hitting on guys, laying it on thick, actually going somewhere secluded, and doing all the sexy sultry flirtation in the world, and then ripping the rug out from under guys' feet with 'whoa hey I just want to be friends, you thought I was coming onto you?', those stories are mostly about women who get off on cruelty."

"I mean that's fair," Gabe replied, "and it's not like I thought Ellen was going to do that. It's just...high risk, high reward scenario, you know? What if I was wrong? You can't un-grab a woman's tits."

"That is also a fair point," Ellen said. "I'm just glad it worked out."

"Would anyone like to hear the story of how Chloe and I first had sex?" Gabe asked.

"We haven't *had* se–" Chloe let out a startled sound as he kissed her on the mouth.

It was a long, pleasant, impassioned kiss.

When he pulled back, she was left looking bewildered and frustrated and very aroused.

"You fucking *pervert,*" she whispered harshly, "did I say you could kiss–"

Gabe kissed her again and then slipped a hand up her dress. At some point he had realized that she was not wearing panties this time around and so he had quick and easy access to that sweet goth pussy of hers. She gasped and jumped as he ran a fingertip between her lips.

"*Gabe!*" she hissed, breaking the kiss, blushing badly.

"You've been pushing my buttons all fucking night, Chloe," he replied, slowly rubbing her clit and making her squirm and moan. "The time has come to pay the price."

"You filthy fucking pervert," she whispered, starting to pant. "What makes you think-*ah!*" she cried as he slipped a finger inside of her.

Holy fuck was she wet.

"Make some room," Gabe said, and Ellen and Holly immediately shifted away from him.

"You're going to do her right here?" Emily asked.

"If everyone's okay with that," Gabe replied, fucking her harder and faster with his two fingers now.

"Go right ahead," Abby said.

"I would very much like to see this," Sadie murmured.

"Perfect," Gabe said, and pulled his fingers out of her. He pushed the straps of her dress down and yanked on it, exposing her big pale breasts. "On your knees, Chloe."

"You fucker!" Chloe cried, trying to cover herself.

Gabe pulled her arms away and pushed her down onto her knees before him. He snapped his fingers in her face twice. "Suck, Chloe. You've been a bad girl all night long and now it's time to own up to that."

She glared daggers at him, her pale face flushed badly, her mouth set into a firm, angry line. Then, without a word, she reached up and began undoing his pants. He saw Sadie stand up and then move over to the couch he was sitting on, apparently wanting a better view.

This felt unreal, but he was very locked into the moment.

Chloe looked like a pale goth goddess.

Her breasts swayed and jiggled as she worked him out of his pants. She looked like she wanted to say more, to keep arguing with him, but she didn't. She leaned forward and dragged her tongue slowly across his head a few times, then slipped his cock into her mouth. Gabe settled his hand over the back of her head as she began bobbing it.

Chloe tried to shake it off but he just tightened his grip, clenching his fingers around her midnight black hair. She made a noise of complaint but obediently kept sucking him off. The pleasure was hot and wet and perfect, burning wonderfully into him as she kept working. He waited until she'd coated his dick in a thick film of her spit, then pulled her back.

"Okay," he said, grabbing her by the shoulders

and turning her around, "on your hands and knees."

"I can't believe you're making me do this in front of all these people," she growled as she moved, assuming the position.

"Don't act like this isn't what you want, you fucking whore," he replied, falling to his knees behind her. There was a nice open space between the two couches and he intended to make full use of it. He flipped up her dress, exposing her nice, pale ass.

"*Gabe,*" she whispered harshly.

"Shut up, Chloe," he replied. "Now," he said, shifting forward and rubbing his head slowly between the wet lips of her vagina, "have you been taking your birth control?"

"Yes. Why?"

"You know why," he said, and penetrated her.

She cried out as he slowly pushed his way into her. Everything seemed to drop away and slow down as he got inside her. Gabe had been thinking of this exact thing since the moment he'd laid eyes on her.

With Ellen and Holly, he'd naturally wanted to fuck them as soon as he'd seen them, but his fantasizing and love of Ellen had gone on for so long that it had become an entirely different thing by the time they'd actually made love.

With Holly, certainly there was a lot of lust there, but hot as she was, to him at least, she was more cute than seductive. He'd felt something different about her when they first had sex. Something more than lust.

With Chloe, though...

It was different. It was way, *way* more about the lust. An almost angry lust that seemed to consume him. She really had been pushing his buttons all week, sending him pictures that were suggestive but never actually showed much of anything, teasing him endlessly.

And they had already discussed, in no uncertain terms, the specifics of the sex. After some consideration, Chloe had said that she was comfortable with zero protection, and with him filling her pussy with his seed, and with an audience, though a limited one.

"Don't come in me," she complained, then cried out as he pushed deeper.

"Chloe, shut *up!*" he snapped, and smacked her ass hard enough that she let out a little scream of surprise.

"Fuck, I *felt* that," Ellen muttered quietly behind him.

"You're so mean!" Chloe complained.

"Only because you fucking make me!" he growled, and slapped her ass again.

And then he was inside of her, all the way inside of her, and his hands were on her hips, and he was watching himself disappearing into that sweet pink pussy of hers. Chloe moaned and shuddered against him, panting as he fucked her, pushing against him, forcing him deeper.

She was like a dream inside, the sex something out of a fantasy.

Gabe had been transported to paradise and for some long, amazing stretch of time he drove into her again and again, furiously pushing into her hot depths and enjoying every second of pleasure. The sounds Chloe made were deeply gratifying to hear and the feeling of her moving against him, not just inviting him deeper but demanding it, were even more so.

At some point he stopped fucking her and she let out a cry of frustration.

"What the fuck!?" she demanded.

"Shut up!" he growled, grabbing her and pushing her down so that she fell flat, then rolling her over so that her tits were out and bare to the world.

"Come on, legs up," he said, lifting them.

"I don't like this position!" she complained.

"I don't care, Chloe! Stop being a mouthy little fuck and do as you're told!"

She bared her teeth at him, looking genuinely angry for a moment there as she raised and spread her legs, and then she seemed to completely lose her concentration as he penetrated her again and began railing her hard and fast. Her mouth hung open and her eyes went wide. Except for the sounds of pure ecstasy escaping her mouth, she almost looked catatonic with bliss.

Gabe kept going, holding on furiously to his orgasm, because he wanted to stretch this moment in time out, wanted to enjoy it more and longer.

But fuck her pussy felt so good!

And the knowledge that five other women were watching this in mostly rapt silence was just pushing him even harder over the edge.

He at least managed to make it until she had one hell of a hard, full-bodied orgasm. Her whole body jerked and she cried out, letting a long, loud, sustained screaming moan of total rapture as her inner muscles clenched and fluttered madly, and she became hotter and wetter and the pleasure overwhelmed him utterly.

Gabe cried her name, laying his hands on her big, pale breasts as he started to come along with her.

The orgasm felt seismic.

His whole body seemed to light up with total, mind-shattering bliss as he started shooting his load into her. He filled her up, pumped her full of his seed one hard, furious, powerful contraction at a time, his cock jerking and each time releasing a heavy spray. He gave her everything, orgasming for what seemed to him to be a very long time.

Gabe began to come back to himself as it faded away. His whole body felt like it was humming faintly with pure pleasure. He found himself staring down at Chloe, who was looking up at him, her hair a wild mess, her eyes wide, her body slicked with sweat as her considerable chest heaved, catching her breath.

He realized someone was nearby, almost beside him, and saw Emily.

"Hi," he managed.

She laughed. "Hi, Gabe."

"What, uh...do you want something?" he murmured.

"Yeah. Abby and I want to keep you both from leaking your semen all over our carpet," she replied, holding up a damp cloth.

"Oh...okay."

"You okay there, Chloe?" he heard Ellen asked.

"Uh...lemme get back to you," she murmured, making everyone laugh.

"Here, Gabe, pull your big dick out so I can...mmm, actually. Chloe, do you want me to lay the cloth over your pussy or do you want to?"

"You can do it. I'm...so out of it right now," she murmured.

"Okay. I know you aren't into girls so I won't make it weird."

"Thank you."

Gabe pulled out of her and Emily did her thing. He let her get on with it, laying on his back, staring up at the ceiling, feeling the faint lingering high and the brand new, ridiculously potent high of sex washing through his body.

Ellen suddenly appeared over him, looking like a giantess more than ever with him laying on the floor and her peering down at him from her full height.

"Hi babe," he murmured.

"Hello, sweetheart," she replied, grinning. "That was so hot."

"It sure felt like it," he managed. "Um...I want a shower. Chloe?"

"Yeah, I need one, dude. You made a *huge* mess in me. Honestly it's been forever since I've had to deal with this."

"Come on, you two," Abby said, "I'll show you to the shower."

"I'll bring your clothes babe, go on," Ellen said.

"Thanks," he replied, then stumbled off after helping Chloe up.

A few moments later, he found himself encased in a tiny world of hot steam with a naked, tired-looking Chloe. For a moment they just looked at each other, then Gabe held open his arms, beckoning to her. She immediately stepped forward and embraced him. They stood there together, naked and wet and satisfied, hugging.

"Thank you," she whispered.

"For what?" he replied.

"Doing everything right and being safe."

"Oh. Well, you're welcome. I take it you're still feeling good about this whole thing."

"I am. I was worried I wouldn't. I was worried I'd be feeling a rush of guilt or fear or shame or some other awful fucking emotion right about now, but I'm not. I just feel...good. Really good. And I know it's not just the sex and the weed, although that's definitely helping. Mmm, here, sorry, I *gotta* clean your fucking nut out of my pussy."

He chuckled and let go of her. "I understand."

"I'll bet you do given how much you probably bust inside your girlfriends," she muttered as she pulled one of the showerheads down and put it up under herself. She exhaled hard and shivered harder, putting one of her legs on the side of the tub and gripping his shoulder with her free hand. "They have such a nice shower."

"They really do," he agreed.

For the next several moments, they both went about cleaning up. First themselves, then each other. Gabe noticed that Chloe seemed different. He realized that it was because all her sass and argumentative nature was completely gone. She almost seemed a little lost.

"So, what happens now?" he asked, then chuckled. "We seem to be asking that a lot."

"Well...this is kind of uncharted territory for me, so I appreciate it," Chloe replied.

"Uncharted how?"

"I have *never* been with a guy, even casually, who already had a girlfriend, let alone two. Let alone who *also* had a side piece. A *married* side piece." She was tilting her head back under the shower now but abruptly she looked at him, running her hands over her head and squeezing the water from her hair. "You're really weird, you know that?"

"I guess," he replied.

"I mean that in a good way. It's just...why aren't you more of an asshole?" she asked.

"You think I'd be with Ellen if I was an asshole?"

"...that's a good point. It's just, I've met guys

who are 'ladies men'. I mean actually successful at sleeping with several different women, not just lying. And, unerringly, they are assholes. Maybe it takes some time to expose it, but it comes out. They're dicks. They let it consume them and quickly come to think that they're just God's gift to planet Earth.

"And they manage what they manage because I'm sad to say there's a lot of dumb and desperate 'pick me' women out there and these fuckwads have a lot of natural charisma and practice at tricking and seducing. Here's the thing though: I can always tell. I always have some sort of sixth sense about it. Like something's just *off* about them. And I'm always proven right...except for you. I know for a fact that you've slept with several women, and you are *actively dating two,* so either you're a god-tier actor, or you just aren't an asshole."

"So which is it?" he asked.

She laughed. "I want to believe you just aren't an asshole. I mean, I *do* believe it, but I'm also a terminal cynic because life has shit on me a lot and I have very little faith in the human race...but you asked me a question. Where does that leave us? What happens now? And the answer is...I don't know, Gabe. I'm still not sure. About some of it, at least. I have settled on a few things."

"I'm listening."

"Number one: I'm willing to commit to not having sex or being romantic with anyone else. I mean, I was already doing that, but I'm willing to commit to you while I figure this out. And, before you ask: no, I'm not asking for the same thing. Because *clearly* that isn't going to work. Second thing: I am willing to seriously investigate the possibility of dating you, and not just casually either.

I'll talk about it more, but later. Third and final thing, and I know this one for absolute sure: I want more sex. I want a *lot* more sex from you...how does that all sound?" she asked.

"I mean, fantastic to me," Gabe replied. "I know that I want to have sex with you, I know that I want to date you, and I know that I want to get to know you more. I want you in my life, Chloe. But I also know that I want you to feel comfortable with it and take as much time as you need to get everything figured out."

She smiled and embraced him again. After a moment, she kissed him, and he happily returned the kiss, leaning into it.

When she pulled back, she had a different look on her face. "I also know one other thing right now."

"What's that?" he asked.

"I want you to fuck me again in this shower."

Gabe kissed her and pushed her up against the wall, and she moaned as he did.

ABOUT ME

I am Misty Vixen (not my real name obviously), and I imagine that if you're reading this, you want to know a bit more about me.

In the beginning (late 2014), I was an erotica author. I wrote about sex, specifically about human men banging hot inhuman women. Monster girls, alien ladies, paranormal babes. It was a lot of fun, but as the years went on, I realized that I was actually striving to be a harem author. This didn't truly occur to me until late 2019-early 2020. Once the realization fully hit, I began doing research on what it meant to be a harem author. I'm kind of a slow learner, so it's taken me a bit to figure it all out.

That being said, I'm now a harem author!

Just about everything I write nowadays is harem fiction: one man in loving, romantic, highly sexual relationships with several women.

I'd say beyond writing harems, I tend to have themes that I always explore in my fiction, and they encompass things like trust, communication, respect, honesty, dealing with emotional problems in a mature way…basically I like writing about functional and healthy relationships. Not every relationship is perfect, but I don't really do drama unless the story actually calls for it. In total honesty, I hate drama. I hate people lying to each other and I hate needless rom-com bullshit plots that could have been solved by two characters have a goddamned two minute conversation.

Check out my website
www.mistyvixen.com

Here, you can find some free fiction, a monthly newsletter, alternate versions of my cover art where the ladies are naked, and more!

Check out my twitter
www.twitter.com/Misty_Vixen

I update fairly regularly and I respond to pretty much everyone, so feel free to say something!

Finally, if you want to talk to me directly, you can send me an e-mail at my address:
mistyvixen@outlook.com

Thank you for reading my work! I hope you enjoyed reading it as much as I enjoyed writing it!

-Misty

Made in the USA
Monee, IL
08 December 2023

48578820R00233